Praise for *A Tree for Antarctica*

"With engaging writing that is inviting, not confrontational, realistic but not bleeding heart, V. J. Michaux brings attention to the urgency of needed change regarding human impact on climate. This is reflected in the challenges faced by Dal, Naija, and Walt as they navigate seemingly insurmountable odds. The book engages within the confines of individuals, while articulating broader implications for the whole planet."

—Dr. Donald Johanson, paleoanthropologist and discoverer of *Australopithecus africansis*, or "Lucy." He won the National Book Award for *Lucy: The Beginnings of Humankind.*

"V. J. Michaux has written an intriguing page-turner. How her engaging characters navigate our landscapes to come is both enjoyable and also unforgettable. A must-read book."

—Liv Arnesen, the first woman to ski solo and unsupported to the South Pole (1994). She is the author of *Skiing into the Bright Open,* soon to be published in English, and with Ann Bancroft, *No Horizon Is So Far.* She was the first woman to cross the Antarctic continent (with Ann Bancroft, 2000-2001). Arnesen and Bancroft reached millions of youth on their Antarctic crossing and continue to combine adventure with education. More about that on www.bancroftarnesen.com.

"V. J. Michaux mixes fictionalized characters impacted by and trying to mitigate the state of the world produced by advanced climate change with scientifically realistic scenarios, creating both an enjoyable and informative read."

—Dr. Paul Andrew Mayewski, director and professor at the Climate Change Institute of University of Maine, author of five hundred scientific publications and two popular books: *The Ice Chronicles* and *Journey into Climate.* He was the first to lead scientific climate expeditions to "the Three Poles"—Arctic, Antarctic, and Everest.

"As the imperatives for action on climate change enter a critical phase, it is brilliant stories like this that engage, inform, and influence. Treat this as a reconnoiter, and buckle up for an eye-opening encounter—even for a seasoned polar explorer."

—Pen Hadow, arctic explorer, ocean conservationist, and author of *SOLO, The North Pole: Alone and Unsupported.* His epic feat of arctic exploration in 2003 has never been replicated.

"V. J. Michaux has created a spine-chilling novel, supporting her picture of the future with well-researched facts within a five-star narrative. *A Tree for Antarctica* is an enthralling page-turner. I consider this book one of the most important to be written recently on the subject of preserving the world we live in. As important a message as *Silent Spring*."

—Alfred Balm, art historian, conservationist, and author of six books including *The Fake Rembrandt* (soon to become a major film). His latest is *The Expedition*.

"A well-written, informing, and above all intriguing novel."

—Rosamund (Pom) Oliver, polar explorer and former film producer (*Hoodwink, Cathy's Child, Biggles*). She was a member of the first all-women's relay team to ski from Canada to the North Pole, and also of the first all-female team to ski the whole distance from the Antarctic coast to the South Pole.

"A brilliantly inventive novel, following Dal Riley on his most dangerous mission of all, in which he carries hope and the future of the planet with him—and the chance of failure is high. The characters are rich and interesting, showing the best and worst of human nature. It is a tale of hope for survival against the odds. A gripping page-turner."

—Ann Daniels, British polar explorer, writer, and speaker, has numerous firsts and six North Pole treks. In 2002, she and teammate Caroline Hamilton became the first women to reach both poles in all-female efforts. She co-led the Caitlin Arctic Survey, and received an honorary degree from Staffordshire University for her environmental work.

"V. J. Michaux's eloquent and compelling depiction of our planet in the not-too-distant future is a prompting to all that now is the time to take action and work together to mitigate the effects of climate change."

—Lorie Karnath, president of Next Breath, former president of the Explorers Club, author of books on science and exploration, and founder and managing editor of *Molecular Frontiers Journal*.

"During our thirty-plus years spent studying penguins and skuas in Antarctica, we documented more than 50% declines in two penguin species populations, and we clearly linked these to climate warming. The scenario presented in *A Tree for Antarctica* is very plausible, particularly if we do nothing to curb the use of fossil fuels. We should definitely see this book as a wake-up call to what is possible in the future."

—Wayne and Sue Trivelpiece, US Antarctic Research Division, NOAA-NMFS (retired). Article in *Proceeds of the National Academy of Sciences*.

A TREE FOR ANTARCTICA

V. J. MICHAUX

ARCTIC TERN PUBLISHING | VAIL

ISBN 978-0-578-89344-0
Library of Congress Control Number: 2021907574

Cover art by Sarah Bereza
Design and production by Chris Crochetière, BW&A Books, Inc.
Printed on 100% PCW paper by Friesens in Canada

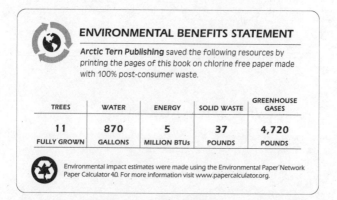

ENVIRONMENTAL BENEFITS STATEMENT

Arctic Tern Publishing saved the following resources by printing the pages of this book on chlorine free paper made with 100% post-consumer waste.

TREES	WATER	ENERGY	SOLID WASTE	GREENHOUSE GASES
11	870	5	37	4,720
FULLY GROWN	GALLONS	MILLION BTUs	POUNDS	POUNDS

Environmental impact estimates were made using the Environmental Paper Network Paper Calculator 4.0. For more information visit www.papercalculator.org.

And then we heard the Emperors calling.
Their cries came to us from the sea-ice we could not
see, but which must have been a chaotic quarter mile away.
They came echoing back from the cliffs, as we stood
helpless and tantalized.

—APSLEY CHERRY-GERRARD
  The Worst Journey in the World

1

The last Riley in Charleston said as he packed up in 2110, "Sadly, it is impossible to live down here anymore. The water cannot be held back."
—*Greater Charleston News and Courier:* Local Memories

OCTOBER 10, 2295

One hundred eighty-five years later, Major Dahlgren Riley III grabbed the stick of his bouncing aircraft and switched Onboard Cognition to OFF. With gusts like this, he preferred to fly the plane all by himself. Flying was the one area of his life where he could always take charge. Especially when a situation got tricky, Dal wanted to be in total control.

His plane yawed wildly in the shifting gusts over Valparaiso, Chile. Formerly at thirty feet elevation, the historic city had long since slid under the rising South Pacific.

Dal buzzed past Edificio Borde 3, once the tallest building in Valparaiso, noting how its twisted top floors punched though the sea's surface, the same way the spire of St. Michael's Church did back in Charleston. He flew on, looking for a rocky hilltop located between the new shoreline and a large refugee camp in the agricultural valley of Quillota, Chile. Somewhere among the hills east-northeast of old Valparaiso, thirty-six members of an extended family had held out on their homestead for too long. Now they clung to an exposed hilltop and waited for Dal.

When he approached the presumed pickup area, Dal scanned the water and peaks below, searching for the refugee family and any other stragglers. Off to the east, huge fenced-in mounds the size of small foothills shimmered in the glaring sun. They edged a series of large, brine-filled lakes. These were the Montañas y Lagos de Sal, composed of the detritus from desalination plants, waste that was no longer allowed to be pumped back into the sea. Beyond those man-made hills rose the dry Andes Mountains. Their former snowcaps and cascading rivers had once quenched the thirst of Valparaiso and watered the fruit and vegetable farms of Chile's coastal plain.

Dal squinted to take another look out his side window. This time he spotted the stragglers, clustered on a water-skirted peak. Immediately, he made another pass over them. The recording viewer on the bottom of his aircraft showed the outstretched arms of the people he was to save, all wearing their best clothing, their anguished faces turned to the sky, pleading for him not to leave. He made one more pass to determine where he could set the plane down.

That's when he saw the young woman holding her baby up for him to see. *That could be Ana someday,* he thought. His mouth went dry. Children in distress did that to him every time. Dal looked down at his controls and gathered himself for what was next.

Forcing himself to concentrate, he began to drop slowly onto the very spot that was most congested—the top of the peak. There was no other place to land, and if he did not land there, not one of these people would survive the night. The IRC (International Rescue Corps) was stretched so thin that no one would search this area again. There was no one else to help them climb aboard, either.

Then Central Cognition Control broke in, the not-quite-human voice speaking melodically through his earphones: "Why did you turn off your Onboard Cognition Control? We are here to help you. Please turn Cognition Control back on." Dal ripped off the earphones and slung them into the empty copilot seat, as he usually did at times like this. Gripping the stick tighter, he continued descending toward the hilltop.

When he was close enough, Dal turned on the loudspeaker and ordered, *"Muevete! Muevete!"* while the plane dropped steadily. The family scrambled away, crying and fleeing down the sides of the hilltop. This plane had no basket because there was no one to man it, and Dal had to land right where they stood. Some of the family stumbled toward the surging waters below, but others caught and held them, clinging to rocks and each other.

With the plane's data flow and bottom viewer, Dal managed to land in the center of the small hilltop—a hilltop so tiny that both ends of his deployed runners extended out over air.

He pushed a button that opened automatic doors on each side while keeping the top rotors moving. This was a VAHL (Vertical-Alternating-Horizontal Landing) aircraft, built especially for rescue work. The top rotors helped Dal hold the plane steady and also kept all the added weight that was about to surge aboard from throwing the plane off to one side and dragging everyone off their perch.

The refugees lined up where they could, and a grandmotherly woman took charge of their loading. Because of this, the refugees' scramble into the hold was more disciplined than other chaotic flights Dal had managed in his eight years of flying rescue missions.

"*Más rápido, más rápido!*" he yelled through his loudspeaker, using two more of the few Spanish words he knew. Two men lifted the mother and baby on board first, and they sat down on the floor. Then came the other children. Finally came the adults, oldest last, sitting on alternate sides of the aircraft to balance the weight. They probably had heard about this protocol through frequent civic broadcasts. Clearly, the family members had prepared themselves for this moment.

"*Solo personas!*" yelled Dal, as he studied two men remaining on the ground. Against all of the rules that they should have known, they were busy selecting small bundles from a pile to sling through the open doors.

"*No, no!*" Dal commanded. "*No macetas, no macetas!*" he yelled through the speakers, his voice rising.

Hearing these words, the men stopped and looked at each other in confusion. Precious time was wasting. Dal broke into a cold sweat. He was desperate to take off before the wind got any stronger. His finger hovered over the button to shut the door. These two big guys might have to be left behind. He steeled himself at the thought.

A young man from the rear of the plane threw himself over the back of the seat into the empty co-pilot's place. He shouted into Dal's right ear, "They think you mean 'No flower pots.' Say, '*No maletas,*' not '*macetas.*' Even better is '*No equipage.*'"

Dal bellowed again through the loudspeaker, *"No! No equipage!"* He stared straight ahead with his fingers pressing into the stick. The two men saw the rotors speeding up and the plane's vibrations increasing. They threw the bags aside and scrambled aboard. The doors slammed shut. The plane lifted off.

Phew! At least there had been no shouting or fighting this time. Leaning forward to glance at his passengers in the rearview mirror, Dal could see one of the two men he had nearly left behind, his big shoulders shaking with sobs while he held tight to the young woman with the baby. Dal licked his dry lips. That would have been a bad mistake. It would have haunted him for years, like others he had made.

Within minutes, he landed the plane beside the teeming refugee camp in the elevated Quillota Valley of ancient farmland fame. All over the world, productive farmland was being converted out of necessity into new migrant camps. This huge, congested camp looked like countless others on every continent Dal had seen before.

He noticed Black Coats strolling around the camp, ostensibly keeping order. Their red laser guns were sheathed but still obvious. It had been the Black Coats' official task to acquire this land and prepare the camp. Now, their work over, they still hung around. Black Coats always managed to eat the best food, drink the best *pisco,* and find items "left behind" to sell on the black market. Nearly every adult in any situation of turmoil around the Earth had a personal story about the Black Coats, who were part useful officialdom and part ruthless mercenary. One rarely knew which hat a Black Coat wore in any given encounter, so they inspired both hatred and fear.

Dal walked quickly to the local IRC commandant's headquarters to report on his mission, happily anticipating a reunion with his favorite superior officer. Commandant Velez had spilled artificial coffee on his buff-colored uniform and was rubbing vigorously at the spots with a small cloth. "I don't know why this swill is still traditional in the services. It's not even real coffee," he said. A broad smile crossed his weathered face when he looked up and saw Dal. He dabbed at his shirt a few seconds more.

"Today you have saved one of our most prominent families from destruction," Commandant Velez said. "They were stubborn people and ignored all our warnings. But they are wonderful people, still.

Muchas gracias in every language to you, my friend." He took Dal's hand between both of his. Then, chuckling, he said, "I am very sorry to have to tell you this, Major, but I am obliged by IRC regulations to admonish you for disobeying your Cognitive Control system and for ignoring a message from the Center ordering you to reconnect with it." The commandant smiled even more broadly as he winked at Dal and shrugged.

Dal nodded solemnly, his eyes wide: "Yes, sir."

This was a ritual. These words had been spoken to him at every IRC camp where he delivered refugees. Nevertheless, if he ever chose to wear them, Dal's chest would be covered with medals commending his successful missions. All IRC officers knew that. Dal and the commandant sat and chatted for quite a while.

THE NEXT DAY, Dal flew the plane back to its home base in Bentonville, Arkansas. To make sure he would not be assigned another long overseas mission, he made an appointment to see his wing's commanding officer, Lieutenant Commander Leslie Gonzales, who had flown many rescue missions herself before assuming this position. She walked slowly across the room and greeted Dal with an outstretched hand. Her grip was crushingly strong, but he knew to expect that and steeled himself to return the same.

"Welcome back, Major Riley. We always get glowing reports about your missions assisting other nations. I could certainly use you right here in North America at times, too. However, sadly, I see that you have asked for a discharge, effective immediately after you take your accrued vacation days. They add up to, let's see"—she glanced down—"seventy-five days. That's roughly three and one-fourth months, once weekends and holidays are added in. Did you never have any leave at all? Not in eight years?"

"Not much, ma'am."

"Well, I'm sure your family will be glad to see more of you then. Where do they live?"

"Orangeburg, South Carolina, ma'am."

"There's a lot of rescue work still going on in the Low Country of South Carolina. I hope your family members are all right."

"Yes, last I heard, ma'am. We live high enough."

"Good. We will be very sorry to lose your skill. You handle unforeseeable situations very well. Not everyone can be so flexible. Can't I convince you to stay on?" she asked, a hopeful lift in her voice.

"No, ma'am. I'm sorry."

"That's a real shame." Lieutenant Commander Gonzales took a step back, looked Dal up and down with narrowed eyes, and folded her arms across her chest. "We are dangerously understaffed, you know. I am authorized to offer you a bonus of one year's salary at the end if you will stay on for just four more years."

"Thank you, but no thanks, ma'am. I am the last surviving pilot from my training class of thirty-six South Carolina boys. I want to keep it that way. Surviving, I mean."

Commander Gonzales stiffened and unfolded her arms. She held her clenched fists at her sides, then raised her right arm and opened a cold hand for Dal to shake again. He felt sorry for her, with her crushing burden of responsibility. Rescue work was not like flying in a traditional war. This work promised neither truce nor treaty, nor any end in sight. He realized it must get harder for her to bear every day, as it had for him. Dal hated adding to her burden by leaving the Rescue Corps, but he was resolved. And most important, Ana might not wait forever.

"Best of luck to you in whatever you choose next." She paused. "This work is extremely specialized, you know." She leaned in, as if to confide in him now that she could. "I can't imagine how someone like you, who excels at rescue flying, the hardest flying there is, will ever be able to fulfil your need for adrenaline and productive thrills again. Not after this."

She lifted one side of her mouth in a half smile. "One additional warning for you, Major," she said. "In civilian flight, they will not tolerate your disabling the Onboard Cognition Control the way we have."

"Thank you, Lieutenant Commander."

Dal emerged into the hot, dry day and disappeared into the milling throng at the camp. He had not told Commander Gonzales that he already had an exciting job offer guaranteeing astoundingly high pay. Or that the woman he loved—and was way overdue to marry—was waiting for him back home. At least he hoped she was.

DAL HOPPED A FLIGHT that evening to a base outside Columbia, South Carolina, and arrived so late that he needed to sleep over in the BOQ. The next morning, having had little sleep for many nights, he did not get going early. This was as close to home as he could fly in an IRC plane, so he rented a beat-up sun car to take him the rest of the way to the family farm outside of Orangeburg.

Dal sat back in the car and felt the joy of freedom rise in his throat. A new life was about to begin. He pounded the seat with both hands and whooped, "Icy! Frigid! Yowzah!" over and over until he got it all out. Only then did he sit back and ponder what would come next.

When he arrived where the highway branched off toward Old Summerville, his car slowed down behind a long convoy of buses. He expected to lose them once he turned off onto One Chop Lane, but the dusty buses turned that way, too. They plodded on ahead of him, taking every subsequent turn he was going to make.

Dal clenched and unclenched his stick-hand repeatedly. But this time he could not turn off a meddlesome OC and take charge. He was trapped. He had to follow this road-clogging horde. The road was deeply pitted, and the car lurched in and out of holes. Dal couldn't pass because another unending convoy of empty buses crowded the road coming in the opposite direction.

After way too long, the car arrived at the farm and found a place to park itself between supply trucks in the outer reaches of what used to be one of the Riley family orange orchards. This was as close to the old house's address as the car would take him. Dal got out and slammed the car door hard, causing a minor dust storm to cascade down the sides.

His mental stew about the slow drive and the long walk ahead of him added to the oppressive heat. His six-foot frame slumped briefly as he panted like one of the resident iguanas. Then he gathered himself up and started walking toward the distant farmhouse. Almost mid-October, it was still too hot in Orangeburg, South Carolina, to walk around outside before sundown.

Ginger-colored dust kicked out from beneath Dal's boots. It hung in the air, floating with the voices he heard coming from green-domed tents lining the new stepping-stone walk to the house. He saw new walkways like this one threaded throughout the area and figured they must be necessary for when the rains came and the whole place turned to mud. He had seen walkways like these before in camps, but never here, never all across the farm. "What the hot fuck is going on?" he muttered.

Dal turned his head slowly to take in the whole scene. The farm looked just like the places he had left behind, the places he wanted to forget.

With his brow knit, a small, worn duffle in his right hand, and his left arm raised high as a general acknowledgment to all those calling out from the tents, Dal began to walk toward the low farmhouse off in the distance. Something about that looked odd, too.

He lowered his left hand, wiped it on his pants, and plodded on. Dark patches formed under his armpits and down his back. Sweat dripped from beneath his hat, rolled down his head, and dropped onto the path. Dal avoided looking at the tented camp covering the gently rolling land where eight successive generations of ex-Charlestonian Rileys had tried to raise everything from medicinal tobacco to rice to cattle to, most recently, orange trees. Right now, though, he worried more about his parents than the farm.

A tiny red ball skidded past Dal's feet, followed nimbly by a small girl who darted in front of him so fast that he nearly tripped over her. When he stumbled, she stopped and pointed solemnly to the ball resting by his foot. Dal smiled at her, picked up the ball, and placed it in her grimy hand.

"Hi there," he said.

The girl flashed a quick, snaggle-toothed smile and ran off toward a large, open-sided tarp located near one of the camp cisterns.

Like everything else, the play tarp was dusty-dull. A young woman with heavy-lidded eyes jumped to her feet and officiously jammed her arms on her hips. *Look out,* Dal thought. His smile waned. Some of the woman's light-brown hair stuck to her perspiring neck while the rest was held back from her eyes by sunglasses atop her head.

"Hey!" she yelled at the child. "Don't you be leaving the shade now! You don't want me coming after you, do ya? There's gotta be *no* leaving the tent until sundown. You don't have your hat or glasses on, neither." The young woman looked around to see if a Black Coat or anyone else had observed this child's disobedience of the rules, for which she would be held responsible.

The children's play-tarp swayed wildly, activated by a group swinging around the supporting poles. Other kids swatted flies from their dust-caked faces and sucked from holes cut in the ends of shriveled oranges. They squeezed hard to get any juice out and then ripped them apart to chew the dry pulp. Air blowers pushed coolish air and dust around under the tarp.

A quieter group of kids sat on the ground playing jacks beneath the drooping roof. They watched intently as the little girl jumped back under the tarp, successfully evading the young woman who swatted at her with a long, slow sweep of her thin arm, missing dramatically.

"You sure have your hands full there," Dal called out with an encouraging lilt in his voice.

The young woman lifted her thin mouth into more of a grimace than a smile. She tilted her head and mouthed back, "Yep."

"Doing a fine job, keeping those hats tied around their necks like that, much less on their heads, in all this heat," Dal said. He had seen camps where kids had no hats or sunglasses at all. He had even seen children with cataracts. He might have had a longer conversation with the woman. This had been his work milieu, too. He got it. He understood the difficulties. But she turned away to frown and wag her finger again at the little girl.

The small, impish child grinned at Dal once more and waved the little red ball aloft to show the woman why she had left the shade of the tarp.

The woman looked back at Dal, her dry mouth turned down and wrinkles held tight between her eyebrows. He smiled at her and took a step in her direction. Maybe she needed a little encouragement to carry on. She didn't react as he expected but kept on frowning and staring at him. This was not the typical Southern behavior he was used to. So un-Southern it was, not to smile back at all.

He stopped, unsure what to do. "Well—bye now," he called with a small wave of his left hand. Then he trudged on, looking neither left nor right anymore.

Finally, his right foot landed on the blue-painted bottom step of the porch, and he paused. The paint was chipped and worn in places, not fresh like the last time he had been home. And there were more steps up to the porch, indicating that the whole house was higher off the ground than it had been. Still, this was home.

He climbed the last two steps, took a kerchief out of his pocket, and grabbed the doorknob with it, pleased at having remembered to do so. The knob, baked all day in the sun, was blistering hot.

2

Populations in Motion: Our correspondents and photographers show how entire new societies can form in the turmoil of migrant camps. They discuss what this means for traditional governments.

—*National Geographic,* comm edition cover story, September 2295

OCTOBER 11, 2295

The front door jerked inward out of Dal's grasp. Risa Riley stumbled over the threshold and into the arms of her surprised son, yelling all the while: "Jim, Jim—where are you? Dal's back! Where are you, Jim? Get on over here!"

"I'm a-comin', Risa," Jim Riley called back. "Too hot for an old man to hurry." Instantly, though, he appeared from around the edge of the house. His hat was wet, and he struggled up the stairs with a pail that looked to be filled with damp dirt. Dal hurried over to help.

"Set that down careful now," Jim said.

He grabbed Dal, squeezed him tightly, and pounded his back with sun-spotted fists. He kept his sunglasses on. Dal noticed that his father's chin trembled a bit.

"Welcome back, son," Jim said. "How long you staying this time, Dal?"

"Tell ya about that inside, okay?"

His parents exchanged glances and followed him in. All of the window shades were drawn against the brutal afternoon sun. Dal and his father kicked off their boots and lined them up on a cloth. The tile floor felt good. They mopped their hands and faces with cold towels stored near the door. By the time Dal and his father joined her in the kitchen, Risa had set out ice-cold lemonade and Dal's favorite bread, made of home-grown bananas, on the simple wooden kitchen table.

"Now, Dal, tell us everything," Risa said. "We want to hear all: where you been, what you been doing, and just, well, you know—everything."

"No, first off, you need to tell me what's going on outside," Dal said. "I know a refugee camp when I see one. Are you both doing all right? Did they pay you to take this land? Any Black Coats hereabouts bothering you?"

Risa erupted, "Oh, you haven't seen the least of what's been happenin'. Been a great big mess since right after you left last time. I know you are an important person, out saving folks all over the place, but we wish you'd come back here, marry Ana, and settle down. We really could use you right here, Dal." There it was, all out on the table. Faster than usual, too.

"Um, well—" Dal took a big bite of the banana bread. "Mmmm"— he paused to swallow it—"now I know I'm home. Wasn't sure where I was when I saw what's going on outside. Who are all those folks?"

"These ones are from Upper Summerville, near the original camps down in the Low Country. That's where the Barrier Islanders and Charleston people first went, ya know. Now they've all had to move up higher. Ya heard? The sea is up to Monck's Corner now. And that pretty Pinapolis? That's an island, can you believe it? You'll hear a lot of Charleston accents out there in our camp. We take good care of 'em. Have to." Risa grimaced, her lips closed. She had a trace of Old English notes in her voice, even though it had been eight generations since the Rileys had lived in Charleston.

"Bet you do," Dal said. "Take good care of them, I mean."

"They're gonna be sent to a new camp in Croft State Park, near Spartanburg," Jim broke in. "Don't know what we'll do for income then."

"I see you elevated the house," Dal said.

"Yep, had to," Jim said, his voice rising. "A big project that was."

"Why did you bother with it?" Dal asked.

Jim sighed. "Ofttimes when we have a good rain, it's a real gully-washer. Comes down in sheets, carrying off my topsoil. That's why we had to raise the house up a few feet just in case. The house did okay, but our fields sure have been covered. All them dried-up creeks and braided, swampy rivers fill up and spill over now with 'bout every hard rain. Comes three or four inches in an hour, regular, and that much don't soak in like it used to. Plus, we get it flowing down from upcountry. Can regular be near as bad out there as that big 2015 flood and all the hurricanes since."

"What about those people outside, Dad? What will they do when it rains?"

"God only knows," interjected Risa.

"They're supposed to be moved afore another big storm comes 'round," Jim said. "Might be another batch in here after 'em, though."

Jim was on a roll.

"We got a drought going now, but just wait. When a cat 5 atmospheric river comes, all the upstream water connects with the new sea level, wherever that might be. Lots of fields been lost to salt incursion down there by the new beach. I tell ya, you wouldn't want to build a dock anywhere. Might be underwater before you ever got to fish off it even one time."

Fishing—now that's a happier subject, thought Dal. "Are you doing any fishing, Dad?" he asked.

"Not many blackwater bass left—just a few now and again. They always was mysterious fish, ya know. Livin' at different depths, dependin' on the temperature. Anymore, they don't come out that much. Rarely does one come to a lure. Some still do catch 'em—at least say they do. Fish tales likely." Jim snorted, his eyes wide and face bleak. "I haven't had much luck with it. Thinkin' on givin' it up, permanent."

"Don't do that yet, Dad," Dal said. He asked more gently, "And where are the orange trees, Dad?"

"Oh, some few are still out there. Prob'ly you couldn't see 'em for all the tents. With leaf drop and root rot and the soil washin' out and gettin' so salty, I got to face it: We've prob'ly had our last orange harvest. Mind you, with what we get for the tent camp from the gov'ment, though, our finances are pretty much even." Jim looked down at his worn hands. "You got no interest in working the farm, anyway, so it doesn't matter."

Dal searched for a subject that wouldn't depress his parents. Before he could find one, Risa said, "Now it's your turn to talk, Dal. So, where ya been?"

"All over. Places where folks stayed too long, mostly. Places in chaos and, well, you know."

"Why don't you come work here?" Risa said. "We certainly qualify, with chaos and refugees and all that. We got it all right here at home, big-time. Aren't folks here as worthy of help as people in those far-off places?"

"Sure they are." Dal placed his hands flat on the table. "Listen, Mom. I snatch strangers from danger. That is what I do. It's much easier if I can't understand what they're saying. If I don't know their language, then at least I'm able to concentrate on what has to happen. It's better if I don't understand a word of it. Just imagine if I were working out there." He swung his arm toward the kitchen window. "Think about this, too: you can lose friends and make enemies for life if you have to separate folks from their homes and possessions. That is what I do for a living. Rather, that is what I *did* for a living." This was not exactly the way he had meant to tell them.

"Whatcha mean, 'did for a livin'?" Jim leaned forward.

"I quit the Rescue Corps My time was up and I didn't reenlist. Have other plans now."

"What do you mean?" Risa sat taller. "You are a major. You have a good career, been promoted regular. Good jobs are hard to find, unless you want to go to work on the Moon Electric Relay Band or somethin' like that."

"Sure, but I want to live a long life, too, Mom. I never told you and Dad how dangerous my job was."

"Well, I'm glad you quit then," said Risa.

"I am, too, son." Jim patted Risa's hand.

"Don't you worry, I already have another job. After I go to meet the guy, it is mine to accept. Pays a lot."

"That's excellent, Dal," Jim brightened.

"Sounds wonderful. What guy?" asked Risa.

"Name's Mori Taktug. Lives outside of New Churchill, Manitoba, Canada."

"What on earth kinda name is that?" Risa asked.

"Part Inuit-Cree-Dene and part Japanese. I looked it up."

"Lord, have mercy—help me! Where did you hear of this man?"

"He commed me out of the blue. Wants me to fly somewhere with long summers and do something about helping draw down CO_2. I'll learn the details after I get up there and see him. I am to train to fly a new aircraft and help out with planning, so I figure it will take a couple months total. It's legal and all that."

Dal paused. Should he tell them this part? "Only odd thing is this: Mori is 141—nearly 142—years old. Born in Gillam, Manitoba."

"Don't you think you should call him Mr. Tukkak, or Kakak, or whatever his last name is?" Risa said. "I have never met anyone who is 140-something years old. The only way you be that old is to have paid a ton for one of those gene treatments at birth, and those have been outlawed more than a hundred years now. Some of those people had way too many kids. Don't tell me he is one of them! Must be one of the last ones alive. You better make sure he's going to live long enough to pay ya," she chuckled.

"You be careful, Dal," his father said. "This sounds strange."

"I managed to live eight years in the Rescue Corps, didn't I?" Dal replied. "Soon I'll have even more to live for if all goes well tonight."

"What are you getting at?" his mother asked, her eyes wide. She prayerfully clasped her hands together in front of her breast, and Dal knew exactly what that meant.

"Okay, here it is, Mom. Your best news ever. I am going to answer all your prayers and ask Ana to marry me tonight. That's why I really have to clean up, eat, and run. She doesn't even know I'm here yet."

"Oh, happy day! About time!" Risa beamed.

"Damn!" Jim Riley slapped his hand down on the table and ran out of the room. Dal heard the front door slam, and his jaw dropped open. This was not the response he wanted. His Dad loved Ana. What was up?

"Bet the dirt in his pail dried up," Risa said. "Happens all the time when he forgets and leaves it out there. Takes no time at all in this heat." Risa got up and hugged Dal hard. "I am so thrilled, Dal—thrilled as I can be for you and Ana. And for us, too."

Jim came back in and sat down, perspiring heavily.

"What was that all about, Dad?"

"No big deal. Only a little extra income lost this week."

"Let's not talk about that," Risa said. "We're celebratin' tonight, Jim."

"How do you know she'll say yes?" Jim scowled. Then he laughed. "Just kiddin', Dal. You know we gotta be happy about this. You can start trying to have that gran'baby, which your mother here can't wait to get her hands on."

"Why'd you run off like that?" Dal asked.

"Risa has a little USC Extension Service job is all. First, though, when are you thinkin' to have the weddin', Dal?"

"Don't you think I'd better ask Ana first? Maybe we can get married in January, once I get into or else finish this job. That timing is good, I figure. What do you think?"

"Sounds perfect to me," Risa answered.

"While I have just a minute, tell me about your Extension Service work, Mom."

Risa lifted her chin proudly. "Jim digs some moist dirt wherever he can find it once a week. I study it under the microscope, and you would not believe what I have found. Besides lots of pesky triatomine insects—God help us if they ever get inside this house; they carry Chagas disease, ya know—I have found many new species migrating north and a couple of species never seen at all before. I photograph 'em and send the photos along with the samples and my write-up to the USC Extension Service. Many of our regular insects have either moved on northward or gone extinct."

"Maybe they'll name a bug for her one day," Jim chuckled.

"Naw, Jim. I am trying, that's all"—Risa swatted at him and swallowed hard—"trying to do my small part and help document all the ecological changes that keep on comin' so fast. So that one day maybe"—Risa paused again and caught her breath. Her voice got higher. "One day maybe, just maybe, we will be able to understand what exactly has been happenin' to nature around here."

She began to clasp and unclasp her hands. Her wrinkles deepened. Dal sat back. He recognized this behavior immediately. He had seen it happen all his life at the very mention of "nature," not a word used much anymore. His mother was one of the few people he had heard say it, and usually that was when she was getting upset. He surely didn't use that word. Too many unhappy connotations. He knew better than to say it. He also knew how to help his mother come out of her depths.

"Mom, do you still have those old films playing in the living room? The old Serengeti ones, and the ones about the Arctic and all that? Do you still bring the kids in from school with their teachers to see them and to hear you talk about all those animals and how they inhabited different ecosystems and such?"

Dal knew exactly how to talk with his mother about her "nature films," although he only did it to cheer her up. He hated admitting, even to himself, that the old films she loved so much represented a big downer for him. He had spent hours and hours sitting beside her in the darkened living room watching those "nature films" when he was a little boy. Risa was at her most cheerful in those times. Her sadness about environmental losses eventually washed over him, too, until he left home and gradually found a way to avoid being sucked down with her: keep your mind busy with a purpose.

Jim also had tried to help his wife with her "environmental melancholy," as the doctor had eventually diagnosed it. But Jim was not as useful at that as Dal was.

Risa leapt up from her seat and headed toward the living room. "You will be getting married soon. I know Ana will say yes, and that is the happiest news for many a year, Dal. What on earth am I sitting here talking about ol' bugs for? To answer your question, yes, I do still have those films."

She waved her left arm for them to follow. "Let me show you how I reedited and put together some of the best clips. Come on, you're gonna love this. Your baby one day will love 'em, too. Come on now." She waved again for Dal and Jim to follow her through the swinging kitchen door to the darkened dining room with the buffalo statues on the table, and then beyond into the living room.

Before they even got to the living room, Dal could see light flickering off the walls and ceiling. The light emanated from a continuous flow of filmed wildlife that covered top to bottom of the long interior wall. The film spooled across the other walls, too, creating a cyclorama alive with moving creatures in scenes from at least two hundred years ago. Some were much older than that. Dal knew every frame of every film.

The house, the films, the old family albums on the table filled with photos of people wearing bathing suits and lying out at the seashore to get a "tan"—all of these things were antiques from a past that no longer existed. Once again, Dal felt oppressed in the midst of his mother's lovingly assembled memorabilia. He knew he could not stay here for long.

Must be bad if she keeps these films running all the time now, he thought. This film was of the caribou migration to the North Shore of Alaska: crossing the wild Yukon, eating until stomachs were swollen with flowery grasses, flicking off mosquitos with their tails and shivers, and giving birth to the next generation of awkward caribou calves on the seaside plains near Barrow, framed by an oil apparatus in the background. Dal looked for the lumbering bear that sometimes skirted the herd, as well as for the Arctic fox pouncing on lemmings. *Aha! There they are . . .*

He turned away, unable to watch this prior reality come to life again. Neither could he show his mother how much these memories affected him, how they had always affected him, and how he knew there was nothing at all to do about the loss. He wished his mother would put "nature" aside and go on, the way most people managed to do.

Risa was all smiles now. "Just last week, the fifth-graders from North Orangeburg Elementary came over here to see the films and what we have done to preserve this home. They all, every one of them, just loved the movies. I gave them homemade animal crackers. Of course, they would watch anything for those. But I think they were truly appreciative." Her voice was joyful again with these memories.

"That's all great, Mom. You do wonderful things helping people remember and take care of the world we have left. Even though, as they say, 'It ain't quite what it used to be,'" Dal foolishly added. Then, seeing her face fall again, he stammered: "But remember, Mom, it still is a really beautiful world! A world with amazing and brilliant sunsets and lightning whipping through the rain and ocean waves so huge and majestic. The light coming through the foam flying off the top of breaking waves is just beautiful. Beetles up close are beautiful, too. You have to appreciate what we have here and now. Okay, Mom? Okay? Okay. I better go clean up, eat, and get over to Ana's."

Dal finished, hugged his mother, and left before he could do any more damage, making his way down the long hall beyond the living room, where Risa had framed and hung a chart of the extinction of elephant species, starting with the woolly mammoth thousands of years ago down to the Asian and African species in the twenty-second century. The light from a herd of running zebras spilled into the hallway. It lit up Dal's face as he looked away and moved past them.

THE OVERHEAD LIGHT swipe was where it always had been, but nothing else was the same in Dal's childhood bedroom. No more great-great-somebody-made quilt. No more thin, lumpy twin mattress smelling of teenage sweat and dogs. He punched one of the pillows on the new double bed. Super soft—his favorite. He sat down to try the man-sized easy chair by the window but immediately jumped back to his feet and looked around in desperation. Where in this new room was the thing he had to find?

He hoped it had not been lost in the makeover. Surely not. His face red and heart pounding, Dal tore through the bedside drawers. One drawer was full of old mementos, so he turned it upside down on the bed. He had to find that ring.

"Aha!" There it was, way back in the desk drawer along with a box of grass paper from the old days when people wrote notes out longhand. Perfect. The ring box was discolored, the lid a bit askew.

All the better, Dal thought. Ana loved antiques, especially old books and paper things. She collected books. *She'd probably collect old newspapers, too, if they still existed,* he thought with a wry smile.

The ring box was wrapped in darkened, fragile paper, which Risa had told him was "air-mail paper." This paper was covered in script explaining that the ring was a family treasure, made in the 1930s.

When Dal had first seen the ring sitting on his old desk five years ago, he hadn't thought much of it. He was sure his mother had put it there as a little nudge for him to get married. But how could she have expected him to have married Ana then, when he was still in the Rescue Corps and bets were good that he would have left her a widow?

He opened the box and the ring fell out into his hand. It was 18-karat gold with a raised center holding six small diamond pieces in a circle and one larger diamond in the middle. There was a black Art

Deco design engraved on each side of the band. This ring was perfect. Ana would love it, especially the fact that it was so old. *Gold looks great on redheads,* Dal thought.

This led him to another idea. He took a piece of the old grass paper and a pen out of the desk and laboriously copied in block print the message from Mori Taktug, the message that he hoped might lead them to new and better lives. *She'll think this is really " far above water."* *No one writes by hand anymore,* he thought with satisfaction.

Dal reread his hand-copied message from Mori, looking for any mistakes. It looked fine.

October 8, 2295

Dear Major Riley,

I have been awaiting your response to my first comm for 14 days and therefore assume that you must have been occupied by other very important matters. [*Well, yeah,* Dal thought.]

I would very much like to have you on board for my new confidential project to assist CO_2 drawdown. A reply with your intent will be necessary by midnight of October 11, and you must arrive here by October 12 if you are to have a chance to participate in this unusual opportunity that I am pleased to offer you.

The schedule needed for this work requires long seasonal daylight in order to be successful. We face a tight schedule to get started: You must train in a special aircraft, help plan details, and form a working relationship with your crew before you embark on the month-long mission. Your crew relationships will be critical, as you will be working alone with them in isolation most of the time.

You will not want to miss this chance to use your proven skills and judgment and carry out an important mission that will be just as exciting and yet safer than those you have done in your work for the IRC. In addition, you will have the satisfaction of knowing you are doing something good for the earth as a whole. I cannot say more here, but I look forward to explaining the rest to you soon in person, should you accept.

I hope to be hearing from you immediately. If I have not heard from you by the date above, I am afraid that I will have to consider my second choice.

Travel instructions and a packing list will be sent to you upon my receipt of your affirmation of intent. I have most of what you will need here, so the packing list will be short.

With hopeful anticipation,

Mori Taktug
Willow Park House
New Churchill, Manitoba, Canada

P.S. I will quintuple the International Rescue Corps salary that you would receive in your next rank should you consider shipping over.

Dal leaned back and stared at the new yellow and bluish-grey Rothko copy hanging over the bed. It was meant to induce serenity, but his mind raced. He did not feel his knees pumping up and down and his heels repeatedly lifting off and falling back to the floor. *How did Mori know my IRC service time was about to end when he wrote me?* he wondered.

That last line in Mori's comm was the final hook. He tried to decipher the old style. *What sort of person writes like that? He sure used a lot of words to get his point across.*

Dal quickly tapped back his reply on his armband.

Mr. Taktug,

Thank you. I am indeed interested, and will arrive on October 12 to hear more. Please send travel instructions ASAP.

Regards, Dahlgren Riley

What is this going to involve exactly? he wondered. *Mr. Taktug said he needed a lot of daylight for the work. Sounds like a trip to the far south. Hope it is to someplace cool, where I have never been before. No more Amazonia. No Micronesia, Africa, or India. And no Chile.*

He opened the bedroom door. The house smelled like chicken and dumplings and something else he couldn't place. At his feet sat his dusty bag, filled with newly clean clothes.

Dal dragged the bag into the bedroom. He turned on his shower to tepid, perfect after the scorching day. He hummed as dirty water fell around his feet. After pulling on clean khaki pants and a blue shirt to match his eyes—he liked the way Ana always mentioned his eyes when he wore a blue shirt—Dal shoved the ring box into his deepest zippered pocket and secured it there. He folded Mori's note, put it in another pocket, and hurried to the kitchen.

THIS TIME THE TABLE had a Provençal cloth on it and was set for four. Dal sighed.

"Who's coming?" he asked.

"Just Uncle Leo. I called him while you were showerin'. Cousin George and Ernst can't make it. They're out on Coast Guard deployment. Live in Monck's Corner now."

"Okay. Just a reminder that I need to get to Ana's as fast as I can," Dal said. He lifted the lid on a big pot of his favorite but rare dinner and savored the smell. His face emerged glistening from the steam.

"Thanks, Mom. Rarely get this good a meal," Dal said.

"Neither do we, but this is a special night. My prodigal son has come home, and we have killed the fatted chicken." Risa laughed and waved a large wooden spoon aloft.

In strode Dal's father, all cleaned up in a fresh shirt, with his taller and heavier brother Leo behind him. "Look who the cat drug in," Jim boomed.

"I heard somebody special was here and had to come see for m'self," Leo boomed back.

Soon the kitchen was full of competing sounds with everyone talking in the traditional Southern, overlapping way that had become difficult for Dal. He had lost the knack of absorbing several conversations at once, as well as any trace of small talk that he might ever have had. He just watched, not wanting to draw things out a minute too long.

When he abruptly sat down, they all joined him. Dal shoveled a dripping spoonful of chicken-and-dumplings into his mouth and kept his face happy while he considered how he could get away fast.

"You look all spiffed up. Going to see Ana later tonight?" asked Uncle Leo.

"Yep, soon," said Dal, quickly lifting another huge spoonful. As long as his mouth was full, he could not be expected to say much.

"Better give her a comm first, Dal," Risa said. "A girl likes a little warning."

"Yep, she'll need time to chase off the other guy afore you get there," Leo said. Then, "Just joshing."

Dal bounced his eyebrows twice and kept on looking at the bowl while he ate.

"Well, I been expectin' a wedding invitation from you all one of these days anyway," Leo continued. "Both George and Ernst are married now. Could take 'em years for those two to have their child, so we're glad they got started. How old is Ana now? Gettin' on at—what is she, thirty-two?"

"Thirty," mumbled Dal as he scooped up another piece of chicken from his bowl. "Same as me."

Why did Mom and Dad have to ask Leo over tonight, of all nights? he thought.

Leo dug around in his own bowl. "Say, Risa, did you give the lad here all the dang chicken or what?"

"Course I did!" Risa exclaimed. "Lay off, Leo."

"My boys are plenty disappointed that they couldn't join us tonight," said Leo.

"Why couldn't they?" asked Jim.

"They're working night and day with the Coastal Commission on the latest remapping project, trying to keep nautical charts up to date with the new sea levels and shorelines and depths and all that. Even with satellite input and cognitive assets running the robots, it's a constant effort to make sure folks hear about new navigation info. Those elements can shift every day, especially after a storm. It's important work. Just like your job, Dal."

"Tell us more," Risa said.

Not now, Mom!

"Well, their favorite project so far was mapping the dive spots around Old Charleston, so they don't have to go search for bodies near St. Michael's spire and the Four Corners no more. Remember how you used to love to dive there with them, Dal? A lot safer now. It's hard but good work. A sure career. Not going to end abruptly like so many things do. Sort of the way your work is, too, I expect, Dal—right?"

"Yep," said Dal, taking another helping. "Never a shortage of work in the refugee business." He didn't want to go into all that now.

Leo started to speak again, but Dal abruptly got up from the table, scraping his chair noisily across the floor. "Sorry. Got to go now."

"Not before my peach cobbler!" exclaimed Risa. This was one of the few things on earth that would make Dal sit back down.

Risa removed the dumpling pot and gently lowered a big, hot cobbler with juices bubbling up over her homemade biscuit crust. The three men stared at it when she stepped back to get a clean serving spoon.

"Where'd ya get enough peaches for that?" asked Jim.

"I got my secret sources," Risa said, smiling through her long fingers covering her mouth. South Carolina peaches had once been the tastiest peaches in the whole country. Maybe on the whole earth. "From way up north" was all she would say.

Right after his last swallow of cobbler, Dal was up again. "Hate to miss the rest of this, but I got to go. Thanks for this amazing food, Mom. And thank you for coming, Uncle Leo. Say hi to the guys. We'll get together and dive again one day. I'd like to see that new Charleston Underwater National Park." While he spoke, Dal went around the table, first hugging Risa, then shaking hands with Leo, and finally patting his father on the shoulder, where his hand lingered.

A first shaft of lurid sunset slid across the floor and colored his father's face. Dal walked over to the sink and drew the kitchen curtains together before he left.

3

SAME EVENING

Dal stepped off the porch and strode the gauntlet of the camp back toward his rental car. He tried not to stare at the massive tent settlement now humming with life. The worst of the sun was over for another day. Dust and people were everywhere. So many people. Only a few lounged or laughed.

Most scurried along, staring at the ground as if deep in thought as they pursued one necessity or another: perhaps to refill a water jug or claim dry rations for the evening meal; to line up for the communal cooking burners or, if one had lost his own armband, to use a camp-wide comms band; or a child might be in line for a swing. There were also lines for the bathrooms and washrooms, for the camp infirmary, and for the machines to wash clothes. The possibilities for waiting were endless. And no one wanted to be the last person in line.

Dal preferred to look up and concentrate on the riotous sunset spreading overhead. This was his favorite time of day. The explosive color made him feel as if the universe might be friendly after all. Sunset smacked of possibility, of a better day tomorrow. He never tired of looking at it. He loved the sound of the cicadas starting up. Sunset also meant that the heat might be more bearable for the next ten hours or so—until the next sunrise, anyway.

"Dal, is that you?" called out a thin young man with walnut skin and shiny black hair dangling in a wave over one eye. He wore brown shorts and a faded tee shirt with a fish design on the front. Running to catch Dal, he called out, "Wait a few!" Then toward the line: "Hold my place, will ya?"

Recognizing the voice, Dal swirled and walked swiftly to meet him. He could take a quick minute to see his old diving friend. "Andy Thompson, don't get out of line!" Dal called. "I'll stand in line with ya for just a minute." But Andy shook his wet head and kept moving toward Dal. Sweat dripped down his forehead. He wiped it away with his palm as he pushed the hair up out of his eyes.

"No use for me to wait there anyhow," Andy said. "Likely to be all out of fresh sheets. Guess I'll lie on the dirty canvas one more night. Was hoping to put something between me and that cot. Never know who was on it for the afternoon rest. Ticks and bedbugs are every-where, ya know. Even triatomines. God, this place is filling up to overflowing,"

Andy looked around at the camp, his face pinched. "What are you doin' here, lookin' so cool and clean?" he asked Dal. "Haven't seen you in years." He grabbed onto Dal's arm. "Remember I'd take you out to snorkel the spire and tour the ruins? Remember when you caught that eel in a little net?"

Dal laughed. "Sure do. Just stopped to say a quick 'Hi.' "

"Where you live?" asked Andy.

"That's our place over there." Dal jerked his thumb in the direction of the long, low home on stilts, as if to say it was nothing much.

"Oh, lor', nice place," Andy said, squinting into the sunset. "So, we're setting up housekeeping on your land—is that right? I knew it had to be somebody's, but never thought of you guys."

"Nobody has it easy these days, okay?" Dal said. "My folks had their land taken to make this camp, and now they have almost no income." Too late he realized how that must sound to an inhabitant of the camp. He spied a Black Coat watching them. Andy scrubbed the dirt with his toe and looked at the ground.

"Look here." Dal pulled the paper with Mori's comm that he had copied for Ana out of his pocket. He tore a small sliver off the bottom, then fished in his other pocket for the pen from the bedroom and printed a few lines.

"Take this on up to the house and give it to my mom," Dal said. "She's bound to have an extra sheet you can use. Explain our connection, and she'll be grateful that you always got me back to shore in one piece. I remember all the crazy stunts we pulled." Dal slapped Andy on the back and started to turn away.

Andy took the bit of paper. "Yeah, those were the days, right? How long ya staying? We could still do something together, maybe?"

"Not likely this time," Dal replied. "Work, you know. But later maybe. See ya."

Andy cut him off. "Me and the wife got flooded out for good last month. I'm even thinking of joining up with those guys." Andy jerked his head in the direction of the two Black Coats watching them. "At least they get steady pay."

"No, don't do that, Andy," Dal whispered. "They are not your type of people. Something better will come along for you."

"After all my troubles," Andy said, "I find out that big house over there is where my old friend lives. Looks to me like you got it made in a nice home up on a little hill. Above the fray. Sometimes folks like me have to join the BCs just to eat, just to live."

Dal took a small step backward. Andy talked faster. "Never mind all that. Surely is good to see ya, my man. If that's really your dad I saw working around here, looks like he could use some help. Why you leavin' so fast?"

Dal couldn't think of a good way out of this. *Maybe I shouldn't have stopped to talk.* "To tell you the truth, Andy"—he paused. "To tell you the god-awful truth"—he stopped again and looked up at the last bit of orange-and-purple sunset over Andy's head. "Truth is, I can't take the goddamn heat."

Dal kicked the dirt, turned slowly, and walked down the path toward the former orchard and the car.

SUNSET'S COLOR SHOW was just about over. The dull gray of early twilight seeped in, and the cicadas tuned up. As the sky deepened to charcoal gray, tree frogs joined the cicadas and began their cascading roars from the few scrubby pines on the far side of the car park.

Dal clicked the picture of an ice cube on the car key. By the time he got inside, it was cool and dehumidified. He punched in Ana's address, and the car pulled out from among the relief vehicles. Dal smoothed out on his knee the note he had torn for Andy. He evened out the edges by folding the paper neatly under and patted the pocket containing the ring. Excitement mounted. What a tense couple of days. But joy was coming now, he was sure.

The car drove to the secondary road, and then onto Five Chop Road, which in a few more miles led to a shortcut and a bridge across the North Fork of the Edisto River. The river seeped along sluggishly at low water. It was hard to imagine the torrents his dad had described.

Despite the bass being gone, a few fishermen and -women lounged on the high, eroded bank in the dusk, their fishing lines trailing to the water far below. Short pines planted by the city shaded them and their beer coolers. In old Dahlgren Riley's time, dense hardwood forests had lined the river all along here, draping Spanish moss into the rich black water where fish dimpled the surface to eat the bugs alighting there. Dal had that mental picture because of Risa.

The car passed a few other cars. Soon he would be with Ana, and they would share a future together. *That is a whole new way of thinking: a future with somebody else.*

He rubbed both hands up and down his thighs, unaware of this tic, and tried to distract himself from worries about what Ana would think of his new job. He stared out the window while chewing the right side of his lower lip.

The car bumped across another small bridge. All the houses here were up on stilts.

Just about there now! Dal felt his hands getting sweaty and his breath coming faster when the car turned into an area of new construction. Everything was at stake now.

Elevated apartment buildings near Old Orangeburg circled a bermed lake created by draining the surrounding swamps. The buildings had catchy names like "Sparkleberry," "Waboo," and "Stumphole," after the former swamps. Dal half-hoped that this area one day would become a swamp again, exactly like it had been before: full of snowy egrets and blue herons, water moccasins, bullfrogs, and water lilies. And also cypress trees. *Not in my lifetime. Not like it looked in Mom's films.* Then once more he wished he had never seen those films.

He slumped back against the seat, overcome that his eight-year journey to get to this point was over. It was all behind him now. The car weaved as it climbed a tall hill of compacted dirt before stopping in front of the experimental underground structure where Ana lived.

Dal left the car to self-park and ran across the median and through the ornamental grasses to a communications board nestled under a sod-covered roof shading the descent pad to the building. *Lucky no one else is here.* A cooling vent around the board sent up a pleasant blast from below. He punched in Ana's code and immediately heard her voice waft up in a musical "Hello-o-o."

"It's me," was all he said before stepping onto the descent pad. It whirred softly, carrying him down four stories to her floor.

AS SOON AS Dal pulled aside the lift's door, he saw Ana running toward him down the long hall. He started running, too, and Ana threw herself into his outstretched arms. Her oriole-yellow dress wound around Dal's legs. Her wavy red hair covered his face. They kissed long and hungrily.

"Where you been? I missed you so," Ana murmured between kisses.

Dal murmured back, "I'm here now. I'm here." He leaned back just enough to get a better look at her face and saw that her green eyes were moist and a little bit red.

"Whoa, what's wrong?" he asked softly as he stroked her translucently pale face—the only one he had ever seen without a single freckle or sunspot. He was glad that she stayed out of the sun, even if it meant that she would only swim nude with him at night.

"Wrong? There's nothing wrong at all," she said. "I'm so surprised and happy and, well, amazed. It's poetic that you appeared right now. I was listening to some music, missing you terribly. You are an apparition, to show up like this. I have to see, to feel you to be sure it's really you." She laughed and lightly ran her hands over his body. She kissed him again. "Yes, it's you all right. Come show me how truly 'real' you can be."

They half-ran to her apartment door, unbuttoning, unzipping, un-belting clothes all the way. "What's been happening? Have you gone home yet? Everything all right?" Ana asked as they stripped off every-thing. She seemed alert to something different about this visit without warning.

"Just stopped home to clean up and have supper. Yes, all is fine— nothing special." Dal stopped, shocked that he could have given that routine answer at this big moment. "Well, maybe this is special." He pulled out the folded message and handed it to her. "And then again, maybe this isn't all that special. But there is something else, something *more* special that I want to ask you about."

"Now I'm getting confused," Ana laughed. Dal loved her laugh, so hearty but not loud. He held tight to her waist as they stumbled toward the bedroom.

"What is it that you have to tell me?" Ana asked, waving the paper. "What is it? What is this?" She seemed a little alarmed now. Dal began gently pulling her toward the bed. He would wipe out talk, which was not his strength. He would demonstrate how he felt, how happy he was to be with her and how much he loved her.

"Is it about this?" Ana asked again. She tried to shake open the grass paper still in her left hand, while Dal continued to hold fast to her right hand. Unable to shake open the paper, Ana tossed it on a table piled with books. "Never mind," she said. Ana raced him to the bed, where they fell on the comforter in an eager heap.

Together they moved quickly into their fastest and most certain ways to satisfaction, before using other pathways familiar from their years together. Dal expected they would enjoy leisurely experimen-tation when their lives together could stretch far into the unknown future, together every day and night. Tonight, they made love over and over, until they finally fell apart, breathless and laughing. Dal moved out of the three-quarter moonbeam thrown across the bed by the bed-room's artificial window, which as time passed had morphed into a deep night view, controlled to match the actual time and conditions. The branches of a programmed southern pine waved from exactly the right direction and with the same wind speed of the night above: ten to fifteen knots from the southeast.

"Are you thirsty?" Ana asked as she untangled herself from Dal's body and the scrambled sheets. "I need some water."

"Do you have any beer?"

"Sure do—always have your favorite. Because I *always* hope you will come back and surprise me. Like you just did." Ana strode naked into her galley kitchen and returned with a dripping cold Tradd Street Brewery Artesian Beer.

"How did you get this?" Dal sat up and grasped the beer by the bottleneck.

"They finally reopened in Greenville. Not as hard to get anymore," Ana said, smiling as he took long swallows. She climbed back on the bed behind him and kneaded his shoulders with her beer-cooled hands.

"Ooooh, my mysterious man, you are very tight here. Let me fix that for you." She kneaded deeper.

Dal set his beer on the bedside table, grabbed both of her hands, and pulled her around in front of him. "I know a better way you can do that," he whispered, kissing her neck and then her breasts. Ana moaned, and they fell back to making love again.

When Dal finally reached once more for the warm beer, Ana moved to get up. "Let me see. What's in that note? I almost forgot it. On grass paper? Must be a love letter," she said with a wink. She pulled herself up from the bed to her full five feet nine inches.

Watching her lovely naked body sway as she walked to the table by the door, Dal held his breath. He almost felt nauseated. *Okay, this is the time*, he told himself. But it was also when the special bonding of their lovemaking left him bereft of words. Determined to find the right words tonight, Dal waited for them to come to him.

Ana's face clouded when she scanned the letter. Dal could see that she was struggling to control herself.

"May I keep this?" she asked. She slowly folded the paper back the way it was before.

"Sure, just keep it to yourself." He hadn't needed to say that. She would.

Ana nodded very slowly, looking at him all the while. There was a long silence. He would have to be the one to speak first. She was not filling the silence, after all. *So this is new. Maybe this is good?* Ana had given him nothing to react to, nothing to arouse his defences.

Dal considered which, of all the things he needed to say, he should say first. He swallowed and was ready to begin when Ana moved suddenly and stood in front of him as he sat on the edge of the bed. She moved in closer between his knees, held his face in her hands, and whispered, "You know, don't you, that I love you to death."

In their early days together, these words would have caused him to make a joke or chat lightly and leave as fast as possible, lest he get too emotional and reveal his full depth of feeling. Now, though, with her steadiness and love, he was way past all that. He knew what he wanted to tell her—if he could just speak it. Dal put his arms around her and said, "Ana, will you marry me?"

"What!?" Ana yelped and leapt backwards. She peered at him intently and frowned. "Are you serious? Now? How did you come up with this?"

"Yes, I mean it," Dal said, looking into her eyes. She was asking too many questions at one time, so he answered only the most important one.

Ana studied Dal's face for another thirty seconds. It seemed endless to him. "If you are really, really sure," she paused—"yes, yes, *yes, YES!*" Ana drew close again, and they planted kisses like exclamation marks all over each other while laughing and jumping on the bed.

Finally hungry and exhausted, they poured vodkas and ate a snack of leftovers from Ana's fridge. She never served the normal dried meals, and Dal liked her food. She was perfect. He felt expansive, as if he could talk about anything.

"Ana, I resigned from the Rescue Corps."

"Thank God! I worried about you all the time when you were doing that."

"I have three and a quarter months' pay due me from unused vacation, and as you can see there," Dal pointed to the paper on the floor where Ana had dropped it, "the pay being offered by Mori is going to be many times what I would have gotten at a higher rank than I just left."

"That is too much," Ana said. "Makes this sound illegal. Where did this guy get all that?"

"Probably his parents had old oil money, earned before oil ran out. Then maybe they invested well." Dal knew he would never ask Mori about his inheritance. That would be like advertising whaling as one's heritage after the whales were all gone.

"I'm going to visit him and I will scope everything out. If there is anything wrong about the job, I won't do it. Remember, assessing and dealing with risk is one of my strengths."

"But where is it you are eventually going and when exactly will you be back? I need to know. If you're my fiancé, how could I not know? It sounds like Churchill is just a staging area. Where is Churchill, anyway? Maybe it's not safe there. I can't have you going off to dangerous places. Not anymore, Dal."

"Well"—he stopped himself and drew his lips in. This was just the sort of discussion that could ruin the beautiful feelings of the night. But he would get past it somehow. He took a deep breath and blew it out, aware that she was watching him.

"Might as well tell you all my ideas. Maybe we can find a place to live that's more comfortable than around here, if you are willing. I am sort of on the lookout for the best place in this messed-up world for us. And hopefully for our child one day," he added softly, stroking her arm.

"That is a whole lot to absorb, Dal. Immigration is not easy these days if you are not an actual refugee. It takes a lot of money. But that is way down the road. Where exactly is this job going to be taking you?" Ana asked again. "I need to know."

"Like the letter says, training will be in Canada. After that, I don't know exactly where we're supposed to go, either. But I think it might be Patagonia or someplace way south like that. It is not rescue, so maybe it will be ferrying a special cargo or something. At any rate, when I get up there in Churchill, I will find out and let you know all I can tell you."

"But you usually cannot send or receive any comms from your work. Are you sure you will be able to contact me this time?"

"I think so. I hope so—or else I will do it anyway. If worse comes to worst, it won't be long until I am back here with you. Let's get married in mid-January—how is that? After Christmas and when all this is over, even accounting for any delays?"

"January is great." Ana checked her homemade wall calendar, lifting up a couple of pages. She was the last person in all of South Carolina to use one of those, Dal was sure. "Looks like January 18 is a Saturday—and a perfect day to marry the guy I love. Then again, tomorrow would be great, too. Anytime is great. All we need is the magistrate and two or three people." Ana came over and sat on his knee, stroking and kissing his head.

"Ana, I have to tell you why tomorrow is not possible. I have to leave for this job tomorrow." There. He had said it. Flatly.

"What the bloody hell?!" Ana blurted. She picked up the letter and read the dates again. "Oh. I missed that part." She threw the letter down.

"Oh, well," she said. "Let's look up this New Churchill. I want to know all about where you are starting out, at least." Ana grabbed Dal's armband from the bedside stand where he had placed it the only time he had ever taken it off. She read aloud. Dal listened closely because he had skimmed over this part before.

"One hundred and fifty years ago, Hudson Bay's waters finally started flooding, pushed by rising ocean waters, just like all other bodies of water around the world that are connected to the sea. Isotonic rebound from under the bay could not keep up with the inflow, so finally water crept over the banks of the bay, forcing Churchill to move to higher ground." She looked up. "Blah, blah, blah. Let's just skip this promo BS," she said. "But this part about Willow Park Forest and House, and how Mori is the only owner, et cetera, might be good."

She read that to him.

"Okay, here is about Mori himself," Ana said. Dal listened again to be sure he had it right in his mind.

"Mori Taktug: Born February 3, 2154, Gillam, Manitoba, Canada. Father: Ahanu Taktug. Mother: Amelia Yamamoto."

"Christ, Mr. Taktug is 141-plus years old! He's past his allowed limit," Ana exclaimed. "Why anyone would want to live that long these days is beyond me. His parents must have paid for gene therapy."

"Well, it's not legal anymore, anyway." Dal pulled her closer. "I hope we can have a child without help, Ana. Let's get started."

No men or women his age that Dal knew had ever used birth

control, and yet they never seemed to get pregnant until the couple was ready for a child. Usually, conception happened when it was planned for, and a doctor helped them aggregate the male's sperm. Rarely did conception occur routinely, at least not in the former temperate First- and Second-World countries where extreme heat was not a part of their long genetic history. Nevertheless, people were still expected to have only one child, as the earth's carrying capacity was now much lower than it had been before the methane emergency of 2150. Dal was so used to this entire reality that he did not feel it was at all unusual for them to be talking about it openly.

Nor did Ana. "Whatever it takes, I'm ready," she said.

Ana tapped the armband. "Look here. Seems Mori is well educated and even has honorary degrees from McGill. Was on many boards and commissions, mostly about trees and CO_2 drawdown. He helped write the Tree Protection regulations for the World CO_2 Commission. Married once. Wife died in a boating accident on Hudson Bay. They had no children." Ana looked up at Dal. "How sad." She shook her head and looked down to continue reading.

"The original Churchill was a thriving Hudson Bay year-round sea-port. Before that, going back three hundred years, it claimed to be the best tourist destination where one could see North American polar bears when they congregated on shore until ice formed over the Bay in November. The ice allowed the hungry, post-denning bears to get to their seal-hunting grounds way out on the pack ice. The former Churchill was also the site of a famed Churchill Northern Studies Institute, a climate change research facility and the Churchill Rocket Research Range.

"Well, that sounds interesting," Ana allowed. She read on in a mocking sing-song voice: "Today, proud of those glorious traditions, New Churchill is pleased to house Northern Manitoba's famed polar bear and beluga whale museums, as well as a rookery for snowy owls. The famous Tundra Hotel and the Inuit and Native Cultures Museum have all been rebuilt in New Churchill."

"Aha, here comes what I was looking for," said Ana. "Tells me how to come and get your ass if you get hung up along the line!" Dal threw his head back and laughed heartily. He had never heard Ana talk this way, but he liked it. She seemed liberated by their engagement. "Transport to Churchill is available via the commercial rocket port. Vehicle rentals for local use are available."

She put down his armband. "Okay. Churchill sounds safe enough. But don't be gone too long. And try to keep in touch? I'll start on wedding plans and have nightly sweet dreams of you."

Dal hugged her tightly. "Remember," he murmured in her ear, "whenever you are looking at the moon, I will be looking at the same moon, too."

As he dressed, Dal felt the lump in his zipped pants pocket. "Hold on—I was so excited to be with you that I didn't think of this."

Dal took her hand and slid the ring onto her finger. The gold was perfect with her red hair. The ring was too big, though, falling off if she tilted her hand down at all.

"Oh, Dal, it's so beautiful!" Tears came to Ana's eyes. She quickly said, perhaps to hide them, "I can get it sized while you are away." She smiled again. "It looks antique, and I love it. But it's *you* that I love more than anything. And always have."

He held her face close and kissed her again. "And I love you. Forever."

Then Dal was gone, like so many times before. But this time, everything felt different. His step was light. He knew that Ana was happy about their future together, too. He must do what Dahlgren Riley had done eight generations before and find another place for their home.

4

The World Migration Police Force, commonly called "Black Coats" because of their distinctive uniforms, will henceforth be deployed in all airports and refugee locations that service a high proportion of migrant peoples.
—Bulletin #287 of the Human Migration Commission, March 12, 2275

OCTOBER 12, 2295

The afternoon rocket bus from Columbia, South Carolina, to New Churchill, Canada, was overbooked. Sweat dripped from Dal as he waited to load on the tarmac.

Looks like everybody wants to go north and nobody is coming back. Just look at their bags and the extra layers of clothes they are wearing. The pungent odor of old sweat was overpowering.

This loading up and flight was going to take much longer than the advertised forty-six minutes. As a "special passenger," a gift from Mori, Dal knew he would be able to get on first. But he could not get close to the entry door in this mob. The crowd packed tight, and no one would give way for anybody else, so anxious were they all to get into the cooler air of the rocket.

"Those with blue cards, hold them high so we can see you," bellowed a tall robot gatekeeper in pleasant tones. "I know you are all hot, but please make way for them."

The robot picked up an amplifier and began using it to call out over the din. "Remain calm. Everybody will get on this flight. You *will* have a seat. Help us out to speed things up." As happened ever more frequently, a Black Coat stood beside the robot and focused his scanner on every passing face. If a red light did not come up, that person was allowed through.

Thank God for Mori, Dal thought. He liked him already. Dal waved his bright-blue card high over his head and pushed harder. When he got near the door, the robot with the horn grabbed his arm and pulled him into the passageway along with a few others. His grip was metallic. Meanwhile, the Black Coat had fixed on someone else in the crowd. There was a scramble behind him, but Dal did not look around to see.

He climbed up the interior stairs and settled himself near the top exit, hoping to get off quickly upon landing. Most passengers fanned themselves with hand-fans provided at each seat. It would remain stifling until the flight got under way. Dal belted himself in, closed his eyes, and reviewed the past thirty-six hours in his mind.

It had been his best trip home in years. He replayed the ecstasy of his time with Ana and felt it all anew. He smiled at the way his parents had gotten so excited about his upcoming marriage and hopeful about a grandchild. His mom had wept with joy. Dal could almost do that right now, just remembering.

His stomach growled. The flight was too short for food service, but the air was thick with carry-on provisions: fried jellyfish, okra gumbo, seaweed and rice with garlic, bread with marmalade. He dug in his backpack and found the pimento and leftover chicken rollups his mother had rushed to pack for him, and quickly wolfed those down.

Dal did not realize the rocket had taken off until he felt his body pressing down hard into the seat, because this plane had new stabilizing technology. Nevertheless, lift-off was never comfortable. He really did not like rocket flights. Dal popped his eyes open when he felt a moist hand grip his right arm instead of the armrest.

The hand released its hold with "'Scuse me." A red-faced, heavily wrapped young man wearing two jackets and four shirts, from the count of variously colored cuffs at his sleeve, pulled back his hand.

The middle-aged woman to Dal's left had also overdressed, especially given the day's heat index of 119 degrees. Sweat streaked her face. Mori had written Dal that he would provide everything Dal would need except for medications and underwear. Dal appreciated Mori more with every step of this trip so far. Eventually, the air-conditioning caught up with the musty heat and overcame it.

"Are you going north for pleasure?" asked the young man on his right.

"Yes," Dal lied with finality. He didn't want a meaningless conversation now. He preferred getting back to reliving last night.

"I'm movin' up there," the young man continued. "My whole family got washed out from Monck's Corner by Hurricane Abbey last season. We finally got assigned a place in one of the new camps near Orangeburg, but it's no good there. Just a dusty ol' dead orange grove. Too crowded and noisy, too."

Dal stifled a flash of recognition. He decided not to ask.

"I heard life might be better in Canada, so my uncle agreed to buy me a flight up there," the young man said. "If I like it, I'll send for my sisters. That is, if they will let me stay," he added, lifting his chin. "By the way, my name is James."

"Well, good luck," Dal replied, turning on his seat monitor and staring straight ahead.

James leaned into Dal's space to get a better look at the screen images. Dal moved to turn the screen off. James stayed his arm. Dal turned and glowered at James. After all, James had a screen of his own.

"Wait a minute. Just look at those poor devils!" exclaimed James.

Rag-clad figures, emaciated and brown with mud, tugged at bundles of what might have been bodies while the emotionless voice of a reporter noted that more villages in the higher parts of the plain of the Benares had washed away in the deadly combo of rising tide and seasonal rains.

"We're mighty lucky to live in the good ol' U.S. of A., and in the good ol' North American Alliance, I'd say. Wouldn't you?"

By tacking on that "Wouldn't you?" James spoke in the common Southern nonquestion mode. Dal knew James was merely asking him to agree, but he still hated this style. He never knew how to respond to it. The only routinely acceptable response to a nonquestion was to agree, but Dal instinctively rebelled against just going along. Especially about this subject. *Not worth it for transient compatibility,* he thought.

Instead of just ignoring James and turning off the screen, Dal replied bluntly, "That's been going on for hundreds of years now. No surprise to them." He spoke with clipped words, thinking he would put an end to this unwanted conversation. But then he was drawn further into it by his own memories. Later he would think that he probably should have kept quiet.

"Floods have always been part of the cycle of life there," he said. "They've gotten worse, that's all. Monsoons always flood the delta, especially after total deforestation in the Himalayas two hundred years ago added to rapid runoff. Then the monsoon shifted course, so now water also comes directly in from the sea, bringing even higher tides and stronger storms."

James stared at Dal with wide eyes, but Dal couldn't stop until he had finished his point.

"No matter where the water comes from, it's still flooding, same as for eons. And some people's acceptance of fate is just the same, too. As long as they think of all this extra devastation as a force of nature rather than manmade, they don't get angry. Only the people who understand it—understand that we made these floods this bad ourselves—those people get mad as hell."

He stopped abruptly and changed the channel, moving the picture to a continuous tracking of their rocket on the map. He had said too much, riled them both up.

"Whoa, sounds like you know what you're talking about." James's friendly interest asked for more, but Dal was not going there now. He cut the conversation short in a way he had mastered by living outside of the South for long periods of time.

"I need a nap," he said, and switched off the monitor altogether.

After a while, the relaxation Dal usually felt in planes he wasn't flying himself swept his mind into fuzzy whiteness. He knew that clouds would be drifting below, that the blue of their brief orbit would deepen and stars would dot the views in the rocket's small, round windows. He had seen this so often, he didn't bother to look out anymore. Other pictures and sensations he knew to bring up were more compelling.

Soothing images and sounds floated through his mind: the pounding of waves against rock in Maine; sitting by the Edisto River and hearing the whine of mosquitoes intensify before they fell malevolently silent on his skin and he made a game of swatting them before they could bite; the happy sound of tree frogs in a deepening night; and by far the most evocative sensations of all, his last night with Ana.

Within twelve minutes a voice announced that it was time to disembark: "We have landed in Akjuit Terminal in New Churchill. Akjuit is Inuktitut for 'the winter star that rises in the dawn of the day.'"

A CACOPHONY OF unfamiliar dialects roared into Dal's ears when he walked off the conveyor belt into the terminal. Boxes and suitcases lay all over the floor. One could barely walk through it all. Dal carefully pushed a large box out of his path with his toe.

"Watch it—that's fragile," said a small woman with tense eyes who sat on a pile of her possessions.

Looks like they brought everything they own. He had seen intense groups like this before in other places. Most recently in his parents' front yard.

Dal saw a few Black Coats on the edges of the baggage area. They stood stiffly and watched the doors. Black Coats. They seemed to be everywhere now. They sometimes helped enforce new environmental laws, Dal knew. It had taken their brute force to get compliance with the tough laws banning wet rice-paddy cultivation and outdoor pasturing of cattle.

"So, they are even up here," he muttered to himself.

Dal tried to act like a local when he passed through a door between two Black Coats. Wearing only one layer of clothes helped. That had been Mori's suggestion. The BCs checked nearly everyone else's identity, but not his, not this time.

He scanned the crowd for a driver with the "Willow Park" sign that Mori had told him to find. Eventually Dal spotted a large man wearing a green shirt and a baseball cap, holding his name aloft at the edge of the crowd.

"Hello," Dal said, as he flashed his identification. The man glanced at the card. His hat brim was low, so Dal never got a look at his eyes. He grabbed at the small bag in Dal's hand.

"I can carry that," said Dal, hanging on. But the man tugged back, so Dal let go and followed as closely as possible while the crowd surged around them. Together they shoved their way toward the car park. The air was fresh and cool. Still the man said nothing.

"Always busy like this?" Dal inquired.

The silent man spread his hands and lifted his shoulders with down-turned lips in a gesture that said, "I got no idea." Or maybe, "Who cares?" Dal began to wonder if he was a new type of speechless robot.

They stopped at the rear of a sleek black car. Dal recognized this model as one of the latest fusion cars with an expensive lightweight battery.

"What a beauty," he said appreciatively. Everybody coveted one of these scarce cars, especially in the higher latitudes where sun cars might go unused for months.

Since this car was a two-seater with a jumper in the back, Dal got in next to the driver, who promptly fell asleep after the car started moving. They rocked gently over the tarmac for a few seconds before zipping up to speed and careening around the other vehicles.

This jerky movement woke the driver up. He punched a few buttons and looked over at Dal.

"Sorry. I had it set on 'Hurry.' Needed to get here in time to meet you, but we don't have to move that fast going up to Willow Park. My name is Henri Fourchette. I am the general do-everything for Mr. Taktug. Advise you to call him 'Mori,' like everybody else does. 'Taktug' doesn't exactly roll off the tongue. He understands that."

"Happy to meet you, Henri. My name is Dal."

"Yes, I know. Must apologize for falling asleep like that. Was up late last night watching my son play baseball for the Malaperts. They are the best moon team." Henri touched his cap to point out the team symbol.

"Is your son from there?" asked Dal.

"Yes, but only born there. We brought him home right after his birth. He was so premature they didn't think he would make it. See, we didn't expect to ever have a baby or would never have signed on for a moon tour. Money is very good, though."

"That is really interesting," said Dal, who was not at all interested in baseball or life on the moon. He had questions about Mori and his new job in mind.

"So, we raised Lou on earth, and he grew up more muscular than most moon kids do, because he grew up here in our stronger gravity. But because of his birth, he could still try out for their team, and his overall strength got him a spot. Plays up there, domed field and all. Took him a while to master the ball speeds in less gravity, though. Even the dome does not really replicate Earth."

"Wow. And how long have you been here working for Mori?"

"Soon will be twenty-eight years. I take good care of him."

"What does that entail?" Dal asked.

"Mostly make sure he gets his stabilizer meds, that's all. Then run the household. You know, he gave my son a good education," Henri said.

"So, he is doing well?" Dal asked. "I read that he must be nearly 142 years old now. Very unusual."

"Oh, for sure. He's doing great. You'll see for yourself."

"I look forward to meeting him." Dal said. He could see that Henri was a man to keep on your side.

The crush at the terminal gave way to ordinary urban congestion dominated by multicolored housing complexes. The structures were surrounded by trees freshly planted up and down the new streets that wove across the gently undulating land. Huge rounded stones and embedded Canadian Shield stone were often displayed for landscaping detail.

Henri opened his window and waved his left arm outside. "Eight thousand, five hundred years before now, all this land was smashed under the Keewatin Ice Cap. Can you believe it? When the ice left, there was nothing but muskeg bog and stone around here. Not fit for habitation. By now, the muskeg is about all dried up, and the smaller rocks have been used in construction. They had to drill into the rocky shield to make holes for some of the trees. Backbreaking job that was.

"There were a few scrubby trees and willows here long ago, but those have slowly moved north. We brought most all of these trees from way south over the past hundred and fifty years."

Dal was taken with the landscape plantings sparkling in the mid-afternoon sun. Trees, shrubbery, and even flowers looked healthy. Some lived in fissures, some in holes drilled into the stony shield and filled with dirt.

"How lucky to have so many new homes aboveground," Dal said.

Henri's plump cheeks pushed out to each side and he grimaced. "As you saw in the terminal, a lot of you folks are coming up here now. Could be too many. We can't handle everybody, you know. But you must be okay or Mori would not have invited you. He's a very private man."

Dal took it all in. He knew what this had looked like before from his mom's films. Where Arctic willows had once bent their red branches away from the wind and bog cranberry had brightened the wetlands seasonally, now a magnificent mixture of old trees and new saplings of all kinds swayed in the steady winds from Hudson Bay. Shifting growth zones had allowed all sorts of previously impossible plants to take root. Dal didn't know most of their names.

Henri proudly supplied those. "We've got sugar maple, white and black spruce, aspen, birch, and even oak trees. You're at the best time to see them in blazing color, too. We've also got a few conifers left. Those are the green ones with needles. The rest either died out or were moved to more suitable areas farther north. Actually, Mori has a good bunch in his woods, though, because there is a cool spot, with winds from the north that funnel into the property."

"Looks like plants are big business here," remarked Dal. The nearest natural forest of these deciduous trees was too far away for them to have spread here naturally.

Dal was surprised to feel his eyes sting. He hungrily took it all in: the clear blue water rippling between streambanks; the tumbled, tan and gray river-washed stones collected at the curves: the sharp, green grasses; the sculptural skeletons of trees that had already dropped their leaves and fanned against the sky; and the other brilliant trees waving banners of leaves still hanging on.

He let his eyes rest on each new piece of evidence of life, ignoring as best he could all the signs of construction. Where the Deer and Churchill rivers met, the color of trees not native to this land in the past shouted to him against the blue sky.

Dal opened the car window and breathed deeply. His hot, Southern lassitude was gone, gone with his sweat dried up in the cool air.

The car glided around a sharp right curve, past a stone marker, and onto a dirt-and-gravel path. They sped by an old stone guardhouse, where a woman came out to wave but did not stop them. The road entered a much older boreal forest of aspen, birch, spruce, and tamarack that had managed to survive, cool and sheltered where they grew along the frothy creek bed. Dal had never paid much attention to trees, perhaps because he had never seen any this healthy and beautiful before.

"Is this part of Mori's big forest? Part of Willow Park Preserve?" he asked Henri.

"It sure is," Henri replied. "Lucky to escape all that building frenzy back down the road."

"How can he protect it from all the people streaming in to build new housing?" Dal asked.

"This forest was grandfathered into a preservation law here, seen to by his ancestors," Henri explained. "Never to be touched. Cost them a pretty sum to do that."

Sunlight sparkled through the shaking aspen branches and glinted off vermilion leaves already on the ground. These leaves billowed up behind the silent car, their rustling the only sound of its passing. A lone, red-shouldered hawk left its perch and circled cautiously before settling deeper into the woods.

5

The dream of abundant, safe, and clean nuclear-fusion energy dates back to MIT in the 1950s. In 2018, it was declared "the ideal energy source, absolutely necessary to fully replace fossil fuels by 2055," if the earth were to avoid the ecological path we are on today. This incisive book describes how the world ignored calls for a Manhattan Project-styled effort to produce and deliver abundant fusion energy for worldwide use. Fusion arrived too late to save us. With twists and turns in public policy, greed, and skulduggery, this essential history reads like a thriller.

—Book review: *A History of Fusion Fuel: Just a Little Too Late,*
  by Arlie Pritchard; published November 16, 2095

AFTERNOON, OCTOBER 12, 2295

The car nestled gently into the pebbled circular driveway of a large, gray stone house with low wings built out on each side. There were no plants in front to break up the austerity, but French doors and large windows helped. *Those big windows would not work at all back home,* Dal observed.

A slight man with faintly Asian features burst from the wooden front door. He smiled broadly and called, "Welcome, welcome!" His casual clothing looked to be of an unusual fabric, the cut of his clothes possibly bespoke. *Well, that fits,* Dal thought. *Maybe he got hold of some antique cotton cloth and repurposed it.*

The man's age was difficult to determine. His straight, silvery hair capped a face unlined except for deep smile creases between his nose and mouth. His frame was wiry. Dal had expected him to be stooped if he really was Mori and over 141 years old. But this man stood straight at his five feet ten inches. He exuded energy, and his stride was quick. His hazel eyes wrinkled at the edges when he smiled at Dal, deepening his facial creases even more.

"Thank you, Henri," the man nodded, and extended his hand to Dal. "Welcome to Willow Park House. I am Mori Taktug. Henri here will take good care of you—and of us all." He swept his arm around as if to indicate masses of people, although they were alone in front of the big stone home.

Dal had seen similar radiant energy before, a feature of zealots everywhere, so he purposely drew his words out.

"Good to meet you, Mr. Taktug. My name is Dal Riley."

"Yes, I know," the man beamed. "You may call me Mori. Everyone does, except for Henri sometimes. He tries to keep up the standards he thinks are appropriate. Standards from the past, though. Isn't that right, Henri?"

"Yes, sir."

"Please follow me. We have a lot to do."

Dal walked behind at his own ambling pace, determined to stay autonomous in the presence of a man he suspected was accustomed to being the eye of his own private hurricane.

Mori led Dal through a large anteroom paved with black-and-white marble squares. They skirted a round central table topped with a fresh flower arrangement. *Mom tried these. Wilt right after blooming if you can get them to bloom at all back home,* Dal thought. He snapped a quick photo of them with his armband. Dal thought that Mori could not have seen him taking the photo, but Mori looked back immediately and motioned for Dal to keep up.

Nearing the back of the house, they stepped down into a glass sunroom that looked out on three sides to a landscaped garden unfolding down the back lawn. Dal walked past Mori to the glass and gazed out onto the variegated greens and delicate colors, as if taking in a priceless work of art.

"It seems you like the garden," said his host softly.

"It's so beautiful," said Dal, his eyes fixed on the view. "This is the sort of thing we try to paint on our walls at home to pretend that we can see out. We don't use glass that much. It lets in too much heat. I didn't know gardens like this existed anymore." Dal turned to face Mori, who stepped back as if he had been standing too close.

"One day, if I designate no heir, this home and the forest will become a deeded preserve of the government, and they will do what they want with it. But for now, it is still mine. Somehow, I hope the trees will be maintained after I am gone. Not sure if I trust anyone else to do that. So far, I've been lucky to keep alive nearly all of the original forests my grandparents established," Mori said.

"All the national parks have suffered immense die-back, and they can't afford to replant appropriate stock. But I can still keep up this little outpost."

Mori turned away and beckoned Dal with his hand. "We can talk more about that later on. I want to take you somewhere else now."

Dal wondered what sort of priorities made Mori so dedicated to plants just for eye appeal—plants that were inedible and unwearable, especially when human need, as Dal had experienced it, was overwhelming in most of the world.

Mori threw open the rear French doors to a grassy loop around the near garden and set off at a fast clip down a bluestone path that wound through banks of color.

Dal followed, anxious to learn details of the task Mori was offering him. Did Mori want him to fly other tree species up here to fill out his preserve? Or maybe bring in exotic flowering plants from distant locations? Did Mori think that Dal would become his head gardener, or protect his trees? No, that was impossible. Mori was paying way too much for Dal to become a gardener or security guard.

They walked without speaking for six minutes, through cultivated gardens that melted into natural border growth and finally lifted to become the same wild forest Dal had been driven through. Eventually, they came to a clearing in which sat a large yurt. Dal bent down and followed Mori through the tent flap.

"This is where I do my best thinking," Mori said. "It's my emotional home, although it gets devilishly cold in the winter because I have not arranged for heat out here yet. I retreat to the comforts of the big house more than my conscience would like to admit. But we will be able to talk better here for now."

Dal thought maybe this was a museum of some sort. Items of personal use from the Stone Age to the present day were arranged as if someone still used them. Rush mats covered the floor. An early-generation household robot stood dustily near the entrance, as if on guard. A modern, full-spectrum communication wristband like Dal's lay on top of a mangy brown fur skin, which in turn covered a pile of dried grass, with body imprints that suggested it might be a bed.

An old *gamutik,* or Inuit sledge, served as a low table, atop which lay a ragged hardcopy book with some pages turned down at the corners. Dal was anxious about their impending conversation, but in order to appear nonchalant, he picked up the book and read the cover: *On Walden Pond.* He put it down.

Never heard of it.

An iron skillet sat atop the latest solar cookstove, which was vented to the outside through a hole in the top of the yurt. The stove and the tent's indirect lighting drew stored power from two movable solar-battery cells that Dal had seen outside.

Probably Mori has a fusion-fuel battery set up for the big house, Dal thought. *He will need a much larger storage system there, if so.*

The whole scene was confusing as to what century it represented. This place, obviously very special to Mori, seemed to assimilate the history of man in one room. Dal wondered who had used the old implements originally, and as he thought about that, his own foundation in time seemed to slip away.

He tried to recenter himself. This place felt as extreme as his mother insisting that he watch outdated nature films and love them. Dal shook his head to clear it.

Mori crossed his legs at the ankles and sat straight down on a mat. He made it look easy. Dal tried to follow suit but ended up falling with a plop and then painfully folding his knees and pulling his ankles into position with his hands. There was no place else to sit. This was damned uncomfortable. Dal managed to keep his face impassive, even as a nervous laugh welled in his chest.

"Well, let's get on with why we are here today." Mori's bony hands lay relaxed and open over his akimbo knees. When he spoke, his body remained still and straight, motionless in the way a cat watches a mouse.

"Great," replied Dal.

"First, I expect that you will at some point think I am crazy, or at least very eccentric."

Yep, beyond belief, thought Dal. He looked fearlessly into Mori's eyes.

"I am used to that reaction after years of trying to get things done by people in power. But I can assure you that everything we will talk about is on the level, and I am quite sane. The fact is, it doesn't really matter what you think of me as long as you are able and willing to carry out what I ask of you."

Dal felt his legs going numb, but he didn't shift position.

"Contrary to my parents' wishes, I am not going to live forever. So, I must get this done now, for my conscience and for humanity." Mori spoke faster and more urgently. "I am running out of time to do what I believe might reduce CO2 even a little bit for future generations here on Earth. Also, I am running out of time to prevent the trashing of the last great land mass left on this planet.

"We have to do what we can for those yet unborn. Removing excess CO2 from our atmosphere back to regenerative levels will take many, many thousands of years. And meanwhile, the feedback loops of devastation march on. I am thinking way ahead now, you see. Don't you wish that prior generations had done the same?"

Dal nodded. "Yes, indeed, I do."

"Well then, we have to be a bit visionary, don't you agree?"

Here again was one of those manipulative questioning modes that Dal usually resisted. Except on this occasion, he surprised himself by simply saying, "Yes, I suppose we do."

"Okay." Mori leaned back, obviously pleased. "Here is the mission," he said, using the language in which Dal had received his marching orders for the past eight years.

"Your task will be to fly a new aircraft especially designed for this single use to Nuevo Ushuaia, Argentina. There you will pick up a load of ten saplings of a particular species of tree, the relatives of which used to flourish in Antarctica back when it was ice-free, when the continent was part of Gondwanaland before plate tectonics broke it apart, and when it experienced temperatures similar to those today.

"Those trees can be found in the small part that remains of Lapataia

National Park, in the mountains behind Nuevo Ushuaia. I will have a man meet you on the first of the two nights you will spend in Nuevo Ushuaia. He will help with this leg of your journey, and with obtaining and loading the trees."

Dal sat taller now, the pain of his awkward position forgotten and his face wrapped in concentration.

Mori continued: "After you load the South American saplings, which will supplement some I have chosen from this preserve, you are to fly to a predetermined area of newly exposed land in the West Antarctic Island group, where you are to plant them. You will have an approximate idea of where to land but will need to scout out the exact spot that will be most appropriate."

Now that Mori was talking about navigation, Dal was completely with him.

"I want you to plant the trees where prevailing winds will have a chance, over years, to propagate them more widely. You are to camp near the trees for four weeks, take care of them, and be sure they are off to a reasonable start. Then you will fly directly back here."

"I know all about flying, but nothing about trees," Dal said.

"You will have two others on the plane with you," said Mori. "One of those people is a tree-renewal expert who is known for his work with nitrogen-fixing fungi and other things."

"What does the third person do?" Dal asked. He hoped it would be a big, strong laborer. Hauling tree saplings about and planting them did not sound easy.

"The third person will be an informed and wise assistant for any unusual circumstance, including survival situations," Mori answered.

"That brings up another important question: What are the risks? I have a wedding to attend in mid-January," Dal said. "My own."

"To be honest, I cannot predict every untoward thing that could happen," said Mori. "We will make every effort to anticipate them, and that is why you will be here for nearly a month before setting out: to train, to plan for contingencies, and to prepare your kit of supplies. But as I have envisioned the mission and as far as I know at this point, it is straightforward and doable. Of course, you will have to look out for Black Coat interference, but that is true in anything one does, wherever you go on Earth."

"This sounds very interesting," Dal said. "My mother would definitely approve of your goals. So, I guess I'm in." Then he couldn't help adding, "I know it's too early and also presumptuous to ask, but what about after—after this two months of work? Will there be more to do later? I will be looking for something steady after this assignment is over."

"Possibly," Mori replied. "There is always a place for someone like you, and as you saw, this area is booming. I am glad you are able to do this mission. But to be blunt, I do not anticipate that I will plan a follow-on expedition myself, although others might do that once we are successful. My time left here is too short for that."

With those words, Mori rose nimbly to his feet, showing no trace of stiffness. Dal struggled awkwardly to get up and brushed off the seat of his pants while Mori held open the tent flap for him to pass into the golden late afternoon.

As they walked back up the path, Mori spoke warmly.

"Tonight, you are at liberty. Please rest up and get comfortable here. Dinner will be served to you in your suite at eight. Feel free to roam the many forest and garden paths, or to swim in the pool any time you like.

"Tomorrow we will meet after breakfast, which will also be served in your suite at eight. Starting with lunch tomorrow, breakfast and lunch thereafter will be a buffet served in the small dining room, and dinner will be in the large one. We will have time to get better acquainted tomorrow and to talk more about the mission. You will also meet your new colleagues when we start. At 8:30 sharp. See you then."

BACK IN HIS ASSIGNED SUITE with its good view of the garden, Dal went over the entire strange conversation in his mind. He wished he had thought to make a recording of it. He had listened carefully, but he had been slightly distracted by the musty smells of leather and evergreens, foreign to his senses. Did he miss anything? He hoped not.

Dal recalled the sensations accompanying Mori's velvety voice, especially how the yellow light of the midafternoon sun had poured through the hole in the yurt's roof without heating everything to blistering. And how the house finches had chirped loudly outside.

He remembered feeling calm and sure when he declared himself "all in" with the plan. Now, though, in his room alone, his stomach tightened. He forced a few deep breaths. *What am I getting into that I do not see? Well, maybe tomorrow will tell.*

DAYLIGHT FADES EARLY at the sixty-eighth parallel north in October. After a light supper, Dal jogged out his door, turned left past the garden, threw off his robe, kicked off his slippers, and plunged into the pool. He yelled unceremoniously from the shock. He could not take a full breath, gasping instead from the spasms of his diaphragm. The water was frigid. Why was the pool so cold in this opulent setting? Couldn't Mori afford to heat it? Dal had never plunged into cold water before, anywhere.

After a few minutes of thrashing around, his reddened skin throbbed with the false heat sensation that extreme cold can produce. Soon he cut through the water fiercely, warmed and invigorated by the motion. After a few laps, even the top of his head felt warm. He sliced through the turns, pushing off as if pursued.

Half an hour later, Dal floated for one final, languid lap and enjoyed the sound of water sloshing in his ears. He stopped at the end near his towel, reluctant to leave the pool for the cool twilight air.

A small, dark figure stepped out of the woods and crossed the grass at the far end of the pool. The silhouette, wrapped in a heavy robe, was blurred in the near-darkness. Only lights from the pool and those twinkling along the paths let Dal know anyone was there at all. This person's walk was neither male nor female in any distinct way, merely purposeful.

As the figure neared the pool, the robe parted and fell. The water was severed by a simple, clean, remarkably quiet dive. Dal thought he must surely have been noticed, but the nude swimmer with black hair and light brown skin turned at his end of the pool and retraced her strokes with no acknowledgment.

He felt a bit chagrined. Whoever she was, she had not coughed, yelped, or otherwise had to adjust to the Arctic water at all. He hauled himself out of the breeze-rippled pool and wrapped himself in a towel, conscious of every movement and feeling a little absurd. Dal strode back toward his room full of curiosity. Despite a great desire, he did not look back.

The flowers and trees that had colored the day receded into the night's mauve mist. Black was the forest beyond. Only a few of the brightest stars shone through a haze wafting in from the bay. It looked to Dal as if wispy clouds were blowing in, thin strands against the night. They moved a little strangely, though—just enough to catch his full attention.

High overhead, the cloud-like apparition grew, strengthened, and then waved like a diaphanous curtain blown by a breeze. The white changed to pale green, and then turned a darker green tinged with yellow as the waves danced vigorously across the sky.

Dal sighed aloud with pleasure.

For a few moments, he imagined himself to be a caribou-clad Inuit walking beside a dog-drawn sledge far out on the pack ice during the long winter's night, isolated but comforted by the shimmering aurora, which in Inuit culture represents all the people who have crossed to the afterlife.

Or, Dal imagined, he might have been an oil prospector from the twentieth century. He would have come to the cold north to get rich and would have left again as soon as he could, hating most things about the Arctic, except for this sublime color in the night sky—which made him laugh out loud for no reason.

Dal saw in his mind a procession of faces through the ages, all tilted upward. And he thought of his kinship with all of those people, all the people who had ever felt happiness at the capricious wonder of the northern lights. He watched a long time before going inside.

6

This eight hundred-kilometer (five hundred-mile) passage between Cape Horn and Livingston Island is the shortest crossing from South America to Antarctica. In those latitudes, the Antarctic Circumpolar Current meets no land mass during its complete circle around Antarctica. Seas become mountainous. The flow of water in this current is six hundred times the former flow of the Amazon River Basin when it was at its peak in the twentieth century, before the desertification of Amazonia.

—*Comsapediass:* The Drake Passage; last altered 6/3/2294

OCTOBER 13, 2295

This morning a low cloud cover spread clammy fog through the trees. It condensed on leaves and splattered noisily to the ground like rain. Dal and his new coworkers stood beside the conference table in a twenty-by-fifteen-foot den converted into a workspace.

Mori introduced the team members to one another. "I am glad you are all finally here and that each of you has agreed to carry out what I like to call 'Operation Green Antarctica.' Please have a seat and, starting with you, Dal, tell us a little about yourselves." He motioned for Dal to begin.

"I am Dal Riley, age thirty, formerly a major in the International Rescue Corps, from Orangeburg, South Carolina. I have flown many sorts of planes in rescue ops all around the world for the last eight years. You name it. But I have never flown to Tierra del Fuego or to Antarctica. I look forward to this new challenge."

"Thank you, Dal," said Mori. "Dal probably did not want to mention that he specialized in difficult assignments and for that received the Distinguished Service wings. Your turn, Walt." Mori turned to the five-foot ten-inch blond man with a small bulge over his belt and a serious expression.

"My name is Walt Halamore, age forty-two. My family was originally from Halifax, Nova Scotia, but moved to Saskatoon when the Halifax Harbor Barrier failed some years back. I am married with no children. I am a botanist specializing in nitrogen-fixing fungi and tree migration, both historical and present-day. I have written scholarly works on the feasibility of trees surviving on Antarctica. I—"

"Thank you, Walt," Mori said. "And now your turn, Naija."

"I am Naija Arnatsiaq, from up north. Central Ellesmere Island, actually. My age is immaterial," she said with a faint smile. "Mori asked me to come along and help you in any way needed. I am happy to do that." Naija gave a slight bow of her head.

Dal watched her intently because he recognized her. She was the woman who had dived into the pool last night.

The three sat down around a table strewn with maps, while Mori stood in front of a screen on which a blue, green, and brown image of the earth was transmitted in real time from a satellite array. Everyone on earth had seen the original such earth image—the famous "Big Blue Marble" taken by the crew of Apollo 17 on December 7, 1972, the first generation of humans ever to view their home planet from space. It was part of ancient history taught in school and demonstrated for children of 2295 just how snowy the earth had been back in the day—in the far north, far south, over Greenland, and atop the highest mountains everywhere, even in Africa. This current image made clear to everyone that now only a tiny and diminishing part of Antarctica was still clothed in white year-round.

Mori rotated the image and zoomed in until the West Antarctic Islands and the East Antarctic land mass filled the screen. Then he backed off a bit to include the tip of South America and a chain of circular storms moving slowly past the outstretched arm of the Antarctic Islands, as the former Antarctic Peninsula was now called. Some larger islands, such as King George Island, had names, but most small islets did not.

"These storms, which you see here and here"—Mori tapped the screen—"are usually about a day and a half apart. Therefore, it will be best if you can fly over from Ushuaia between those storms. On calm days, the Drake Passage is called 'Drake Lake' by the ice shippers. They would try never to haul an iceberg in one of these storms, because a rolling berg can capsize a vessel. Investors lost a lot of ships in the early days of ice hauling."

Mori found a calm area between storms and zoomed the camera in to show two large robot-controlled ships with thick towing nets that encircled a small, pitching iceberg. Dal wondered just how much of the berg would be left when it finally reached its northern destination. But obviously this ice-hauling system worked well enough to continue the practice, and it did manage to get some water to Australia, Arabia, and Africa. If ice-hauling didn't result in good water reaching some parched place, no one would go to the trouble.

Mori put down the clicker. "To summarize, our mission is to plan in detail and carry out an expedition to an area that I will designate. This will be in former West Antarctica, on land that is connected to the mainland continent but is and will remain ice-free. There you will unload and plant several species of trees that stand a chance—not a complete guarantee, but still a reasonable chance—of surviving and propagating in the climate, light, and nitrogen-deficient conditions that prevail on those new lands at this time in history."

Dal looked around at the other two. He wanted to laugh—it sounded like a film script. He stifled that laugh out of politeness. There would be other reasons not to laugh later on.

Mori continued. "The last time tree survival was possible in Antarctica was maybe 280,000 years ago. No one knows exactly when, but dated fossils show that it *did* happen—and at a time when the world was not even as warm as it is today.

"The general area I have selected for you to plant the trees has been reliably ice-free for thirty years. I have had my eye on it. Here, southwest of Mount Vinson." Mori circled a large area with the laser tip. "Due to nearby protective rocky outcroppings and the mountainous backdrop, ice from what is left of the central Antarctic dome will not sweep down to the coast again in this direction until the CO_2 level drops way back down. In other words, not for at least hundreds of thousands of years.

"Glaciologists project that this area will remain ice-free until then.

The icebergs you just saw being hauled away are remnants of the re-maining ice dome of East Antarctica, where a few bits are still to be found and removed via the Weddell Sea. The warming we have now will not abate in foreseeable time, as you all know. You must realize that our species is at stake in this situation."

Dal knew this but had never heard it presented so frankly before. *Mom is right to be upset,* he thought.

"You will be working on the ocean side of these barrier mountains." Mori tapped the screen again. "You will be far away from any ice your-selves. Our trees will have ice-free and ever-warming conditions here. Once CO_2 levels return to those of our ancestors, snows will return naturally, and the ice dome will slowly build up again. That will drop the sea levels around the earth and give us more usable land." Mori paused for dramatic effect. The room was deathly quiet.

His voice was low when he spoke next. Dal had to listen closely to hear him. "But that may be too far away in time for humans. That will take just too long."

Mori's voice rose again: "So—now is the time for action! We must plant trees in Antarctica that will survive, to show that it can be done and that Antarctica can and should one day be filled with trees to pro-vide us with a huge, oxygen-producing CO_2 drawdown. This is within human power and initiative. It will not repair everything, but it will give us hope at least."

Dal slid forward to the edge of his seat, put his elbows on the table-top, and leaned in, spellbound. Nevertheless, a doubtful part of him thought, *Only a few trees will do nothing.*

He listened closely while Mori continued as if aware of Dal's un-spoken feeling that theirs would merely be a token effort against huge chemical and geological forces that had spun out of control. "There is yet another compelling reason why we must take this action now. We must do what we can to keep this huge, unused land mass from being scarred and overrun by mining and extraction. Let me explain." Mori began to pace.

"We can and do get necessary minerals from asteroids and other spatial bodies. But it is much easier and cheaper to dig them out of our own earth. Many people want to continue that practice, even though it ruins desperately needed land. Those same people are pressing for mining operations to ramp up in Antarctica, just as they did in Greenland. We simply cannot allow that to happen."

Mori raised a bony forefinger high in the air. "The mining proponents and their thieving crews *can* be thwarted. By us. Yes, by just the four of us here."

Who is the fourth? Surely he cannot go.

As if reading Dal's mind again, Mori said, "Count me amongst your crew, as I will be with you in spirit. 'We few, we happy few.'"

Something about this last remark made Dal's skin crawl. He could not remember exactly where he had heard that phrase before. Something desperate about St. Crispin's Day was all he could come up with.

Mori looked down at his complex four-inch-wide armband. "It just so happens that a small, obscure law is on our side, and will add to your safety."

He read from the band. "'The Air Purity and Food Production Enhancement Act of the World Climate Commission of 2294 states in part that—'" He paused to look up at them, then peered down at his armband again. "'—any large land mass containing live trees may not be used for mineral or like extraction in any part thereof.' Well. You can imagine how this is driving the extraction folks crazy."

Dal had never heard of this law.

"I am convinced that our plan will help the whole earth recover, even if we can plant only a few trees this time. This will be just the start. If we succeed, mining operations will never be allowed to gain a foothold there. Magnates will not be allowed to jump in and desecrate Antarctica. In time, others will be encouraged to plant trees there, as well. I envision the whole continent covered with trees, just as Israel covered its hillsides with forests, one tree at a time. And all that will happen because we will have saved Antarctica with our first effort. Your effort."

Dal watched Naija gaze at Mori, her face aglow.

"We must act immediately, before the mineral cowboys descend on Antarctica. They are writing extraction leases right now, just the way oil, gas, and coal profiteers did—at first unwittingly, and then, once science was clear, with full knowledge of the horrible ramifications. They brought us to where we find ourselves today. Humankind has not changed, but our circumstances certainly have. The law I just read to you says that lands proven to support trees may not be disturbed. So we must make that proof happen and show that trees *can* survive in Antarctica. Let no one say we didn't try!"

Dal felt as if he were in an old-fashioned revival tent and that what Mori preached was true and compelling. "For now, the miners' petitions are tied up in International Court, as are claims from Chile and Argentina and others. Also, for this brief period in time, where trees are concerned—just as it does currently with human migration—international law overrides national law. So, I repeat: according to current international law, wherever trees exist, mines and destruction may not be founded."

Dal looked around. Walt was chewing a thumbnail and Naija remained still, almost not breathing.

"Black Coats are everywhere, monitoring all tree survival. That is part of their job. They also are supposed to keep miners out of Antarctica until all the permits are assigned." He stopped to look around. No one spoke.

Finally, he asked, "You get it, don't you?"

"Not really, Mori," Dal replied. "Please explain what you're getting at."

"You tell them, Naija," said Mori.

Naija looked at Dal. "All right. You see," she said in her rounded accent, "we know from experience that Black Coats mostly think about lining their pockets. They are especially subject to bribery. And the extraction industry can and does bribe them. Black Coats will, for a big fee, lie and help people get permits to mine an area before a full study is completed. Even now, companies are trying to get permits for Antarctica." Naija spoke slowly and quietly, in sharp contrast to Mori when he was fired up.

"Yes, that's it exactly," Mori broke in. "We have to beat them to it, before permits get pushed through with Black Coat help and ruin the place for eternity. You will need to watch out for Black Coats all along the way. Even though they are 'supposed' to help preserve trees, they will *not* be on our side with this.

"If you are successful, our live trees will protect the whole continent. By law." Mori stopped to let that sink in.

"It took too long for people to understand that humans must have trees to survive. It helps us now that, finally—and hopefully not too late—international law fully protects trees. It does *not* help us that the enforcement arm is so corrupt." Mori bowed his head. He looked tired.

Well, that settles it. Mori is definitely not even part robot. Those guys don't get tired, Dal joked to himself, trying to relieve his built-up tension.

Mori walked slowly toward the door and then turned back. "Well, you three get better acquainted now. All you know is each other's names. You will soon need to be friends as well as coworkers. Lunch is ready in the small dining room any time you want it."

Dal sat back in his chair. He had never heard anything like this. Lieutenant Commander Gonzales had prophesied that he would not find exciting and meaningful work again such as he had back in the Rescue Corps. At this moment, it looked to Dal as if he might have found the perfect job, after all.

The man named Walt spoke. "Well, what do you think?"

Dal moved his head side to side, as if to say, "Jesus, can you beat that?" He wanted to hear what the woman with the unpronounceable name had to say. But she sat still, gazing at the slowly rotating images of the earth.

Walt filled the vacuum. "I knew Mori would come up with something interesting. But this is way out there. My botany career is going nowhere, but if his idea works, I'll get a fresh start. We might all become famous. Maybe not in our lifetimes, but in time for our grandchildren."

"When did you meet Mori before?" Dal asked.

"Saw him in Saratoga, New York, a couple years ago at the UN Species Migration Council. I was a minor speaker, and he was hassling everybody about how trees need help, we need trees, and all that. As if we didn't know that already. He's been around the fringe of the scientific community for a long time with this same general mantra. I think he's gotten fed up with official channels. Plus, he's running out of time."

Dal looked over the top of Walt's downy hair at the image of the earth turning through its 360-degree orbit. He hoped Mori was not listening in.

Shifting his position away from Walt, Dal ventured: "I think Mori is brilliant. But this was also a pep talk, to keep us motivated. Most expedition prompts tell you the risks right away and emphasize safety actions one should take. Mori hasn't mentioned risks at all except to say, 'Watch out for Black Coats.' I don't believe that is full disclosure. Take it from me: it's very risky to head anywhere away from North America right now."

"He may not know all the risks," Walt said. "This is a first-of-its-kind sort of thing."

"That's true," Dal replied. "Another thing, though: who exactly is going to plant the trees? We will at least need one laborer to go with us to help plant them."

"I think we three together will be able to manage that," Naija said. "I'm stronger than I look."

Dal lifted his eyebrows but chose not to dispute her words.

He was accustomed to noticing details and had observed that Walt habitually bit his nails down to the nub, leaving his fingertips pink. This little item concerned Dal. Also, he saw how Walt sat, with a smooth forearm concealing the bulge of his stomach protruding above his belt. Was he trying to hide a lack of conditioning?

"I hope they will be small saplings, then, as I don't see us three doing all that manual labor." Dal tried to sound light, but he was deadly serious.

Walt broke in as if he hadn't even heard Dal. "In case it's not obvious to you, Mori is really, really, really old. His ancestors were obscenely rich, and because he was an only child, he inherited everything. With that big cash advantage, Mori has already outlived his 140 allowed years and is hiding it well. Ha! And we just get ninety. Oh, well, I emphatically do not want to be sent to live on one of the colonies just to get to live past ninety. Not worth that. Where was I?"

From the corner of his eye, Dal saw Naija squirm in her seat and look out the window. He agreed with her body language.

Dal broke in as Walt took a breath. "It sounds like Mori is hiring us to carry out his dream for him. I can honestly say that it does sound worthwhile. I have never been offered so much money to fly, either. But we will all earn it. This will not be simple."

Walt interrupted, overtopping Dal's last words. "There is a certain lag time before one knows whether or not an artificial introduction of plant life on newly exposed land will take hold. I think Mori wants to be around long enough to go back to Toronto and say, 'See, I told you it would work.'"

"He may not have enough years left for that," Dal interjected.

"Maybe not," Walt squeaked between sips of water and wiping his wet chin with the back of his hand.

Dal again wondered if the room was bugged and Mori knew what they were saying about him. He felt sorry for him.

The sun ripped out from behind a tree as wind pushed back the fog. It blazed through the window and into Dal's face. He moved his chair back out of the glare.

Naija shifted in her seat, arranging her small body so that she occupied more space before she spoke. "Mori is neither crazy nor self-aggrandizing," she said evenly.

Walt looked at her piercingly.

Dal liked Naija's implicit rebuke. Her voice was quiet, with the words rounded in the middle and clipped at the end, the way he had heard speech sound in old films of North American First Nations people. He hoped she would say more.

"Mori is doing a penance related to what he thinks is a proper role for man in relation to the natural world. It comes a little late in his life, and it may be uncertain in outcome. But at least he is trying. And to him, this is a spiritual as well as a practical quest, practical for the good reasons he has outlined. You will not hear him talk about the spiritual part."

Naija took a deep breath and continued. "Because of his feel for nature—"

There's that word again, thought Dal.

"—we in this area have always thought of Mori as a '*quablonut* who knows something a little,' or a 'spiritually powerful white man,'" she concluded with her inscrutable smile.

"You're kidding, aren't you?" Dal looked directly in her eyes.

"Oh, no, I am not." Her eyes were soft brown, set in an oval, flattish face with high cheekbones. *An unusual face,* Dal thought. *Seems very sure of what she says.*

"That doesn't make any sense to me," Walt interjected.

"You will come to understand," Naija shot back.

"I am not into mystery," Walt said, sternly separating each word. "I never thought of Mori as spiritual when I would see him armed with charts, surveys, quotas, and data up the wazoo. I think you're wrong about that, Naija. I will not risk my neck for another man's morality. I am going along with this only for the science myself."

Seeing Naija's face harden, Dal moved to defuse the mounting strain. "Well, what about my question, Walt? What brings you here, if you don't care about the spirit of what Mori wants to do?"

Walt flushed. "I've, uh—well, truth is, this is an amazing opportunity for any biologist. It is not whether I agree or disagree with all the humanitarian stuff. I was shocked when Mori approached me and asked to talk. I'm not what you would call a household name, although I have published some papers on tree migration and thermal karst erosion. In nontechnical terms, that means tundral erosion after permafrost thaw."

Naija got up and walked toward the dining room, her jaw set.

Things were not starting off well for the three of them. Dal thought he might have to find a way to bring down Walt's superciliousness. He jiggled his knees up and down to diffuse pent-up energy. Expecting more from Walt, he put his hands on his chair arms as if to rise and follow Naija.

But before he could move, Walt pulled his chair up to block Dal's exit and leaned in to him. He spoke more quietly, as if he had a secret.

"This is the perfect time for a big, unheard-of field experiment. I want to be part of it!" Walt tapped the arm of his chair with his fist and sat back again, satisfied. He looked to Dal for a reaction.

Dal moved to get up again, but Walt put a restraining hand on his knee. "No. Listen. Please. I could ruin my standing in the bio community if I get caught doing this, breaking other laws Mori didn't even tell us about, such as the prohibitions against uprooting healthy trees. But hey, if we are successful, this might be the ticket for me. I might even get a Nobel Prize." Walt laughed, but Dal figured he really meant it. Then Walt asked, "Why are you here, Dal?"

"I'm a pilot, and he needs a pilot. Seems like a good match. But I've got to watch the risk-factor thing. I'm getting married soon."

Walt kept his hot hand on Dal's knee. His eyes reddened and his chin quivered until he got control of himself again. "Well, there is one other little matter. Just between us, okay? Marriage can be hard. My wife, Ellie, told me I should go anywhere and do anything Mori wants. I expected her to worry about danger, but she was unfazed. She just wants me to go. Go anywhere. She tells me I need an 'adventure.'" Walt took a quick bite of his thumbnail. "I commed her last night. Don't tell Mori. She's been playing indoor tennis every single day. Has been for months now. Has a handsome young instructor. I met him. Keep all this under your hat, okay?"

Walt's shifts of mood and manner worried Dal. He nodded reassuringly as he gently removed Walt's hand from his knee and stood up. Dal had thought that Walt might be a wild card. Now he understood why. He excused himself to follow Naija into the lunchroom next door. His stomach growled. Low blood sugar made him feel weak, and this was no time for that.

NAIJA AND HENRI stood chatting by the buffet.

"Hi," Dal said. "Say, Henri, what all do you do for Mori here? Looks like a big operation." Dal gestured toward the large buffet, the rooms, and gardens.

Henri nodded to Naija, as if to indicate that she already knew what he was going to say. He swallowed a big piece of bread. "I do just about anything Mori asks, which is less and less these days. He seems to be slowing down a little. If you think he looks good now, you should have seen him in his prime."

"Yes, Mori does look good," Naija said. "You are doing a great job, Henri."

Must be old friends, Dal figured.

Henri explained, "I learned to give Mori those stabilizer injections as soon as I started working here. Mind you, Mr. T has been to every corner of the world and had some wild and risky times. But he could never bring himself to stick his own skin with a needle. So that is my most important responsibility. After that, I fit all the rest of this in, second-tier."

"What sort of name is Taktug?" asked Dal. "What does it mean?"

"'Foggy,'" Naija interjected. "It was often foggy where Mori's father's family came from in ancient times, so they took that surname."

Henri continued between chews. "My little medical assistance is the lifeline for Mori. He doesn't ask for much, and he is doing just fine. Mostly keeps to the grounds now, not taking off for Toronto or New Shanghai. Or anywhere, really."

"Do you think Mori will be around long enough for us to finish our work?" Dal asked Henri once Walt and Naija had left to circle the buffet.

"Oh, sure. Sure. I'm not going anyplace," Henri said, "and I'll take good care of him, don't you worry. He has been darn generous to me and my boy. I never forget something like that." His eyes followed Walt and Naija. "Actually, I never forget anything."

DAL WALKED BACK toward his room after lunch, taking the outdoor route under the dripping branches. The ground fog had lifted and continued to waft away on a light breeze. Only a few cottony patches held on amongst the shiny spruce and fir needles before tearing away to join the fog bank out over Hudson Bay. Sun dappled the ground unevenly, promising a more colorful afternoon.

Dal found a large rock already dried by the sun and sat down overlooking the edge of the garden yet out of view from the house. His mind swirled with all the strangeness around him, and his stomach roiled with the unusual food. He knew just what he needed to calibrate himself: a comm and then a rare, enjoyable outside jog.

Turning his armband to transmit, Dal began a comm to Ana, taking special care to keep his RECEIVE switch off. He did not expect Ana to break the usual rules and try to locate his exact position. *But then again, she just might do that. We have a different sort of life between us now.* He enjoyed that thought for a few minutes. Then he began a voice comm. She would really love that.

"October 13, right after lunch. Hi, Ana. This comm is probably a surprise, arriving so fast. I miss you so much and have an overwhelming urge to hold you. First off, this job is going to be perfect for us, and I am very glad I came here. The place is nice—beautiful, really. And the temps are more reasonable where I am. It will not be an easy job, but we will be just fine. There will be three of us going together. And it is a worthwhile thing that I will be doing. Mom would love it. That's all I can say now, because this is a very secret operation at this point.

"More later when I can sneak another comm. Hope the wedding plans are coming along okay. Don't let Mom push you around on that. I'm thinking of you in your yellow dress. And also thinking of you without that yellow dress. Dreaming about our whole last night together, and of all the ones in our future. I love you so much. 'Bye for now."

Dal tagged the SEND button and felt better than he had since leaving Ana's apartment.

7

The USDA announces it will cease providing plant-hardiness maps and planting schedules to citizens. The changes in plant zones have occurred too fast and are too erratic to quantify the data in any meaningful way for use by the general public. An announcement will be made if we are ever able to resume this activity.

—usda.gov, Re: Plant-Hardiness Maps, March 2243

OCTOBER 27 AND 28, 2295

For two weeks, the trio in Willow Park worked all day every day, harder than Dal imagined would be necessary to organize such a small expedition. But then, Dal had never done any expeditionary planning before. This expedition was complicated. It involved assembling, checking, and rechecking endless items: long supply lists; flight routes; details about Ushuaia and Tierra del Fuego; Black Coat evasion tactics; emergency procedures; food; caloric and nutritional requirement charts; sun protection; hygiene and water-purification kits; appropriate clothing; a medical kit; bedding; tarps; titanium-alloy plates for a portable hut; camp pots and heat cubes; a shovel and small dolly; tree stakes and rope; tree nutrients and nitrogen-fixing compounds; et cetera, et cetera. On and on the lists went. A few old-fashioned items were added by Mori, including, of all odd things, a strong magnifying glass to start a fire in case matches or food-heating cubes failed.

"What the devil are we supposed to do with this, Naija?" asked Dal. She was the most likely to know how to use it. He waved the magnifier in the air.

"I'm too busy doing up the med kit now," Naija said. "I'll show you if and when we need it. Unlikely to be used. Could even be a joke."

"But you actually know what to do with it?"

"Sure I do. Later, Dal, okay?"

"Rescue Ops involved none of this bullshit," Dal sniffed.

For two weeks, they pored over maps of Tierra del Fuego and Antarctica: old maps from when the ice had been intact, and new satellite transmissions that showed changes on a daily basis. They became familiar with ship and air traffic over the Drake Passage between South America and Antarctica. Dal really liked this navigational part, with which he had plenty of experience.

What he did not enjoy was trying to understand the arcane legalese of the World Court as it related to the Antarctic Treaty and the Law of the Oceans. With these statutes changing frequently in response to new petitions and conflicts, Dal thought it all to be a waste of time. Also, it looked to him as if they would go ahead with their plan, regardless.

He enjoyed most of their discussions—if they didn't involve long-winded botany talk from Walt. Most of all, Dal enjoyed hearing Naija say almost anything in her unusual accent.

On this sparkling, late-fall day at the sixty-eighth parallel in Canada, their chats began on an especially upbeat tone. "Where did you learn all this?" Dal asked Naija after she had regaled them with tales of food-foraging in cooler regions. The tales seemed useless, since there would be nothing to forage where they were going. Nevertheless, whatever was said in Naija's voice was worthy of Dal's full attention.

"I taught meself it all," Naija said with a little smile. "You might say I was home-schooled until university. Here is a good titbit for you: did you know that the original inhabitants of Tierra del Fuego wore no clothing? They covered themselves with animal fat and warmed themselves by large bonfires. This is why Magellan named the region 'Land of Fire.' They even carried fires in their canoes, and they may have been the first humans to cross to Antarctica in those same canoes. All with no clothes at all, except for the occasional luxurious fur coat. How do you like that?"

"I'm speechless," Dal laughed.

"Very cute," Walt interrupted. "Dal, you were questioning if trees can actually live well in Antarctica? Well, back in 1992, paleobotanists discovered the fossilized remains of a deciduous *Glossopteris* fern forest on Mount Achernar in the Transantarctic Mountains of Antarctica. The forest had flourished at latitude eighty or eighty-five degrees south, with only half a year of full sun and half a year of full darkness. We do not know how. But nevertheless, it shows there is some real hope for our project." Walt occasionally had something very interesting to say, Dal allowed.

"Great, Walt," he replied. "Just remember this: we are not going to stay long enough to see a grand forest take hold. We are going to go in and out as fast as possible. As soon as our trees are staked and looking good, we are gone. I'd say three weeks max. If they are stable, there's no need for us to linger and watch 'em grow," he said with finality.

"Oh, no. We are not hurrying anything along," Naija asserted, looking to Walt for support. "We are going to plant and monitor those trees very carefully. We have to do this right."

"Anything can happen if we stay too long, and I'll be flying that plane on *my* schedule," Dal replied, looking down at his nails with a gesture of confidence that his was the ultimate power. "Just be sure that you two chickadees don't miss takeoff when it's time to go."

"Dal, you know perfectly well that you committed to a month down there," Naija said. "We are going to need every day of it. And," she warned, "Mori can always get another pilot."

"Not now he can't," Dal replied. "We can't even fill up the Rescue Corps slots. There aren't many like me around."

Dal desperately wanted to finish the job and get back to Ana. He was looking for any time corners he could cut and still do the task well.

"Tomorrow I start training in the new plane. He really can't replace me now, Naija. Not if he wants this done in his lifetime."

There was no reply to that.

THE NEXT MORNING, Walt and Naija spent hours in a shed going over lists of food and supplies and weighing and packing small squares of artificial cheese and other high-calorie, nutrient-rich foods into small daily pouches. This was an expedition prep that had not changed much in hundreds of years.

While they were thus occupied, Mori took Dal down a different path to a gate Dal had seen on his solitary walks. The heavy gate held together a ten-foot-high wire fence and was secured with a big, rusty lock of the old key type. Mori fumbled to open it.

They were headed to the runway, and the plane that Dal would soon be flying to Antarctica. He walked bouncing with anticipation. "So, what do you have for me—some old thing from the 2160s? Maybe a Mongolian make?" Dal glanced sideways at Mori with a half-smile.

"Ha!" Mori replied. Dal could see part of a short wing, but most of the plane was hidden by a turn in the path. Even with only that, though, he could guess what they had. "Where'd you steal this thing, Mori?"

Dal had flown a lot of optional-rotor, vertical-landing aircraft, but always a well-used plane. This one was brand new, built in the lower seventy-two states.

"How many seats, Mori" Dal asked.

"Four."

Why four? We are only three. Is Mori going after all? Maybe a laborer? Hope so.

"My man in New Ushuaia, Bill Hernan, will need to go with you for one very short leg to pick up some more trees," said Mori. "That is all. No more crew once you fly to Antarctica." Again, Mori eerily seemed to read Dal's mind.

The plane's insignia proved a connection to a megayacht registered in the Argentine Malvinas: *Aurora*, a common yacht name implying "a new beginning." They were to tell immigration officials when they landed in New Ushuaia that they had come in for sightseeing from that yacht. The actual yacht would be stationed off the coast to verify the tale if needed.

This plane, like all those Dal had flown before, could land vertically with the lightest touch by using the soft antigravity thrust controls. Also, it was capable of hovering and horizontal flying and landing. There were optional wheels and runners, and deployable rotor blades for slow hovers, takeoffs, and landings. However, Dal would soon learn that superficiality from a distance was where commonality with his experience stopped. The stored sun-battery range for this plane was huge, sufficient to see them all the way to ninety degrees south and back to fifty-eight degrees north, several times across that eight thousand-mile one-way distance. That in itself was enough to keep the plane out of the hands of the public. Mori's planning for this mission had achieved miracles in procurement.

A man of medium height wearing a leather aviator jacket and cap stepped down from the pilot's side. *Leather? No way,* Dal thought. *Only in a museum.*

"Did you buy him that outfit?" he asked out of the side of his mouth as they approached. This time Dal did not expect an answer, and he didn't get one.

"Please meet Aron Weeks, Dal. He will show you this aircraft's special features. I want you to fly maneuvers in it yourself every day until you leave. I have arranged cleared airspace for that if you stay north of our latitude.

"Aron has been filled in on your experience and abilities, and he has read your résumé. He says that with your qualifications he can get you up to speed in forty-eight hours. But since we have more time than that, I want you to train in this plane every day." Mori turned to Aron. "Aron, I have plans for final departure at 0730 on November 17."

"Guess we are finally getting down to brass tacks," Dal said. "Good to meet you." He liked the amiable face of his new instructor. Suddenly, Dal felt himself on the verge of laughing, but he turned it into a cough instead. How funny that Mori had adopted flight-speak with that "0730" bit.

Aron motioned for Dal to climb in. Dal had not loved the "school" part of flight school but knew he would have to pay attention now. This intricate hunk of beehive-coated titanium alloy was going to have a lot to do if it was going to get them all back home safely again.

Mori left them. Aron rapped a knuckle on the side of the plane. "I know. You basically know how to fly planes that look kind of like this. But this one is special."

Dal bristled. *Know a lot more than basics, Buster,* he thought. "What did you do before instructing? Where did you serve?" Dal politely asked Aron.

"I am an official HVTOL antigravity-potential flight instructor. They decided not to waste my knowledge in service so kept me on to teach others. I always work on the latest birds, right out of production.

I couldn't keep up so well with the newest stuff if I were off flying around someplace."

Dal again said nothing.

"I also fly Mr. Taktug around, although he seldom goes anywhere now," Aron said. "His own plane is an older version of this one. It's in the hangar," Aron added, his chin high. He turned to point out some orange dials that Dal had never seen before.

"This unique compounded-titanium shell is nonreactive to avoid detection devices. You will be able to move about unobserved by scanners that track all normal commercial air and sea traffic. Only photographic satellites would be able to find you, and it is unlikely that anyone would be looking for one small plane in the trillions of images they take every day, especially because they will not have any reason to be looking for you whizzing by where you are going. Your sonic boom is washed out by the plane's supersonic laminar-flow design, so you are soundless at this plane's full speed of Mach 1.5. But you will not need to go that fast, and you should not.

"The plane can fly higher than our lower atmosphere, but it will be best to stay down here for your mission. I recommend that. Higher altitudes are okay for those who don't mind detection. With fewer unscheduled flights up there, they get the most scrutiny. You would very much rue being followed, at least as the mission has been explained to me."

Dal listened carefully, excited by the plane's capabilities.

"There are cognitive fly-bys built in to improve stability and performance when the plane transfers from one flight mode to another. You can fly top speeds, then quickly convert to heli for closer observation and landing. Even the props are soundless. The batteries are solar and therefore lighter than fusion ones, plus they will be perfect where you are going with those long, long days for a month.

"Once you leave Ushuaia and arrive in Antarctica, you will have nothing to worry about, as there is no one there now. Just stay out of other people's airspace until you get to your destinations, and you should be golden. On return, bypass New Ushuaia and head directly back here unless you have an extreme need to stop. Makes for a longer flying day, but by then you will probably be ready to come home anyway."

"You bet," Dal agreed. "But what about all the old Antarctic bases? Palmer, McMurdo, Bellingshausen, South Pole Station, Vostok, King George Island, the British Antarctic survey stations. Even little old Patriot Hills. Are you sure no one is there minding any of them?"

Dal had learned about these bases from evenings spent reading in Mori's Antarctic Library. "Antarctica was attracting settlers and crooks, last thing I heard. Anyone hiding out now, refusing to leave?" Dal asked.

"Naw. Believe it or not, there's really not supposed to be anyone at all there now," Aron said. "Everybody left gradually when the ice melted, wildlife vanished, and things got really soggy. Nobody knows quite what to do with the place. No country can afford to go to war down there right now, so the whole area is quiet."

Aron sighed. "I could go into more detail on that, but let's stick to my main objective for today and get you into the air. I'll go up with you today, and all the rest will be solo." Their heads bent together over the cognition panel and the intricate notebooks now spread open across their laps.

"You will have one day to fly to New Ushuaia, a brief hop nearby, and then another short trip over to Antarctica. This plane can reach Mach 1.5. But I strongly suggest you not exceed 768 miles per hour. Sonic-boom suppression is built in, but it is better not to try your luck. Your waves might be detected by a sensitive plane nearby, even if the sound is not heard."

"How do the rotors handle those speeds?" Dal asked.

"They retract to embedded. Only to be used at slower speed for takeoff, landing, approaches, and hovering," Aron answered.

After a couple of hours, Dal came to value Aron. He asked him, "Are you always here? If I have any questions along the way, could I give you a comm?"

"Sure, if communication is part of the plan. I don't think you will need to, but yes. If I don't answer, Mori can find me instantly," Aron added. "He asked me to stay nearby for the whole time. Just in case."

8

Lab-grown meat, which debuted in 2013, is now worth buying. Costs are finally lower than fresh, slaughtered meat. Originally, lab meat cost $325,000 per ground patty. Our modern lab meat has nutritional value and safety equal to or better than live-grown meat. The first patties looked dull and tasted bland, but improvements have been made in appearance and taste. Nevertheless, even these new "meats" are largely frowned upon and are eaten only on special occasions.

—*Consumer Reports*, January 2070

NOVEMBER 12 AND 13, 2295

Dal enjoyed the flying. After a few days of training in this responsive plane, he felt as if they were one object in the sky. The days passed quickly. Nevertheless, he was anxious to be off and then get back home to Ana.

One sparkling night at dinner, which was always elaborate by Dal's standards, he eyed the platter of caribou steaks coming around the table again. He felt queasy at the thought of another night of meat, as luxurious as it was. At first, he had gorged himself. His family's relative affluence assured them sacks of lentils, dried hydroponic algae, and special dry-farmed rice whenever a shipment arrived. But real meat, except for the rare chicken or occasional "test-tube" meat, had not been a featured item in Riley family meals for more than a hundred years.

"Where do you get all this meat, Mori?" Dal asked after Mori offered him a second serving of *tuktu*. "We only have meat a couple of times a year, and never like this."

"This is overproduction from the original small caribou herd on this property. Have you seen none of them on your walks? Must be hiding from you." Mori laughed. "With no natural predators left, they overproduce by anywhere from eight to twenty per year. I keep a little of the meat but mostly share it with the Inuit or medical institutions. Naija's people have received three caribou per year ever since she was born—isn't that right, Naija?"

Dal watched Naija hold her breath and nod with her eyes down. There was a lot he didn't know about her special relationship with Mori and Willow Park. Obviously, there was something.

Mori seemed in a reflective mood. He put his elbows on the table and his fingertips together. Looking pensive, he spoke slowly and clearly, with none of his usual drive.

"I hope you have been absorbing here some feeling for how life and nature used to be," he said. "That will help you feel what you are doing and why. If I were to try and explain the emotional underpinnings of this project, it could be difficult, as these things can be very personal. When I tried to get this same work done through international agencies, it was a hard time for me. Walt is aware of all that, I'm sure.

"Anyway, I hope each of you will find some important personal meaning in this mission before you embark on it. For it *will* be difficult, and meaning helps one get through difficulty.

"In spite of your careful planning, and the best technology that money can buy, nature remains a grand and unpredictable force, best encountered with enthusiasm born of respect and affection. You will be meeting her on close terms of drama and geophysical retribution in the wildest place that remains on this earth."

What a speech, Dal thought. *I can't accept any of that, won't go there mentally. Too much like my mom.* He shifted uncomfortably in his chair. Naija's eyes remained devotedly fixed on Mori.

"Those of us who were lucky enough to see nature in a state less affected by humankind could not help but be awed," Mori continued. "There is scarcely any place left now that has not been changed by our activities, from several miles into the earth to the heights of our atmosphere.

"Where can we find awe today? Awe—the underpinning of every

great religion. We now look to the skies, to celestial majesty, for traces of a God that we used to find right here on earth." Mori paused.

Dal thought again of his mother and her films. She would be weeping by now. But he would not let what Mori was saying get to him. He had to have nerves of titanium to carry out this mission and get back home. He would ignore this talk the same way he had shut out the cries of refugees on his rescue flights in order to do his work the best he could.

"If I am honest with myself—" Mori paused again. "If I am honest, I might even say that this mission for the Earth, which you are about to carry out, technically constitutes human interference in a very, very long natural process. We must not forget, however, that it was we humans who shoved earth onto the path of this process and all that we are experiencing as a species now. By comparison, your efforts on the newly exposed continent of Antarctica will be palliative, benign, interesting, and potentially beautiful." Mori's voice dropped to almost inaudible. "And to be honest, in fairness I must admit to you that it could also be futile. That is a possibility. All of our work could end up being nothing more than an offering on a windswept altar."

Oh, Lordy, thought Dal. *He and my mother would be quite the pair.* He felt very uneasy after this talk of sacrifice. He had the impulse to flee this dinner and run to his bedroom, the way he had fled from the caribou and zebra migration films on the walls at home, the way he had run from his mother's rapture followed by despair. Had he come all this way just to be confronted by the same thing again?

"But we will persevere!" Mori's voice was strong again. "I salute you on your spirits of adventure, and I wish I were going myself." He raised his glass in a toast.

It was an astonishing performance. For the first time, Dal began to worry in a way that turned his hands clammy. He really wanted to go to Antarctica. But he must come home again.

BECAUSE IT WAS RAINING, Dal skipped his after-dinner stroll around the garden and walked through the house to his room. Lights automatically came on when he entered each hall and darkened behind him when he exited. He walked down the long hall where their rooms were. A shaft of light moved with him as successive overhead lights clicked on and then off with his steps. Coming toward him down the hall was another beam of light, out of the glare of which vaulted Walt's voice. Their lights merged and then separated again. Walt had stopped to chat, but Dal had not.

"I didn't get what the old man was talking about there at the end, did you?" Walt asked.

"I don't know," replied Dal as he kept walking. He felt afraid and unsure, and he didn't want more confusion interjected into his churning mind right now.

"Good night." Dal opened his door.

"All right, then, good night," Walt replied.

LYING IN BED, Dal turned onto his stomach and threw his right arm out across the sheet. The bed was large and lonely. It took a long time, but he finally fell into a deep sleep. He dreamed of a bumpy, thin causeway through a turbulent sea, where waves hung high on either side, about to break over him. He must run through them fast to safety and not fall or be swept away. It was a dream from years ago, an archaic part of himself bubbling up again—at once both hopeful and terrifying. In the dream, the waves never touched him, and Dal always got across the causeway to the other side.

THE NEXT MORNING, crows squawked raucously outside his open window. Dal stretched and recalled the dream. It clung to his mood like a reluctantly greeted old friend, indicating that he was the same since childhood in some essential way. *Why did I have that dream right now? Thought those were over.* Thinking it useful to put aside introspection, he determined to forget about it and went to breakfast.

Alone in the breakfast room he lifted a spoonful of grain, the breakfast of his childhood, and felt, rather than saw, another flashback. What could be bringing this on? Fascinated by these old memories and what his brain was allowing him to recall, Dal mind-raced back to the late 2270s.

Every year the extended Riley family took a holiday at the seashore. They went in midwinter, when the weather was cooler and the worst storms were over.

He was the small boy sitting on a warm sandy spot on a beach, wherever the shore might have been that year. Maybe he was around five? The whole family would have been somewhere nearby. They would have found a new, safe beach for the family tents used during those February holidays. Dal loved the days spent playing with his cousins in bodysuits and hats, jumping in the water's edge to cool off.

Their mothers had been overprotective, he felt. Later, as a teen, Dal would defiantly take off the full-coverage suit after sundown and rebelliously swim without it. This became his adult preference, too. Even though he had not swum in the ocean in ten years, he still relished the memory. Now, he had heard, the ocean had a slimy feel and an odor, as if algae might be growing nearby. It was not exactly as it had been when he was young.

Dal remembered the water at the shoreline, where it washed over dirt, concrete, and tree stumps. On a sunny day, the water might be blue instead of greyish green. It might even be clear if there was no wind at all. One had to be careful going in and look for a patch of sand amongst the debris, or check for dark shapes of ruins under the water before diving in. Since everyone crowded into the few nice places, they always sent a family member out several days before the trip to stake a claim.

On this one hot day that Dal remembered so clearly, he heard the waves crashing noisily. Towering above, they seemed like live monsters coming toward him. Dal reckoned from his adult perspective that they were actually maybe only two feet high. His father ignored Dal's wails and his mother's protests and carried him across the froth at the edge, out into the breaking waves. Dal remembered the feel of his father picking him up. And then the sound of his mother protesting: "Don't do it, Jim. Jim? Stop, okay?"

But his father carried Dal off, laughing and trying to calm his fears.

Dal clung to his father's neck, wrapped his legs around his waist, and pushed himself tightly against him. Jim jumped up and down with each wave, often timing his jump so that a small wave could break over both of them for fun. Dal screamed and laughed in a hysterical mixture, just short of tears.

DAL STOPPED EATING and held his spoon. He studied the bowl.

"NO, NO, JIM—don't *do* that!" his mother had called out, cupping her hands around her mouth. Over his father's shoulder, Dal could see Risa standing at the water's edge. He saw her run down and wade in.

He felt himself being lifted high over his father's head. He clawed to keep hold of his father but felt himself wrenched away. His father had thrown him. Suddenly water covered Dal. It rolled off the top of his head and into his eyes. The salt stung. Dal bobbed up and down, his flailing arms, wrapped in flimsy flotations, suspended where he had landed. He sputtered and coughed and cried. He was alone in the deeper water, across the breaking waves from his father.

Jim backed off toward the shore with the next larger, cresting wave. A bigger set was coming. He called to Dal: "Swim to me. Swim to me, boy. Swim. *Swim, dammit!*" His father for some reason had not—and did not—come out to get him. Dal struggled and cried and swung his arms around ineffectively.

"Move those arms, Dal. Kick, kick!" Jim yelled over the roar of the surf, rotating his own arms above the water to demonstrate a swimming motion, his feet firmly planted on the bottom. Finally, Dal managed to move in the right direction, and another wave drove him into his father's arms.

"Atta boy! See? You made it—see? You gotta know how to swim, you hear? Everybody in this family has gotta know how to swim." Jim repeated this over and over, more gently each time. He held tight to Dal and waded back to shore.

Only years later, during a chitchat with his uncle while sitting in a seventeen-foot skiff after surfacing from a dive over Charleston—only then did Dal learn that his father could not swim a stroke himself. Dal never told his father that he knew this. It would not be worth bringing up now.

DAL SCRAPED THE BOWL one last time with his spoon. He felt satisfied and calm, reassured that he could take care of himself.

MORI PERCHED IN the big easy chair that everyone liked. By the time Dal walked in late for the morning meeting, Naija and Walt were already there, so Mori started immediately.

"Yesterday the World Court issued a new directive binding all nations interested in Antarctic operations to cease activity immediately within two hundred miles of the Antarctic coastline. Now they say force will be used to ensure compliance until all land claims are adjudicated and procedures are established for dispersing the continent's resources.

"This wrinkle makes it even more urgent to get our project going ASAP, because as soon as those claims are adjudicated, the Antarctic gold rush will be on, and we will have no chance at all."

"They probably just want to avoid armed conflict," Walt interrupted.

"Maybe so," said Mori. "But as I was saying, the closest anyone is supposed to come to shore now is two hundred miles, at which point floating ice may be harnessed."

"Pretty wasteful to let all that good water melt into the ocean," Dal interjected.

"Yes, seems so to me, too. And dry nations are appealing. Australia, India, and the African Congress have already proposed a seventy-five-mile line for harvesting float ice.

"Nevertheless, this complicates things for us a little bit. No one else will be there to bother you, for sure. However, you will not want to get caught in Antarctica illegally, as then you could receive a prison sentence. So could I, for having sent you.

"But even worse than time in prison would be the revocation of your travel passes. Being condemned to stay in one place is a terrible hardship these days."

At this, Dal felt a prick of concern. His hope, his mission for himself and Ana was to find a better place to live, after all.

"So, given all that new info, I think we should activate our plan earlier," Mori said. "The authorities are not quite ready to enforce this yet. Dal, are you feeling secure about flying the plane? Aron thinks you are ready."

"Yes, sir," Dal replied, as he traditionally did when accepting a hard mission.

Mori's face was flushed. Dal thought he looked upset, and a little older. He felt sorry for Mori, because his whole mental construct, which had kept the plan within the bounds of his law-abiding character, was now in danger. And with that push into illegality, his reputation, life's work, and reason for being—perhaps even for staying alive—was threatened. If Mori pushed on now and got caught, he would be considered an international outlaw. They all would.

"We will not get caught, Mori," said Dal. He was determined not to allow that. Dal was used to last-minute wrinkles before an operation. He had often been told of bad actors in an area, or dangerous weather coming. This news did not feel so different from those other preflight sessions. He would—no, they *all* would return, just as he always had. And not as outlaws, either.

Naija looked around at the others. Walt looked down at his hands. Dal stared out the window at the branches blowing in the steady northwest wind. Nobody else said anything. But Dal knew he was still in. In the same way he had always volunteered for the hardest, most impossible rescue missions, this added danger pushed him forward. And he expected from experience that when it was all over, the reward would be that much sweeter.

Mori stood up. Naija and Walt left quietly. Dal went over and stood beside Mori. Together they watched the satellite image of Antarctica and the surrounding ringlet of low-pressure storms riding the West Wind Drift, those prevailing westerlies that circle the globe in the forty and fifty degree latitudes south—the strong and persistent winds that isolate Antarctica completely, that pile up seas unchecked by land, and that over thousands of years had deterred colonization.

"You know what, Dal?" Mori said softly. "Those swirling storm patterns remind me for all the world of the clover chains I used to weave with my cousins on fair summer days. One hundred thirty-five years ago that was, now."

9

Curiosity will conquer fear, even more than bravery will.
—James Stephens

NOVEMBER 14, 2295

They scrambled and were ready to go in forty-eight hours. Before their last dinner with Mori, Dal had sent Ana a jaunty comm telling her they were leaving the next morning, how much he loved her, that he would be home in no more than four weeks, and not to expect any comms in the meantime. It would be too risky if transmissions were intercepted and traced to their location, so she should not comm him, either. Sort of like the long comm blackouts in the 20th century for naval personnel on nuclear submarines. *If they could stand it, so can I,* Dal reasoned.

All their gear had been loaded the day before, including fourteen saplings selected from Mori's forest. There was nothing to do this morning except mill around drinking coffee. The important things had already been said. Dal paced up and down. He wanted to get going, but Mori insisted they wait until the light was good for photos.

While he paced, Dal looked down at the simple little spectrum-watch on his wrist and the large patch of white skin surrounding it, where his larger armband had always been. He had only ever taken that band off to make love. Now he felt naked without it. He deeply regretted the night before, when he had complied with Mori's request. No, it had really been a demand.

Once again, the whole episode got Dal's back up, just remembering. It happened at their last dinner, a sumptuous affair with fresh flowers, real silver, candles, farmed fish, caribou, fresh greens, moon rice, and a special dessert Dal had not eaten before: chocolate mouse—or was it moose? It seemed named for some extinct animal, anyway.

"Made from preserved, real chocolate," Mori had remarked. "Henri has it frozen for special occasions." Fungal cacao blight had wiped out cacao production years ago, so all Dal had ever known was artificial chocolate flavoring. This was lick-the-dish good.

"This is the most important meal I may throw for the rest of my life," Mori had said, smiling at them, his arms open wide.

"Now don't say that, Mori," Naija said. "You have years to go yet! The most important dinner we will have together will be when we all land back here again after giving those trees a new home. So you'd better be ready for us. We will be very hungry. Dried meals and protein bars are going to get old in a hurry," she joked.

"You're a surprise a minute, Mori—usually it's only dictators who have real chocolate," Dal said, regretting it immediately.

This morning he was still sorry for having said that. He was also thankful that he could remember anything at all about the night before, after the great wine.

Mori had circled the table, pouring a couple of ounces of red wine from a heavy crystal decanter into each oversized glass. Swirling his, he instructed: "This is what real Oregon pinot tasted like, from grapes grown where they were supposed to be, before they had to move north. Or before being grown in today's computerized nurseries. Remember this taste. It's from the first press that ever used the special preservation process we have today. In"—he picked up the bottle from the sideboard and looked at the label again to double-check—"ah, 2069. So, this bottle is 226 years old, and it is as good as it was after the first four years in the bottle.

"Wine today simply cannot compare to this. The original earth minerals, weather, and strength of sunlight where grapes and wine production evolved together over the ages no longer mesh like they once did. And we cannot recreate a natural wonder like that. This is very special. Enjoy."

They sipped slowly, and Mori brought out a second bottle, an unheard-of display. Dal took it easy with just two half-servings, knowing he had to fly the next day. "Where did you get this, Mori?" he asked.

"My ancestors bought a lot of it long ago, before the vineyards had to move so far out of their natural range. They could imagine the world we would live in today. And I try to imagine the world of tomorrow." He looked down at his glass. His head nodded and his eyes closed, then opened again. "I can remember too much of the past, what we had before the latest sea level rises and all that. It's not so good—to look back too much. Best be thankful for what you have now, and try to keep it. That's my advice to young people." His words were slightly slurred.

Dal remembered Henri banging through the swinging door from the kitchen with a tray of coffee. They were all a little bleary but came back to life with the steaming cups. Speaking as if he had not quaffed any wine at all, Mori dropped his demand in the softest of tones.

"I think in the interest of your safety that you should leave your fancy armbands here. You can pick them up when you get back," he announced over the stubby, flickering candles.

"Nope," Dal said. "I always wear mine. Will be nice to have it if something goes wrong." Walt vigorously agreed.

"In this case, though, you will get into more trouble if you wear them," Mori said. "I have thought a lot about this. Imagine: You three are going to stand out in New Ushuaia anyway. If you walk around wearing sophisticated gear, people are going to wonder who you are, where you came from, what you are doing, whom you are talking with, what messages you are sending, and so on. Not many people have armbands like those down there at the tip of South America, and if they do, they are either Black Coats or gangsters. Someone might even kill you just to get their hands on one of those."

"Which proves my point," Dal countered. "Those are exactly the times it would be helpful."

"Whom would you call for help?" Mori replied. "Me? Henri? Aron? If you are officially detained, International Amnesty will see that you get your communications through to me. And when I hear of it, you can be sure my help will be immediate. If a renegade gang detains you, though—and there are plenty of those down there—you will not have time to do anything. Because the very first thing they will do is take that band. And if it's the Black Coats, same thing. Only divine intervention could help you. Believe me, the chances of your being harmed along the way are negligible if you leave those armbands here. Otherwise, they are red flags.

"Henri, please give them their new watches." Henri carefully placed a small armband resembling a cheap watch in front of them.

"I had an old-fashioned, Perseus-style communication installed on each of your watches. The button is on the left side. Press it firmly—it will transmit here to a relay device and immediately send the message directly to my band to tell me if there is any trouble. Try it now. See how my armband lights and vibrates?

"The Perseus was an emergency notification system from the old days and is extremely reliable. It will tell us to come to the location from which the signal was emitted and whisk you away. The relay receptor will be located in my outer office.

"Perseus is quite useful. It says in effect, 'Come and get me now,' along with your coordinates. You do not need to repeat the message because it is saved and repeated on the relay. It also transmits *only* to this receptor, and my band. I will be watching for any such message every hour of every day and night while you are gone. If I am asleep, Perseus will wake me up. Henri will be attentive to the main device, as well."

They all sat motionless in thought. Dal was uneasy, but Mori made sense.

"This truly is your best hope for assistance, believe me," Mori continued. "You really cannot even comm out on these new watches. But neither could you have commed me on your sophisticated ones once you leave here because your comms surely would have been intercepted. Just the way I know all about your comms to Ana, Dal. And yours to Ellie, Walt."

Dal jerked his head up and stared at Mori, trying to remember exactly what he had written to Ana.

"Don't worry, Dal. I know you did not spill the wrong beans. That was all harmless. And it showed you love Ana very much. I hope you will invite me to the wedding.

"Again, remember that you must save that button for only an

extreme life-or-death emergency. Aron will come immediately to your position once a message is received. Do not expect that watch to do anything else.

"Also, always remember that this is a secret expedition, and you are to make no calls home by any other means until it is over. This band does not have that capability, either."

Dal didn't like that part, but he was committed now. Also, unease was a familiar feeling in his work. He was skilled at thrusting it aside. Dal thought perhaps someone else might speak up, but no one did. The Perseus as described by Mori sounded reassuring enough. Plus, Mori was right: some criminals would indeed go so far as to try to cut his arm off for his full-spectrum armband. That had been tried before.

So far, Mori had shown great care for their comfort and safety. No reason to doubt him now. Plus, Dal knew that Mori would never needlessly endanger Naija. She was the first to take her armband off and lay it on the table. Then Walt. Finally, Dal slowly unfastened his armband and placed it beside the others.

DAL CONTINUED TO PACE in and out of the long shadows of the rising sun, looking down repeatedly at his puny new watch. It was hard to get used to. At last, Mori said it was time. Henri zoomed in for close-ups of their faces with the video.

They shook hands all around and hunched out of the way of the blades to take their last steps into the plane. Dal showed Naija and Walt how to adjust their earphones. Naija shook off his help and looked comfortable in the plane, as if she had been there before.

Dal had given them terse emergency instructions earlier: "Keep your head down when getting on board or leaving whenever the blades are deployed. If we are going to crash, I will say, 'There's a problem,' at which time you should bend over and cradle your neck. As soon as we hit the ground, step down from the plane as fast as you can and run. Go straight out from the sides or to the front, never to the back. Got it?"

He revved the engine until the viciously rotating silent blade atop the plane whipped the trees behind them into a rattling froth. They lifted off, hovered briefly, and slowly gained height. Mori waved them out of sight. His smiling face shrank to a pinpoint and then was lost in the enlarging view below.

Dal retracted the blades and switched to vertical equilibrium. They rocketed away. Everything on the ground blurred—first the garden, then the forest surrounding the house and garden, then the tall gray buildings spreading out on all sides right up to the shiny river and the bayshore. At traveling speed, features in every direction were soon lost in the ever-present brown haze that lay close to the ground and was easily visible only from a plane or a high promontory.

Thirty-two days, give or take a few, and I will be back in your arms again, Ana!

10

Babies worldwide must be protected and cared for like never before. Because, like never before, they are increasingly hard to come by. We need the next generations.

—WHO Special Bulletin, September 2294

NOVEMBER 14, 2295

Ana Chambeau had carried a bottle of sparkling water with her everywhere she went for the past few days. It was within easy reach now as she traced the route to the Riley farm. Her car knew where to go, even though she had only been there a couple of times in all the years she and Dal had been together. His visits in and out were achingly short, and they had more privacy at her place. But soon they would be together for days at a time, for months, and for all the years stretching ahead, too.

She smiled at this thought and sensed that the roadside view was prettier than ever before. The day was cooler and the birds were louder. Luckily, the threat of a hurricane had passed far out to sea last week, and the high-pressure system that had pushed it away now cooled Orangeburg just enough to make it tolerable for her to be outside during daylight.

It was good that Dal had not written again and, above all, that he had not said Ana could go with him, as she had once wished he would do. Wherever he was going, that would be impossible for her now. With her own parents gone, Ana wanted to get closer to Jim and Risa.

However, she didn't want to tell them her big news yet. Dal didn't even know.

Ana sat back, caressing her abdomen with her hands. How would she tell Dal? She would have to think of some special way and not just blurt it out. Would he be thrilled? Ana knew he would. She herself was ecstatic, relieved by this happenstance. Now she could avoid the long, uncomfortable, and often disappointing process of sperm aggregation and artificial insemination that so many of her friends had gone through.

Ana smiled when thinking about her friend Gina. Gina was called "miracle girl," the only other one in her group of friends who had been able to have—in her case, not just one but two—children naturally with the same man and without medical assists. For this, Gina was a minor celeb and was given free diapers, baby food, and such, even though more than one child per couple was frowned upon by many.

Risa and Jim will be crazy happy. She couldn't wait to tell them. Still, Ana wanted to keep the news secret until she could tell Dal, and that might not be until he returned. She decided she would make only one visit to his parents before she started to show. She really had to wait and tell Dal first. He deserved that much.

Only two days past her expected period, Ana's hands had shaken when she fumbled with the wrapper to open the strip test. Then she'd gone in for official confirmation, and her whole life had changed.

Heavens! What is all that mess in the orange grove? she wondered. *Tents and lines of people, with buses wallowing through those muddy ruts, bringing in still more people, more stuff. Dal didn't mention any of this. Of course, we were kinda busy.* She smiled again, remembering that night. Those memories got her through the long days.

Good thing it drizzled just now, Ana thought. Blowing dust would have been worse than the mud. The rain had cooled off the front-door knocker, so she put her handkerchief back in her pocket and was able to grab the knocker with her bare hand. Jim opened the door, pulled her inside, and called out, "Risa! It's Ana!"

"Oh, my, what a surprise!" Risa popped out of the kitchen, a half-empty bag of dried lentils in one hand and a measuring cup in the other. "Is everything all right?"

"Sure is, Mrs. Riley," Ana replied. "I just wanted to say hello. And let you know that I haven't heard from Dal again since his last comm, the one that I called to tell you about. So I guess he must have taken off for the next part of his job by now. I'll have more time to work on the wedding instead of checking for comms every minute, right? And no worries about the wedding," she hastened to add. "I have it all under control."

"How nice of you to drop in, Ana. How about a cup of tea and some of my cheese-flavored sticks?"

"That will be great, thanks," said Ana. Right then she felt a vicious rumbling in her stomach. Acid rose in her throat.

She could barely get out the words, "Where is your powder room again?" Risa pointed. Ana rushed in, hung onto the sink, and breathed deeply, finally stifling the urge to vomit. She was lucky to have avoided a major retch right in front of them. *I've gotta get out of here fast. Risa is so savvy, might suspect something. Must tell Dal first!*

Ana emerged from the bathroom with an even paler face. "Had some bad jellyfish last night that didn't agree with me," she said. "No telling where it came from, but I could not refuse to eat just a bite of it to be polite. I better get back home. Sorry about this quick visit. Maybe another day." Ana threw the front door open and was gone in a flash, running back to her car. She vomited on the other side, out of view from the house.

Back in the kitchen, Jim remarked: "Well, if that don't beat all. Who would eat anything from that ocean around here right now?"

Risa stirred her lentils into the boiling water and smiled her knowing smile. "Nobody, Jim. Nobody in their right mind would do that. Ana's way too smart for that."

11

Harmful algae blooms, or HABs, occur when colonies of algae grow out of control and produce ill effects in people, fish, shellfish, marine animals, and birds. Human illnesses caused by HABs can be debilitating, even fatal. Pesticides, toxins, and waste increase the occurrence of these so-called "red tides," which are on the rise worldwide.

—NOAA educational material, August 2018

NOVEMBER 14, 2295

Far from the ground, Dal's relief at finally being under way smoothed his forehead, relaxed his jaw, and eased his stomach. No more surprises from Mori. He knew what to do now. He could call upon years of training and experience. He expected nothing he had not mastered before.

He wished Ana were in the seat next to him rather than Naija, as companionable as she was. *Just as well that Ana's not here, though,* Dal thought as he remembered the risk profile of this mission. With a lot of the plane's gear located over his head, this particular flying machine was susceptible to rolling over to the right and spinning around; plus, they carried a heavy load and had more to pick up in Ushuaia. It was all going to be very interesting.

The atmosphere inside the cockpit became friendlier than at any time during their weeks together on the ground. Naija sat beside Dal with her small backpack at her feet. Walt had the double backseat to himself but spent most of the time leaning forward between them. "You really don't need to lean in so close, Walt," Dal said through his headset. "We can hear you just fine using these." He tapped the mouthpiece. "And belt yourself in back there."

"What's the flight plan, Captain?" Naija asked.

"We are heading south now," he replied, "across the Gulf of Mexico, slicing Mexico at its narrowest point to the Gulf of Tehuantepec. Then we'll have clear sailing over the Pacific in a south-southeasterly direction until we arrive off Cape Horn, which I will circle and approach from the east. To arrive, we will fly up the Beagle Channel, the same way Darwin sailed it.

"There are more direct routes, but this way we cross a minimum of borders. I wish we could fly down the spine of the Andes and take a look, but we can't. I want to enter Ushuaia from the eastern sea and mix up with the traffic from Islas Malvinas. If we were to enter via Chile, the Argentines would intercept us for sure. Those two are often suspicious of each other, especially in competing for Antarctica."

Walt shoved a bag of dried fruit forward over the seats. "Want some?"

"Thanks." Naija grabbed a handful and poured some into a kerchief, which she quickly shaped into a little bowl and placed it on Dal's leg so he could keep his hands free.

"Wow, you have no end of talents," Dal said.

"This is just the tip of the iceberg," Naija replied.

The sound of wind as they flew, the mountainous clouds billowing ahead, the green dials on the panel, and the sour-sweet taste of cherries in his mouth wrapped Dal in contentment. He was in his element, far above the melee on earth.

"What does your family think about a nice girl like you going off to the bottom of the world on a crazy jaunt like this?" Dal asked Naija.

"You mean what did they say?"

"Yeah, what did they say?"

"They don't really know where I am. But they would all trust Mori to keep me safe."

"So, your mother knows Mori, too?" Walt asked. "How did you all meet?"

"Mori has been close to our family for three generations. My great-grandmother on my mother's side met his father on his first trip to the far north. Mori's father encouraged Mori to visit before it changed too much. Mori got to know us, the Inuit, and also those few of the Dene and Chippewa people who had moved up to Ellesmere to get away from the crowds taking over down south. Most people think that there are no Inuit left. We are supposed to have all intermarried and lost our identity."

"That's certainly what I thought," said Walt, chewing into the earphones.

"Maybe that's what people want to think," Naija responded. "Multi-culturalism of the twentieth century became expensive as national policy once immigration picked up so much by 2200. The government stopped supporting our ethnic identity altogether.

"My mother always said, 'No matter what happens, it is important that some things be remembered.' She taught me what she knew. I am not completely Inuit, but I am strong in tradition." Dal listened closely. Naija's earnestness permeated the plane.

"I remember my grandmother telling me how Mori brought them protein after hunting ended forever," she continued. "Mori paid out of his own pocket for my education in Winnipeg and saw to it that I had ticket money for the commute. He arranged advanced medical care for my village, beyond what people normally get. And above all, he listened carefully. He was willing to learn. He endeared himself to us so much that after a long time, people started to call him *quablonut.*"

"Look at those clouds!" she broke off, poking Dal with her elbow. Towering gray columns approached from the left. On the right side, the curve of the earth etched through the sky like an inverted bowl.

"It's okay," Dal said. "I know all about that from the morning report. There was a seasonal storm in the eastern Gulf of Mexico shown in this morning's weather bulletin. We will stay far to the west of it. This one is gonna strengthen to a cat 7, so we'd better move along," he said, veering sharply away.

Walt rustled around in his bag and came up with what looked like a walnut.

"Lookie what I smuggled aboard," he exclaimed, thrusting his arm between the front seats.

"What is that?" asked Naija.

"It's the tiniest camera I could get."

"What the hell did you bring that for, Walt?" Dal asked. "It can only be incriminating. Bad news if you take pictures of us and they surface somewhere."

"How about in twenty years?" Walt replied. "Might be okay by then, and it will be proof of what we did. What if I die and don't come back? Ellie won't have to appeal for handouts, won't be using Scott's last words, either. None of that 'For God's sake, take care of our people' crap."

"You've read too many of Mori's books, Walt," said Dal. "You should have been out exercising instead. I'll wring your neck if I'm ever in any of your shots." The reference to Scott was unfortunate. Dal had started that book but put it down once the ending was obvious. He'd seen the photos, though.

"Don't worry, Walt. I'll take plenty of pictures of you—digging holes, carrying trees, building irrigation channels—all the fun stuff," Naija joked.

"I can't believe you think I am going to do all the planting, and Dal here thinks he is just the high-and-mighty pilot," Walt shot back. "You might be tiny, but you're as strong as a robot."

"Okay, okay," Dal laughed. "It's all going to work out. We will all work together and get it done as fast and as well as possible."

The storm was far behind them now. Dal cut a sharp left, tilting lower over the ocean. The surface roiled with whitecaps whipped by a thirty-knot wind. "Maybe I can show you something interesting," he said. "This ocean view gets boring, staying so high the whole way."

"Remember, we are not to go near the coast, Dal," Walt warned.

"Trust me, it will be okay," Dal assured him. "We have plenty of getaway power. Plus, this plane is almost undetectable."

Walt slid back in his seat and clapped his hand to his forehead.

"We're going a couple of miles out from a little island, Punta Aguja, which used to be a high cape connected to the mainland of Peru by a fertile plain," Dal said. "Rising seas made it an island. I worked down here a few years ago. Nobody lives there anymore."

"The sea looks pink!" Naija said. "What on earth is that?" Just ahead the water turned from the inky blue of deep ocean to the turquoise of shallows and then faded off toward the shore in pinks to brownish red.

It looked as if a large whaling station in full flensing operations had tinged the water red with blood and whale bits. But they all knew that was impossible. Only a few endangered orcas and humpbacks remained anywhere.

"My mother told me about the last whale hunt of our people," Naija said. "It was ceremonial, and my grandmother was sad when it ended. Killing the whale was a sacred connection to nature, she used to say. I argued with her about that, but she believed it. She told us how water would turn a beautiful pinkish red." Naija's voice drifted off as she stared down at the red sea.

Dal hadn't meant to introduce such a wistful memory as this seemed to be. "Well, what you see here is called a red tide," he said. "It's colored by an algae that poisons any shellfish you eat. A person can actually die from eating something from these waters, or from breathing the fumes. Just imagine."

"*Pseudo-nitzschia*," Walt crackled through the earphones.

Dal continued: "Years ago, a red tide would last a season or so and then stop. But this one has been here for fifteen years now and taken over the whole area. Everyone had to evacuate. Still, from up here it looks awesome. Like a reflection of sunset in the water."

Suddenly a green light flashed in front of Dal. He reached out to focus the screen onto a smaller sector representing the mainland seventeen miles away. Two tiny blips appeared on the screen. Evidently those planes did not have antidetection capability. The blips moved parallel to the coast at 1,700 meters elevation, drifting back and forth across their territory. *Maybe they're on a routine patrol,* Dal thought. The two planes turned.

"What's that?" Walt asked, his eyes clamped on the blips. He gripped the strap over his head as Dal turned the plane into a sickening spiral turn. He leveled out and throttled up for a fast retreat seaward, forcing Walt and Naija back in their seats.

"I told you not to go near the coast," Walt said through clenched teeth.

"Clam up, Walt," said Naija.

"Goddammit, how did they detect us?" Dal mumbled to himself. Why were they seen? Would all the other new high-tech assets really work in a pinch? He hoped so. Especially the Perseus. Sweat beaded his forehead while he took evasive action. Under hand control, the plane turned and wobbled in the sky. The blips hovered where they were for an instant, and then pursued.

"Damn," Dal muttered again. Maybe they had some unknown technology. Aviation advances were happening every day.

Everyone stared at the screen, watching the blips close the gap. Dal's hands tightened around the stick. His thigh muscles tensed, as if he could run away through the air. He held his breath at first, but switched to deep breathing to keep his brain oxygenated.

Shit! Why? Why'd I do that? Dal rebuked himself silently as he accelerated to maximum potential. If they could just get to two hundred miles out and weren't lasered into oblivion, he would breathe normally again.

Walt had lain down in the back seat by now, unable to watch. Naija picked her backpack up from the floor and hugged it.

A long minute and a half later, Dal's shoulders relaxed and a slow grin spread across his face. He turned around to give a thumbs-up and saw Walt curled up in a fetal position. "For god's sake, Walt, what are you doing?" Dal laughed when Walt hastily sat back up. The plane settled into their southward course. The screen was blip-free again.

"They turned back at a hundred and eighty miles out," Dal said. "Maybe they thought we were Argentines showing off in their air space."

"Maybe you'll avoid the coast now?" Walt said.

"Oh, man, that was something!" Naija's eyes shone. Energy bounced around the cabin.

"Have to hand it to ya—you sure pulled that one out." Walt's damp hand shook Dal's shoulder.

"Nothing like a close call that works out. You two might as well take a nap. I'm going to keep it boring from now on."

He stayed far offshore while Naija and Walt dozed after their adrenalin surges abated. Dal struggled a bit to stay awake, too. He poured artificial coffee from his thermos and sipped it, allowing the cognition panel to fly now.

Dal passed the next hour thinking of what he might do for work after this gig was over. If this tree scheme worked the way Mori hoped, perhaps he could be in charge of other pilots flying to and from

Antarctica to plant more trees. He could run the whole show from Canada, flying down only now and then to keep his skills sharp. Dal pictured himself and Ana in a little apartment outside New Churchill, on a street lined with trees and flowers. He imagined Ana doing her remote teaching from home. They could walk outside together.

He forgot about Walt, who lay out of his peripheral vision. Naija rested her head on her crumpled jacket, which she had balled up and pressed against the window. He felt as good as alone now. He pictured making love with Ana outside under the aurora, and lingered over the details of that. That was a great idea. They could actually do that if they were to live up there.

12

In 2018 it was predicted that by 2050, 68 percent of the earth's population would live in urban areas. Now that number is 93 percent. Climate-forced migration has ensured this movement to urban living. In many cases, people have migrated to entirely new cities, most of which did not exist in 2050.

—*New York Gazette,* May 2292

SAME DAY, 2295

Dal took control back from OC and turned the plane sharply east into turbulence. "Thought it was about time for you two to wake up," he said. Naija and Walt stretched and came alive.

"I wanted to go over the arrival plan again before things start hoppin'. A quick review now: we need to evade full inspection at landing. If we can manage it, we are not to open the cargo hold until we load up more trees in Lapataia Park day after tomorrow. We don't want people to realize we have a load of trees. In Lapataia, Walt"—Dal jerked a thumb in his direction—"you will mastermind the loading of the trees while Naija and I deal with whomever we have to. Got all that? Okay. We must look for a man sent by Mori who will approach us and help with everything. His name is Bill Hernan, and he will meet us at a bar. Naija has that detail in her instructions.

"Soon we will start feeling the winds over the Drake Passage, and we will come in a few kilometers south of the Horn before we change heading to north and northwest to duck into the Beagle Channel. We'll approach New Ushuaia by going past Puerto Williams. That way we only have to deal with one country's close-in airspace. Take a good look. This area is all new to me, too, and changing fast."

Dal nosed around Cape Horn about twenty kilometers out to sea, beyond the protective lee of the land. They bounced violently in Beaufort Scale winds of force eleven. Thirty-foot waves crashed below, and huge ships strained to move their icy cargo northward. As the plane passed Cape Horn, Dal changed course again toward the north, and soon again to the northwest. Finally, he slowed way down.

The moss-covered end of South America, remembered by generations of pioneers as a miserable sea passage to California, was now just a small nub of an island that tilted the tip of South America toward the southeast. Unimpressive for all that it was so storied.

"Looks like a lot of action down below," Naija remarked sleepily. The choppy sea heaved with bobbing ships of many types, all straining toward the northeast to Africa and beyond. From their high vantage, the tumbling sea resembled a sink of green, soapy water.

The plane tilted again, this time to the west-northwest. They rounded tiny Nueva Island and skimmed by Picton Island before entering the Beagle Channel. These formerly large islands were now mere rocks, their vegetative fringes submerged under ever-widening seas.

Dal slowed the plane even more and, once they entered the Beagle Channel and were out of the worst winds, deployed the rotors. The water of this broad channel was smooth and steely gray. The channel widened to meet steep, glacier-cut hillsides lining the misty spectacle on both sides.

"Puerto Williams is over there," Dal said, jerking his head to the left. "They moved the town, and now it is mostly inside that mountain."

Ahead in the west, the sun peeked out from clouds and glinted between two high peaks in Chile. Shafts of gold penetrated the low, metallic-colored sky, casting a subdued and reverential mood. The scene reminded Dal of his mother's descriptions of a Gothic cathedral saved from unendurable gravitas by heavenly beams of light pouring through its stained-glass windows.

His headset crackled with air-traffic controllers' orders. Faster craft whizzed by, hurrying to land. At a lower altitude, personal antigravity air conveyances streamed up the channel. Dal hoped he could fly amongst them without hitting anyone. Because there were so many, he decided to stay high until the last minute. Numerous light VTOLs darted about between new cities coming into view high up on the hills of both sides of the channel.

"I can't believe it is so congested down here," remarked Walt.

Air streams from rocket buses lingered vertically over a leveled mountaintop before twisting apart in the wind. "That's the Fuegian Transport Base," Dal said. "We'll land there."

In the water below, ferries and barges choked the channel between Puerto Navarino and Puerto Williams on the south side and New Ushuaia on the north. It might have been the busy Hong Kong Harbor in an earlier time.

Naija's voice broke into the stream of talk coming over the headset while she ruffled through her bag for their itinerary. "Here's where we are stay—oops, sorry," she said as Dal cut her off with a slice of his hand in the air.

He listened intently for the signal Mori had given him. It must be mixed up in all this gibberish. Ah, there it was: Mt4-Aurora. That was painted on the outside of the plane. They were a private plane from the megayacht *Aurora*, coming in for dinner and sightseeing. That was the story. Mori had assured him that an actual yacht *Aurora* would be out there in the South Atlantic with instructions to verify them if needed. Nevertheless, Dal worried about keeping the details straight. Honesty was so much easier.

How would he control his face and be convincing if he had to lie the whole time he was here? Dal considered himself an up-front type. Even though he could keep things to himself, lying was not something he did well. People always knew, even if it was just a white lie, so he seldom even tried. Therefore, he planned to avoid talking to most other people while they were down here.

He muttered aviation lingo into the mouthpiece. Meanwhile, Walt unbuckled, heaved himself over the back of his seat, fetched their larger packs from the rear, and pushed them forward to behind his seat. He went back and closed the curtain covering the cargo space; they needed the cargo to remain unseen. Often, private planes could get away with that because inspectors were so busy.

Naija turned around in her seat and gestured to Walt, asking if the trees were all right after the tossing the plane had taken. He mouthed back, "Yes," and held both thumbs up. He made a tying motion to indicate that the ties still held them fast against the walls.

Just in case anyone did get a glimpse of the cargo, Walt had concocted a story about a botanical study comparing trees from similar latitudes in North and South America. False entry permits supporting this confab lay in his folder, and he had a few small field instruments with him to look the part.

Dal glanced back. There were dark wet blotches under Walt's arms. He must be nervous, too. One thing for sure: they did not know enough about local customs and immigration procedures. These could change daily, what with people on the move around the world the way they were.

Could a nervous guy like Walt really come through? Something about the atmosphere near Churchill had filled Dal with optimism. But out here every problem seemed magnified. He would have to recapture some of his usual confident audacity.

Dal had no more time to think about it. The headset crackled again with "Mt4 Aurora, Mt4 Aurora, cleared to land by tube 3, 110, east." Dal repeated their instructions in his monotone pilot voice.

Then he took the plane down.

Walt removed his earphones and spoke rapidly to Naija: "Let's let Dal take the lead in the airport. If we have to speak, we are just knownothing tourists, in for a quick lark." Then he put the earphones back on. His shoulders straightened, and his gaze clamped on the horizon.

"We are staying at the Beagle Hotel, and according to Mori we are to meet Bill Hernan at a bar called Natural Selection," Naija reminded them during a break in the babble from the tower. "It's by the waterfront, but atop a mountain. We can take the cable car down from the terminal to our hotel. Once we are off the top, everything is extremely steep. Look how they have shaved the summits off these mountains to make some flat land."

The plane touched down. "Let's get past these guys," Dal said as he opened his door, pushed himself out, and dropped onto the runway.

Half a dozen men and women and three menacing German shepherds on leash converged around the plane. A red stripe down each leg and a patch over the right pocket identified them as UN Immigration workers. Behind them stood several more men, unmistakable in their Black Coats uniforms and holding tiny laser pistols casually in their hands.

"Those with the stripe are Argentine," Dal whispered to the others. He looked at Naija. She could not stop watching the Black Coats. "At least they're not aiming at us," Dal whispered. "Don't look so scared."

"No hablo español," Dal said, stepping forward with his arms flared in an awkward shrug. He gave them the most disarming and helpless smile he could muster.

"No problem, Mr. Riley," said a small man with dark hair and bags under his watery eyes. He glided to the front of the other officials and held out his hand to receive their flight manifest and passports.

"We all speak English here. You will find this a very cosmopolitan place, now that the whole world is interested in Antarctica, our lands to the south." Dal already knew that both the Argentines and Chileans had always considered the wild continent 1,260 kilometers to the south to be an extension of their countries.

"You may follow me." They walked past a row of uniformed officials toward the hangar where noncommercial visitors were processed.

A cart rumbled up to their plane when they were about a hundred yards away. Walt turned to see that the cart had stopped near the cargo door. He opened his mouth to shout something, but Dal grabbed his arm and gave him a warning look. Walt turned back toward the hangar. Dal hoped no one had noticed Walt's alarm.

Whoossh! Suddenly a sound like a firehose whipped all of their heads back around to see the horrifying sight of their plane simmering in a cloud of gas.

"Just bug spray," Dal whispered under his breath. "Trying to kill any spores that might contaminate the ecosystem here. At least they haven't sprayed us yet, like they did to people arriving in planes in the twentieth century."

"You should have told us to expect that," Walt whispered back.

The hangar was enormous and empty. *Probably used for parking planes during the long winters. Bet winds can really whip across these shaved-off mountaintops,* Dal imagined. He walked through the echoing space toward a desk and a counter off to one side and put his bag on the counter as instructed.

"Where are you from?" asked the flat voice of one who had said this too many times to care.

"The yacht *Aurora.* Registration 953072, from Port Stanley, the Malvinas." Dal had practiced that considerably.

"Reason for visit?"

"Pleasure," Dal answered, as he always did no matter what his mission. Usually, "pleasure" aroused fewer questions than did "business."

"Pleasure? You must be the only traveler coming here for pleasure right now. What's to do? It will be too muddy to hike for another month yet." The interrogator chatted in what had become a pleasant, conversational tone. This change of attitude alerted Dal more than the flat, uninterested question had.

He paused, unsure what to say. Hot breath blew on his neck, and Walt pushed him aside.

"*He* may be here for pleasure, because he finds a good time wherever he goes. *I,* however, am a university professor on sabbatical, and I therefore am de facto on business at all times. The business of learning. No pure pleasure trips for those of us who would add to the fund of information for the next generation and who will take back what we learn here to nurture the minds of the young. No pure pleasure trip for those of us who are curious about every part of the world: its people, its flora, its fauna, its geology, its—"

"Okay, okay, that's fine." The once-again-bored interrogator cut Walt off in midpontification. "I hope you will find something here worthy of your great intellect. How long are you staying?" he asked, looking over Walt's head at Dal.

"Two nights."

The interrogator continued to stare at Dal, as if he expected more.

Finally, Dal added, "We wanted to see the area, spend a couple of nights in town."

"Three North Americans arriving by way of a yacht from the Malvinas, flying over for a few days' entertainment. Um, well, stranger things are happening around here lately, I can assure you.

"And you?" The handsome, dark head turned away from Dal and inclined toward Naija, who stood composed and quiet.

"I am with them," she said, flashing a brilliant smile and lowering one eyelid in such a slow movement that Dal was left unsure whether or not she had actually winked at the man.

Scarlet crept up the man's neck, and he quickly looked down. His stamp resounded solidly on all three passports with impressive precision. *"Tienen buenos dias, señores y señorita. Bienvenidos a Argentina."*

DAL PUSHED THROUGH the turnstile without waiting for Naija to go first, so anxious was he to get out of there. He hurried through a human-sized door cut into the vast wall of the hangar. The door was painted white and propped open with a rock, which Dal kicked in glee as he emerged into the cool humidity under metallic gray clouds. In the west, gold rimmed the edges of a huge cloudbank. Somewhere above them, beyond the clouds and the mountains, the sun still shone intensely.

Naija and Walt caught up.

"Slow down, man," Walt said under his breath. "Look normal instead of running off like that. I thought you were used to tight situations."

"Not this kind. I'm not much of an actor—unlike you, apparently. But, hey, it worked. I'm buying you a *cerveza* as soon as we hit that bar."

Naija beamed at them. They all linked arms and fairly skipped over to a ticket booth near the edge of the mountaintop. Ahead, rusty cables dropped sharply out of sight. This old cable car was a popular attraction in New Ushuaia, both for the 360-degree views and for the slow, old-fashioned ride up and down, taking people beyond the tree line and across a boulder field.

The land below the boulders fell away in a green strip down the mountainside, left natural to enhance the ride. Except for the little bit of green below the cable car, the rest—and all the other nearby mountains—displayed a mass of development. Every inch had been terraced, burrowed into, or cantilevered from, producing a jumbled skyline of hasty urbanization.

Far below them, water filled the cirques between mountains and swamped the low places. The rising, gray-green sea completely covered the docks, the homey waterfront cottages, and the painted, corrugated-iron buildings of the old town of Ushuaia.

Several jagged mountain peaks could be seen in the distance. *Probably in Chile,* Dal suspected. The majestic peaks, their snowfields and hanging glaciers long departed, drew his eyes to the most distant horizon. He asked Naija, "How do you think all this would have looked when capped with snow?"

"I don't know," she replied. "Pretty, I would expect. We didn't have much snow, either, even where I lived in my mother's and grandmother's time."

The nearby mountains ended just as this one did, sliced straight across at 1,800 meters. Dal braced himself against the strong wind while he looked around and waited his turn to enter the cable car. Several other mountaintops appeared to be active transportation hubs as well. The rest of the cut-off mountaintops sprouted buildings that resembled mushrooms, dome-shaped to withstand the harsh wind and weather.

An attendant came up behind and pushed them in to pack the cable car full. Dal's stomach inverted when the crammed car plunged over the side and took a free fall before catching up with the slack cable line. After that trauma, it continued down more slowly. The faces around Dal had shown no fear at all throughout the ordeal.

Despite his churning stomach, Dal was exhilarated at being here— and being alive in a new situation. Naija pressed against him in the crush of families, couples, and random travelers, none of whom paid the least attention to them. Most of the people had dark hair and eyes like Naija's. It occurred to Dal that she could pass for a native-born citizen here.

Walt swayed against his neighbors and chatted animatedly with a tall, beefy man next to him. The man wore a backpack, which hit shorter people in the head whenever he moved. Dal wished Walt were not quite so gregarious. *He acts like this really is a vacation.* Dal shifted his weight from one foot to the other, but when that caused him to press harder into Naija, he shifted his weight back again.

He looked over at Walt once more. Walt was still yakking away. Dal frowned to signal him to knock off the chatter, but Walt still wouldn't look his way. Dal worried that Walt might say something that would draw attention to them. He would be so happy to leave this place, with its nerve-shattering traps. He wanted to be any place where he could be in control again. Like flying.

13

A new outbreak of unidentified infectious disease associated with the triatomine insect, otherwise known as vampire bug, *barbiero, chinche,* or *vinchuca,* has been detected in the Americas. Report any high fever to local authorities when it is accompanied by rash, headache, and lassitude. If leading to somnolence, the illness can be fatal. The nocturnal bites are sometimes, but not always, accompanied by itching and local inflammation. Strong insect-repellent use is recommended at all times in sleeping areas where these disease vectors are present.

—*World Health Bulletin,* winter 2294

THAT EVENING, NEW USHUAIA, ARGENTINA

I'm ready for that brewski you owe me, Dal." Walt bounced on his toes as he hurried along on an adrenaline high. Outside the hotel, he peered up at the climb to the bar. "Yikes."

"Yep," Dal said. It was chilly up here in the damp wind. They each had brought one nice outfit as directed by Mori, just for this stop. Otherwise, all they had was rough camp gear and no good jacket to wear with these nicer clothes.

Dal gripped the cold metal railing and looked up the ladder. It zigzagged out of sight, up into the mist in the general direction of the bar that served the best drinks to go with the best views in New Ushuaia. "It's up there?" Naija asked, pointing a wavering finger. "Natural Selection? Are you sure?"

"Yes," said Dal. That was where they would meet Mori's local contact, who would lead them to a small cache of trees found only in the local national park—trees similar to those that thousands of years ago had survived in Antarctica.

Dal stared up the ladder. He had no idea what this contact looked like, only that he was an old friend of Mori's.

One little detail that Dal had never told Mori or anyone else was that, unless he was encased in an airplane, he was afraid of heights. He never went near the edge of anything. Dal put his foot on the first rung of the ladder and blew out through his lips. He kept blowing out every few steps as he climbed and never looked down. Naija moved nimbly ahead of him.

Better at climbing, just like she was at swimming in cold water, Dal thought. *Where are her limitations?* The lights of Ushuaia twinkled in and out of the fog that swirled off the channel dizzyingly far below.

"We'd better come back down to our rooms the less-adventurous way," Dal yelled up to Naija. "Let's take the mid-mountain cog rail. Especially after a couple of drinks."

"If you like," Naija yelled back, never slowing her pace.

Breathless and thirsty, Dal finally reached the top landing. There stood Naija, hands on her hips, not panting at all. They waited five more minutes for Walt to arrive.

"Egads!" Walt gasped.

The trio entered the bar through an arc of blue light. The air inside was dense with machine-made smoke, through which they could make out a trio of Brazilian musicians galloping through a Latin melody that blew through Dal's ears straight to his pelvis. Waving hands in the air, his body gyrating in sync with each dancer he passed, Dal made his way across the dance floor to the bar. He grabbed onto the bar as if it were the rail of a pitching ship. Naija covered her nose with her hands, coughed, and wiped her eyes.

"You've never been in a smoky room before, have you?" Dal said. "There aren't antismoke laws here, apparently. I don't really know what this stuff is." Dal offered Naija a napkin from the bar.

Before she could answer, Walt jabbed Dal in the ribs. "So, what do you want while I have this busy man's attention?" Walt grinned at the bartender and pointed at Dal. "That guy is paying."

"Gin and tonic—Bombay Sapphire gin," Dal said.

"Hey, mate, this is the last fuckin' outpost at the last end of the fuckin' world. And haven't you heard yet? Bombay took a dive." The bartender rasped like an old cabaret singer. "We've got generic gin— that's it."

A friendly voice. Aussie. You never know where you'll find one. "I'll have to make do then, I guess. No worries," Dal said. He turned back to Naija, who still wrinkled her nose and breathed in shallow puffs.

"The smoke won't hurt you in small doses, but if you're not having fun, we can leave as soon as we find him," Dal murmured in her ear.

"No, I don't want to miss this. And we can't leave fast, anyway. Might look suspicious. I'll have a dry kir royale, please." Naija coughed into her elbow.

Dal turned back to order this drink he did not know and saw that the bartender had gone back down the bar again. He frowned, for an instant chafing under the strain of trying to be so many things at once, none of which was quite himself—a man on a secret mission, a professional pilot looking for a contact, a buddy to Walt, and whatever he was to Naija. He waved to get the bartender's attention.

"The lady will have a dry kir royale," Dal yelled, as the bartender set Dal's G&T down and trotted off again. "Do you have that?"

"If you don't mind twist-off-top fake bubbly, we sure do," the bartender called back over his shoulder.

Should let her order her own drink, Dal thought as he knocked his glass against Walt's. *She is capable enough.*

"Who's ordering the fancy drinks? And, if I'm not mistaken, in the accents of an American Southerner—just a trace?"

Dal looked past Walt to see a thin, very tan and weathered woman with streaky gray hair. She had broad, cracked fingernails and was using them to scrape the salt from the rim of her drink.

"I see you don't like salt on your margarita," Walt observed in a disgusted tone. "My friend here ordered the kir. Excuse me, I didn't get your name." His face was set and unfriendly.

"It really does pay to be nice to people down here," the woman replied. "You can't tell who is who. It's too dangerous to have enemies in a wild place like this. My name is Erica Thorstinsdottir." She held out a rough hand, which Walt politely shook, apparently chastened.

Erica stared hard at Dal, and he realized immediately that this woman was looking for a fantasy, not him. This had happened before.

Self-confident women gravitated to him, and then tried to take him over and make him over. It never worked out, because he was never interested in them. Only in Ana, since he was fifteen years old. As he thought about her, Dal began to feel his feet planted more securely on the floor.

"Ushuaia is where you can meet someone from anywhere, I've found," Erica said. "I've only been here two weeks myself. How about you?" She lifted her glass in Dal's direction.

"Just arrived," Dal said quickly, using the truth as much as possible, as they had planned to do. He hoped he would not forget to use their made-up names.

"Are you with the Migration Board? I heard a new office is opening here soon, and a bunch of scientists are coming in. I'd like to find them and talk with one."

"Nope," Dal said, bobbing up and down to the music, pretending to be more interested in the beat than in conversation. Perhaps he would ask Naija to dance.

His posture with Naija informed Erica that they were together, and her manner shifted accordingly. She stuck out her hand to Naija.

"Hi, I'm Erica."

"Hello. I am, uh, Nancy." Naija smiled. This was the first real welcome any of them had given to Erica, whose face then relaxed.

"Well, Nancy, you are very lucky to be here with friends. It's bitterly hard to be alone, thrusting oneself on strangers just to have a little human contact. I could always find a robot, but there is nothing like another human. An odd feeling—to be alone in a place as crowded as this."

"Yes, I guess it must be. Why are you by yourself?" Naija asked.

Oh, Naija, no! Dal tried to transmit to Naija silently. *No extraneous conversations. She could be an incognito Black Coat.*

Erica looked pleased to begin what Dal feared would be an entrapping story. She looked at each of them in turn.

"My country sent me down here. I was most unwilling." She fairly spit the words out. "You see, I'm an epidemiologist studying new vectors and diseases. Supposed to find out what insect is responsible for the new fevers showing up in Iceland brought by climate refugees from around here. We have a quite large new mosquito never seen there before, a variety of the *Phospora ciliata*. It used to be harmless, but perhaps it is carrying something new. I am supposed to study the relationship between this mosquito and any new diseases here. But my superiors have no idea how hard it is just to get around."

At that, Dal's interest perked up. He leaned forward to hear her better over the din of the bar.

Erica locked eyes with Dal and elaborated: "Everywhere I try to go, it is either straight up or straight down, or across some water, or knee-deep in a bog. I don't know how these people stand it. The living conditions down on the lower slopes are miserable, especially when it rains.

"Also, the mosquitos and other bloodsucking bugs. Yetch! Take the triatomine bug. They will eat you up, I tell you. Some people grow anemic just going to bed at night, and those little monsters are resistant to all our attempts to kill them. Also, anywhere the wind is not blowing at least fifteen knots, you are in trouble from mosquitos.

"We once thought mosquitos might be eradicated by gene-drive manipulation. Guess they showed us, huh? A few species made it through, and here we are." Erica spoke louder to overcome the music. Other patrons gathered around to hear what all this was about.

"Do you think I was prepared for this? I assuredly was not. Was not even issued standard insect repellent or a little head net. Such negligence! I just might sue—if I get back to headquarters with any of my blood left."

"Where did you find the head nets?" Walt asked. "We only have repellent."

"In any store. Most people here know to take the right gear when descending to the valleys or going up into Lapataia Park. But where are you going? You may not need to have protection, depending on exactly where you are going."

Dal jumped in. "We have no destination in mind, really. Just looking around. We may not get off the mountaintops, actually," he said with a forced laugh.

Erica looked skeptical. "How very eccentric. No one comes here just to look around. It's too far from everything, and too unpleasant. You cannot camp or cross-country ski here anymore. Say, I *know* you are from the southern part of the U.S.A. I studied in a communicable-disease lab in Atlanta once. I liked it there. Where are you from exactly?"

"South Carolina." Dal started to sweat. He didn't know how far to go before he would have to start lying. Just then he felt himself being pulled backwards. Naija dragged him onto the dance floor. Her grip hurt.

"I just have to dance whenever I hear this song," she called back to Erica.

Naija had saved him. "Maybe this is one of the mysterious talents Mori told us you have," Dal laughed. "He said we would not understand until we needed you."

Holding her stomach with one hand and taking mincing steps while wiggling her hips in a mock rhumba, Naija danced toward Dal, backed away and repeated the step, moving more elaborately with each pass. Dal tried to copy her but eventually fell back into the same shuffling movements he always called dancing, no matter what the style of music. Naija doubled over laughing at him.

"What do you mean, you love this song, Naija? I'll bet you have never heard this music before. They don't play this stuff in Churchill." He couldn't help it. He loved the way her smile crinkled her roundish face without making her eyes disappear.

"Saved your butt, didn't I?" she whispered. Suddenly her smile faded.

"Local Officials and BC are all over the place. Look!" she commanded.

Dal scanned the periphery of the room, noting a dozen or so persons dressed the same as the airport attendants had been. They must have just arrived. He hadn't seen them earlier. Also striding back and forth were several large men in the familiar Black Coat uniforms.

"Probably here to keep rowdies from breaking too many glasses," Dal said. Then he wondered why he felt he had to reassure Naija. She was proving quite sturdy on her own.

"Oh yeah? Watch those two." Naija cocked her head toward the same scene that Dal had been observing with increasing tension. Two Black Coats signaled back and forth across the room while speaking into their armbands. Then they began to walk slowly through the crowd, nodding and smiling at the sweaty dancers who hastened to move out of their way. They were headed right where Dal and Naija danced slowly.

The BCs' eyes looked fixed on them. "What shall we do now?" Dal whispered to Naija. "Let's run for it!" he said. "We can slip away more easily than those large guys can fol—" He gripped her hand but she held him back.

Dal stopped midword when he saw that the BCs' eyes were not on them any longer but rather on another couple a few feet away. The Black Coats converged, shoving Naija and Dal aside to get at the couple, who quickly separated and ran in opposite directions. They were stopped at the doors by two more Black Coats, who gripped their arms hard behind their backs and marched them outside.

No one else on the crowded dance floor appeared to have even noticed this commotion. The throbbing music and dancing continued unabated. Meanwhile, two more Black Coats took the place of those who had left with their prisoners and stood against the wall, guarding the doors as if nothing had happened.

"I cannot believe we just saw that," Naija blurted out.

"Shhhh," warned Dal. "We're all right. Let's act like everybody else. And try to find our fucking contact." This was an entirely new sort of danger—not what he was used to.

Dal looked around for Walt. There he was, still at the bar with his back to them, trying to get the bartender's attention for another beer. Erica was not in sight.

"Let's go rescue Walt before someone else latches onto him," Dal said. Placing his arm around Naija's waist, he began to pull her off the dance floor.

"Erica wanted to latch onto *you*, you know," Naija said.

Dal ignored that. He thumped Walt on the back. "Sorry we left you that way, ol' buddy," he said.

"Erica finally found a scientist and went off with him. Lucky guy," Walt said, wiping his brow.

Dal heard a deep voice behind him. "So, are these your friends, Robert?" Robert was the alias Walt had chosen. Perhaps the voice spoke to Walt. Dal turned to find himself belly to belly with the same large man Walt had been so deep in conversation with on the cable car.

The traveler had cleaned up his act considerably. His scraggly beard was now neatly trimmed, his tanned face clean and perfumed, and his clothes upscaled for the evening. A long, beige net shirt hung over a grey bodysuit underneath. The man's large hand reached out and gripped Dal's in a display of strength, which Dal returned with equal force.

"Bill Hernan is my name. I think you have been looking for me. Friends of Mori?"

"Mori who?" Dal asked warily.

"Mori Taktug. Who else? Nobody else has a name like that," Bill Hernan chuckled. "He will be proud of you for being so careful."

He leaned closer. "Did you see the goons drag off that couple? In the middle of a sexy dance, too. How uncivilized. Might never see them again. But don't you worry. They were probably smugglers or ice haulers without a license. They take that real serious down here. There are big bucks in shoving that ice around the ocean. They were criminals. Not like you guys at all."

Naija rolled her eyes and remarked, "Oh, you never know."

"No fooling me, young lady. I'll take good care of you. Mori and I go way back. And he told me to take care of all of you, but you especially. How's he looking lately?"

Dal watched Bill's face. He had a slight Spanish accent. Might be a local. "He looks good. Did you expect otherwise?"

"Well, as I said, we go way back. And Mori goes back even further than I do. A lot further. He must be about at the end of his time, unfortunately. I was happy to learn he was still kicking when he contacted me about helping you guys out.

"Say, would you like to show me to your hotel rooms? It's noisy in here. No place to conduct business. Smoky, besides." Bill drew a large, rumpled but clean handkerchief from his pocket and handed it to Naija, who was still wiping her eyes every few minutes with the wadded-up napkin Dal had given her.

She put the disintegrating napkin on the bar and took Bill's handkerchief with a grateful smile. Bill gazed at her intently. "You sure look familiar. How did Mori find such a pretty young thing to come way down here? He always knew how to pick 'em. He always got the pick o' the petri dish, I used to tell him."

"We are all professionals," Dal couldn't keep from saying. "Naija was hired for her abilities, not for being 'pick of the petri' or anything like that."

Naija looked at him unhappily.

What have I done, now? he wondered.

As if to underscore Dal's overreach, Bill replied softly, "Why, of course, I know that. It was just a manner of speech, an old devil's way of appreciating exotic beauty. I apologize for any misstatements." He bent over Naija's hand and kissed it, still looking at her face as if trying to remember something.

Dal couldn't believe it. This whole scene was such an anachronism. He half expected Naija to knee Bill in the balls.

"Let's go," Dal said. He wanted to leave this room, this situation, this feeling of things being not quite right.

"We'd better leave separately," Bill said. "Meet you in your hotel lobby in, say, twenty minutes? Mori told me where."

Abruptly, Bill pulled back a few feet, no longer acting as if they were friends. He boomed out, "Hey, have you tried the dark beer from Puerto Williams? Great stuff. Give that a try while you're here. Have a good trip. It was nice to meet ya." A Black Coat on another task shoved past Bill, who quickly slipped away and wandered, seemingly without direction, in the crowd. Dal watched as Bill sidled up to a woman standing alone.

"Check this out. It'll be good," he said to Walt in a low voice. "She has a date already. I saw him."

Dal watched Bill try to get something going, only to be ignored when the woman's date returned with two drinks. Bill wandered away again. He repeated the rejection theme several more times. Finally, he left, going out the door with his shoulders slumped in defeat. Dal had to admire Bill's act, for he was sure now that these social failures were an elaborate ruse to pave over his departure.

Staying together, Dal, Naija, and Walt meandered slowly through the dance floor to join a stream of people exiting via a door topped with the flashing symbol of a train track. An even larger number of well-dressed partygoers flowed into the bar through an adjoining door whenever the bouncers would admit a new group.

Once outside the human crush, Dal cleared his lungs of smoke in the cool air of the mountain tunnel. He could distinguish six different languages being spoken around him. These were the determined night-sounds of people badly in need of diversion. He listened in on a few conversations, hoping to learn something, but he could only grasp a word or two.

Fortunately, the map on the tunnel wall was in English, still the universal language in this area for commerce and navigation. Naija deciphered their route and set off, with Dal and Walt following her. They threaded around clumps of people, walked over a small bridge, and finally jumped between the closing doors of a full train. It sped off, careening down the spiral tunnel on a hissing column of air. This express train made no stops at the many side tunnels.

The moist floors of those side tunnels glittered with pools of light at the intersections when the train throbbed past, appearing to arouse no hopeful stirring in those who waited. *They must know this train never stops for them.* Dal turned his face from the glass back to the interior where his companions were.

They reached the bottom in one hundred thirty ear-popping seconds. Everyone spilled out into an underground tangle of streets and movable walkways. Once more, Naija consulted a wall map before hiking off briskly down a narrow tunnel and through twisting pathways; soon they were in the warm lobby of their small hotel.

There sat Bill on a scruffy, wine-red circular couch, talking with a woman dressed in close-fitting athletic garb. Dal guessed that she must be at least eighty, though well preserved. He wondered how old Bill was. It was so hard to tell with most people.

"Ah, here you are." Bill rose stiffly, turning his back to the woman. "Hope you find him okay," he said to her. She listlessly waved goodbye.

"Poor lady, she's had the worst luck. She came down from Porvenir two months ago, after the water broke through the levees and covered her house. She hopes her brother will take her in, even though her sister-in-law hates her guts. Problem is, she can't find him. She went by and saw his yard is underwater now, too. No telling where he went. She should have called ahead, because he's not answering his armband, and the Migration Board has no record of his movements. Plus, she is nearly out of money. Maybe I'll give her some cash if she's still here later on."

"I wouldn't do that," Walt replied as he punched the button for tube eight. "She probably tells that story to every softie, looking to hook a fish like you." The door opened, and Walt stepped in.

"Listen, amigo," Bill said. "There are plenty of stories like that here, and they are mostly true. Where have you been, anyway—in a time warp? Don't you know what goes on?" The vacuum door slapped shut, and they shot up to their suite.

Soon they were settled in the largest of their rooms with an adjoining sitting area. Dal sprawled in a straight-backed chair with, his legs stretched out in front. What a day. Was it nearly over? He couldn't feel what time it was in the interior of this mountain without the stars or northern lights. There was not even a scenery simulator like Ana had in her home in place of windows. He wished he were in her apartment, sleeping in her bed with her right now.

He sat up and yawned loudly, too tired to cover his gaping mouth with his hand. His eyelids drooped again. He roused himself and took charge.

"I understand we are supposed to scope out where to pick up the cargo tomorrow, Bill. Then, day after tomorrow, you somehow help us load up and get out of here. Are you all set for that? What is your plan?"

"Ah, yes, on to business." Bill winked at Naija, who had a grim expression. Dal wondered what conversation he had missed.

"All we have to do tomorrow is go out to where I have stashed some saplings on the edge of Lapataia," Bill said. "You'll have a chance to check out the lay of the land and where we will have to fly the following morning to pick up your cargo. We'll start out by ferry and then hike to the site. We may see some refugees or even Black Coats along the way, but let's hope not. Just play it cool and follow my lead the whole time."

He continued: "It's much better if I keep you out of New Ushuaia tomorrow. Authorities are jumpy here, as you could see at the bar. People here expect Chile to reclaim all it can of Antarctica, starting with the high ground closest to where their bases were in the 1970s. They built some very nice domed huts and called them research stations, and claimed a wedge from the coast to the pole for about 150 years or so, whether or not anybody actually lived there full time. Well, of course they usually did conduct seasonal research. Even one time there was an idea to empty the large lakes under the ice and make nice homes out of those. That idea, of course, sounded insane to us here."

"Spoken like a true Argentine," said Walt.

Bill ignored him. "Industrial spies, money launderers, and madcap scientists are all rooting around here looking for loose change. I can hardly stand to go out and about anymore. That's not like me at all." He winked at Naija. "It's awful what greed can do. Greed and the climate can be awful forces for bad."

"Is it all that awful?" Walt asked. "Seems a stimulating place to me. You know, 'May you live in interesting times' and all that." Walt seemed uncommonly energetic. Red spots lit up his cheeks, and his eyes glittered.

"Yeah, stimulating, sort of, but this used to be such a nice place," said Bill. "Even in my parents' day it was better than now. My ancestors came here quite by accident. The first one, William Lore, came here in a shipwreck, back when an entirely new life was possible on this earth. I suppose one day someone might think of Antarctica that way." Bill looked pointedly at Naija and added: "Someone like Mori, perhaps."

What does he know already? wondered Dal.

Bill then turned to Walt. "Walt, I think you must be a city boy."

"Of course. Isn't everybody?"

"Yes, that's about right. But I mean at heart, my lad, at heart."

Something in Bill's meandering talk bothered Dal, but he couldn't focus on that now. He was exhausted. He stood up, determined to get some good sleep before their big day tomorrow.

14

Any live tree or sapling over three feet (0.91 meters) tall may not be cut down, uprooted, or *in any way* harmed without permission of the Local Tree Authority, which is an official arm of the UN Temperature Modulation Board. Each LTA must assess and report the CO_2 drawdown ability and oxygen-generating capacity of every tree in its jurisdiction before any action to remove, transport, kill, or damage said tree may be carried out. A breach of this regulation is punishable by imprisonment or death.

—October 22, 2295, regulation 3,862 of the *UN Temperature Modulation Code*

NOVEMBER 15, 2295
NEW USHUAIA AND LAPATAIA NATIONAL PARK, ARGENTINA

Dal slept like the dead, but he had crazy dreams all night as his brain worked to file away all the data from the wild day.

"Come on, man, we've got to move it!" Walt shouted as he shook Dal awake. Walt held in his hands the pillow with which Dal had covered his head; the blanket he had kicked to the floor lay in a crumpled pile. Dal arose unsteadily. He shivered. The best way to warm up was to move, so move he did.

In ten minutes, they managed to meet Naija in the lobby. Dal looked rumpled and half-asleep as he squinted in the daylight. No time for either fake coffee or real food. They had a boat to catch.

The wide hoverferry crossed and recrossed a brand-new cut, created by dark-green ocean water surging up between the rugged mountains to the west of Ushuaia. Trees and moss clung to the sides of the mountains until their high granite summits burst free of the green chains.

These summits reminded Dal of films of Mayan temple ruins rising out of the jungle.

At each floating ferry station, the entire passenger complement changed. Dal thought he and his companions looked more conspicuous every time the ferry emptied and refilled. No one else crossed as many stops as they did.

"Bill acts as if he and I have met before, and I know we haven't," Naija whispered to Dal. He decided to stay close to her today. He assumed that Bill was coming on to her.

Bill stood near the controls and chatted up the ferry operator, a red-eyed man with streaks of gray in his dark stubble. He wore an oily yellow jacket, damp with early-morning condensation.

"Looks like the usual crowd, huh, Jake?" Bill said. "Don't you ever get any interesting passengers? How do you keep yourself awake on this boring run?"

"You think this is boring 'cause you don't know the half of my job!" bristled Jake. "I got to ease this ferry up to them docks just right or the whole thing will crumple like a pile of toothpicks, popping all them folks waiting to get on right into the drink. There'd be hell to pay then. My ass is on the line every time I cross this damn dirty water. That there's enough to keep my eyes open." A grinding cough cleared Jake's throat before he spit over the leeward side.

"Once in a while I get some nice scenery to wake me up good, though," Jake said. He cocked his head toward Naija, who hung over the side watching a family of ruddy-headed geese bob on the water's opaque surface. Despite having sprayed on copious amounts of insect repellent, she still slapped and scratched at her bare ankles and neck every few minutes.

Dal watched a ring of red welts rise on her neck. A very large dead mosquito lay plastered there, the tendrils of its contorted legs tangled with wisps of hair that spilled from her short ponytail. A smear of bright blood marked her white shirt collar where she had slapped one. This mosquito was much larger than any Dal had ever seen before, although he had seen some big ones swarming in South Carolina after especially bad floods. "Bill, you got those head nets we asked for?" he asked.

"No, nothing open yet."

"Here, Naija, use this repellent again. Put a lot on," Dal ordered. The last thing they needed was somebody getting sick down here.

He took out a wipe and gently removed the gore from Naija's neck. She turned away from the geese. Dal lifted her bloody palm and carefully rubbed it with the cloth. Naija looked at him acceptingly. Feeling the eyes of Walt, Bill, and Jake, who had all stopped talking, Dal stroked more roughly, then put Naija's hand down. "Slather lots of that stuff on now," he repeated gruffly.

"Them pesky skeeters ain't even fully waked up yet," Jake said. "They're out 'cause it's overcast. Just wait 'til sunset if you think they're bad now." Then in a low tone he said to Bill, "Seems those skeeters know a tasty bite, huh? Not goin' for ol' pickled meat like us." Jake rocked back and forth with the rhythm of the boat, laughing soundlessly at his own wit.

"Yeah, I hear they're drawn to estrogen like bees to honey," Bill said, jabbing Jake's ribs and joining his mirth.

Then he remarked casually, "You know, I thought I heard your name back in New Ushuaia, Jake. Yep, it was someone in the Natural Selection Bar. Come to think of it, that was a couple of Black Coats talking, actually. I wondered why a BC would know the name of a regular guy like you. Even though you ferrymen get around, it still struck me as strange."

Jake looked up sharply, his eyes narrowing: "Come on."

"No, really. I heard them saying, 'Jake—the run from West Dock to Lapataia.' I heard that. Have you been carrying Black Coats up to my neighborhood regularly? Are they perchance watching you for some reason?"

"I swear, I ain't done nothin' for 'em to care about!" Jake spat again. "There was a few of 'em on board last Monday. Went west to your stop and never came back down. They got no cause to be after me, so I nearly forgot about it 'til you mentioned them sons o' bitches just now. You sure you heard them BC speak my name?" Jake's scraggly eyebrows drew together, creating more furrows.

"Yep, sorry, my man. It had to be you," Bill replied. "You know me—I wouldn't josh you. I live up here, too. We got to stick together. If I hear anything more or see anything else, I'll be sure to let you know. And vice versa, okay? The average citizen is helpless if we don't watch out for each other. And keep this between us, don't you know?"

"I hear what you're sayin'," Jake replied. "I'd hate to have to leave here and run. I got this good job and a tiny piece o' ground up high that I plan on terracin' one day. It's straight up and down right now, ya know. My kids will be pissed if we have to leave. There's nowhere to go to anyways. But those BC guys, they got no mercy. I know of folks who's done plum disappeared off the face of the earth after one visit from 'em."

"Okay, then, let's both be on the lookout for any BC and report to each other what we notice," Bill said. "I'll help you any way I can, Jake. Here's my signal where you can call me." Bill lifted his sleeve and pressed one corner of the screen on his armband to illuminate his local ID. Jake punched it quickly into his own grimy, primitive band. He looked behind him fearfully, even though there was no one else on board the ferry now.

THE FERRY EASED neatly into the last western stop. Jake watched grimly while his four passengers trudged up uneven stone steps set into the eroding bank.

"You scared the devil out of him. Was that really necessary?" Walt asked Bill.

"Jake? Oh, he'll be all right," Bill replied. "We need extra eyes, and his are some of the best around. Trust me, we do not want to be caught doing strange things up here. And whatever Mori is up to with those trees is bound to be strange. I've known him almost a century, remember? Mori is a weird old duck."

Walt's eyes widened and his back stiffened.

Bill laughed and slapped Walt's taut shoulder, seeming to enjoy the effect of his words.

THE WALK UP from the ferry to a high col on the edge of Lapataia Park was yet another steep climb. Drops of sweat slid down between Dal's shoulder blades and trickled to the small of his back. He breathed in fast and blew out with force—one step for breathing in and two steps for breathing out. For more than three hours, he had watched Naija's calves tighten and release in front of him and seen her buttocks strain into mounds of shifting strength positioned almost level with his head, so steep was the trail. It looked easy for her. Occasionally she stooped to scratch one of the deep-pink mosquito bites around her ankles.

They sometimes climbed pitches of huge prehistoric stone steps set into the hillside by barefoot natives who had worn only grease and occasional guanaco robes against the cold of an earlier time. Dal had thought he was in shape, but this was a challenge.

Just when he wanted to call for a break, they topped the lip of the col. There the trail leveled off, curving to the right. They squished across a boggy creek in the high col, where the trail petered out completely.

Dal stood in a verdant hanging valley, one of the last glacial scoops before the gray peaks around them rose into the clouds. This valley had been filled with ice only a few hundred years before. Dal guessed this col to be several thousand feet above the tree line. The ground was soggy, the dirt black. White and yellow wildflowers of great delicacy splattered across the springtime grass here in the Southern Hemisphere. Occasional huge boulders, dropped here when the hanging glacier had melted, sprang out of the soft earth. They climbed up on one boulder, which still steamed from morning dew. A nippy breeze sprang up and blew the small, puffy clouds to the east. The sky would soon be aster blue.

"Your cargo is over there, behind yonder granite boulder," Bill said, pointing to the largest boulder in the valley. It lay at the far end, near a jumbled outflow of gray rubble avalanched from one of the peaked stone summits that rimmed the col. "Nobody else ever comes up here. Let's get a breath, and then go over there. It's farther than it looks. You're probably not used to looking through clean air where you come from."

HALF AN HOUR LATER, Bill leaned jauntily against the huge, Ice Age–rounded boulder. It towered more than nine feet above him. With one foot crossed over the other at his ankles, Bill flipped his right hand up and out into the air in a dismissive gesture toward a cluster of small trees standing in root bags. "So, this is what you are going to so much trouble for. I picked these out myself. They are the best small but hearty specimens—just what Mori asked for. Me and my guys dug them out night before last and dragged them up here for safekeeping. Mori told me this had to be kept a big secret. I told Mori what a backbreaker it was going to be. I told him that to keep this all a secret on top of the labor would be doubly hard. But he was not fazed. He just emphasized that it was very important that we follow his instructions to the letter."

Bill continued, "What are you going to do with them? Take 'em back to his place?"

"Don't you know?" Naija asked.

Bill hesitated a second. "Why, sure! You think ol' Mori would keep a secret from me, his best buddy from the old days?" he exclaimed.

Dal looked hard at Walt and Naija as if to warn them, but that was not necessary. They kept quiet.

"I know how much Mori liked his gardens, that's all," Bill said. "Figured he would want a few of these oldest species from down here for his collection. Some people say that trees sort of like these used to live in Antarctica millions of years ago." He looked rapidly from one to the other. No one reacted. He shrugged, pushed himself away from the boulder, and walked ahead of them back to the edge of the col, where he stopped before starting the quad-wrecking pitch down. "Enjoy this view," he said. "This is a beautiful place."

It was indeed lovely. Dal sized up his landing for tomorrow. He would have to come in carefully over the edge of the col, not land in too wet a place, and get close enough to that huge boulder to load the ten small trees. He might have to do it all in near darkness, too. He was glad to have seen this place in full daylight.

The entire stop here in Tierra del Fuego was, in his view, way too risky just for these pathetic trees. The plane already reeked with evergreens. Did they really need these added ones? They looked no more special than the ones already on board.

Walt, however, was very excited by these particular trees.

"Those are great specimens, Bill. Mori is going to be very pleased. Never saw any of them before."

"Well now," Bill said, "that makes my day, young man."

Dal couldn't wait for tomorrow to come. They would hurry to get up here early, load the trees, and be off. They would plant them as fast as possible, wait a reasonable bit of time, and go home. Home to Ana.

He wanted to flee this end spit of South America, with its omnipresent laser-armed Black Coats, its desperate, termite-mound cities, its steep and watery land that smelled of rotting vegetation. Bill was helpful, no question about that. But Dal wanted to get far away from him, too. Away from his fake cowboy style as well as his troubling questions.

If we can take off tomorrow without incident, the rest is gonna be a piece of cake, Dal thought.

THE HIKE DOWN was hard on the knees, even relatively young ones. They arrived late for the ferry at the dock, but Jake had waited for them. He paced the wide back end of the ferry, hands jammed into his jacket pockets and his neck drawn into his shoulders. Jake repeatedly sucked his lips into a reverse pucker, making them disappear and reappear while he morosely watched the sun slide down to the horizon.

Dal watched him with apprehension. Had Bill upset him too much? Did Jake have bad news for them about the movements of the Black Coats around here? He crawled inside his worries, staying alone with them. Naija looked so untroubled that he began to wonder just how observant she was.

Bill sauntered over to where they sat. "Jake says the Black Coats went back to Ushuaia at midday," he told them. "We're lucky to have missed them. We'd have had to strike up a conversation. And you guys don't seem too good at that.

"The Black Coats told Jake they would come back to see him tomorrow. That's why he's so nervous. I kinda wish I hadn't baited him quite so well. He's liable to do something dumb, all wrought up like he is. Might draw attention to himself and us, too. Anyway, they are coming back up here, and we don't know what their business is or if it has anything to do with us. Let's all be alert and careful.

"By the way," he added, "did you know it's doubly illegal to dig up any living tree here? Fuegians are desperate to keep the little greenery we have left, what with the lower latitudes all clambering for it to replenish what they've lost. I'll find myself in deep shit if you don't get those saplings out of here before dawn. From what I know of Black Coats, they don't like to get up early. So best we do, and beat them up here."

Dal nodded in agreement. "It will be easy for me to find that hanging valley," he said. "I could find a cup in the ocean with the incredible nav equipment in the plane. Still, landing could be tricky in the dark with all those rocks and no lighting. I hadn't planned on landing in a high boulder field before dawn and not being able to use my lights."

"I'll be with you," Bill said. "You'll need me to help get the plane released before 8 a.m. So that means I need to go with you tomorrow anyway. You can leave me up there and I'll find my way home.

"Aw, I can see that all this talk is making you uptight," he observed. "Nothin' I hate worse than that. I know a tiny locals' place with great duck and authentic pisco sours.

"Jake!" Bill called out. "Which stop is Deseado's at? I usually get there on the Intramountain Line, not from the water. Let us off there, will ya?"

THEY CHOSE A TABLE in the corner. Despite the international flavor of this last outpost on the Pan-American Highway, the Latin habit of late dining still prevailed, so the restaurant was almost empty. Dal sat across from Naija so he could watch her face. That way he could tell if Bill was annoying her.

A small collie belonging to the only other people in the restaurant padded over and lay down under their table, which had been salvaged from a restaurant in Old Ushuaia. The table rocked unevenly when the dog shifted positions. Plexiglass covered the wooden surface, which had been deeply carved by twentieth-century patrons.

For at least a hundred years, Ushuaia had been the final port of call for cruise ships, which liked to call their trips "expeditions." Passengers often went out in town to celebrate after the rigors of their sea voyage to Antarctica. Upon returning to a green land of trees and flowers and grasses and visible life everywhere—land with an overwhelming variety of smells beyond merely penguin guano, a land of sensual bombardment so very different from the pristine, awesome beauty of icebound Antarctica—on arriving here those travelers were permitted to carve their names into the wooden tabletops while they drank their pisco toasts, thrilled to have been among the relatively few to have stood on the frozen continent.

Dal expected he would have a few stories of his own to tell once he got home. He couldn't wait to tell Ana about everything. There was already so much to tell her, and they had not even gotten there yet. He stabbed his fork into the steaming mound on the plate. The oval platter was piled high with saffron-colored rice flecked with tomatoes and topped by a knuckley stew, chewy and unrecognizable. The food tasted vinegary and pungent. He liked it, liked this restaurant.

Dal started to think about the odd way Bill had stared at Naija all day, as if concentrating on something through her and beyond.

Suddenly Bill slammed a big, flat hand down on the table, rocking it and shaking Dal's knife off the edge of his plate. Everyone grabbed their sloshing drinks. The dog ran out from underneath the table and sat on its haunches, watching them from safety.

"Sons o' bitches, I've got it!" he exclaimed. "No matter what they tell you these days, urging everybody to take those mind-booster supplements, the brain just isn't what it used to be after you pass a hundred. You wait and see. Sometimes it seems I can't remember squat." Bill shook his head. "Well, anyway . . ."

Could this be swashbuckling Bill, admitting to a vulnerability? Dal wondered. *What might have caused this development?* Walt and Naija had stopped eating, too.

"I must apologize for annoying you, little lady," Bill said. "I've been trying to figure out where I'd seen you. I had you mixed up with someone else, who certainly could not have been you because I met her only one time—and that was eighty-some years ago."

Naija put her fork down and sat very still. Walt perked up from his fatigue and leaned forward. Dal kept on eating.

Bill began: "So you will understand, you need some background: Mori and I met in the UN Volunteer Service in the South Pacific, doing some water rescue and resettlement work. To make a long tale short, we became friends. The sort of best friends you become through shared hardships. After our enlistment was up, we started putting together land deals to sell to climate migrants. Some migrants had money and could see what was coming. We were doing great when Mori up and quit the business—just like that!" Bill snapped his fingers.

"The way it worked was like this: Mori would locate a good remote parcel, and I would negotiate the financing. There was still a lot of land in the Northern Territories, as that part of Canada was called then, when we started out. And people were hungry to buy—people from Polynesia, Asia, the Netherlands, the US, even South America. They knew that any land far from the sea, even if it was melted permafrost or peat bog, would be a finite resource. And the smart ones studied and knew how everything was changing and would continue to change in different parts of the world."

Dal methodically ate on, his fork clanging against the plate. He looked at his dwindling food and wondered when that satiated feeling would kick in. Anyway, Bill wasn't saying anything an average student didn't already know.

Bill continued his story. "On this one occasion, Mori and I happened to be nosing around some high ground near Repose Bay in northern Canada. We fixed our sights on a planned community we would build there, with a sports park, schools, and shopping. Everything would be aboveground, of course, like in the old days. I tell ya, we would have had a fabulous market response to this idea. Probably would have presold everything, even before the amenities got built.

"I had equity investors lined up for the chance to participate. And then—well, you won't believe this."

"What?" asked Walt, enthralled. Naija sat very still, her face so pale that her mosquito bites looked redder than ever. She picked up a piece of bread and began breaking it into pieces.

"Mori and I were at dinner one night—eating grilled arctic char, I remember. Funny how the details come back. Anyway, Mori struck up a conversation with our waitress, a local woman from farther north, who also turned out to own the little place.

"Mori walked her home after work, and he didn't come back to the hotel that night. Not at all. I hadn't paid much attention to her. She didn't seem special to me at the time. For years after that, I tried to remember details of how she dressed and talked. I tried to imagine how she did it—how she made Mori and me give up millions in profit. I nearly forgot what she looked like—until I saw Naija. You see, Naija, you look just like her. And no reflection on you, Naija, but she had a dreadful impact on ol' Mori."

Dal stopped eating at this and held his fork suspended over his plate.

Bill continued: "When Mori finally did show up around mid-afternoon the next day, all he could talk about was what a beautiful, remarkable, spiritual, interesting person that woman was.

"He would say irrelevant things like, 'Bill, did you know that the Inuit have lived here ever since the Ice Age?' or 'Bill, the Inuit believe they were once one with the animal spirits.'

"At first, I tried to talk some sense into him. I'd say, 'Mori, you know good and well there has been no honest-to-God Inuit culture for a very long time. Not since so many of them died off with the third flu or heated homes replaced the igloo. Get a grip, man.'

"But Mori probably didn't even hear me. He kept saying, 'I had the most incredible night.' Then he would tell me more about the local people, how they were a remnant of the original Inuit, and how they were essentially superior to the rest of us.

"I would say something provocative to try and bring him out of it, like, 'Too bad this wonderful woman wasn't around in the 2060s. Maybe she would have kept her people from insisting on their tribal hunting rights.' Or I would say, 'You're just talking fairy tales now, man.'

"Mori was in love, and I know how that screws your mind up. It happens, and I could sort of understand that. But then he changed his mind one-eighty on our deal. And that I could not understand—not at all.

" 'I cannot buy and sell this land after all,' was the whole of Mori's explanation. Said that to me, his fuckin' partner! Excuse me, Naija," Bill said. "He actually had come to believe, on the basis of what must have been one hot night, I'm telling you, that our land still belonged to the Inuit. Never mind that you could barely find a pure one anywhere.

"And damned if he hadn't already used part of his inheritance to buy the parcel that we were planning on developing together right out from under me. He signed it over in trust to the Canadian Indigenous Peoples Board before telling me about any of this. What did he think

Rosemary would say when he got back home? I don't think Mori ever told her the whole story, because I know he returned to Repose Bay many times.

"You can maybe imagine the position I was in, with Dutch investors supposed to fly in that very day to look at the site."

"You must have been livid," Walt remarked.

"Yes, I was indeed, Sonny. But the funny thing is, I never can stay permanently mad at Mori. He is always so earnest about everything. About things that might seem nuts to me. He was just doing what he thought was right, weird though it may have been. It was a shock at the time, and right awkward to tell the Dutch to turn around and go back home.

"But in the end, all it cost me was potential earnings on just one of our projects. Hell, we had already made a fortune. Although I frittered mine away since. I ultimately decided our friendship counted for more."

"What does this have to do with Naija?" Walt asked.

Naija studied her plate while she tore her bread into smaller and smaller pieces. When the bread was as crumbled as she could make it, she picked up and ate each crumb separately, her eyes squinting in concentration.

Bill tried to bring Naija back by addressing her directly.

"Well, as I said, it couldn't have been you I saw in that restaurant, Naija. You're too young, and much prettier, too. You just remind me a lot of that woman. Your voice or walk or something."

Naija still said nothing and picked at the breadcrumbs.

Dal watched her anxiously, wondering why she didn't look up, laugh, and defuse the growing tension the way she always had before. He broke the silence. "Seems understandable enough how you could get confused, Bill. I'm all the time seeing people I think I know. It happens when I'm away from my family and friends."

"Bill lives here, and he's not one bit lonesome," Walt said flatly.

"Let it go, Walt," Dal injected. He put his napkin on his plate and called for the check. "We'd better wind this up early. Tomorrow is going to be a long and busy day."

"Can't have you oversleeping this time," ribbed Walt.

Bill took charge. "Four o'clock, then. That's a.m. I'll give a wake-up call on your armbands. Say, where are they? I haven't seen any of you wearing yours since you got here."

"We didn't bring them," Dal said.

"What do ya mean, you didn't bring them? What on earth were you thinking?" Bill exclaimed.

"Mori said to leave them. Our armbands are too advanced and would only cause us trouble down here." Naija was back.

Bill shook his head and stood up to go. "Okay, I'll call those antique-looking watches you have. Hope they work."

DAL WRAPPED THE HEATED ROBE around himself and stepped into the dark. A jet of warm air and a moving light accompanied him twenty feet down the dank hall. He knocked. Walt's voice said, "What is it?"

"It's me. Dal."

A crack the width of a security chain appeared. "Why aren't you in bed yet?" Walt's voice was gravelly with sleep. He cleared his throat.

"Let me in, will you? We have to talk."

Walt rattled the chain loose, opened the door, and Dal stepped inside. A nightlight lit the room from the floor, casting an eerie glow upward across Walt's face as he ran a hand through his hair.

"It's late, so I'll be quick," Dal said. "In the interest of harmony among us, I think we should forget it all. Never mention again all that stuff Bill had to say about Mori and the Inuit tonight. It's plain to see that it has nothing to do with Naija. Nevertheless, it seems to upset her to hear about it. Maybe she didn't like the unflattering way he spoke of her people."

"Okay, no problem," Walt said. Cocking his head to one side, he swiveled to go back to bed.

"I just think we don't need any distractions," Dal continued. "We don't need anything from the outside to upset us until we get back from Antarctica."

"You won't get problems from me," Walt replied pointedly.

"So, I think we should go on as if tonight didn't happen," Dal repeated. "I think Naija will feel better if we do that."

"You would know," Walt answered. He turned wearily back toward his bed again.

"Do we have an understanding, then?" Dal persisted.

"Do I have to draw up a contract or something? Didn't you hear me the first time? I said I wouldn't mention it." Walt whirled around, fully awake now. "You don't have to act as if you are the only decent person here. You aren't the only one who can put the team first. Just make sure you remember that the team is bigger than you and Naija."

Dal was blindsided by this.

"Don't worry, Walt. It's the three of us who have to finish together. That is what counts most."

Walt silently reached out his hand for Dal to shake. His hand was warm, dry, rough, and pleasant, not moist, clammy, and soft, as Dal had imagined it would be.

15

As of November 16, 2295, ferries to Lapataia Park may be appropriated with little warning if needed by the Black Coats and other officials. There has been a tree theft from the park. If you are traveling to a stop on that line, you are advised to plan alternatives for your return trip so as not to be stranded overnight.

—Posters newly nailed up around New Ushuaia

NOVEMBER 16, 2295
LAPATAIA NATIONAL PARK, USHUAIA, ARGENTINA

The next morning, they all managed to meet at the bottom of the cable car by 4:30 a.m. It was not open yet, but a couple of workmen were loading one car full of the day's supplies and breakfast items for the tiny concession at the top of the cable.

Bill strolled over to the man who looked in charge. Acting as if it were the most natural thing in the world, Bill offered the man cash for an unauthorized ride. The young man looked around, gave a quick nod, and the four of them sneaked into the cable car and hid behind the cargo boxes.

Once at the top they slipped out and, hunched over, and ran to the private aviation sentry shed. "Wake up, man! We're getting an early start up to my place," Bill called into the shed, not able to rouse the sleeping guard who was supposed to be watching the electronic fence monitors that had been placed around all the aircraft. Any slight motion would wake him if the area were breached. But tonight, apparently, not even a rat had crossed. Dal had no idea what sort of alarm would go off if they were to sneak by the sentry and run out to the plane. Better not find out.

"I've had it with that sickening ferry," Bill said loudly to the sentry sprawled on his cot. "This time I have a friend with me who can fly me back home—in that honest-to-God real plane over there, no less. You remember me, I know. I make this trip often enough, don't I?" He shook the groggy man. Then he tried an outright lie: "Don't you forget this. I sure won't forget you. I'm a retired Black Coat. Have lots of friends still in service."

At this the guard stirred but still did not get up. Must be drunk. Bill continued his tirade. "My old bones won't take the damp wind you get hit with in a personal air conveyance. You got to be young to fly around in those things. I got better sense than to go that route, don't you know." Louder yet: "My wife is waiting for me up there. Gotta go. She'll get worried." Bill paused, then just inches from the guard's face, shouted: "She just might call the damn BCs herself!"

At this, the guard roused himself and stumbled over to unlock the gate and disarm the sensors. He stopped before pushing it open, perhaps wondering whether he should do so or not. Bill edged up close behind him, slapped him on the back, whispered a few words in his ear, and palmed him some cash. The guard stepped aside and they ran in. Dal deployed the soundless rotors for their short flight.

It had been too easy getting to the plane. *Doesn't anybody care what we're doing?* he wondered.

The stars shone dully. Cloying humidity allowed no twinkle to show through, flying low the way they were, navigating by sight in the predawn. As they gained altitude, the stars became more interesting. This morning, however, there was no time to look at them, or for the Southern Cross, which Dal thought should be out there low in the sky.

Bill spread his hulk over the right front seat and flapped his arms about, directing Dal back to the high col. Dal was thankful this would be their last stop before Antarctica. He had programmed for the general park, way back in Canada, but not that col.

"All right, go between those peaks there," Bill yelled, heedless of the mouthpiece attached to his headset. Dal winced. Walt tapped Bill's shoulder and pointed to the mouthpiece. "He can hear you in a normal voice with this."

"Okay, stay to the right—thirty degrees right," Bill said.

Dal would rather have had a detailed flight plan. It was fine to fly visually in daylight, but he could see little in the predawn except for dark blotches of the mountains that quite suddenly filled his windshield whenever he got close.

Bill seemed to know every twist. "I know you can't see it yet, but go up another two thousand feet, level off, and put her down."

"Put her down where?" Dal said. "I just see black." He turned on the searchlight and a gray granite cliff face loomed. He veered sharply away, just missing it.

"Switch that blooming thing off!" Bill commanded. "Do you want to tell the whole bloody country that we are out here at this hour? Black Coats are nothing if not wickedly curious. They show up when least expected. Now go on up another two thousand feet, turn ninety degrees right, and go deep into the col valley. Put her down there, just like I told you."

Soon, as Bill had predicted, a faint circle of lights located far back in the col valley, therefore invisible from lower elevations, steamed in the dampness. Dal maneuvered through the valley to hover over the small illuminated spot, and there he settled the plane.

Three dark figures bent over and rushed toward them. Dal stiffened. His hand moved down his leg to where he had stashed a knife, contrary to Mori's prohibitions against weapons. It would be no use against lasers, he knew. Nevertheless, he felt better for having it.

"Those are my guys," Bill said. Dal moved his hand up again and opened his side door. Bill pulled up his sleeve and studied his vibrating armband. He read aloud the tiny transcript of Jake's message.

"Jake must be all excited. He's saying, 'Six Black Coats are hiking up from your stop. Just got off my ferry. More of them than last time. They asked me if I saw you come back this morning. I said you must still be in town. Where are you? They're not interested in me.'"

"Aw, shit," Bill squeaked out the side of his mouth. He threw open his door. *"Rápido ahorita,"* he yelled to the men who squatted under the blade as it slowed to a stop. Walt threw open the side cargo door from the inside. Bill got a glance in before Walt could close it again.

"Shit! You've already got a bunch of trees in there!" Bill exclaimed.

"I thought that plane smelled good but figured you were using air freshener for the john or something. Those trees look like the kind Mori had around his house in Canada when I was up there years back."

Dal knocked on the cargo door, and Walt reopened it a crack.

"Let's load up fast, Walt," Dal said softly.

Bill stood with his arms crossed, staring at his feet and deep in thought. Meanwhile, the three local men hurried to help Dal and Walt load the saplings—the saplings Bill had collected at Mori's request in honor of their long friendship.

Dal frantically pulled and pushed to load the saplings as fast as he could. Suddenly he felt his hands being torn from the eighth root ball he was struggling to heft onto the ramp, where Walt could drag it inside to a place for Naija to secure it. Two big hands dragged Dal backwards, spun him around, and slammed him into the side of the passenger door. A red-faced Bill shouted at him, his spit flying.

"What the fuck are you up to? Trying to pull one over on Bill Hernan? Huh? You aren't taking these trees to Mori, are you? You aren't taking them anywhere! Not till I get some answers. Mori hasn't responded to my comms since you got here. Yeah, I commed him all right.

"I had to find out what you bunch really are up to. Now I see all that greenery you got stashed inside this plane. Did you con Mori? Steal his goddamned trees? What for? What bloody business are you up to? Tell me now!"

Dal could feel Bill's heat and smell the artificial coffee on his breath. He brought his hands together and punched Bill's midsection with both fists. Then he pushed his fists up between Bill's arms, which still held Dal's shoulders pinned against the plane. He shoved out and splayed Bill's arms apart.

Dal ducked under Bill's swinging fists and slipped behind him. Bill tried to steady himself and turn around to face Dal, but Dal kicked one of Bill's legs out from under him and fell on top of him, forcing him to the ground. He felt Bill's large body go limp beneath him.

Dal got up and stepped back, panting heavily. He was trained for hand-to-hand combat but not used to it. Bill didn't get up.

Naija appeared from the depths of the hold, her figure framed in the cargo door. Her hands were covered with dirt from the new saplings. "What in the world are you two doing?" she screamed at Dal, seeing Bill sprawled on the ground. Bill's workmen paced nearby, preparing to enter the fight. Dal drew his knife from its hiding place.

He had no idea how to use it for this, how far to plunge the metal into a human body, whether he should slash or stab, come from below, or descend in an arc from above. How many wounds would it take to render someone harmless to him and Walt and Naija? He gripped the knife handle tightly.

"Don't worry, little lady," Bill called up to Naija in a husky voice, gallant once more. He waved off his men. "Just a little tussle here." He groaned as he crawled up on one knee, then lifted himself up heavily, dusting off his pants with hard slaps of resignation.

Dal moved back around the plane toward his open door, still gripping the knife in his left hand. Bill limped along behind him. A smile worked its way across his face.

"Seems you aren't going to tell me what's going on," he said. "I'll have to get a fake refugee visa and go see Mori myself. If you have done him wrong, there is no place on earth where you can escape me," Bill warned, grunting through his words with pain.

"Shut the cargo door, Walt," Dal called.

"There are still two more saplings to bring on," Walt replied. "We can get 'em fast if you can get those little guys do it."

"We have enough," Dal said. "Just shut the door. Do it now!" He reached in and started the rotors. The blades spun and the plane vibrated. Bill ducked and made no more threatening moves.

Once Dal was in and reaching out to pull the door shut, Bill approached in a crouch and called up to him: "Hey, let's not part on bad terms. If the Black Coats show up like Jake says they might, it's just as well that I don't know what you are up to. I can always say that you forced me at knifepoint." Bill's lips stretched into a macabre grin.

"After all, we have a mutual friend," he continued. "Mori would not want us at odds. We've had some nice camaraderie here despite these little squabbles." Bill edged slowly forward, bending over to avoid the whirling blade. He extended his hand up to Dal in reconciliation.

Dal hesitated. Finally, he reached his right hand across his body to accept Bill's gesture of good will. Bill's hand was strong and moist. The grip felt loose and friendly—before it suddenly tightened hard! Dal saw Bill grit his teeth and heave himself backward with all his might to drag him from the plane.

Dal drew his left foot up to kick Bill away. Bill saw it coming and lunged to his left to escape the full force of Dal's kick. He still had a strong hold on Dal's right hand, and Dal had to grip the back of his seat with his left arm to try and hang on. He was pulled halfway out of the plane when Walt grabbed onto Dal's left arm from over the seat back and held on.

Then Dal bent his right knee and gave a series of quick jabbing kicks to Bill's head and shoulders. One landed right in Bill's face. Bill fell to the ground and this time did not get up. By now, Dal was fully stretched with his body hanging out of the plane. He kicked both legs for leverage, and with Walt pulling, was soon back inside. Dal reached out for the door once more and tugged hard to close it. Immediately he could see through his left window the imprint of their landing spot, which was proof that they were no longer on the ground. Dal looked across his right shoulder to see Naija busily working the hand controls for one of the two throttles and the control plate.

"How did you learn to do that?" Dal asked. She gave him a slow, tiny smile of pride at their smooth liftoff.

"I watched you," she said. "It's not that hard." Then she added sheepishly: "Well, no—actually, Mori insisted that I have emergency takeoff and landing lessons with Aron before we left. Just in case of, well, of anything. But all I know is straight up or down, no dips or turns. I can't convert from rotor to speed, either."

Dal had already taken over on manual. He tipped the plane, and they veered steeply away.

"Look back down there!" Walt yelled.

The people on the ground had become mere dark spots in the rich light of dawn that spread across the valley like spilled olive oil.

Dal counted five dark figures. Then there were six. Numbers seven, eight, and nine scrambled over the lip of the col to stand on the almost-level, boulder-strewn ground. Dal gained more altitude, then trained the scope back where they had just departed.

Six of the figures surrounding Bill wore the uniforms of the Black Coats. There was no need to touch Bill, as their laser guns were ready. It was all so peaceful.

Dal saw them look up when Bill pointed to where their plane might have been if visible but for the rapidly accumulating distance and the morning haze. All three of them watched Bill give a big shrug and throw his hands up as if he knew nothing about anything. Maybe he had told the BCs he was trying to stop what looked to be a theft of trees. His workers already had fled down another path.

Bill disappeared over the side of the col, surrounded by an armed escort for the long climb down. The plane zipped past so high that it was invisible and continued on. Out of Argentine airspace. Due south.

16

Utilizing the fastest ships on the ocean, diminishing quantities of Antarctic ice have been moved north at record speed during recent months. This formerly endless supply of fresh water has created a new class of ultrawealthy investors, and water-futures bidding remains high. Nevertheless, just as happened with oil, this "gold mine" will soon come to an abrupt end.

—*Economic News*, December 15, 2261

SAME DAY
OVER THE DRAKE PASSAGE AND THE WEST ANTARCTIC ISLANDS

Dal spoke their heading into the onboard navigator. The temperature and humidity controls turned red, indicating that they were adjusting to the changing environment and were now over cooler seas. Dal stayed high and kept the honeycomb detector-shield activated, even though he did not expect anyone to follow once they were out of Argentine nautical territory. Not even Bill had guessed where they were going.

Bill. What would happen to him? Walt, Naija, and Dal kept a funereal silence after seeing Bill be led off by the Black Coats. *Bullshitter Bill will probably come out all right.* Dal kept telling himself that.

But would Bill tell the Black Coats about the trees in the plane and how most of them were from Canada? Would a meddlesome underling looking for a promotion ultimately figure out where they were going and alert whatever Black Coats oversaw Antarctica?

"I think those BCs have plenty to do without worrying too much about us," Dal said to no one in particular, though he was far from sure.

"Do you think we should call Mori and tell him what happened?" Naija asked.

"Oh, my God, no way!" exclaimed Walt. "No transmissions from us to Mori unless it is a true emergency and we need them to come and get us, remember? I would call Mori in a minute on our little emergency button if that would be useful. But I don't think it's a good idea at all to give away our position when we are basically invisible. No one really knows where we're going except Mori. Let's not call him until we're finished."

Dal agreed.

Naija gave Dal a stony look. "Bill may be taking the heat for us at this very moment," she said. "When we get back and tell Mori that the last we saw of Bill was his being marched off by Black Coats—Bill, his old friend—do you really think Mori will be happy that we did nothing? That we didn't even call him? Maybe Mori could find a way to help him."

"Bill won't need any help and, anyway, remember—we don't have back-and-forth comms. It's just an emergency button." That was all Dal could say. He was back to basics. The hell with trying to be the nice guy. He could still feel the strain in his right arm where Bill had tried to yank him out of the plane. He massaged the arm as if to remind Naija of their struggle.

She looked away and stared out the window, sitting as far to the right of her seat as she could. They would have to settle this, Dal knew, or it could be a miserable four weeks ahead.

He took the controls back off auto. At least this gave him something to do. Like the pole-to-pole migrating arctic tern, Dal's favorite bird from Risa's films, they flew straight across the roiling Drake Passage toward land at the bottom of the world.

Dal had not been able to luxuriate in daydreams of Ana for two days now, what with all the excitement since leaving New Churchill. Now Ana came up like a vision, filling his thoughts. He wondered what she was doing. He fantasized about their future together. It would be heaven, he was sure. The hardest part of this mission must be over now.

He pulled up a view of the ocean below. It was restless, a dull, dark green flecked with white spots that grew and quickly disappeared. Dal zoomed the bottom lens in closer for a better look. Mountainous waves, forty-five to sixty feet high, swept across the Drake Passage. These waves circled the globe, unmitigated by land. Not even the shifts in ocean currents occurring elsewhere had changed this prevailing movement. They flew on, well above the winds that howled below them.

Walt and Naija began to watch the screen, too. A ship wallowed into view, rolling horribly as it zigzagged its way northward. It turned slightly to nose into the biggest waves at an angle, trying to avoid a disastrous capsizing or pitchpoling. Dal honed the picture tighter until they could see the robot navigator's hat and face between the sweeps of windshield wipers on the bridge. He looked so humanly worried that Dal began to feel sorry for this one. Some robots brought that emotion out in people, given that they were assigned the worst jobs. Occasionally, when a wave collided with the downward crash of the vessel, cascades of water covered the bridge and then poured off the ship.

"Aren't we glad we're up here!" exclaimed Walt.

"Oh, yeah," said Dal.

"Look how many," Naija said, as more ships bobbed into view. "One, two, three, four—ten . . . twenty . . . thirty-eight."

The ships spread out like a fan, heading for the west coast of South America and for Africa, to Saudi Arabia and her sister states, two ships to each berg.

"Water ships. I've seen 'em tied up in different places," Dal said.

"Amazing," Naija replied. "Tell us about all of your adventures some time."

It was good to hear her sounding normal again. Dal slumped a bit, glad to have left New Ushuaia behind.

The plane began to toss about in conflicting currents right before they crossed an invisible line in both air and ocean. Once they had crossed the Antarctic Convergence, the tumult began to calm down. Humidity dropped. The sea became azure blue, but wind still whipped the top of the water into a bubbling stew. This shifting convergence line, where colder Antarctic water met warmer northern seawater and all creatures could tell the difference, was a weaker demarcation than in times past.

Dal focused the screen on an ice station located south of the convergence. The water around the station's platform resembled a crowded bazaar, as tugs hauled smaller bergs and bergy bits up to the larger water-transport ships, which would then melt those small bits of ice and store the water for transport rather than losing it to melt.

They had to work fast. Every day that ice floated in the ocean, money melted out from under the bottom of what little remained of the grand ice of Antarctica. And if a big berg sat too long, it would not just melt, it might capsize, endangering any ship lashed to it. This was dangerous work, but lucrative.

"Bet they are scrambling now. Aren't we within two hundred miles of the Antarctic coast yet?" Naija asked.

"We surely are, especially if you count the islands," said Dal.

"How about an early lunch?" asked Walt.

Dal was about to protest that they would land soon, but they had eaten no breakfast. He heard determined rustling from the back seat. Walt opened the vacuum-packed algae sandwiches and leaned over to spread them on the fold-down space between the front seats. He popped the automatic heaters in cans of pea soup and set them down carefully. Dal slurped his straight from the can. The green rimmed his upper lip, and he clowned a big grin at Naija, who laughed until her soup rocked.

"Look out, you're gonna spill it all," Walt chided.

Dal's immense tension was gone. Safety and food—one needed not much more than that. Except love, and he always had Ana for that, no matter where he was. It had always been like that. "Life is good," he said.

Naija licked bean paste off the ends of her fingers. Her lips scrunched up delicately in the way that angelfish used to nibble at coral. Dal would have told Naija how charming that was, but without having had the benefit of his mom's films back home, she wouldn't get it. *What?* Did he think of those films as having been a "benefit?" That was something new.

Naija wiped her hands on a napkin and used the balled-up remnant to scratch an inflamed bite near her ankle. Even with the unsightly patches of red showing against her brown skin, her ankles were beautiful, their small bones curving upward to support strong, sculptured calves. Dal was used to being with Naija now. She was not as powerful a presence as Ana, though. He turned his head to observe her while she stared down at the clouds below. They looked like skyscrapers with windows reflecting yellow sunlight.

At that moment, watching Naija, Dal missed Ana more than ever. But, he thought, *I'll be back in her arms in another twenty-eight days or so, and hopefully before that.* Before he had time for any more comforting thoughts, he had to deal with a compelling necessity: find a place to land.

The powerful plane flew over a cluster of tiny islands that once had buzzed with as many as thirty scientific stations. These rocky outcroppings now lashed by the sea had previously been called King George Island, the gateway to the former Antarctic Peninsula. The crossing had been easy. No one had followed them.

DAL SLOWED THE PLANE and brought out the rotors again. They still had an interesting distance to go that was worth a closer look. Over the glacially gouged bottoms of new bays and inlets full of seawater they flew; over rocky islands, glinting with minerals where the moraine deposits had been washed away by surging waves; over muddy flats of fine alluvial dust and colloidal bogs, where higher tides combined with meltwater from the interior to create treacherous mudflats of finely powdered stone dust; over brown etchings that looked like striped ribbons, where the glaciers and ice shelves of West Antarctica had forced their way downhill and thundered into the sea. They flew over ancient mountains, the end of the Andes, freed from their epochal shrouds of ice. And finally, they flew over occasional tiny patches of lichens and mosses that showed green in some of the wet valleys. They were among the first humans ever to see all this. Wanting to see as much as he possibly could, Dal took them down even lower.

The coordinates for several likely landing sites had been computed and set. Still, Dal preferred a hands-on landing, using vision to supplement the computers, especially when he was landing somewhere new and untested. Someone might have beaten them here, but he hoped not.

"Those early explorers had all the fun," Dal said. "There aren't many places left where you can be the first. But this might be one."

"Maybe," nodded Naija.

"Not likely," said Walt. "But nobody is here now for sure."

Soon they would unload their cargo, work hard to get it all properly planted, stay the required weeks that they had promised Mori, and then return home to normal life again. This time Dal would be going back to a new life with Ana. Walt would go back and patch things up with his wife. Dal wondered what Naija would go back to.

The lower they went, the more the plane, slow and under rotor, swayed against the katabatic winds blowing off the land and turning the Bransfield Strait into chop.

Mori had shown them pictures of Antarctica the way it had looked before the Great Unhinging, which is what the final loosening of the massive ice shelves that held back the glacial ice had come to be called. Antarctica back then was a subtle, raw world of white nothingness, beautiful in the extreme. But when they flew lower, what Dal saw sweeping beneath them looked more like the aftermath of a massive volcanic eruption.

Rivers of mud seeped where glaciers had cracked and groaned their way to the sea. On both sides of these great avenues, dirt piled up high and uneven, as if a giant excavation were under way. Moraine dust turned everything either gray or tan and could be seen swirling in places. Much of former West Antarctica now lay under water. The water was clear and dark blue, except where dust turned it dingy near the shores.

Dal skirted Anvers Island, the gouged surface a testimony to the last desperate era of surface mining on earth. He saw the three anvil-shaped peaks of the island, unmistakable still from the photos, but sunken and distorted. The land looked like a poor slum on the edge of a serene blue contrast. An uninhabited, gaping wound.

No life moved. No raucous penguins in the millions. And in the sea, no whales slowly bubble-net feeding on small fish or scooping up krill in this, their former austral summer feeding ground.

"Maybe we should have brought grasses along, too. Something besides just trees," Dal remarked. Had Mori realized what it really was like down here? How desolate it seemed without visible life? For the first time, Dal could grasp Mori's passion to plant something here.

All three became absorbed in their own thoughts at the sight of this once-glittering continent now so barren and sad. The ice was gone, and the nearest human habitation was some six hundred miles away. Also, far away, if alive at all, were most of the marine and air creatures formerly adapted to this place when it had been covered in ice and snow. Yes, it was clear: Antarctica would have to start over again—as something else.

IT FELT AS THOUGH they'd been flying slowly across the same drab landscape for hours. Actually, it had only been twenty-two minutes. Walt spoke: "There. Up against those mountains. Those are the Ellsworth Mountains. There's Vinson Massif to our northeast, the highest mountain in Antarctica. Wow, look. Just a tiny spot of snow is still there in a crevice on top!

"Remember the kind of landing we picked out from the satellite photos?" he asked. "How we decided it might be better to plant the trees closer to the old Antarctic Peninsula, where it's warmer? We saw some plateaus and deep bays with beaches rimming these mountains. There was enough land to plant trees without having seawater incursion anytime soon."

"Gotcha," Dal replied. "Let's get even lower in our quadrant and pick out a place to land. If we don't like it on closer inspection, we can leave and find another."

Dal loved this part—tricky landings in a new place. He would fly the plane manually, just like in the old days, the way Neil Armstrong had taken over on the moon when his fuel ran low and the surface was uncertain. This place looked like the moon, after all.

"Farther on over there is a better configuration, with more land. It's flat there," Naija offered, pointing to a place a few miles southeast of their location.

They all agreed that the distant area might have more possibilities.

"But the only water source looks to be that small creek," Walt said. "Let's inspect this area more closely. If that water supply or anything else seems inadequate for the trees, we can move on."

Dal switched to vertical descent so they could land on the plain. Beyond that, the land sloped sharply up and flanked the mountain behind.

When they climbed down from the plane, Dal could feel that the earth was a bit spongy. Reddish lichens colored some of the rocks farther up the mountainside. Other small areas were green with moss, a pretty effect after all the brown and gray they'd flown over.

"Looks good to me," Dal said.

"Sorry, Dal, I think we're going to have to move on," Walt soon countered. "The way the sun circles here, this area will be in the shade too much of the day, and the trees need full sun now. They will have to spend a lot of the year with no sun at all."

"Why don't we camp here and study our charts again before going to another site," Naija suggested. "We're all tired, and Dal, you need to rest after your scuffle."

"I like that," said Walt. "That gives me time to analyze the water from that creek and feed and water the root balls. They've had a rough go."

"I'd rather just stay here and plant the trees," Dal said. "Looks good enough to me. But as I'm not a biologist and have been outvoted, we'll do what you two think best. This time. The next stop will have to be it, though. We could look forever for perfection," he said, scrubbing his toe in the sandy soil with irritation.

It didn't take long to make a temporary camp for one night. Just the basics would do.

17

The CIB has decided to fund an advertising campaign to promote immigration to Siberia as a good alternative to Canada. Greater New Khatanga, in its new site at eighty meters above sea level, should be a consideration for some of the many people looking for a high-latitude lifestyle instead of overcrowding our own land.

—Canadian Immigration Board, minutes of monthly meeting,
  July 2295

NOVEMBER 17 AND 18, 2295

USHUAIA AND NEW CHURCHILL

Bill Hernan stumbled as he tried to step over the heavy wooden threshold set in a grimy wall of peeling plaster. He had been released after only a few hours of beatings and questioning. He was lucky.

The threshold he tripped over was part of the door to the Old Prison Museum, now moved far up the hillside from its previous location in the lower old town. It was being used as a prison once again, this time run by the Black Coats. It was full.

Bill's bloodshot, purple-rimmed eyes watered in the bright sunshine. His face was distorted and swollen. He limped from a sprained back. He grimaced and moaned when he bent over to fit his bulk into the battered old sun car and immediately lay down in the back seat.

Carmina Hernan patted Bill's haunch with her right arm across the back of the front seat as she drove away quickly.

"Oh, Bill, *mi vida, mi ángel*. You look *muy malo*. Wait 'til I get you into the *baño caliente*. You will feel *mucho más mejor*. Much, much better. I have some *aqua ranchito*-raised *merluza negra* waiting for you in *la cocina,* too."

"Carmina, darlin', black octopus is too damn expensive," Bill said, grunting between words. "What are you thinking?"

"No, no, we can afford it now, and you deserve this!" she replied. "We have the money. But tell me, how did you convince the Black Coats to let you go?"

"I just had one story to tell, and lucky for me it was the truth. I was able to hang onto that story through everything they tried. No, you don't want to know what they did." Bill shook his head, seeing her anxious eyes looking back at him and her mouth opening.

"Somehow, the fact that I was telling the truth finally got through to 'em. I still have no idea what those North Americanos were really doing down here. I did my best to help them, just like Mori asked me to." He paused, deep in his troubled thoughts. "Then this happened to me.

"Of course, I had to tell the BCs I'd been duped," Bill continued. "Made me look like a friggin' fool. I said those three crooks must have forged all the papers they showed me to make the tree transfer look legal. Truth is, there were no papers at all. I trusted Mori. What a dope. Still, I don't know whether I was lied to or not. He never actually told me what the trees were for or where they were supposed to go. I just thought, well"—he lifted his head a little. "Is the money here? Did he pay us?"

"*Sí. Mucho dinero.*"

"I assumed the trees were for Mori's place up north," Bill started again. "But when we loaded them up, they already had the plane nearly full of trees from up there at his spread. All those were northern varieties. And I saw stakes and shovels, too. It makes no sense to fly all that down here and back again. Now we got us one big puzzle. *Big* puzzle." He frowned.

"Like I said," Bill repeated, as if rechecking his memory, "Mori never actually said that the trees they picked up here were for him, but I thought that was the idea. He seemed to be so adamant about what I was supposed to do—exactly which ones to take and all that. I thought they must be for his own place. He loves that forest up there so much. I took them for him, right out of the Lapataia National Park—what's left of it."

Carmina drove carefully to avoid detection, nodding at everything Bill said.

"Everybody knows there is nowhere except far in the north or far in the south to transplant those trees. Just about everywhere else is too hot or too crowded. It would be insane to go south to Antarctica with trees—or to go there at all right now, the way things are. So, what is actually going on? Beats me."

Despite Bill's uncertainty, there was new resolution rising in his voice as he tried to explain all this to Carmina.

"Oh, *mi amor pobre,* do not think of it anymore," she said.

"No worries," Bill replied, trying to calm the fear he could hear in her quivering voice. "I might be better off if I never do understand, anyway." He paused and scowled. There was something more he could not yet let go of.

"*Sin embargo!* Mori owes me an explanation—that he does!" Bill's voice rose to a shout as he banged his fist on the back of the front seat. "On top of that, I'll have to forge some tree-authorization documents for those bastard BCs right away. Said they'd come back for me if they don't have them in hand within forty-eight hours."

Carmina tightened her grip on the control wheel and looked straight down the dirt road.

"You can bet I'll get to ol' Mori as soon as I can," Bill said, digging his broken fingernails into his palms as he stared out of the dirty window. "I'll get it out of him one way or another." Dust trailed the car. For once, Carmina was glad for the choking, blowing dust. It made it harder to be followed.

AFTER A LONG SOAK and his favorite black octopus served warm, with last year's potatoes that Carmina had saved from their garden, Bill seemed almost normal. He had watched as Carmina carefully saved the eyes of the potatoes she peeled, knowing she would plant them again soon.

He relished her warmth and comfort when she lay down beside him. Even though it was early evening and the sun was still high, she felt so comforting next to him. Bill knew Carmina would get up to finish her chores once he fell asleep. It was late spring down here, light until very late. Time to put in the new potato crop. It was impossible to buy seeds anymore, and he did so love her potatoes.

IT WAS DARK when Bill crept painfully out of the house and down the hill to comm Mori without Carmina hearing.

"Mori, that you? Bill Hernan here."

"Bill, *amigo!* How are you?"

"I been better."

"What do you mean. Are you sick? Is Carmina all right?"

"Yeah, yeah, she's okay," Bill said. "We've seen better days, though. The BCs are all over me. Listen up now. Those three locos you sent down here to get trees for your preserve up there in Canada? Well, they ought to be getting back there before long. I got them what you asked for and helped 'em load it up. But holy Christopher, Mori—I saw as they were leaving that they had a plentiful load of trees already!" Bill gripped his arm tightly near his armband, as if he could hold Mori's attention across the miles.

"Perfect. Thank you very much, Bill," Mori said.

"No, no, I don't want any thanks," Bill interrupted. "Because I don't know what to make of it. I thought those trees were for you. I think they have ripped you off and are going to sell all this stuff on some black market. Tried to stop them, but all I got for my trouble was a few broken ribs and a black eye. The pilot I heard them call Dal even tried to pull a knife on me."

"You didn't hurt anyone, did you?" Mori asked, his voice sounding strained.

"No, no, *amigo,* listen up: didn't I just say they hurt me? Me! Your ol' buddy. What's wrong with you, Mori? Are you getting tetched in the head or something?"

"Bill, now don't you worry about a thing," Mori said. "They are doing me a big favor, just like you have always done. It is all under control. One day I will explain everything."

"How about you explain it right now?" Bill demanded. "I was just let out of a two-hour goddamned physical interrogation and could be taken back at any time now that the BCs know all about me. I lied to them. Said I have official approvals to collect those tree specimens. I told them I didn't have the approvals on me but that I would bring them in within forty-eight hours. That's the only reason they let me go. That and the fact that the jail was packed with other prisoners. They'll come asking me for those papers, and if they find out it's all a lie, I'm done for. I didn't tell Carmina, but we have that hanging over us," he fibbed.

"Did you say they were not the Atmospheric Police but the Black Coats? How did they get onto you?"

"What are you—deaf, Mori? Yes, it was the BCs. Must have seen the trees missing on patrol. Maybe they found the holes we dug, even though we tried to fill them in. Probably my guys didn't disguise the holes well enough. You know, they count those things around here—count the trees. They also questioned Jake, my boatman, without any mercy, like I feared they would. He told them I had gone up there with your unholy threesome. Now I'm in a world of trouble, Mori. What is this thing you got me involved with? You owe me a full explanation."

"I will have some certificates drawn up and sent to you, to show to the BCs when they come around again." Mori said. Then he reconsidered.

"No, wait," he said. "I have a much better idea. I will send my own pilot, Aron Weeks, down immediately to land at your farm and bring you and Carmina up here. He can be down there by 4:30 a.m. your time. He will get you completely out of danger. Then we will have good-looking approvals drawn up, not just a rush job. I am very sorry not to have thought of that before now, but this should cover you for sure forever. You really do not want a second interrogation. I've heard that each one gets worse."

"True," Bill said. "But tell me what this is all about, Mori. Need I repeat this? You owe me an explanation right now."

"As for a full explanation, that will have to wait a while, Bill," Mori replied. "I'm sorry, but you're truly better off not knowing anything more right now. In a month or so, when it is all over and done, I will tell you everything. That you can count on."

"In a month? That's a long time."

"For now, just know this, Bill. What you did is a noble thing, good for our earth that is going through so much on account of us all. This good deed never would have happened through regular channels. One day you can be proud that you were a part of all this. If you understood, you would probably agree."

"Bullshit, Mori! This isn't being like the partners we once were, before the land deal when you screwed me over so badly. I forgot you could be this high-handed." Bill waited, breathing hard, but Mori gave no answer.

"All right then," Bill finally said. "Send your man down right away. We will have our bags out by the gate and be ready in three hours." Then he shouted, "You'd better not go and kick the goddamned bucket before you tell me the whole truth, Mori!"—and cut the connection.

Carmina had heard Bill's raging voice and crept out to meet him. She hugged him close in the damp darkness, then went in to pack their few clothes, knowing that Mori would provide everything else they might need.

BY 6:00 A.M. New Churchill time on November 18, Henri was pouring Bill and Carmina cups of steaming coffee in Mori's breakfast room. Mori came slowly in to greet them. Bill jumped up to shake his hand, then winced when he hugged Mori with one arm. "Thank you for this, Mori. I'm all beat up. You on the other hand look pretty good, considering," he said.

"You look terrible yourself," Mori said with a wan smile. "I hate what happened to you. Truly never expected that."

Henri sidled up and whispered something in Mori's ear.

"Come around after breakfast and see me in my bedroom," Mori said. "Henri just told me it's time for my shot." Mori turned and left. Bill and Carmina looked at each other.

"He isn't the same man," said Carmina.

Bill nodded. "Sad to see him fading away. We better get those tree approvals done fast. I'll ask Henri to get them from him ASAP and we can go right back. Wonder who he's going to leave this spread to. Pretty nice place, huh? Can't be long for him now." Bill's voice wandered off as he looked out the window, thinking.

Carmina wiped her eyes at the thought of Mori fading away. They strolled back to their rooms, which were so nice and comfortable that they no longer felt quite as eager to get back home.

THIRTY MINUTES LATER Henri came to take Bill and Carmina to Mori's bedroom suite. They walked the beautiful passages, Carmina peering right and left, trying to take it all in. They passed through Mori's outer office, where a small white disc sat blinking with red and green lights. It was out at the edge of the desk, where it could be easily seen by anyone passing by, seeming to say, "Look at me!"

The strange object caught Bill's eye. "What's that thing, all lit up like a Christmas tree?"

"It's the Perseus—one of Mori's new gadgets for communication," Henri replied. "It sends important messages directly to his armband." He knew better than to say what sort of messages. He instinctively did not trust Bill.

Henri opened the large double doors to the room where Mori lay propped up on six pillows in his big bed. Mori opened his eyes and lifted his head when Henri arrived beside him and touched his arm. "They are here," Henri said. He pushed the pillows down behind Mori's back so he could sit up straighter.

"I am so glad you are here and are safe," Mori said. "I must tell you this to explain my lack of energy. We received an official notice yesterday that my stabilizing injections will be cut off on December 16. I've been expecting that would happen one day, but it still came as a shock. Puts everything in perspective—right, Henri?"

"Indeed, it does, sir." Henri shifted and looked away, blinking rapidly.

"I decided to start taking half doses immediately so I can still be here to celebrate when our mission folks get back. I can last a little over a month like this, maybe five weeks. Don't look so mournful now, you all," Mori implored. "I've had too long a life anyway. There is just this one thing more I must live to see: the success of the mission and Naija's safe return. That is why I must stay alive."

"I'm glad to still be a little part of your life, Mori," Bill said. He was thankful, but it was not in his character to grovel. And he couldn't help adding, "It would have been better if I hadn't got beaten up, though." When that was received well, Bill went further: "So what the hell is it all about?"

"I explained before, Bill, I cannot reveal what my team is doing until they get finished and there is proof of success." Mori sounded weary of having to say this once more.

Henri shook his head and frowned at Bill, as if warning against starting any conflict. He took a step in Bill's direction.

Carmina put a restraining hand on Bill's arm. Bill threw it off. He strode two long steps to the bedside and grabbed Mori's near arm, his right arm where his armband was hidden under his sleeve. Bill's grip was crushing.

"Listen, Mori, you and I, we go back together a long, long time. So you simply can't treat me like an old shoe again, the way you did with those land deals back in ancient history. I've stayed loyal despite all that. Even got myself beat up on your account, and right now you are not giving me my due. You owe me better. You owe me an explanation. And that is the very *least* you owe." Bill's voice was low, more menacing than if he had exploded.

Henri wedged himself between Bill and Mori. Mori didn't answer Bill but laid his head back and closed his eyes.

Bill threw Mori's arm down hard, turned, and stomped out, letting the heavy double doors clash noisily. "Shit. Shit!" He glanced at the attention-grabbing disc when he went by. In his fury, Bill picked up the twinkling object and hurled it across the wood-paneled room.

The disc slammed into a marble column on the fireplace and smashed into bits, most of the sound drowned out by Bill's roaring anger. A few lights continued to blink green and red, but in seconds all of them went dark. Carmina had hurried out after Bill. She paused just long enough to shove the broken mess under the skirt of a nearby upholstered chair with her foot.

HENRI STAYED WITH MORI, patting his limp hand and talking in a quiet voice. "He's a hothead, Mr. T. You know that. Don't let him upset you. I'll get his tree approvals and send him back home whenever you say."

"I am not sure when to send him back," said Mori. "Cannot risk his getting jailed again down there. Bill will calm down. He always has before.

"But do keep a close watch over that Perseus for me," he said. "That is vital. You understand that, right? Watch that thing all the time. I will feel it if my armband responds to a call, but I still want you to do that and double-check. They should have arrived down there by now and might be planting those trees." Mori's voice was thin with fatigue.

He ran his tongue over his dry lips again before asking haltingly, "Yesterday—they landed—right?"

"Yes, sir, unless they had to look around a little for the best location for those trees. But I'll bet they're planting them right now, as you said," Henri replied in his most soothing voice.

Suddenly Henri saw blood come through Mori's sleeve and drip on the sheet. He gently rolled up the sleeve and stared at Mori's armband, which was now loose due to his lost weight. Bill must have smashed and rubbed the band into his delicate skin because there were several long, bleeding cuts on Mori's arm.

Henri carefully removed the band. Mori lifted his head to protest, but laid it back down when Henri said, "I promise I will wear this band for you, sir. I'll keep it on night and day. If a signal comes in, I will hurry right to you—you can count on that. This band cut you badly and could cause an infection. We want you in good shape for when they all get back. There will be a lot to celebrate. I know how much those trees and Miss Naija mean to you. You can count on me."

Mori was too spent to argue. He could trust Henri. It had been a big day already, and it was only nine in the morning.

Henri hurried out to get dressings for Mori's bleeding arm. He rushed so fast that he didn't notice that the Perseus was not twinkling on the desk as usual. When he returned with the dressings and suddenly did not see it, he felt his heart constrict.

He called in the housekeeper, who said she had not seen it. Then he had no choice but to go to Bill's room. Carmina was there alone.

"Miss Carmina, have you seen that little white blinking disc that sat on the edge of Mori's desk? We need it."

"No, Henri, but I saw a little piece of white on the rug near the chair by the fireplace. Maybe your *muchacha* put it under the chair?"

"No, she would never do that," Henri replied. "Everyone knows it is very important."

"If she broke it, she might have done that to keep Mr. Mori from anger," Carmina said. She began to shake, and her eyes brimmed with tears.

"How would she possibly break it, Miss Carmina?" Henri's voice was soft now, as if interrogating a small child.

"She might have gone *loco* about something and thrown it," said Carmina, her voice tremulous and her hands clasped tightly together. "Please do not tell Mr. Mori she did this. I'm afraid for her sake."

"I heard a little crash as you and Bill left the room," Henri recalled. "I thought maybe you had bumped into something. Was that it? Did you break it?"

Carmina wept openly now. "No, it was Bill. He threw it. But if you tell Mr. Mori this, it will upset him, and that might kill him. He is *muy enfermo*. And if you accuse my husband, Bill will also be upset and tell Mr. Mori. Either way, it is better for you to say *nada*, say *nada*. I do not know what the little thing is for. Only a machine. But if it is so important, do not tell either of them, please. That is *muy importante*. No say *nada, nada*."

"I must tell Mr. Mori," Henri replied. "He has to know this."

"No, you must not," Carmina pled. "Not if it will kill him. Mr. Mori is so sick now. Anything more might kill him. And telling him can help nothing. If this is so important, come, I will show you where it is, and you can take it now to get it fixed *pronto* or buy another, okay? Remember to say nothing to Bill. He does not know this machine is very important. And it is best he not find out. Or we do not know what he will do. This is best for everyone, for us all, and especially for Mr. Mori. Our secret. Okay?"

Henri faced an impossible situation. What seemed right could be disastrous, and what seemed wrong might actually be the right thing to do. He was paralyzed with indecision. But first he must go get the Perseus back online. Right away!

HENRI CONTINUED TO FEEL the weight of his huge responsibility and the secrets he held. It was an intolerable burden, but one he owed to

Mori to handle well. He wore Mori's armband faithfully, never taking it off for any reason. Later, his sleep was troubled every night by worries of what could possibly have happened during the four days it took him to get the Perseus repaired and back online. He tried to dismiss these forebodings as unlikely, while he continued taking excellent care of Mori.

18

For hundreds of years, landing has been considered the most dangerous phase of flight. Current statistics tell us, despite safety advances in
all areas, that it is still true.

—*Aeronautics Monthly,* September 2295

NOVEMBER 17, 2295

ANTARCTICA

Dal woke early, his sleep cycle disturbed by the change in hours of
sun. All three being tired and sore from the previous day, they
dragged themselves up to breakfast. Dal tried to work off his stiffness
from the fight by walking along the shore.

In two hours, they were back in the air again, looking for an op-
timum place to fulfill their mission. Dal noted that their sun battery
was holding up well, a hopeful sign that they might be able to avoid
an emergency recharge on the way home. Black Coats could be out
hunting for them right now. They might have to return by an entirely
different route, which could be longer.

At breakfast Dal had made clear, "We can't fly around looking for
the perfect place too long today."

"Just a little farther," Naija said, pointing to the southwest of their
camping beach. "Over there is a beachfront configuration similar to
yesterday's, except the land is much wider and flatter. Then it rises, but
with wide shelves and hanging valleys that could be good for longer
sunlight."

Ahead Dal saw two miles of dark beach lying flat between large brown gouges down both sides of a mountain that the altimeter pegged at 7,254 feet high. Beyond the mountain on the inland side they could see two alluvial rivers that joined and drained away to the east. Dal buzzed over a big, sunny, glacier-gouged valley on the lower shorefront side of the mountain. A valley stream emerged as a waterfall only seventy-five feet above the flats. There was moss there, too, and a pool below. "Might be a good place to plant," Dal said. "What do you think, Walt?"

"Looks good. Plenty of sun with no obstructions. The water test I did in that other valley was fine, with no adverse minerals. This watercourse is probably similar, coming from the same mountain range."

Apparently, the ice had left this area early during the glacial unhinging, and the exposed land below them was not in danger of washing away in cascading meltwater from the interior. The waterfall and the mountain both looked easy to climb. "Yes, this might be a good place, but we should double-check before landing," Dal said.

Naija and Walt both gave thumbs up. The setting, although being the same moraine granite-and-dust color as everywhere else, looked even more perfect the closer they came. The plane nose-dived to the left when Dal passed over the flat area again.

"Look at that." Naija pointed to a dust plume blowing off the mountain's peak. But no dust seemed to be blowing across the beach on the wide, flat area where Dal thought to set the plane down. A minor curiosity. Probably the wind was stronger up high, and the land might be a little moist, holding the dust down the same way it had yesterday. The controls indicated only light winds at ground level. This looked to be a wide and perfect runway of packed dirt.

Dal decided to try for a level spot near where the skirt of the mountain began to slope gently upward. Beyond that, the ground rippled with heavy pleats. This location was also close to the waterfall that misted about a tenth of a mile away on the left. And it was close to the big, sunny, hanging valley—not too far to haul the trees. There probably wasn't a more practical or picturesque spot in all of Antarctica.

"All right!" yelped Walt. Naija applauded and beamed at Dal. They had come farther than mere miles could indicate. They were about to stand on fresh land, and no one except an old man in Canada knew where they were. The cockpit crackled with the excitement of explorers within grasp of their prize.

Dal concentrated on the plane's every vibration. If they caught any strange winds from the mountain, he could move out quickly. He knew that Antarctic mountains could funnel their own wind, especially down here where, when the land was covered with ice, katabatic winds could roar down suddenly with the strength and sound of a locomotive.

He tensed, prepared to bolt the aircraft away if necessary. But the wind stayed steady at eight knots from the southwest. He nosed the plane into it, hovered, and began the rotor descent—a hundred feet, fifty feet, thirty, twenty. Dal took it slowly, even though everything looked routine. He had made much harder landings before—on pitching ship decks, on windy mountain peaks, on little rocks lashed by waves. This was so easy that it might have been boring were he not landing in Antarctica, the land peopled only by imagination.

The plane's deployed runners settled gently. It was a perfect landing. The runners sank in a little, indicating that the surface was a bit soft, but Dal had expected that from yesterday's experience. Then he saw the dirt surface outside his window fracture into thick rings, as if a rock had been thrown into a sludgy pool. The runners settled in and disappeared. Dal pushed the rotor speed to lift off, but the plane was held as if it were tied. Indeed, the nose began to tilt down.

Dal broke into a cold sweat. He worked every thrust vigorously, but instead of lifting off, the plane listed. He could neither right the angle nor take off. Abruptly Dal threw the blades into full stop. He could see their future.

"What the fuck?" screamed Walt when the fuselage tipped. The big blade atop was slowing when it struck the slush on the starboard side. The blade sliced through with a "schmucking" sound, filling them all with horror before it twisted and snapped apart. Loose metal pieces careened madly over the top of the plane, ripping open the roof to the sky. Mangled shards of metal shot around the cockpit like bullets.

The crunching and ripping sound of their slow-motion disaster ricocheted for a long time in Dal's ears. He reflexively cradled his head and covered his neck with his jacket and hands. How long would it be before that awful sound stopped?

Finally, all was deadly quiet, as if life, and even Dal's heartbeat, had stopped. No one spoke. The wind whistled faintly across the jagged hole in the roof. A thin, distant roar could be heard, perhaps the sound of the waterfall carried on the breeze. Gradually, that sound and the wind in the open hole gained enough prominence to draw Dal back to the reality of where he was.

He lifted his head to look around. Naija was hunched over toward him. What could she be thinking now? She touched his hand tenderly, where blood from deep scratches dripped off the tip of his thumb.

"Looks like you're mostly all right," she said. But Dal knew he was not all right. None of them could be all right here like this. He quickly pushed his "Perseus button," as Mori had called it. There it was, under the red dot on the left side of the unimposing watch that Mori had insisted they bring. Dal held down this last link with civilization—and with Ana—as hard as he could.

19

To live is to be slowly born.
—Antoine de Saint-Exupéry

THE SAME DAY, ANTARCTICA

Walt moaned from the back seat. Blood from his right knee oozed through the center gap and down onto Dal's seat. "My leg is jammed between the seats," Walt cried through clenched teeth. "My knee is stuck. It won't come out."

"Dammit, why weren't you belted in?" Dal asked.

"My knee is stuck and it won't come out," Walt said again. "I just wanted to see better, and I thought you knew what you were doing. It looked safe."

"Put your head down, Walt, and take deep breaths," Naija said calmly. She was scrunched to the left by her caved-in side, so she couldn't turn around completely.

Dal took a quick inventory. Amazingly, they had all escaped decapitation and serious open wounds, although Walt's condition was not clear. The control panel, however, had been ripped open by an oblique thrust of blade debris. Even more worrisome, Dal saw that whatever else might have escaped the blade's damage lay completely smashed under the overhead transmission, which had fallen directly atop the computer console. There went the power for communication and navigation. Dal's insides turned cold. He swallowed a retch that bubbled up his esophagus.

"Lower your head between your knees if you can, Dal," Naija said.

"Your face is very white." She watched Dal's color improve when he did so. Her eyes followed his stare to the mangled cognition panel.

Walt moaned again.

"Let's get out of here," Dal said, his instinct being to flee the wreckage. He unbuckled his belts and started moving toward the hole in the roof, where he saw a bit of blue sky. As he moved, the plane groaned and its loosened parts creaked loudly. Then it canted further to the right.

Walt screamed, "Holy mother of God!" and crossed himself.

Dal carefully pulled himself up to stand on the wrecked console and stuck his head through the jagged hole in the roof. Though the air was cool, the sun shone with unexpected warmth.

"Here, take this to pad the edges," said Naija, handing her jacket up to Dal. "They're sharp." Dal used it to cover the sharp metal edges of what he assumed would be their escape hatch. No way could they open the doors, not knowing what was outside.

He looked around, unsure what to make of their situation. The plane was definitely wrecked, but what was this unstable, dun-colored surface they had landed on that had been their undoing? What had sucked the plane in, and what kept it more or less afloat now? How far away was solid land, and in what direction could they most efficiently cross over to it?

"You okay up there?" Naija called.

"Stay put a few minutes while I check something out," Dal called down. "There's not room for all of us to be up here at once."

He threw a piece of debris off the top of the plane and watched it disappear into the thick, muddy solution that surrounded them. The top of the moraine quicksand was disguised by a dusting of fine soil, a ground, colloidal moraine dust evidently blown there over time by winds from the mountain. He looked around, taking in the whole scene.

What Dal heard was his own heartbeat muffled in his ears when he carefully slid back down into his seat.

"Naija, when we leave the wreck, you will have to wiggle over this hump and come out from my side," he said. "I will help you then. But first, let's free Walt. Walt, I need you to get me some of those stakes from the back. You know, the ones we brought for the trees."

"How do you expect me to get back there when my leg is jammed up here?" Walt grunted.

"When I count to three, Naija, pull your seat to the right. Walt, you will have to pull backward on your leg to free it, and I will pull my seat to the left and push your leg at the same time. Get a good grip, now. Do you understand? Okay—one, two, three—PULL!"

Dal jerked his seat to the left and shoved hard on the top of Walt's knee with his right arm.

"Augh, stop, stop!" Walt yelled, throwing his head side to side in pain. His knee remained stuck, and the plane wobbled frightfully.

Naija pulled a tiny pair of scissors out of a small pocketknife and sawed at Walt's pants until she was able to rip the fabric apart. Then she tugged at the ends of fabric until his swollen, mushy kneecap was exposed.

"The cut causing the bleeding does not look deep," she said. "It gapes open like that because your knee is so bent." She poured hand cream from a small bottle down the sides of Walt's wedged leg.

"What else have you got in those pockets of yours?" Dal asked. Naija cocked her head but didn't look up until she made sure the cream was covering all the right places.

"Cut out the flirting, and just get me out," Walt said, gritting his teeth.

"Now then, let's try it again," Naija said. "This will hurt, Walt, but only for a second. Take a deep breath and, one, two, three—PULL!" Naija pushed fiercely against his knee, and Walt's lotion-greased leg popped free. He fell backward into his seat, moaning. The plane rocked back and forth but settled. "Thank God," Walt panted.

"What do you mean, thank God?" Dal said. "Thanks to Naija!"

"Yeah, whatever." Walt grimaced with pain and rubbed his hands across the seat.

"Listen, people," Dal said, "we can handle this." He hoped it was true. He spoke slowly and carefully. "I landed on some unstable ground, more like quicksand. It appears solid, but it is not. We have to be extremely careful exiting because the plane could be sucked under. We don't know where the bottom is. So please do exactly as I say.

"Now, Walt, I need you to drag yourself back to the cargo area. Get a couple of stakes and some of that twine we were going to use for staking up the trees. Move carefully, and try not to make the plane shift. It seems to be balanced on a rock or something in the back."

Walt groaned. "The only way I *can* move is carefully," he said. He grasped the back of his seat and hauled himself over it, using his left leg to hoist himself up. Dal heard a heavy thud and a cry of pain as Walt fell to the floor behind his seat.

"Move as gently as you can," Naija called to Walt. The plane rocked sickeningly again.

Walt struggled for a full five minutes, and neither Dal nor Naija could see what he was doing. Finally, a stake waved in the air above them. Naija grabbed it. Then came another, and another. Next Walt threw a small spool of landscape twine across the seats, and it stuck on a metal spike that used to be part of the console.

Naija handed Dal her small knife, which he secured in his pocket. He stuck the stakes out of the roof, shimmied himself up through the hole again, and pulled the stakes up. Sitting with his legs dangling into the cockpit, he lashed the stakes together to make a long probe.

Then he lay on his stomach and inched out to the nose of the plane, where he jammed the probe into the mud. It did not hit bottom.

Dal tried again from both the right and left sides. This was more difficult, because the fuselage tipped frighteningly with the side-to-side weight changes. Still no bottom. It was hard to hold the stake firmly because of the mud collecting on it. He wiped his hands on his pants.

"What's happening?" Naija yelled, her voice piping.

"Figuring stuff out," Dal yelled back. "Tell you in a minute." Were they marooned on this crippled plane in a sea of mud? He would not carry that thought forward. They had to get off. That was the only thing certain right now.

Dal crept back over the rear roof of the plane, probing the mud every two feet. He worked around another gaping hole in the cargo roof. About eight feet from the end of the plane, the probe hit bottom at less than the depth of one stake, so Dal figured the bottom might be about nine feet below the surface at that point. He prayed the ground under the plane would angle up sharply beyond that.

After more probing, Dal determined that the plane was indeed suspended over a shallower part of a dust-topped bog, with the tail resting on a large boulder located a couple of feet beneath the opaque surface. The boulder probably had been carried there by glacial discharges in recent years. Maybe there were other boulders under the surface, too. He scanned the shore. Rocks and boulders, some as large as cars, studded the higher ground. Other places looked swept clean down to bedrock.

Dal sat down gingerly on top of the plane, holding his mud-plastered probe. He was now covered in mud, too. He moved his hand from the side of his face, where he had cupped his cheek, and pushed his hair back, leaving a dark streak across his forehead and up into his scalp. He sat there for ten minutes more, thinking.

Suddenly, this mud-streaked apparition thrust his head into the cockpit through the hole in the roof. Dal told a startled Naija and an ashen Walt, "I know what we must do."

20

Scared is what you are feeling. Brave is what you are doing.
—Emma Donoghue

THE SAME DAY, 2295
ANTARCTICA

// "Twist it to the left—now, to your right. Yeah, that's it. Now roll and
bend it—help me bend it 'round. Okay. Now push it through.
Stop! We're rocking too much. Okay, let's try again. Push. Slowly,
slowly now." Dal and Naija struggled to maneuver thin titanium-
alloy plates onto the roof where Dal sat. The plates were to have been
used for their temporary shelter. Now Dal had another plan for them.
He sat on them one by one as Naija worked them up through the hole
in the roof.

Walt made his anguished way again and again to the rear of the
plane. He dragged the lightweight, four-by-eight titanium sheets to
the front and pushed them over the seat to Naija by kneeling on his
left knee with his right leg extended awkwardly. Naija had wrapped an
elastic bandage around it while Dal was topside. Only a small red stain
showed through the bandage.

After a struggle, Dal held eight of the fourteen titanium sheets under his foot and called down to his companions: "I can't come back
down or these will slide away. We may be able to get to a place where
we can walk if the slope of bedrock continues up at the same pitch
under this bog the whole way. I can see what seems to be solid ground

about forty feet away, beyond the tail section. There are boulders and rocks there, too.

"Naija, you come up here first. Walt, be ready right behind her to climb up when I tell you to. Naija is going to lay these plates flat on the top of the bog ahead of her and then walk carefully across them. She'll go first, and we'll proceed after her, from lightest to heaviest.

"Be careful, Naija. Don't let the corners angle down or they might break the surface tension and start sliding under. We're counting on that tension and very little thrashing around to help us. We need these plates to float on top just long enough for us to walk across. Walt will go right after you.

"Walt, when it's your turn, you will have to move fast," Dal shouted down into the plane. "No matter how much pain you are in, put it out of your mind for five minutes from the time I say, 'Go.' Your life depends on it." *And my life, too,* he thought. "Any questions?"

Naija looked up from the destroyed cockpit and shook her head. "No, no questions." She had a look of intense concentration but seemed calm. He hoped she would be able to control the plates in the breeze. Each plate had to work in order to cover the whole distance. There were six more left in the cargo space as backup—in case any of them went under before it was Dal's turn to escape.

Naija stretched her arms up. Dal locked wrists with her and lifted her, keeping one foot firmly on the plates. Naija was light, but also strong and sturdy. He held her close once she stood on the small area near the hole in the roof. She gripped his waist until the rocking stopped. Then Dal carefully helped her turn around to face the tail of the plane and the ominous distance to shore.

Naija had to do the hardest part and go first. Dal wished he could help her. By far the biggest, he would go last. He might even have to try running across the plates, and he had no doubt that they would buckle and probably sink under his weight.

"This is the plan," he said. "Lay them out one at a time, end to end, with a small space between them that you can bridge with your stride. You may have to wade through at the end. Spread your weight and avoid standing on the edges of the plates. Must be done delicately."

"I know, I know." Naija seemed impatient, eager to get going. "Just the way my people used to cross thin ice-floes during the Arctic spring-melt of old times." She smiled at Dal reassuringly, as if off on a longed-for adventure. Then her face resumed a blank stare of concentration, and she edged forward with the delicate balance of someone crossing Niagara Falls on a tightrope.

Naija carried the plates crosswise close to her body. They were nearly as tall as she was. At the end of the plane, she carefully peeled one off. It flapped up like a sail. She tottered. The plane rocked. Dal bit his lip and held his breath.

Naija struggled to nose the first metal plate into the prevailing breeze. Dal took one step forward to help her but stopped himself. She would have to figure this out before she stepped off the plane. She wouldn't have this relative safety out over the bog, where she would be alone trying to control all the plates. After several minutes, the wind died between light gusts, and Naija succeeded in placing one plate atop the deep muck that separated her from solid ground.

Dal watched her reach out ever so slowly with her right foot. Was she too afraid to do it? He would have called out encouragement, but something told him to keep quiet.

Naija took a long step off the plane. It was a muscular movement worthy of a gymnast or a ballerina, her whole body weightlessly suspended for what seemed an eternity. She landed with the lightest possible touch. The first plate quivered. Dal let his breath out with relief. She was in the middle of the first plate, and it was not sinking. This just might work!

She had to move faster now. It was difficult to hold onto the remaining plates while laying the next one down, especially when the wind caught them. She developed a routine. Holding the other plates with her elbows against her body, she half squatted and carefully placed the next one into position. Once it was laid out in front of her, she rose smoothly and lightly stepped onto it. Behind her the plates formed a curious wake, askew and drifting a little out of line.

"Walt, your turn is coming. Get up here now," Dal commanded when he saw this drift begin. Naija was not yet to shore, but every step she made pushed the plates farther apart.

Dal pulled Walt up. Walt wrinkled in pain. His face was chalky white. He stood up on one leg, but he would have to use both legs to make the crossing. He would have to walk evenly if the plates were to stay on the surface long enough for Dal to have any chance at all to make it.

"Walt, ol' Buddy," Dal clasped Walt's shoulders in the most reassuring grip he could manage. "It's up to you, man."

Just then Naija staggered through the last four feet of thigh-deep mud and made it out. She threw up her arms up in victory.

Dal stuck two mud-caked fingers in his mouth and whistled back. Walt raised an arm to wave, which immediately threw him off balance, but Dal caught him before he could slide off the fuselage.

"Easy going there, Walt," Dal said. "Do exactly like you saw Naija do. Spread your weight by keeping your feet apart in a wide stance, but stay away from the edges. No jolting movements. Walk steadily and as fast as you can with good balance. And if possible, push some of those plates back in line for me when you leave them."

"Rather a lot for a man with one leg," Walt winced.

"At least you still have both of them attached to you," Dal said. "Forget about that little injury. Think life or death. Use your legs as if they're both fine. Once you get to shore, we can fix you up. For now, put your considerable brilliance to work." Then Dal had an idea.

"Try this: Pretend you are in the last hundred yards of a single-sculls crew championship. You are slightly ahead, and you know you can win if you try. The pain has started. It's strong, and it'll be with you until you win the race. Until you get to the finish line. You must arrive at that beach over there and be victorious. That's the finish line. Your pain is not an injury. It means that you're using your body to win. It means your mind is strong, stronger than your pain. You are better than the rest. You're ahead!" He turned Walt around toward the rear of the plane, unsure whether Walt could relate to that scenario.

Walt stepped out gingerly to cross the plane, toe first and dipping slightly on his bandaged right leg. He stopped and crossed himself. Dal thought too much time was passing. He was about to shout for him to hurry up when Walt straightened.

He made a smooth rowing motion with his arms—once, then twice. Walt began a measured rowing simulation with his arms, and between those he inserted steps: first left leg, row, then right leg, row, then left leg, row, right leg, row, on to the end of the plane, then onto the first plate and across the second. Walt moved like a flightless bird trying wings that were meant for another medium. With every plate that Walt crossed, Dal's estimation of him rose, and with it his hope for them all. He was strangely moved, considering the situation. *Brave companions.*

It was in crossing the last plate that Walt's injured leg buckled under him. He cried out and fell off the plate, and was covered with mud up to his neck before he could find any footing. The edge of the last plate was shoved under; Dal watched it slide away with frightening speed.

Naija waded back to help drag Walt out, while Dal headed down into the cargo space to grab two more titanium plates. After quickly sifting through the stores for a few light items, he strapped on a pack of food bars. At the last minute, he included a tiny two-ounce bottle of brandy meant to celebrate their completion of the mission. If that were to weigh him under, well, so be it.

He must hurry. Did he have everything he could take? Oh, the water purifier. Shouldn't need it here. No animals to spread giardia. He left it.

One more quick look around. His eye caught a glint of sunlight coming through the broken roof and falling onto the trees. Those abominable trees were the root cause of their plight.

The trees stood upright where they had been tied to the walls. Some were straight and some were a little askew. The white spruce nearest Dal shivered in the faint breeze that poured deep inside the plane. The tree's needles were a dusty blue-green in the sunlight—an arresting change from the brown all around them outside. Dal paused only an instant over this glorious life in the midst of mud and destruction.

It was the only other large life that Dal had seen in Antarctica, and they had brought it with them. The sun would never set on these trees while he was here. Unless they stayed too long. All of these observations overlapped and went through him in a flash. He turned to go.

By now the plates that were still floating on the bog were coated with a slick film. Dal slid across the first one, fighting to stay upright. He could feel it sinking out from under him. As soon as he jumped to the second plate, the first one slid away and was sucked beneath the mud. The second plate also sank alarmingly fast as he left it. Dal was bigger and heavier than the other two. Did he need to jettison any of the supplies he carried? Not yet, he decided.

He strained to lift his weight higher and to stay atop the tilting, slippery plates, jumping fiercely from muddy plate to muddy plate, each leap more difficult. The extra effort drove both him and the plate he landed on deeper into the muck.

His heart pounded in his chest. He could barely hear Naija and Walt shouting encouragement from the shore, their voices drowned out by the sound of his own gasping.

AT LAST DAL lay on the mud-and-rock-strewn shore. Thick mud covered all of their clothes and faces, matted their hair, and even gritted in Dal's mouth; he spat several times to get it out. Lying exhausted on the dirt, the three of them resembled elephant seals in their unattractive moulting stage.

Nevertheless, Naija's teeth flashed white with a smile. Even Walt looked cheered by their success at having left the wreck alive. Dal wished he felt more relieved. He alone seemed to comprehend their isolation from the rest of the teeming world. He glanced down at his little armband, wondering if the Perseus command *"COME GET ME NOW"* had made it through. To make sure, he pressed the knob again.

Dal knew he was responsible for their situation. And he felt quite stupid for having done as Mori wished by leaving his powerful armband back on the table in Canada. Because of its astral as well as global positioning, with that band he could have placed a call anywhere, even to the moon colony, to summon help. This watch would only call Mori, and no one else could intercept the message. Not even the Black Coats would hear the signal.

As if she understood his thoughts, Naija placed her hand on his arm. "We had no way to expect this," she said. "You know that. Don't blame Mori. Or yourself."

Dal's eyes reddened. He looked stonily past her, across the mud flats toward the wreck. No words came. Her sympathy brought him near tears, but this was no time for that. Silence reigned. Every now and then Walt would shift position and groan a little. Maybe half an hour passed this way.

"I'm responsible for wrecking our plane," Dal eventually said. He couldn't stand the silence. It was time to get their feelings out in the open, he said.

"Ah, let's not," said Walt.

Dal waved Walt off and stood up in front of them. "No! You listen to me!" he shouted. Walt and Naija gazed up at him in alarm.

"I'm damned sorry, that's all," he said as he stood in front of them, swaying and haggard with fatigue.

Walt struggled up onto his good leg and limped over to Dal. His feathery hair appeared to be painted onto his skull, and blood streaked his face where he had rested his head on his knee. His breath was stale, and he smelled like wet dirt. He was inches away from Dal's face. Dal wanted to turn away or shove him, but Walt held onto him as he spit out his words through clenched teeth.

"No–prob–lem–man. Now–chill–out–will–you?"

21

On earth, nutritional needs for 12 hours of heavy labor for a male of 180 pounds can be up to 6,000 calories per day. In very cold temperatures, rarely seen now, 10,000 calories may be required.

—*Nutrition Quarterly*, volume 6, issue 9, September 11, 2280

NOVEMBER 18 AND 19, 2295, ANTARCTICA

// 'm hungry," Naija said. "How about you two? Got anything in that pack?" She pointed to Dal's load.

"Yes." He opened it, glad to be able to give them something. The contents belonged to them all, but he had gotten it off the plane, so he took temporary comfort in that. The wreck glinted reprovingly in the never-completely-setting sun. Dal turned his back to it.

Soon they had their one package of dried stew heating in their one pan, with an oil packet and a heat cube thrown in. Naija waved the spoon in the air. "Looks like you got the good stuff for tonight, Dal," she said. "You must be a whiz at the grocery."

"Never been to a grocery," Dal mumbled. "We have to find a way to get more food here. There's not much in that pack. You're cooking up the best of it right now."

"Tell you what," Walt said. "I am never crossing that miserable mudhole again, not for food or anything else. I'd rather starve."

"In which case, you might do that, Walt. Starve, I mean," said Dal. "What if we finish the meal and bars we have here? We know there is plenty more food out there in that plane. What if no one comes to get us in the next four days?"

Walt stared into his empty bowl as if reading tea leaves.

"Someone will come," he said.

"We don't know when, though," Dal said gently. "I already set off my Perseus on the watch Mori gave each of us. Twice. If no one comes in two days' time, we'll know for sure that the bloody thing, which is supposed to be instantaneous, doesn't work."

"Let's each set off Perseus again right now, all together," Naija said hopefully. And so they did.

"Satellite photo scanning will eventually find us," said Walt.

"Why would anyone take the time to photo survey this one area when there is so much data to review in more important places?" Dal replied. "No one is even supposed to be here. Sure, we *could* be found—*if* someone were looking. But who will be? We've covered our tracks pretty well."

"Mori will send for us when we don't show up on time," Naija said. "He will arrange it. He can do it." She stabbed the ground repeatedly with her pocketknife. "I know he will. I just know he will."

"Arriving 'on time' is too late," Dal said. "On time is December 20, or maybe even later, plus or minus a couple of days. If the Perseus comm we sent together just now didn't work, Mori won't realize we need a rescue until we don't come back. Just to be sure, let's all call him together one more time. We'll send our messages and show him our coordinates just like he said we should. Get all mud off your watches first."

Dal waited while Walt cleaned his watch. "We will press the signal button together on three. All right now: one, two, three." He waited another minute and said, "Now let's do it again, but one at a time. Naija, you go. After thirty seconds, Walt, you go." Then Dal pressed his own button for the fourth time in an hour.

"Okay, now that we have done all we can with Perseus, let's go back to the central issue: we have to get the rest of the food out of the plane if we're going to last until help arrives. Somehow, we have to do it. We brought twenty-eight days' worth of food with us. We have twenty-six now because we ate one day's food yesterday. And we are eating one now. Of those twenty-six days' worth, I have just two in my pack."

Dal pointed to the battered plane with his bloody hand. "We have to get out there and bring out the rest of the food in two days' time.

Then we can wait out any failure of the Perseus. Mori will send Aron to look for us if we don't show up on time. Aron might take a while to find us because Mori would have no coordinates for him to navigate. So without that food out there, we're in trouble." He stared out at the wreck, trying to will it closer.

The plane's roof was ripped in two places. The rotor blades hung bent and twisted beyond use. The tail of the plane rested on a submerged rock while the rest of the aircraft nestled into the fine-grained alluvial bog that resembled quicksand. Motionless items might float a while out there, but anything that moved would quickly be swallowed up.

Dal tried another vein, determined to impress upon Naija and Walt the extremity of their plight and spur their help in figuring out how to get to the food supply.

"Sure, *if* Mori is able and *if* he knows we are in trouble, then surely he will send someone to get us. Think about it, though. Bill told us that Mori isn't well, even though Mori never let on about that to us. We do know he's at the end of his allotted time. No ethical doctor on earth is going to do more than help a 141-year-old man die in comfort. And he's almost 142. Most people his age keep that a secret, but not Mori. He might even be assassinated for being over-age. That happens sometimes."

Dal saw Naija's eyes brim with tears. Walt's spoon clanged tat-tat-tat-tat-tat against the bowl, and it took both his hands to stop it. He put the bowl down.

Dal stopped talking. No need to overplay this and bring his companions down with him. He could beat himself all up and down the muddy shore for putting them in this position. He alone had done it.

IT MUST BE LATE MORNING now with the sun so bright, Dal thought. His back ached. His neck was cold. *Hate sleeping on the ground. Goddamned sun. Wish there were a proper night down here. No real dark. No stars. No sleep. Dreamed of penguins—squawking adélies, cooing gentoos. Pink, smelly penguin shit everywhere. Underfoot. Up my nose. Wait— there are no penguins. Damn nature films again.* Dal's jumbled thoughts poured out as he staggered to a standing position from his cold bed on the ground.

Just then a large bird buzzed his head, hit him with its feet, and flew off. He took a swing at it. Dal looked toward the distant sea to be sure where he was. Yes, there it was, the horrible wreck looking perky in the mud, tinged pink by the scattered clouds and sun refracting on dust and moisture in the air.

Naija was already up, sitting on a rock upwind of the spray coming off the waterfall. She was wringing out a piece of cloth. Even after Dal walked over and stood close behind her, she didn't look at him.

She had finished washing the mud from her hair and face, and shivered while she washed her arms in the ice-cold water. Dal considered hugging her to warm her up, but felt she might not like that.

"Were you cold last night?" he asked.

"No, the reflector blanket worked fine," she said. "I hated to get up and out of it, but we have things to do. I hope Walt wakes up soon. We need his help. I was thinking—"

"About what?"

"We have only two days' food on shore. What if no one comes in two days? What then, Dal?"

She didn't need to ask him these questions. This one and more had disturbed his sleep all night, much as he might prefer to blame the hard ground for his restless tossing.

Naija stood up and held his gaze. "You were right. We have to get back to the plane. There are so many things we need out there. We both know that. It could take a while before someone happens along."

"Sure could," responded Dal.

"I have an idea for how we can get back out there."

"Let's hear it then."

"We can make a bridge to the wreck out of all those rocks up there in the scree," she said. "We can roll them down and shove them into place. See how many rocks are partly rounded? It shouldn't be too hard to move them. You can carry the larger ones. We will work from the shore out and drop rocks off the end until we get there."

"The Egyptians had a few more people than we do," Dal said. "And they had log rollers, too."

"Let's get started," Naija replied, ignoring his comment. She had come up with not merely a good idea—it was the only idea so far. "We need to start right away, so we can finish before we are too weak and hungry to carry on."

DAL BIT INTO the dry energy bar, filled his mouth with water, and held his lips closed until the mass had softened enough that he could chew and then swallow it. A whole day's essential nutrients in two ounces, expanding in the stomach when followed by water to provide a little satisfaction. Missing was food with enough calories for high-energy endeavors—such as building causeways out to wrecked airplanes.

They sat on stones around a nonexistent campfire, chewing and talking. Naija was enthusiastic about the day ahead. "We have four of these bars for each of us on shore, enough for two days' food, but that is all. We have to get out there and bring out the rest. And there are other things out there that will make us more comfortable in camp, too."

"Isn't it better to conserve our energy rather than do all this manual labor?" Walt replied. "We might wear ourselves out, not to mention get hurt moving all that rock. Someone will come for us, and we will have wasted our energy."

Dal thought Walt had a point, but asked: "What if they don't get here in the next two days, Walt?"

Naija broke in: "I think we have to assume that we will be here the whole four weeks, and we don't know how long beyond that. Original explorers of this land ended up staying one to three years more than they had planned. We can manage for just a little while."

Walt fell back on the ground as if in a faint. "Heavens, just shoot me now and get it over with." Then he sat back up. "My wife will worry herself to death if we don't get back on time. I dreamed about her last night."

"We all dreamed about someone, Walt," Dal said.

"I didn't," said Naija. "No one is expecting me back except Mori."

"I can't believe that, Naija," said Dal. "Great gal like you."

"It's a long story—not for now," she said with finality.

Dal looked down, filled with sadness for her. Would Ana feel the same sadness if he didn't return? He knew it would devastate her and was determined to save her from that.

THE WORK OF BUILDING the causeway exhausted them all. Dal drank a bottle of water every hour or two. He had to fill the bottle from the waterfall, which took precious time from the main job. He sweated constantly, and his sweat dried up quickly. Salt formed around his mouth and crusted on his face.

Meanwhile, Walt crawled around above the beach from one rocky area to another. He jimmied useful-looking stones loose and sent them rolling down the slope, eventually to stop along the edge of the mud. He became pretty accurate in directing the fall of the rocks, so Naija and Dal didn't have to push or carry them as far as they had the first stones.

They made a sling out of their two jackets, which increased what they could carry together. But it meant Dal had to walk backwards. He stumbled often but managed not to fall off the first few feet they had built out into the mud.

The "Causeway," as they called it, was all Naija's idea, and she kept them hard at it. Mori had been right when he told Dal and Walt that she would have "many contributions" to make. Dal, remembering his recurrent dream of walking a causeway between two huge waves, provided the name as well as most of the sweat equity.

The bog nearer shore turned out to be only eight feet deep until one got within ten feet of the wreck. For some reason, none of the muck seemed to ever dry out. Perhaps there was an underground source for the liquid?

The original section went reasonably fast. Before the first long day's end, they had completed ten feet of a two-foot-wide stone walkway. Its surface was irregular, but as long as they watched every step they took, it was crossable.

Dal's stomach called out for lunch only two hours after breakfast. He tried to quiet the hunger with long drinks of water, but his body wasn't fooled. He suffered until early afternoon, driving himself to keep going whenever he felt weak. If they could follow the work plan closely, they just might be able to finish the causeway before running out of food.

At this rate, though, Dal was sure to lose substantial weight. Ordinarily he wouldn't have minded. But in this survival situation, he knew that every ounce was precious. Despite his greater size and heavier workload, they had begun by dividing their meager food into three equal portions. At first Dal had thought this was fair. But now at lunchtime, with his allotted bites already wolfed down and the others still chewing, he began to believe that his portion was not fair at all.

Still, he didn't want to say anything. After all, Naija was a woman, and Walt was injured. And wasn't it his duty to take care of them? His Southern ancestors would surely have agreed with this. But then again, wasn't it also true that men often died in disproportionate numbers in mixed-gender survival parties, partly for their greater nutritional needs and the uneven burden of manual labor? *We men use ourselves up mercilessly in times like this,* Dal commiserated with himself.

The afternoon involved more backbreaking effort: lifting, pushing, panting, resting for a minute, then shoving or carrying rocks again and again out to the end of the causeway. Once they arrived at the end with a good rock, they heaved it off and watched it fall with a mighty slurp into the bog. Eventually, the rock piles rose above the surface, and they proceeded to fill in the crevasses with smaller rocks.

"Dal, those rocks you just put in rolled away," Naija called out from the shore, hands on her hips.

"They were round. We need more angular ones," he yelled back.

"Walt, send down more irregular rocks with sharp edges," Naija called up.

"Angular rocks get stuck and will not roll down to you," Walt called back through his cupped hands. "Dal will have to come and get those if they are big and you can't do it."

Dal heard this exchange and stomped back down the causeway. He passed Naija without a word or glance and plodded up to where Walt was struggling to free another large stone. Dal strained to pick up a big, angular stone and haul it out to shore and on to the end of the causeway, where he placed it very carefully. It didn't move.

"Great job, Dal," called Walt.

Dal gave him the finger and went back for another big, angular stone.

Naija walked out to help Dal shove the biggest rocks off the end. But mainly she filled in with smaller rocks. She smiled at Dal often. When a rock was especially large, she came over to help him move it, and in the narrow space they bumped into each other with increasing frequency as the endless day went on. The continuous daylight, added to the adrenalin of danger, gave them energy to carry on.

Walt could see all the activity from his isolated perch in the rock field above. Dal gave him little thought except when he heard "Incoming!" or "Fore!" or "Heads up!" or one of the other warnings Walt devised to indicate that loose rocks were tumbling down toward them.

Finally, the sun turned downward in the sky, sending rosier tones over the evening. The sun never completely disappeared, even when it went behind the mountain. It circled around them always, just above the horizon or dipping under a hill for only a few minutes.

THE THREE SAT DOWN for their second shared supper. The squawking, aggressive bird that had first swooped down at Dal now swooped at them all. It landed into the wind, sidled over to them, and, recognizing the most vulnerable, went for Walt's food most persistently. This talent had kept the birds fat back when the place was just a narrow beach surrounded by rock and ice and covered with penguin nests during the short summer. Dal knew the scene of these birds in action, having watched it all unfold on his walls at home, with the birds striding up and down looking for unprotected penguin eggs or chicks. He figured they must need their food now as much as he did.

Walt called them "skuas" and enjoyed talking about them. "A few skuas must still live out on one of the islands left over from the breakup of West Antarctica," he said. "Coulver Island once was a major skua habitat. Way back when, you'd find it loaded with penguin chicks. Seals lived there, too. Skuas found the seals' nasal parasites especially tasty—"

"Ugh, Walt, stop. That's disgusting!" Naija slapped at him.

"—and they stole this gooey, yummy food right from the seals' wet, dripping noses!" Walt finished loudly.

"Gross, so gross," Naija repeated. She faked a punch at Walt's bad knee.

Walt liked to write field notes in a tiny notebook. He also took photographs with his forbidden camera. These things kept his mind occupied. "You know, I think that maybe after the penguins and seals left, some of these smarter skuas might have learned how to fish more efficiently from the ocean. Maybe they changed their diet just enough to survive."

Naija tried to change the subject. "I'm so tired. Let's not go out dancing tonight, okay? Let's just put on some music, snuggle up on the couch, and watch the wall screen," she said.

"Aw, that's too bad," Walt said, picking up her thread. "I was raring to go dancing until you pooped out."

Dal was sure Naija had meant dancing with him, not Walt. But he wanted to keep Walt included, so he said, "You guys don't stay out too late now," and rolled up in his reflector blanket as if to go to sleep. He was beat. And he was still hungry. He wondered if the others were hungry, too. They had built about half of the distance. Ahead lay the deeper bog, and the unstable plane. And only one and one-quarter days' food lay buried in a rocky cairn, out of the reach of the skuas.

22

Using speeds of movement for the Ross Ice Shelf at the time of death as a reference, it was estimated in 2003 that, moving within the glacier, it would take approximately 275 years for the snow-embalmed tent containing the remains of Robert Falcon Scott and his two fellow expeditioners to reach the sea and tumble in. When glacial speed in the great warming period increased, Scott and the others no doubt reached their watery grave much sooner.

—*Glaciologists' Notebook: The Abandoned Science*, July 2275

NOVEMBER 22, ANTARCTICA

"Your knee needs rest and elevation now, Walt," said Naija. She placed a cool mudpack on it. "As soon as we get to the wreck, we'll look for the medical kit and tissue-repair capsules."

"Bring the food first," Walt said. "I can stand the pain." He slowly pulled himself up and started to limp along the shoreline. "The sprain feels better. Knee just grates a little inside," he said as he hobbled away.

"Walt seems pensive to me, if not depressed," Naija whispered to Dal when Walt was out of hearing. "And this is just our fourth day."

"I get that feeling," Dal said. "We're each on half a bar of food today, and none tomorrow. He's right about food coming first. I can barely move, much less continue building that causeway forever. We better finish it today." Dal stood up, stretched, and hobbled like an old man back to the rock pile. He selected a rock and lugged it down the causeway out to the end.

"Try not to think about it," called Naija. "My people went through months of starvation every spring in the old days."

She ran after Dal, caught up with him, and whispered loudly, "I think we have to give Walt something else to think about, too. An absorbing task to bring him out of his funk. All the stones we could ever use are piled up now. He has no more reason to keep going."

Dal grunted and followed Walt to where he stood the near end of the causeway. "Walt hates not doing his share of the work," Naija said when they got out beyond Walt. "This morning he tried to give me part of his energy bar. 'You need it more than I do. I'm pretty useless right now,' he said. I couldn't take it, though, even as hungry as I was. He would have thought I agreed with him that he's useless."

Dal slid the stone in place. It held. He turned, satisfied and ready to do it again. And again. And again.

"What about Walt's wife?" he asked, thinking of Ana. "Doesn't she keep him going?" Then he wished he hadn't said that. "What keeps you going, Naija? Is there someone or something you think of?"

"Me? I think of my fiancé, who gave up his life to put out a peat fire. He saved a white spruce forest from the big peat fire near Flin Flon, Manitoba. That's what keeps me going, Dal. I want to live and plant those white spruce and other trees out there in his honor." She pointed to the plane, where the top of one white spruce stuck defiantly out of the jagged hole. "After that, I have a big job waiting for me back home—taking care of Mori's preserve when he's gone. I have a lot to think about and keep me going. Don't you worry about me."

"I get how important the trees are, but our lives are more important, Naija," Dal said. "Be sure you take care of yourself, too." He turned back to the shore for another rock. She stayed at the end to chink the holes.

"I SAW WALT trip and nearly fall into that sucking bog when he tried to get up on the capstone at the beach end yesterday," Naija said when Dal returned with another large, jagged stone. "I'm afraid he'd better not try to walk out here. He just wants to be useful. We have to give him something else to do. How about cooking and tidying up?"

"Cook what, Naija?" Dal said. "We don't have the food yet. You've got to be practical and take any food he offers you. Your face is thinner. He's not moving around as much as you are, either."

Naija ran the back of her hand gently over Dal's forehead and down his cheek. She ended with a pat on his shoulder before turning to walk back to shore. Lately Dal always arranged for her to walk ahead of him on the causeway. That way he could watch and catch her if she were to trip on the uneven top. That hadn't happened so far.

THE SUN CIRCLED three quarters of the horizon before they finished the remaining feet of the causeway. Dal's mind wandered as he mechanically pushed and pulled and hauled stones. One image in addition to Ana's face stuck in his mind. Like an errant wail, it kept him moving. He had seen it for the first time in the books at Mori's place.

It was a poignant photo and description of Robert Falcon Scott, dead in his tent with his two mates when they were found on November 12, 1912, eight months after they had died. That was more or less this same time of year. But what a different place Antarctica was back then. The Ross Ice Shelf was not a watery bay, for example.

Scott lay frozen between Bowers and Wilson when their ragged tent was found. His jacket and sleeping bag were both thrown open to the cold, while his two companions looked peacefully wrapped in their bags on either side of him. Why had Scott opened his sleeping bag and shirt to the cold like that? Why was he not wrapped up against the bitterness of that long blizzard that did them in?

The other two explorers in the tent were known via Scott's journal to have died before he did. Dal thought maybe Scott couldn't stand being alone. Maybe, hopeless of rescue, he wanted the cold to carry him off from that great solitude as fast as possible so he could rejoin his companions.

He remembered the filmed ceremonies they had watched at school commemorating the anniversary of the end of the historic Ross Ice Shelf. The bodies of Scott and the others had already floated away, embalmed in some unrecorded ice calving long before expected.

Later, Dal and his mom watched a plaque-laying ceremony on their home screen, with Elgar's "Jerusalem" playing in the background. The ceremony took place in St. Albans Cathedral, England, where a plaque for Scott was placed along with the other graves transplanted from the flooded Westminster Abbey.

Dal had not known this full history back then, of course, until he read about it in Mori's library. It was his mother's inexplicable weeping that he remembered most. And his father patting her shoulder. And himself, as a boy, standing at her knee trying to console her. He still didn't know exactly what she had been crying about.

It probably would not have been for the long-dead explorers. And if it were for a submerged city, why not Charleston instead of London? If for Westminster Abbey, why not for St. Michael's Church in Charleston? Yet Dal had never seen her weeping for those. So just what was it that bothered her? He resolved to try and talk with her about all this when, not if, he ever got away from here.

She was still a puzzling mother. Dal didn't know what she thought most of the time. He knew she was passionate about insects, of all things. And the long-extinct animals that paraded on their house's interior walls. And the ice-covered places that used to exist. All that was a downer for him to live with, really, even though the walls were always covered with beautiful pictures. Why had she not understood that the present is more important? Why had she not been content just to be alive with him in the here and now?

One has to accept the world as it is and go on, Dal told himself. He felt resolutely sure of that. *I don't want Mom needing to cry over me. She is happily oblivious, not aware that I'm here. She doesn't know. Nor does anyone else. Not even Ana. Only Mori can know. What is going on in Canada that Mori hasn't sent Aron to help?*

With this thought, Dal pushed his Perseus button three more times. This would be his last try—he hoped it went through. If a message wasn't received this time, it never would be. *In either case, I will live day by day, and hope.*

23

... Did you know hemoglobin
and chlorophyll have similar structures?
That we're almost trees
almost being us. O hyperemerald cousins.
O o....
Green of the tipping point
between the world being drinkable
and the world being dry.
—Bob Hicok, "The Impulse: To Hold," 2018

NOVEMBER 24 AND 25, ANTARCTICA

Finally, the causeway was completed just enough that Dal and Naija could cross it and climb into the plane. They banned Walt from helping with this part and gave him a shore job instead. "It's for your own safety, Walt," said Naija. "You are too important to risk falling in. We need you for the trees."

Dal and Naija threw things around the wrecked plane in a frantic triage until they had all the food secured in their packs, pockets, and hands. They carefully carried it back to camp, where they laid it out and tallied it as if it were gold.

"Let's have double rations today," said Walt.

"No way," said Naija. "Too shocking for your digestive tract after eating so little. We will start with soup today. Highly caloric, but still soup. Sorry I forgot the pain pills, Walt."

Dal didn't protest eating the soup. He trusted Naija. And Walt didn't protest the missing pain pills, either, once Dal told him it would be hard to balance on the causeway if he took them. They were all weak from the extreme effort of building it.

Done in, they lay about resting all day. Dal got up in the afternoon to dig a bigger sleeping pit, and even that little bit of exertion made his heart race. So much for heavy labor on starvation rations. No one tried to return to the plane for the rest of the day.

THE NEXT MORNING, Dal lay curled in the shallow hollow he had scraped out, with rocks stacked around part of the edge as a windbreak. He turned onto his back and his feet hit the end, dislodging a small rock, which rolled underneath him. He sat up, threw the rock out, and lay back down. Each of them had one of these sleeping hollows, made to size. It hadn't rained yet; they might turn watery if it did. Dal couldn't wait to get the air mattresses out of the wreck. That would happen on the next trip out. Maybe today was the day for that. He breathed fast, and his heart pounded. Was it nerves or physical? He hoped the sensation would stop soon.

"OKAY, WALT," NAIJA SAID. "One, two, three—now pour it and smile." In the absence of champagne, Walt poured fresh waterfall water on the large capstone that formed the first big step up onto their proudly finished causeway. She took a picture of their ceremony with Walt's tiny camera. They were all feeling better after full rations.

They each took a sip of the brandy Dal had rescued, then clapped and cheered, as if this were the New Golden Gate Bridge opening again.

The celebration had been Naija's idea. Dal thought it would be enough of a celebration if they grabbed all they could from the wreck as fast as possible. But she had wanted to mark the end of extreme drudgery, as well as try to restore Walt's lagging spirits.

"I didn't do anything," Walt said, at first declining the christening role. "You two did it all. I'm out of the picture."

"No, you were absolutely necessary," Naija replied. "You rolled down all those rocks, got water, and cheered us up when we were exhausted at night."

She piled on the compliments until Walt finally began to smile. Dal suspected Walt smiled just to humor her so she would stop fussing over him. Walt had at last agreed to join in inaugurating the causeway, and he did his part well.

"I christen thee 'Slippery Rock Causeway,'" he bellowed.

"Great name," Dal said, slapping Walt on the back.

"I can't wait to get this leg healed so I can go out there with you two," Walt said. "You've done all this together. It's not that I was left out of the fun—well, actually, let's face it: I was."

"Sure, right, Walt, it was all a lot of fun out there," Dal said. "Unloading the cabin. Wading through things. Carrying boulders. Wish I had had an injury instead."

Walt shoved and punched Dal playfully. Dal punched him back lightly. Walt took a good swing, Dal weaved, and Walt fell to the ground. Dal pretended to trip over Walt and fell down beside him, laughing when he pulled Walt to his feet.

"Watch out, you two—don't get hurt," Naija said wearily.

"Enough fun and games—we have work to do," Dal said. "Get ready for incoming, Walt." Dal grabbed Naija's hand and walked slowly onto the rough causeway to begin their salvage. Walt sat on the capstone at the shore and waited.

"SHIT! WE DID make a dog's dinner out of this place," Dal said. Twisted and cut metal lay strewn all over the inside of the plane. The instrumentation was sliced wide open, eviscerated beyond repair. Dal couldn't pass by the comm system without trying to revive it. There was no response, of course. He hadn't really expected any. No light, no whirring, nothing coming to life. It was as dead as they all could have been if not for their extraordinary luck.

"How did we survive this?" Naija whispered. "Do you believe in any gods?"

"Not really," Dal said. "But some things can make you wonder."

They climbed over the bent seats back to the cargo area.

"Look at those saplings," Naija said. "They're still good and alive!"

"It's only been four days," Dal replied. "Of course, they are." He saw, however, that many of the branches drooped and the floor was covered with fallen needles and leaves.

"They need water," Naija said.

Dal took her hands and looked into her eyes. "Hold on a minute. I'm thirsty. You're thirsty. Walt is thirsty. We're hungry, too—horribly hungry. And tired. Too tired to care about trees yet. So, don't go wasting your pity on those trees. What's wrong with you and Mori, anyway, all worked up over trees? We wouldn't be in this godforsaken place if it weren't for those fucking trees." he immediately wanted to retract that when the realization hit him again: he was the one who'd wrecked the plane.

Dal's voice grew tighter and cracked. Naija held him tightly, her cheek against his, and stroked his lower back. Her breath was in his ear. She moved slightly and kissed his head. Then she pulled back and slid to the floor. She patted the place beside her, motioning for him to sit, too.

"Okay. We have privacy out here. Ask me anything," Naija said.

The plane rocked gently. "Better sit opposite," said Dal. He was not into talking right now. *Not a woman who likes to talk about feelings, please no,* he silently prayed to the god he did not especially believe in. At first, Dal could think of nothing to say or ask her. He sat down against the other wall to keep the plane from rocking.

After a bit, he said, "Well, there is one mystery I would like to know more about. You. Do you remember when Bill upset you, talking about the woman Mori met up north in Canada who ruined his business, and then Bill went on to insult the Inuit? If it doesn't make you uncomfortable, can you tell me about all that?" Dal asked.

Naija smiled slowly, as if she'd half-expected this. "Sure. Just between us, though—you must agree to that."

Dal nodded. "Of course."

"The woman Bill described was my great-grandmother. Mori is my great-grandfather. I did not know this until after his wife died. Mori did not want her to know, because they had no children of their own, and he thought her knowing about me would remind and depress her. Whenever he came up to visit us, he couched the trips as a charity project for our community. That is what I believed, too, for a long time.

"Mori told me all this fifteen years ago, after Rosemary was gone and when he began to think about mortality. He sent me and many members of my extended family to school in Winnipeg so he would have well-educated progeny capable of carrying on for him. He gave many others who were not related to him an education, too."

"Mori asked Cornel, my fiancé, and me if we would carry on his work of preserving trees for CO_2 drawdown after he dies and do our best to care for what is left of his forest. All that fits into my culture anyway, so we accepted."

Dal looked around the wrecked plane. He didn't know what to say.

Naija stood up abruptly and cocked her head toward the messy pile. "Let's get to work now." The talk was over.

"HEY, WALT!" DAL YELLED from the causeway. "Inch on back to the campsite and be ready to sort this stuff out. We're coming in with the first load."

The top of the causeway was slippery and uneven, more like walking over wet rocks in a stream than on a real walkway. Dal had filled his pack and arms with what he thought was most urgently needed. He first took all of the dried food he could manage. Then he added the shovel, the one large pail, and more tree stakes to dangle from the pack. Last, he tied a seat cushion onto the top.

Naija slowly emerged from the hole in the roof after him. She was carrying the rest of the food, two lightweight tarps, three blankets, deflated air mattresses, the medical kit, and another seat cushion. Her pack was higher than Dal's but weighed less.

The wreck wobbled again with their departure. Dal resolved to try and better stabilize it tomorrow. They would come back again to get everything else that might be of use. Maybe he would to try the communication panel again tomorrow, even though it looked completely destroyed.

He gave the hull one last glance. At least they hadn't been crushed along with it. Was this only their seventh day here? It seemed like forever. They'd been lucky, but he didn't expect the luck to last. Nothing in his life so far had made luck seem the least bit dependable. He would have to depend on himself.

Dal jumped off the capstone at the beach end and was surprised to sink so far into the muddy shore. He had landed eighteen inches above the high-water line, and yet it seemed slushier than on previous days. What did this mean? Probably nothing. Or maybe just the incremental rising and falling of the sea? He filed that observation away, slogged up the shore, and climbed the additional rise to their campsite. The heavy pack made him waddle side to side, like an adult penguin returning to feed the young.

Sweaty and out of breath, Dal dumped everything on dry ground. Walt limped over faster than Dal had ever seen him move.

"We'll have a good meal, tonight," Dal panted. Naija had dumped her load there, too.

"What took you two so long?" asked Walt.

"We had to sort through a big mess out there," Naija answered.

THAT NIGHT DAL SLEPT peacefully, unaware of any dreams. The air mattresses from the wreck made all the difference. Tomorrow, he reckoned, after shoring up the wreck a bit more and bringing in another load, they could start to build a shelter. He had gone to sleep thinking of that. Although Naija had other ideas of what they should do first, Dal was determined to prevail.

Building a secure shelter out of what they had at hand had come to him while he was out in the plane with Naija. With that stimulating purpose top of mind, he banished any more thoughts of Mori and trees and loneliness. Most of the titanium plates were at the bottom of the bog, but there was still plenty of rock.

Dal drew a diagram in the shore mud. The shelter would have stacked-stone sides, and they would use the last few titanium panels they had in the wreck for a roof. They would be held in place by more stones resting on the side walls. Although light and pliable, the panels were exceedingly strong. They would have to figure out how to bend the edges down and make sure the roof stones couldn't come crashing through the top. He would experiment with that.

At least they wouldn't have to use inverted boats for shelter the way

Shackleton's men had been forced to do on Elephant Island, where they survived for 137 days before rescue came. Dal knew their physical and weather situation was much better now, but the absence of any land or marine animals was a huge problem. There were no other food sources beyond what they had brought with them.

Dal hoped that the three of them would not be here long enough to eat all the food. Maybe they should start a ration plan now. Surely Mori would send Aron in time, but maybe they should ration anyway, just in case.

24

From the time Ron Naveen of Oceanites wrote in April 2017 of "only 12,000,000" Antarctic penguins still living in Antarctica, we have watched until their populations are now completely devastated by loss of food and habitat.

—"State of the Antarctic Penguin," *Journal of Extinctions,*
    spring 2117

NOVEMBER 26–DECEMBER 4, 2295
ANTARCTICA

It was their eighth full day in Antarctica. After a dinner of reconstituted stew with a fancy name but the same bland taste as all of the other dried food, Dal sat in his usual pose: slumped in a sandy pit with a cushion under him and a blanket around his shoulders. His skin was tanned copper by the never-setting sun.

The cascading waterfall was delightful to hear in the background. When Dal hiked high enough, he could see Ross Bay leading out to the Southern Ocean beyond. It formed a deep-blue horizon line a long way off beyond the boggy ground in front of them. Dal hated the bog. Treacherously, it had initially looked solid and so deceived him into crash-landing in this awful place. No inherent beauty could take that memory away.

Rocks of many colors, types, shapes, and sizes lay strewn about, moved here by natural forces. Many others had been strewn around by Walt. The largest rocks left huge gouges in the earth. The ancient ice that did the work of hauling stone to this area was now a part of the vast, enlarging ocean beyond the bog.

Dal liked the mountain view best. There was not much to do in the evenings, when fatigue took over. He usually sat alone, observing things around him and trying to think of some way to get out of there. He had begun to appreciate the smallest signs of comfort. Or if not really comfort, at least familiarity. The three of them gradually turned the extreme wildness to their use.

They had built a shelf of stone, the shelter was going up, the cooking area was set up, and they had improved their sleeping pits. All of this made for everyday sights and routines, which Dal had read were vital to maintain in a survival situation. The waterfall provided all the clean water they would ever need. These things created a certain comfort, but Dal still rebelled at the thought of getting used to this place.

Of course, there were the mountains, impressively massive, of sparkly, hard granite with white and black flecks and occasional clear lines of quartz running through. A volcanic mountain far off in the distance regularly let out smoky puffs.

The sunlight was never oppressive, always circling low around the horizon, though the circle lifted a little higher every day. Dal appreciated the sun here. He wished he still had his good armband to record these observations. Even old-fashioned paper and pen would do. He might be too busy to write down his impressions and thoughts once he got back. Despite the hardship and constant threat of danger, Dal vowed never to forget a few things about this unforgiving place.

Every few days they had seen rain falling somewhere, but oddly it was never over their camp. The clouds seemed to hang on top of the mountains, get stuck there, and dump moisture mostly on the north side. Plenty of water made its way down to them in streams and rivulets, though. Some of the moraine ground near the stream had good dirt deposits and might have been ideal for planting the trees. Dal thought maybe they should do that—plant the trees. Someday, but not just yet.

Naija strolled over to where Dal sat thinking about all he was in danger of losing back home. "Okay," she said, "we have had enough rest. We are eating regular meals. We have almost every last thing we could pry out of the wreck piled up over there on shore. Except for one more thing. And you know what that is."

"Not now, Naija, not now. Anyway, the dolly is broken, you know,"

Dal said, waving her away. He was gone, deep in a restorative reverie of Ana.

A DAY LATER, when they were gathered for breakfast around their "fire ring" with no fire, Naija looked for support from Walt.

"Walt, you know how important our mission is," she said. "If we can get the trees growing here, it would have positive repercussions for the whole world. Think of your career when we get back."

"Did you bring out the nitrogen-fixing compound and organic fertilizer yet?" Walt asked. "I see the shovels, stakes, and rope."

"No," Naija replied. "Dal told me it was too heavy for right now, and we ought to save our energy—right, Dal? I can't lift that stuff, and the dolly is broken, you know." Naija stared at Dal, who continued eating.

Walt peered up from his porridge. "I can help plant them now," he said. "I'm getting nimbler every day, and I haven't done much to help—at least not like you two have."

"Alright now. Just who do you folks think is going to haul those trees out of the plane, drag them down the causeway, find the best site, dig the holes, and stake 'em up? Not you two, that's for damn sure," Dal said, slamming his tin bowl down. "And I'm not ready to do it yet, as important as those trees are.

"We have to think about the 'what ifs.' What if we don't know how long we have to stay here? It's clear now our messages did NOT get through. Mori is thinking everything is just fine, so he'll wait until after we should have returned to come look for us. That could take a few days more at the very least. And we don't have extra food for that, much less calories enough to do heavy physical labor on top of surviving.

"We must keep minimally fit but also save energy. We should only do those things that directly benefit us. *Us*, not the trees. Like it or not, this is not a high-and-mighty mission for trees and the planet anymore. This is now just a routine survival situation, and I've seen enough of those to know. We can't forget it for a minute. Saving ourselves is numero uno. Case closed."

Naija replied evenly: "It's a shame just to let the trees die out there after coming all this way for the single purpose of planting them to start new life here and potentially save a whole continent."

"We have a hut to finish first, Naija," Dal said, before turning to Walt.

"Remember that mossy place we saw from the plane before we landed, Walt? The one in the hanging valley above the waterfall? I was thinking we should go up there and see if there is any peat underneath the moss that we could cut into blocks and stack to dry out, the way they used to do for fuel long ago. I read about it. We can take our time with that, and it will give us just enough exercise to stay fit and able to stumble to a rescue plane. Peat might be useful besides."

"We have 138 heat cubes now," Naija said. "That is at least as much as we have food. What will we need peat for?"

"Didn't I just explain?" Dal asked. "We don't know when we can actually leave here. Our messages apparently did not go through. The Perseus must be dead. And Aron could look for us for a long while before ever finding us.

"The weather is good now, but what about wintertime? It will be dark, and we'll have to keep warm. We'll have to heat water to drink and cook. We ought to ration food and heat cubes, too, and I recommend we start doing that this week."

Walt coughed. "Are you nuts?" he said. "We can't stay here that long! Until winter? No way can we do that. My wife will worry herself to death. She may go off with someone else if she thinks I'm not coming back. Plus, I can't stand even the short days of winter back in Canada without my special light. Having no daylight at all is just not possible for me. Not possible! I would rather die if it comes to that."

"Don't worry, Walt," Naija said, patting Walt's shaking hand. "Mori will figure out that we are stranded and send for us. Dal, I am sure that if we ever did burn peat, that would bring on the Black Coats for sure. Dirty stuff. Completely outlawed. The atmospheric sensors would catch it and find us. No good."

"Maybe we should do it then," said Walt.

"We're not quite desperate enough to hand ourselves over to the Black Coats yet," Dal said. "Might never see our loved ones again.

I merely meant that cutting and stacking peat could be a purpose-ful light activity, that's all. Better than just sitting around waiting for something to happen."

Dal wished he had Naija's faith that Mori would figure it all out in time. He hoped Mori would not die before he could rescue them. Remembering Bill's comments about Mori's age and health made Dal draw his jacket closer and zip it up.

Tomorrow he would bring up the peat-cutting idea again. And he knew Naija would bring up the trees again, too. She was determined to plant them as soon as possible. Dal also wanted to get the mission done somehow or other. Thinking to avoid daily arguments about it, he decided to negotiate.

"Naija, how about this?" he said. "When rescue arrives, we can ask whoever comes to get us to help plant the trees. We need the help any-way. Meanwhile we can keep them alive while they're still out there in the plane. It's easier to water and feed them there than it will be to haul them out. Plus, just the act of bringing them off might destabilize the whole wreck. It'll be nearly impossible for anyone to find us if that wreck goes under."

"Right," said Walt. "Okay, I agree with Dal now." The matter seemed settled, at least for the moment.

NAIJA AND DAL kept going back out to the wreck every day, ostensibly to be sure there were no usable scraps left in any little cracks. They brought back random knobs and pieces of plastic. And sometimes they carried back fallen leaves and pine needles for their beds. At Naija's urging, Dal lugged heavy pails of water out to the trees every other day.

While Naija and Dal lingered in the wreck, Walt limped back and forth on the shore, or sat on a rock staring at the dusty but still glim-mering wreck at the end of their uneven, rocky bridge. He twisted his wedding ring on his finger and stared down the causeway. Sometimes he rambled over the rocks at the bottom of the mountain behind their beachfront, looking for routes upward that he might be able to man-age. That was how he verified the small, peaty bog that he proudly reported during their meager lunch the next day.

"That's wonderful, Walt," said Naija.

"Might be useful—glad you checked it out," said Dal.

"I'm going to try to walk on the causeway tomorrow," said Walt, flush with success.

"Don't you do that, Walt," said Naija, pointing her finger at him sternly.

"Maybe if I help him?" asked Dal. "How about that, Walt?"

"Don't need help," said Walt. "I can do it by myself."

Dal stood up and towered over Walt. "You are an important member of the team, Walt. We will need you especially when it is time to plant the trees. We can't risk losing you by your slipping off the causeway."

Naija rose from her squatting position and began to dance slowly. She bent over in swooping circles with her arms flung out like a big bird in flight.

"What on earth are you doing?" asked Walt.

"I am calling on the wisdom of the snowy owl to keep you from endangering yourself," sang Naija.

Dal hooted and clapped.

"Can you also ask Father Owl to let Mori know we need help now?" Dal sang back to her as she swirled and swooped.

"I'm switching my message to that immediately, yes," Naija sang. "Walt has received enough wisdom by now not to go drown himself in mud." She continued to swoop and bend in her graceful dance. Before long, Dal joined her. Walt stood up and waved his arms, weaving from his waist and sending a message to Mori, too.

"WHERE DID YOU get those rips in your pants?" Naija asked Walt two days later.

"Just a slip, that's all," Walt replied. He adjusted his prized tan Tilley hat and drew the string tighter under his chin.

"Not out on the causeway, I hope," said Naija.

Walt just smiled when Naija launched into a safety lecture. Dal watched it all, bemused. Walt was walking more steadily than ever, he thought.

"MAYBE I'LL TRY it again tomorrow, if my nerves hold up." Walt squinted up at Naija when she and Dal found him the next morning sitting on the capstone end of the causeway with his legs over the side and his feet muddy.

"It's still too uneven and slippery out there," she said. "Best not to go any farther."

Dal turned his face away when she said that so Walt couldn't see his smile. Truth was, he and Naija enjoyed the time alone out there in the wreck. After watering the trees or some other convenient chore, they would sit on the floor talking, one of them on each side of the wreck to keep it stable.

By now there was no practical reason for them to return to the plane together, but Naija still went once a day anyway, just to look at the trees. Dal said he went with her for safety, and every other day he carried the watering pail. Today had started out like all the other days with a careful walk out to the wreck.

Dal had given up expecting the comm system to come back to life. Nevertheless, he still went forward and turned all the knobs and pushed every panel on each visit. Today, when Naija looked forward from the cargo area, she saw Dal punching the broken panels in frustration.

"What are you doing, Dal?" she exclaimed. "You'll cut yourself on those jagged places."

Dal grabbed the closest panel hanging off the console and with both hands ripped it off and tossed it through the open roof. It clattered across the top of the plane, then slid into the bog. All the comms portals were destroyed beyond repair. The Perseus was a failure, too.

Dal climbed to the back and dropped down to the dirty cabin floor. Tears edged out of his eyes, and he rubbed them with thumb and forefinger, as if tired. Naija sat down beside him and cradled his head in her arms. She wiped the mud from his face and gently kissed his cheek. Dal hugged her tightly, and then his shoulders began to shake in silent sobs. He cried for Ana, for his mother, for his father, for everyone he knew and feared he might never see again. Neither of them spoke a word. He felt Naija's quiet presence through his despair.

After a while Dal gathered himself, and Naija left to scrape any fallen tree needles into a pile. He reached around for little pieces of debris they had missed before, climbed out, and threw them overboard, watching until every last speck was sucked down. Only an occasional item stayed afloat longer than the rest. Then he walked carefully back down the causeway with Naija, strode wordlessly past Walt sitting at the nonfire ring, and stopped beside the rock pile. Dal bent down to pick up another large, jagged stone and lugged it back down the causeway. He dropped the stone strategically near the tail of the plane to try and stabilize it. That wreck really must stay afloat if they were ever to be found.

It was a battered shell now, with nothing left inside except for the trees, tree supplies, and the broken dolly. After his next trip out with a stone, Dal swept an armload of tree needles into his shirt and carried them to shore to make a fragrant matting for Naija's bed.

"DAL, I THINK Naija is right," said Walt at breakfast. "Planting those trees now is the best thing we can do after we finish the hut. Even before we cut the peat."

"You just don't want to dig the peat, do you, Walt?" Dal said. He looked at the date on his watch. December 4. He knew Walt could not deal with the thought of winter darkness, which peat brought to mind. But it was early December, not even the brightest high summertime in the Antarctic. They had months to go before shorter days would begin, before darkness would squeeze around their ever-shorter periods of sunlight, squeezing down until there was no sunlight at all.

"No, it's not that," Walt replied. "Imagine if we don't ever get to leave here. At least we will have left an imprint. Better that than to have nothing at all come of what we've been through."

"None of that," Dal said. "We're going to be rescued, so let's just stay in shape to be able to stand up and walk to the plane when it arrives." His jaw was set. He had none of the usual crinkling around his eyes.

Dal continued: "If Mori doesn't send Aron to rescue us by December 17, we might have to draw attention to ourselves. I've been thinking that at that point we should start a fire, using refraction if our matches don't work. That will draw the Atmospheric Police. They monitor the whole earth. Since we're not supposed to be here anyway, someone will come running."

"And I know just what you will propose to burn!" exclaimed Naija. She jumped to her feet with clenched fists. "I would die for those trees! As long as I have a breath in me, I will not let you do that!"

"Burning the trees might in the end be the best way to save us," Dal said, standing up and facing her. "It will save all our lives, even if we have to deal with Black Coats in the rescue party."

"I don't know about that," interjected Walt. "Might laser us first and talk later." Then he said, "Sit down, you guys—giving me a crimp in my neck, looking up at you two."

Dal remained standing and began to pace around the ring. "I only propose we burn the trees *after* it is completely clear that no one we can trust is coming. To show that I have good faith about this, I also think we should be selecting the exact planting site and digging the holes right now, while we still have energy for that. I will start tomorrow. Right after we dig the holes, we should institute three-fourths rationing.

"I won't mind so much if the Black Coats come by then, if we'll have waited as long as we could for Aron. Anybody at all will do by then," Dal concluded.

This was his last-ditch plan for getting back to Ana, or at least getting word to her of what had happened to him. She was planning a wedding and waiting for him, oblivious. What would she do if he never came back? This thought destroyed Dal. He imagined her at home in her yellow dress. She would be reading and listening to music, but she would look up at the door every few minutes, one ear cocked to hear the airlock open and his footsteps coming down the hall.

WALT PROUDLY LED them up to the site he had selected for the trees. It had the best soil he could find, but it was in the hanging valley, near the rippling stream that formed part of the waterfall.

"Couldn't you find an easier place to get to?" asked Dal.

"This is a beautiful spot for them," said Naija. "Sheltered from wind, yet fully open to the sun. I love it!" She leaned against a tree stake and panted. Her face was flushed. *Was it the exertion?* Dal wondered. No, she had looked like that at breakfast, too. He remembered that she hadn't eaten her whole allotment of food, either. He decided to keep an eye on her.

"Dal, would you bring the bags of nitrogen-fixing compound up here?" Walt asked. "I can be preparing the soil."

"I see my future," Dal joked. "Just the mule again, right?"

"You got it," Walt said, a grin spreading over his face when Naija hugged him. Walt pushed her away. "You're way too hot a chick for me today."

Dal made a point of hugging her, too. She did feel unusually warm. Maybe it had been the steep walk up there.

"Please dig holes a bit small now, Dal," Walt said. "We can enlarge them later. I just need enough soil to mix my compounds."

"It might take me a couple of days to dig holes, carry water for the trees, and get that compound up here, Walt," Dal said. "We're supposed to be on lower rations after tomorrow, you know, so we don't run out." Dal set to digging two holes and afterward began lugging the nitrogen mixes up. Walt got to work measuring and mixing the proper planting soil in piles.

THE NEXT MORNING Dal climbed up to the hanging valley right after breakfast to knock off the rest of his digging chore before he got too hungry. He'd thought Naija would try to come up, too, but she stayed down below, sitting on the capstone. Her hair was stringy and damp, and her shirt was already sweaty, well before any exertion.

Dal yelled down to her, "Wait for me! I'll come right down to help with the watering." He wondered where the new antibiotics were in the medical kit. That was all he had to give her, although they were often of no help against emerging diseases. Even the newest antibiotics quickly became useless. At least there was old-fashioned aspirin, and maybe an immune-system booster. As he ran down the hill, Dal's legs felt wobbly at the thought of Naija being ill.

25

The majority of babies born in countries where populations are not culturally accustomed to high heat levels are now conceived via IVF, iPS, cloning, sperm aggregation, and/or using an artificial womb. "Normal" human pregnancy is increasingly likely to be an accidental event.
—*Journal of Obstetrics*, July 2263

DECEMBER 4, 2295
ORANGEBURG, SOUTH CAROLINA

Ana Chambeau had a decision to make. Every night since he had left, she'd prayed for Dal, as always. But for the past two weeks, she had felt uneasy, as if God might have turned a deaf ear to her. At first she thought her feelings might be hormonal because of the tiny person growing inside her. Being a woman of action, however, Ana would not sit with her turmoil for long.

"Hello? Is that you, Ana?" Risa Riley answered tentatively into her new armband. She barely knew how to use it. It was a gift from Jim in celebration of their grandchild to come, even though she had not been properly informed. They had not seen Ana since her quick visit weeks before.

"Hi, Risa—yes, it's me. I wondered if we could talk about a few things concerning the wedding. I would ordinarily pass these by Dal, but since he's away, I thought you might know what he would like best. We didn't have time to discuss details before he left."

"Of course, dear," Risa replied. "Fire away. Would you like to come over here? Or I'm happy to come to you."

"Well, that would be so nice, but I need your answers right away," Ana said. "And I may be catching a cold, so it's better if I don't share it." She hated lying to Risa, but she didn't want to see her in person, as she might figure out Ana was pregnant. Or Risa might notice how on edge she was. This way, Ana reasoned, she could ease into asking about Dal and not cause Risa to worry.

"You take care of yourself, Ana, especially now. Have you had your universal viral vaccine?" Risa asked. "Do you need any hot soup?"

"No, thanks for the soup, but I'm really okay," Ana replied, "and yes, I had my shots. I'm making the guest list now. Can you please tell me how many people you think Dal would like to invite to the wedding?"

"I have no idea," Risa said. "I think you might want to keep it small and family-oriented, especially now."

"What do you mean, 'especially now?'" Ana asked. "Is everything all right? Have you heard anything from Dal?" She struggled to keep her voice calm.

"No, honey, not a word. But that's not unusual at all."

"You have no idea when he'll be back?" Ana asked.

"Not really, but surely before the wedding," said Risa "He's not going to want to miss that!" she laughed.

"Okay. What about attire? Does he have a formal suit?" Ana tried again.

"He might from his Rescue Corps years, but Jim doesn't have one. It really will be easier on all of us if this is a low-key and casual affair. Particularly better for you."

She has got to know! Ana thought, or else Risa wouldn't keep harping on that theme. Still, Ana wouldn't admit she was pregnant until she got to speak with Dal. "If he calls, let me know then, okay?" she said.

"I will surely do that, yes," Risa replied. "Jim and I are very, very happy you two are getting married. We didn't have a chance to properly tell you on your last quick visit, you know."

She sounds aware. I know she is! thought Ana. But still she wouldn't let on.

"I'm so glad you are happy," she said. "Dal and I are totally happy, too. I look forward to spending the rest of my life with him," Ana added, choking up over those last words. Getting control again, she said, "I'll take a guess at the number of guests and put a list together. May I run it by you later?"

"Don't you worry, Ana. We've seen Dal disappear without a single comm for two or three months at a time. I'm sure everything is all right."

These words brought Ana very close to tears. Risa could really get next to you. "Okay, great—'bye for now," Ana said, signing off as quickly as she could.

She sat very still, her thoughts swirling. Then she opened the drawer in the table next to her bed and took out the grass paper onto which Dal had copied Mori's letter. She reread Mori's comm, then listened again to Dal's last voice comm from Canada.

"You might not like what I'm about to do, Dal," she said aloud. He had told her not to try to comm him back, and she never had before. When she finally tried in desperation, his armband didn't respond. Things were so different now from what they had ever been before their engagement. She really must know where he was and that he was safe.

Within 20 minutes, Ana had booked a rocket flight to New Churchill. Sadly, it would not leave for ten days. All flights to Canada were overbooked, as usual. She vowed to call back every day to check whether there was a cancellation. She lay down on the bed and hugged the softest pillow there, the one that Dal liked best.

26

A stone marker will be dedicated on Saturday, December 7, at 1 p.m. to those heroic firemen who finally extinguished the Hudson Bay Lowlands Peat Fire. This fire had burned for thirty-eight years, increasing respiratory illnesses among our citizens. The ceremony will be held in Seahorse Gully Square at noon. We hope everyone will turn out to honor our heroes.

—Public announcement by Hudson's Bay Watch

DECEMBER 5, 2295
NEW CHURCHILL, CANADA

Henri rushed down the hall to Mori's suite. At the anteroom door, he slowed down and took a few deep breaths. It had been way too busy at Willow Park House since Bill and Carmina Hernan had come to stay. Henri fervently hoped they would go back home soon. Mori had succumbed to Bill's plea to stay for a while in order to avoid the Black Coats back in New Ushuaia. Even holding the papers he needed, Bill continued to say he felt safer here with Mori.

"Yes, you can stay as long as you need to," Mori had said. "I put you in this fix. But you must never cause an uproar here again." Of course, Mori didn't know that Bill had broken the Perseus. Nor that Henri had gotten it back from repairs four days later. *No need to upset the boss,* Henri told himself. *Must keep him as healthy as possible. And I got it fixed, after all. Only took four days. Goes to show how kind Mori is, that he let Bill stay on. What sort of person would ever have thrown a delicate machine like that Perseus relay across the room?*

Henri quietly opened Mori's door. Mori was lying on his side in bed. "Sir? It's time for your shot now."

Mori rolled to his back and stretched his thin lips across his teeth. "Thank you, Henri." He held out his arm. "Where is my armband?"

"I took it off you because it cut you, remember? That day back when Bill grabbed your arm so hard? Now it's too big and heavy for you. Don't worry, sir. I check the system every hour and wear the band all night and day."

"Very good," said Mori. "I must know if Naija or any of them call me and are in trouble. Immediately, you hear. Miss that girl. She's my solace."

"I know, sir. I will certainly do that, Mr. T."

"About Bill—"

"Yessir?"

"I want to put him in my will. I realize I didn't treat him right over that land deal long ago. I want to leave him some money. And you know that I'll take good care of you, too, Henri."

"Thank you, sir. But no worries or hurry about that. You are not going to leave us." Henri's voice grew strained. "Now please turn over for your shot. You need to stay strong, at least until Miss Naija comes home."

"You are so right, Henri. That reminds me: Will you please make a contribution for me to the Firefighters Fund? There will be a ceremony in town soon commemorating the Great Peat Fire. And you remember that poor Cornel, Naija's fiancé, was killed fighting to save the spruce trees in that awful fire near Flin Flon. We must honor all our firefighters." Mori closed his eyes as he turned.

"Yes indeed, sir. I am planning to go to the ceremony to represent this house. That was a terrible time for her and for everybody." Henri pushed his sleeve up to check the time, as the medication had to be given precisely on schedule.

There was Mori's own band, large and blinking normally, tight on Henri's pudgy arm. Henri worried that if Bill ever found out what this band was for, he would try to steal it, or try to ruin either the band or the Perseus relay again.

Mori still didn't know about the fiasco with the broken Perseus. Henri was relieved that no signal had ever come through after the

Perseus was repaired. Everything must be fine in Antarctica. He did worry a little about whether anything bad could have happened during the four days when the Perseus was completely down. At least Bill still did not know where Dal, Naija, and Walt had gone. Or that this armband and the Perseus were supposed to be their lifelines.

THAT SAME EVENING, Henri reluctantly carried a big dinner tray to the Hernans' room. "They should come to the dining room," he grumbled. "Just one more thing for me to have to do." He paused outside the door and listened. He always checked before knocking, snooping a bit because he didn't trust Bill.

Mori had told Henri that Bill complained to him about Dal, saying that Dal had beaten him up and pulled a knife on him. Henri didn't believe that, not for one minute—unless Bill had deserved it. That, Henri could well imagine. He had heard Bill speak roughly, even to his loyal Carmina.

Henri put his ear to the Hernans' bedroom door and listened. Bill sounded agitated, as he often seemed to be lately. His voice grew louder. "Carmina, listen to me! I don't care how much you want to go home and tend your garden and see your mother. We're sitting on a G-D gold mine right here, and I intend to stay here until at least a part of it is mine. Preferably all of it!"

"But Bill, *mi amor*—"

"No sweet-talking 'buts' from you," he said. "You're going to do exactly what I say, do you hear? We have to play this cool and stick together. Where is that ridiculous Henri with our dinner?"

Henri heard Bill's heavy footsteps coming to the door and quickly backed away. The door was yanked open and an angry Bill, seeing Henri standing there with the big tray, changed his expression to smarmy.

"Ah, there you are," he said. "Been here long? I didn't hear you come up. Come on in and put the tray there on the coffee table. No need to set our places, we'll do that. Now, off with you. Can't keep Carmina over there hiding from you in her nightgown. We're very tired. Oh, and come back with some more of that artificial whiskey slop, will you? The bar's empty in here."

OVERCOME WITH ANXIETY, Henri trudged up to his rooms on the top floor and lay down on his bed. He covered his eyes with a pillow. He wasn't going to take any "whiskey slop" to that man. He had a new problem to manage, in addition to his continued concern about what might have happened during the four days when the Perseus was down.

Now Henri worried about how Bill might try to get control of Willow Park and the Forest Preserve for himself. All that was meant to be for Miss Naija to carry on Mori's work. He would have to warn Mori somehow without upsetting him too much. He could see that Mori was going downhill on these half-doses of his stabilizer medication. Henri tossed from side to side atop his bedcover. *Oh, what to do!*

27

A sanctioned flag expedition of the International Explorers Club was poised to traverse the Ohio Range of the Transantarctic Mountains in Antarctica from Eldridge Peak to Mirskey Ledge, including a climb of Mount Schopf. This would have been the first such expedition to the area. Unfortunately, the expedition is on hold until the final governing disposition of the continent can be decided.

—*International Explorers Club Journal,* March 2295

DECEMBER 5, 2295

ANTARCTICA

"Couldn't we just plant the smallest ones?" Naija cajoled again. "Ourselves? Now?" Her earlier fever, or whatever it was, seemed to be over. She looked fit and beautiful in her exotic way, although grimy from the dirty task of chinking up the rock walls of their new shelter. The walls now stood nearly five feet tall.

They would continue to build the walls to just over six feet in order to give Dal some headroom. There would be no windows, at his insistence. He had not said why. He didn't want to repeat that they might have to spend a winter here, and it would be cold. The shelter was small, only eight by eight. Hopefully, they would not have to ever use it. In any case, Dal enjoyed sleeping outdoors now.

He patted Naija's cheek to try to get her to stop talking, pointedly ignoring her repeated request, which she advanced in any number of creative ways. "You are the 'No Guy,'" Naija grumped. "Always saying, 'No this' and 'No that.'"

"I thought you were happy with watering the trees in the plane," Dal said. "We'll have more help when Aron gets here."

"Sitting in the plane is not as good for them as being in the ground," she retorted. "Or in the fresh air."

"They get plenty of fresh air and some sun as well through that gaping hole in the roof, Naija."

"Well, whoever comes for us is going to want to leave immediately," she tossed back. "He won't want to stay here to plant trees."

"Maybe, but we'll force him," Dal replied. "We won't leave without putting the trees in the ground first. The trees will be okay for a long time in the plane. I've seen my dad keep orange seedlings alive for months before planting."

"Yeah, sure, Mr. No Guy!

"Walt, can you please find a small rock to fit in this hole here?" Naija called out, pointing to a niche in the shelter wall. She turned her back on Dal. The tree subject always returned, like an itchy nerve. He liked her so much and was sympathetic with her goal, but they must prioritize their own survival first.

THAT NIGHT, WHILE WALT SLEPT with an arm over his eyes to keep out the evening light, Dal and Naija met in the hanging valley above the camp. It had become their other favorite spot. Dal climbed the knoll quickly, going straight up instead of using the switchbacks Walt had worn in when hunting rocks.

The scooped, moist valley could become a verdant meadow one day, Dal imagined, drawing from his mental archive of Risa's films. It would be filled with wildflowers in the summer, especially tall and colorful flowers that live on creek banks, such as bluebells and "butter and eggs." Maybe in the distant future some herd animals, perhaps elk or caribou, would lie in the mountain grass, chewing slowly on white cow-parsley blossoms. The deer would prefer columbine.

No. More likely, hordes of people from the north would swarm into such a lush place. They would tear up the ground for homes and cut down any trees Dal and Naija might succeed in planting. *They might think all of that to be good and necessary,* Dal mused.

He pushed aside these thoughts, which threatened to destroy his happy mood. Up here, Naija never mentioned the trees. It was a place of moratorium. She was already there. They watched the sun skim behind the mountain ever so briefly before reappearing to create dazzling light effects in the air.

THE HUT WAS FINISHED NOW. The plane was empty except for the trees. Each day was just like the one before. There had only been three days so far without a major task. Even with Naija and Walt to chat with, every day seemed endless to Dal now.

Yesterday Walt had killed one of the two squawking skuas that dive-bombed his head. A well-hurled rock had broken its wing. Walt pummeled it with other stones until it lay still among scattered and broken feathers. He plucked and cleaned it and washed it under the waterfall. Then he tried to boil the shattered bird for lunch, throwing it in their one pot along with two heat cubes.

"Yuck. I'll never want to cook in that pot again," Naija said.

"This is a gift from the heavens," Walt rebutted.

Naija spit out the chewy meat, which contained grit and tiny pieces of bone.

"I can't eat it—sorry," she said.

"Nice of you to try and scare up something different," Dal said. He took only one bite.

"It was self-defense, actually," Walt replied. "That creature came at me time and again. Got what he deserved. I'd do it again, even if we wouldn't eat the scrawny thing."

Naija looked at her plate with disgust. Walt seemed to be strung on a wire, his face drawn and his voice tight. Dal thought he'd heard him sniffling in his bag last night. Dal wasn't sure about the sniffling because of the din from the waterfall. But lately he had noticed how Walt's eyes were often red. He was sluggish in the morning and became more animated only in the evening. They had to encourage him to eat all of his portions. Dal knew the symptoms of depression and was concerned.

"How about let's start on the peat today, Walt?" Dal said. "We've been lazing around long enough. Waiting for rescue like this is getting to me. We'll all be better off with a little job to do. Lessons learned from Shackleton, and all that."

"You read too much at Mori's place, Dal," Walt replied. "What's the use, anyway? We're going to be stuck here, and no one is going to come for us. You and Naija have been afraid to say so, but I know that's why you wanted to build that lousy, airless little shed that no one wants to use. We won't be going back to Canada. Why don't we just get the cards out on the table now?"

Naija threw down her plate, the bird remains sliding off into the dirt.

"Now you just listen to me," she said, standing over Walt. "If we burn enough peat, the Atmospheric Police will detect it through their satellites. They will have to check it out. Maybe they will take pictures first. But after the robots inspect the photos and see us camped here, you can bet someone will be here in a flash."

"They may not be the people we want to see yet," said Dal. "A peat CO_2 emission would ruin our reputations forever back home. We could never go outside without someone throwing rotten stuff at us. Maybe we should wait for Aron. But we still could cut some peat and start drying it. That would at least give us something to do."

Naija broke in, almost wailing: "You're right, we cannot burn peat, I know. Or only maybe one little, itty-bitty bit. Peat is such awful stuff. It releases too much carbon, and if it were to get away from us, it would burn for years. We'd never get out of prison. But what else can we do?" She jumped up and threw her arms around Walt, who held onto her tightly, burying his face in her shoulder.

"Do you know any old Inuit chants, Naija?" Dal asked. "If so, I'd like to hear them." This made her laugh. Walt eked out a tiny smile.

"No, but I will make something up," she said, winking at Walt.

Then Walt laughed. Naija had found a way to lighten him up, and Dal was grateful. Once again, he watched her soothe and motivate Walt to action.

PEAT CUTTING WAS HARD WORK. At first, they had thought there might not be any peat under the surface of wispy moss. But after shoveling down through it, they came upon a thin layer of ancient peat laid down thousands of years before.

Dal's back ached from lifting the watery blocks out of the hole, even though he tried lifting from a squat to let his legs do the work.

"Make them smaller, Dal," Naija said. "Smaller pieces will dry faster. Here, let me show you how to shape it." She pushed her way into the hole and shaved the edges of a clump with her knife until she had a piece the size of an old house brick.

"There, that's perfect. If we stack them in a circle with openings all around, like a loose beehive, they will dry much faster and transport easily. This stuff is so wispy, though, it would burn too fast to provide much heat."

They left the bricks stacked close to the cutting area. Maybe they would move the load down to camp once it was dry and lighter to carry. They never considered burning it in the ground, not even if the idea was to summon the Atmospheric Police. Dal knew that ground peat fires could last for decades and do enormous damage to the atmosphere. Everyone was taught about the Great Peat Fires of Siberia. No, this was truly make-work, just something to do. Dal didn't intend to burn any of it. Once they had one small beehive stack completed, they stopped cutting it altogether, afraid that to continue might dry out the valley.

After this, they didn't talk about winter again, even though they had no idea what to expect. There had been reports of snow falling in the interior of Antarctica at the South Pole over the past couple of years, phenomenal amounts falling in what had been an icy desert. In eons of geological time this snow would cause a new ice dome to spread its icy fingers in East Antarctica once again. But would snow really fall and melt here at their campsite this year? Or would chill rain fall instead? Dal had no idea. Anyway, he was not going to be here for it. *This is all crazy to think about. Surely Aron will come before long.*

"I DON'T BELIEVE Mori got any of our messages," Naija said. "Not the Perseus, not the dancing and chanting, not the prayers." She and Dal lay facing each other, up in the hanging valley. Dal had hollowed out a larger nest in the ground, and Naija had filled it with fallen leaves and

needles from the trees in the plane and covered the fragrant crunch-
iness with a camp mattress pad. They started spending an hour here
every night, ostensibly to keep warm before separating for bedtime.

Dal absently stroked Naija's black hair and wished it were that of
his beloved redhead.

"I get the feeling Mori is just not receiving," Naija said for the second time. "He did not answer my chant from last night."

"We can't know if he's receiving or not. Maybe he is," Dal said,
hoping Naija would relax. There was nothing they could do about it
anyway. Dal now believed that Mori had not received the first Perseus or any of the others and that they were truly alone here. He felt
so alone that he wanted to get close to Naija, wanted to feel close to
anyone. He had tried talking with Ana in his mind, but that was not
the same as being with a real, warm person who understood what they
were going through.

Naija sounded worried, and he was, too. It was too much to face.

Tonight, Dal let himself be overcome by the strong smell of pine
needles mixing with her scent. He silenced Naija's gloomy talk with a
slow and careful kiss. Her full, soft lips kissed back, and his light hold
around her grew tighter. Naija pushed her small body fully against
the length of his, committing herself. Her touch was so different from
Ana's that Dal pulled back to see her face.

Eyes only a few inches apart, they studied each other, as if to ask,
Who are you? Are you the one I really love? Dal took in a big breath.
Their gaze locked together in painful realization that the answer for
both of them was, *No. You are not the one I love most. But you are the
one here now.* They held onto each other with determined, lonely, hungry desperation.

Naija's small body felt so unlike Ana's that it took Dal by surprise.
He could never pretend that Naija was just a surrogate. No, she was
herself. She was all Naija and definitely not Ana. Soon after that sank
in, and for a brief space of oblivious time, Dal was transported beyond
caring.

28

Dal still hadn't gotten the hang of sleeping in the never-ending sunlight of late astral springtime. It helped if he drew a corner of the blanket over his eyes or covered them with his arm. The constant light didn't seem to bother Naija as much.

Last night they had slept together in the hanging valley. Naija hadn't gotten up and gone to her separate sleeping pit the way she always had before, and Dal had not wanted to disturb her. She slept as if unconscious. This morning Walt found them together.

It was awkward. Walt went back down and waited for them at the nonfire-ring food station. He stood there, throwing fake coffee and hot water cubes into the one and only pot so that they clanged and the sound could be heard far off.

Dal was concerned about Walt. He had stopped doing much of anything except his food chores. His nails were red and bitten more than usual. He spoke less frequently and spent most of his time sitting on the near end of the causeway, staring out at the hated wreck. In those times, Walt constantly took his wedding ring off and put it back on. Occasionally he would lose it on the ground and call out in panic for someone to help him find it. Most often it was Naija who would run over, find the ring, and console him.

Today Naija was unusually quiet. She walked over to the nonfire ring, picked up their one large pail, and collected water from the nearest runoff. She was struggling down the causeway alone with it before Dal realized and chased after her.

"What are ya doing, Naija?" he called to her. "You know I must go with you for safety when we water the trees. They got watered yesterday, remember?"

"Aron is not going to show up here and report to Mori that we have not done our best," she flung back. "I owe him at least that."

Dal tore across the causeway. "Right now, you owe Mori exactly nothing," he yelled. He caught up to her midway across and reached to take the pail of water. Naija twirled away and shifted the pail to her other hand.

Dal's voice was low. "I think Walt needs our help today," he said. "Maybe we can explore the interior a little bit and take him along. Do something interesting and easy. We have to use our muscles a little bit to keep our health up. We watered those trees yesterday, don't you remember?" Naija silently turned back toward the wreck. "Stop this and save your strength," Dal said as he held her arm. "Your own life is on the line, Naija, and you're worried about what Mori will think of you? I can't believe you're being so impractical. Mori said your skills would be 'invaluable' to us here." Naija looked at him doubtfully. "Yes, that was the exact word. And he was right. But right now, you're acting a little crazy."

"Well, he also said that you would get us here and back again, and that you were the best pilot he could find anywhere," Naija retorted. She jerked her arm away and continued to stomp and stumble over the rocky causeway, lugging the pail and splashing water over her feet. The footing became more treacherous. She slipped, spilling more water, but regained her balance, her hair plastered to her neck from the effort.

Naija's face had been quite red again this morning, though her eyes had been clear. Putting this together with her odd behavior, Dal had an awful premonition. He followed her and reached for the pail again. "I'll help, then, if you're so dead set on doing this right now," he said gently. He wished the trees would all dry up, so they could no longer be a major point of contention between them. Naija steadied herself and, finally letting Dal carry the pail, staggered on toward the wreck.

Despite more carefully worded protests from Dal, the rest of the morning was spent ferrying water out to the root balls of the trees. But first they swept up the dry needles and leaves to add to the beds.

We would sleep better if the trees were all dead, Dal thought. Nevertheless, he carried pail after pail for Naija, who developed a glassy look in her eyes.

THE NEXT MORNING was windy and cloudy. Still, Naija insisted on watering the trees again. Dal thought she looked as though she should spend the whole day wrapped up in her bed. He had taken tea to her early and found her kicking her way out of her bedding and putting on her wind jacket at the same time.

"There is not much time left for me here, I'm sure," Naija said, "so I want to do the right thing." Dal saw that she was perspiring before any real exertion.

"What do you mean, 'not much time for me?'" Dal asked. "You meant to say 'for us,' right?"

"Whatever," Naija replied. She didn't look at him.

"You don't look right today, Naija," he said softly. "Take a rest. I'll see to this after breakfast. We might kill the trees by overwatering. Ever think of that?"

"No!" Naija jerked up her jacket zipper and trudged off to the causeway. Dal followed to help her with yet another heavy water pail. She skipped breakfast, so Dal had to do the same. He could neither tie her down nor keep her from walking the treacherous causeway alone.

WALT WATCHED ALL THIS from his prime seat beside the nonfire ring. He had been measuring their food supply and knew it was dwindling fast. They were on half rations, and still the food stack in the cache grew inexorably smaller.

Walt thought he would agree to further rationing at this point. Maybe he would tell them when they had their meager lunch together.

Meanwhile, he decided to prove his mettle and venture farther out on the causeway today. He could intercept them on their way back. They wouldn't be able to get past him or ignore him. And he could tell Dal and Naija all his worries and thoughts. He was sure Dal had been wanting to tighten up the rationing and would consider it very helpful if he were to suggest it.

Walt picked up the carved walking stick he had made from a dead branch Dal had cut from a sapling when Walt was first injured. He carved a little on it every night using Naija's pocketknife. He rarely needed the stick now unless going downhill, but it might be of help out on the causeway today. He stepped up onto the capstone with his good left leg, using the stick to balance and push off, and moved out slowly.

It's exciting to be out here! I'm about twenty feet out, twice as far as ever before. I'll stand right here until Naija and Dal come out of the plane. But after fifteen minutes, the wind and his unsteadiness forced Walt to sit down on the uneven surface.

It was an awkward situation. His legs dangled over the side and sank into the mud. Now his shoes would be slippery for the walk back. *How can I get up again without falling?* He felt uneasy. *Maybe I should have waited for them at the capstone after all.*

His confidence started slipping. *No, hold on! All I have to do is to wait for Dal and Naija to reappear, and Dal will steady me while I get to my feet. Dal can keep me from falling in, too. Dal can do almost anything.*

With this comforting thought, Walt settled down to enjoy the view back toward the shore and up to the mountains. He hated the plane anyway. *That disgusting wreck!* It reminded him of all the horrors they had been through. He hoped no skuas would come along and attack his head while he was out here. He pulled his special Tilley hat made in Canada down tighter on his head.

More time passed. He reflexively pulled his wedding ring off and put it back on again. *What is Ellie doing now? Maybe it's raining back home. And maybe the indoor tennis courts have burned down. Struck by lightning, perhaps. Yes, that's it!* The idea made him chuckle.

Soon I'll be back with Ellie and we'll straighten everything out. He fervently hoped so. *Hope is not good enough. I have to carefully think through exactly how it will go.* Walt imagined the loving comms they would exchange when he got back to civilization. Then he envisioned walking up to his front door with the "Welcome Home" banner above it and all his friends arriving for the big party Ellie would throw in his honor. He imagined everything in minute detail: the words on the banner, the food, the conversations, the sweet look on Ellie's face.

A gust of wind blew his jacket open, and Walt drew it together again. *Way too much time is passing.* He looked around. "Where the hell are they? You can't depend on anything or anyone," he said aloud. All of his doubts welled up again, and his vision blurred. He started pulling his ring off and on again; this time it slipped out of his muddy fingers, careened off the stones where he sat, and headed toward the edge. Walt panicked and grabbed for it. He missed. He watched as the silver ring, in what seemed like slow motion, hit an uneven stone, bounced again, and plopped into the colloidal bog, where it immediately sank out of sight.

He drew his feet up and lay down on his left side, stretching his right arm out into the mud where he thought the ring went in, hoping he would find it suspended just below the surface. Nothing. He tried reaching again and again, each time a little deeper and a little farther out. Nothing.

That ring was his one solid connection with home. He began weeping and calling softly for Ellie. "We are probably not going to get out of here," he said to her. All his fears and gloom descended to obliterate the tenuous grasp on hope he had struggled to maintain for so long.

Reaching for the ring one more time, Walt extended his chest out too far. With horror, he felt himself sliding off the side of the causeway. Panic took over. It was all his fault. He couldn't call for help and let them find him like this; not even Dal could haul him out, and if he tried, Dal might fall in, too. Feeling himself in the grip of malevolent fate, Walt didn't claw or struggle to grasp the slippery rocks. Instead, he covered his eyes with both hands. *This is how it will end. No one can get here fast enough to save me. Not even Dal.*

As he slid into the bog, Walt remembered something he had heard before: that thrashing about in a bog makes a person go down faster. So, believing he was irretrievably gone, Walt stirred with his arms and legs as hard as he could to get the inevitable over with quickly. He didn't call out for Ellie or Dal or Naija or anyone else. Within a few minutes, all that remained visible was Walt's tan hat floating jauntily atop the deceitful mud, not breaking the surface at all. Soon the bog smoothed over, appearing guiltless and, once again, like a good place to land a plane.

29

"To all ships and aircraft in distress: Avoid landing on any Antarctic island or the continental territory. Black Coats have started inspections for the UN Commission to ensure the area remains free of human or robot incursion until all land and mine claims are final. Penalties will be the stiffest possible."

—Bulletin to all vessels in the Drake Passage or environs, December 8, 2295

SAME DAY, ANTARCTICA

EXHAUSTED AFTER OVERWATERING the saplings, Naija slid down to the dirty floor of the hold, oblivious to the water oozing from the root balls and running in rivulets along the grooved floor. Her hair fell over her face. Dal squatted beside her and massaged her legs.

"You're strong, Naija. You can do it," he said. "I'll support you, and we will walk back slowly."

"Don't you tell Walt that I am sick."

"He might notice, but I will not say a word. I'll tell him you're taking the afternoon off, deservedly. Don't worry about him. He'll be fine without you at his side all the time. I will encourage him a lot. Right now we have to get some meds and food and water in you. You feel hot again." He added, "Don't worry about the trees—they have plenty of water now."

Naija nodded, her jaw slack and her lips parted. Her perspiration mixed with the water on the floor. They rested there for a while. Dal tried talking with her, but soon she could only mumble a few words. "Cornel" was one.

After a rest, Dal pulled her up and, supporting her body against his, climbed over to the exit. Naija held onto its rough edges with both hands, wobbling and gritting her teeth as Dal helped her down onto the causeway.

They began the precarious trip back to shore. Naija kept her head down and her eyes on her feet. They stopped to rest often. When they were twenty feet from shore, Dal saw that the causeway was muddier than earlier that day or on any other. Naija concentrated on putting one foot in front of the other, so Dal thought maybe she didn't notice.

He was on her right side so he could better see the unusual mud marks. Then he spied Walt's hat floating on the bog. His knees buckled, but he caught himself. He almost lost his hold on Naija, but from years of concentrating under stress, he pulled himself together. What was the hat doing out there? Walt loved that hat. It and the extra mud on the causeway gave Dal a bad feeling about all this. He held onto Naija even tighter. He must focus on her.

One more time in the final twenty feet to shore Dal stole a quick glance back to his right and immediately turned back to position himself to make sure Naija wouldn't see Walt's hat floating out there. That might be too big a shock for her. It was too much for him to assimilate, too.

He forced himself to talk to her. "Okay, we're almost back now. Not far to go. You are a celestial star, doing great. What a trooper! You're so strong! Don't worry, Naija, I've got you."

Once off the causeway, they stopped by the nonfire ring, where he positioned Naija to be looking at the mountains instead of back toward the plane. This was not her usual place, but she didn't protest. Her arms hung loosely, and her head drooped over her chest. Dal brought her an energy bar and water. "Where is Walt?" Naija asked in a monotone.

"No idea. Maybe he went back up to the peat—or is looking for skua eggs or something." Dal hoped he was right. He felt nauseous. "After that food goes to work, let's get you to bed for a while. I'll bring you some more meds from the kit. You'll feel better soon. This is probably the same thing you had before, and you bounced back from that beautifully. Might be it's a temporary fever caused by those mosquitoes. Take it easy. Let me pamper you." He forced a smile.

Naija's smile back was wry, using only one side of her now very pale face. There was not the usual light in her eyes.

"Rest here while I organize for you." Dal ran up to her sleeping hole, carrying the pail and her cup. He stopped by their waterproof cache in a small rocky opening to get some aspirin, general-purpose antibiotics, and immune boosters—the new ones that Mori had included in their kit. He shook out her sleeping bag and fluffed it, then positioned the water nearby.

I better dig another sleeping pit for me closer to her, he thought. His hands shook when he set the water down. Things were unraveling too fast—and right after they had reached agreement on how to deal with the trees until Aron came to pick them up. Dal had almost gotten used to the routines in this unwanted camp.

He looked over at the outdoor latrine he had built with its twisting entrance of four-foot high rock walls. It was close to Naija's bed. He had built it for her, to give her privacy. If the weather got too cool, they would have to move inside the hut, but that wouldn't be for a long time, if ever. *Walt's right. The hut is airless and awful.* Then he realized again that he didn't know for sure where Walt was.

THE PREPARATIONS FOR Naija's comfort didn't take long. Dal returned to the nonfire ring to find her lying on her side, asleep. He woke her and almost carried her up to her sleeping hole. "Here. Keep this and blow on it to call me if you need or want anything," he said. "Anything at all."

Dal handed her a small, silver toy whistle he always carried in his pocket. It was a gift from Ana, a play on one of her favorite vintage films featuring two movie stars who had been lovers both in the film and in real life. "Just whistle," he said to Naija. That's what Ana had playfully said to him. But this was not play.

Dal watched Naija swallow the meds and immediately fall back asleep. He ran back down the causeway to where Walt's hat still floated atop the bog. It looked to be a little bit farther away now. With small binoculars he scanned the shore up and down for any sign of Walt, then got on his knees and looked along the side of the causeway.

There, not quite perpendicular to the hat, he saw mud splattered up on the side rocks. This must be where Walt had sat down and his feet had first gone in, Dal surmised. None of the other side-wall rocks looked the same as in this place. The top of the causeway was muddier there, too. There was a big smear across the stones where Walt might have sat down.

Dal hurried back to shore and looked for Walt's stick. That special stick, whittled with designs Walt had made of an evening to amuse himself, was not in sight. Dal walked back to the capstone and found a deep, narrow hole in the mud close to the first rock of the causeway. That might have been where Walt would have plunged the stick to help himself step up. Overlying footprints indented the rest of the beach but offered no other clues.

Back at the nonfire ring, however, the last fresh footprints on top of many older footprints from Walt's usual seat all pointed in the direction of the causeway.

Dal whirled around, hoping Naija had not looked up and seen what he was doing, for she would surely question him. Failing to see her, he slowly turned back around and began following what he now thought might be Walt's last footprints. He picked up the longest tree stake that was left to take with him. The muddy area was a long way out on the causeway—farther than Walt usually went, Dal was sure. What could he have been thinking?

He began to feel guilty for having stayed so close to Naija. He knew Walt had been jealous of their friendship. While he had tried to make up to Walt for that, his efforts must have been insufficient. But what more could he have done? *Oh, cut it out—he's probably off somewhere and all right,* Dal told himself, unable yet to handle this dilemma.

But he didn't really believe Walt was all right. He tried to fish the hat out with the stick. *When Walt comes back, he will be so happy I saved his hat for him. He MUST come back!*

Dal couldn't reach the hat. It had moved too far away. He wished now that it would sink altogether before Naija might see it. He decided that later he would throw some stones at it to make it go under and out of sight.

IT WAS LATE, and the sun at its nadir barely skirted under the mountainous horizon, leaving a golden glow on everything. Dal had been sitting beside Naija for hours, waiting for her to wake up. Finally, she stirred and tried to sit up. He leapt to help her.

"I need to go to the bathroom," she said. Dal helped her pull on her shoes, stand up, and walk to the twisting privacy wall. He held her close to keep her from falling.

"Thanks, I can handle it from here," she said, gripping the stone walls on both sides. The mud plaster had dried to a sturdy firmness. Her voice sounded better, he thought. She was still very warm, though.

On returning, Naija uttered the dreaded words: "Where is Walt?"

"I don't know, actually. Have not seen him. Maybe he's still exploring. He'll probably be back soon." Dal tried to sound light. Naija nodded slowly. He hadn't decided when might be the best time to tell her what he feared, but for sure this was not it.

"You need to eat something." Dal had a plate ready with a portion left from his own supper. He was too worried to notice hunger. She took two mouthfuls, drank some water, and lay back on the ground where she sat. While he was telling her that she must stay awake and eat and drink more, Naija rolled away and fell immediately into a deep sleep. Dal put the plate down, feeling exhausted and very alone.

He covered her food with Walt's plate and a rock to keep any skuas off. Then he carried Naija to her sleeping hole and settled her in it. He crawled into the new one he had dug for himself nearby while she'd slept through the afternoon.

Dal turned his face toward her. Her breathing was regular and deep, which he felt to be a good sign. She was only five feet away, yet there had been no indication at all that she had heard his shovel hitting rocky places or the sound of dirt falling all around when he had built his new bed.

30

Due to increasing conflicts on migration planes and rockets, we recommend that specially trained human attendants fly along with the usual robot attendants on every international flight, beginning as soon as staffing can be arranged. The robots are as safe as humans when functioning as pilots, but we have found that at least one trained human can better handle complicated interpersonal situations, the innumerable permutations of which are not yet adequately programmed."
—UNFAA report, December 1, 2295

DECEMBER 7 AND 8, 2295
NEW CHURCHILL, CANADA

THE GROUND TRANSPORT line at the rocket port in New Churchill was the longest Ana had ever seen. There was never this large a crowd in Columbia. Her rocket had been full, too. She shouldered her small overnight bag and inched forward, surrounded by the same sort of throng that Dal had encountered more than eight weeks before.

No one was there waiting to drive her to Willow Park House. No one even knew she was coming. After ninety minutes spent inching forward in line, Ana finally climbed into an old sun car converted to taxi service.

"Willow Park House, please," she said in her most authoritative voice.

"Tours of the Tree Sanctuary are over for this season, ma'am." The driver's voice was weary, his gray hair matted. The car smelled of his lunch.

"I am not going on a tour."

"You cannot get to the house without passing the gate, and you cannot pass the gate unless you are on a tour. And, they must have your name on a list. Do they have your name?"

"I'm not sure. Let's go see." Ana was confident she could talk her way in.

"I'm telling you it'll be a waste of time if they don't know you're coming. And then you'll have a double fare for me to bring you back. It's a long drive."

"I have the money. Let's just get going!" A very large sum had appeared in her ledger a month ago. From Dal, Ana was sure. She had been saving it for the wedding, but this trip was more urgent. She had not slept well for weeks wondering what to do. Once she decided, nothing was going to get in her way, least of all an unhelpful driver.

"Okay, ma'am, just trying to help." He turned around and punched in the coordinates for Willow Park House, the home of that strange old man he had never seen but had heard about: Mori Tukkag. Or Gattuk. Or Tuktuk. Or whatever. "Old man may not see you," the driver said. "He's pretty ancient now. Nobody much visits there anymore."

By mid-December, the deciduous trees were bare of all leaves, and their sculptural branches reached out in freedom. All the land around the rocket port and along the road was filled with buildings of interest to Ana. When they turned off the main highway and out of the congestion, Ana finally could see the emptiness that had filled her flight with climate migrants drawn from all over North America and beyond.

After a while, the battered car with poor shocks pulled up to an imposing stone gatehouse. A barrier stretched across the private road ahead. A woman in a green uniform with "Willow Park" in script over the left front pocket came out with a clipboard. Ana opened her window.

"Ana Chambeau here to see Mr. Taktug," she said.

The young woman pushed back her straight, dark hair and quickly scanned through a three-page printout. Then she went through it again more slowly. Lifting her head, she said, "Sorry, but we do not have your name here. You will need to make an appointment and come back another day."

The driver suppressed a laugh that ended up in a red-faced, phlegmatic coughing fit.

"I have come a long way. It is very important that I see Mr. Taktug."

"Let's just call him Mori, okay?" the woman said. "Taktug is hard for many people to say, so we all call him Mori here. At any rate, he is not receiving visitors right now."

"Can you please put in a comm to the house and tell whomever answers that I am Ana Chambeau, the pregnant fiancé of Dal Riley, and I really need to know how Dal is. They will recognize his name. He spent an entire month here." Tears welled in her eyes, but she refused to let them fall, setting her face in a determined squint.

The young lady with the clipboard examined her printout again. She tapped her pen against it. Then she dropped her arm with the clipboard down by her side and turned back into the guardhouse, where she spoke into her wristband behind the closed window. She watched Ana intently, talking and nodding as if she were describing her to someone. There was a long back-and-forth conversation.

Five minutes later, she walked back to the car, looking so grave that Ana could not tell if she was going to get through to see Mori or not. But then the gate flew up. The young woman gave instructions to the driver, and off they went.

"Well, I never heard of anybody getting through that gate before," the driver said. "You must be somebody." Ana smiled. One obstacle down.

"WHAT A PLACE," Ana remarked, awed by the stone façade of the house.

"Never seen it before," the driver remarked. "Gatekeeper said to be sure to come back the same way, but I might drive around first. May never get back in here."

"If you don't do as she asked you, you surely won't ever get back in," Ana said. "On the other hand, if you make a good impression, you might get in more easily next time," she added, not sure if he would take this advice or not. The admonition was really to remind herself.

A portly man in an apron came bustling out of the heavy front door. He snapped his dishtowel at the two border collies barking by his heels.

"Welcome, Ms. Chambeau. I'm Henri, greeting you for Mr. Taktug."

"Is he here?" Ana's voice was a little higher and raspier than usual.

"Yes, yes, he is here," Henri assured her. "Just a little indisposed tonight. We will try to get you in to see him tomorrow morning."

"I hope he is all right?"

"He's doing okay," said Henri. "I like Mr. Dal. I did not know he was engaged, and not to a woman with beautiful red hair, either."

They walked together through the house. Ana barely noticed the fine floors and rustic antique furniture in the long, darkened hall.

"This was Mr. Dal's suite while he was here. I will bring a dinner here for you tonight. You can walk around outside all you like. It will be dark very soon, though."

After Henri left, Ana pulled open the drawers and closets to see if anything of Dal's might still be there. She sat down on the edge of the Matelassé bedspread, then fell back among the three layers of pillows that covered the bed. Ana grabbed the closest pillow and held it tight. She pulled one of the white pillows out from under the decorative stack, held it close, and breathed deeply, hoping for a scent of Dal. Then she allowed the tears to come. She missed Dal here even more than she had back in her apartment.

The task Ana had set for herself was so important that she quickly dried her face and eyes with the end of the pillowcase. She would not want red, swollen eyes tomorrow, either, so after dinner she put ice cubes in a washcloth and held it up to her eyes.

Later, she went out for a walk around the garden and was glad she had brought an old jacket of her mother's. She didn't own a jacket herself. The gardens were lit softly by low lights, which showed her that all the flowers were well past their prime. The trees were shrouded in deep purple and black. "Must have been a glorious garden when Dal was here," Ana thought.

She sat on a cold stone bench and shivered. The garden looked pretty near perfect to her eyes. The bed labeled "Dahlias" was all dug up, the roses were pruned low, other flowers were tied up in bunches, and the hydrangeas had been left to dry on the plants, soon to be cut way back. The nandina leaned over, heavy with berries. What a beautiful variety of plants. Here were none of the spikey, deluge- and drought-resistant flowers like those back home. The surroundings were nothing like the dying orange groves and the tent city on the farm, either. *I know Dal just loved all this.*

Thoroughly chilled now, Ana got up to go back inside.

A couple walked into view, emerging from the woodland path, apparently after a stroll. They had a flashlight. Ana sprang to her feet. The big man laughed and the woman with him said in a friendly voice, "Hello, we did not mean to scare you." She had a Spanish-speaker's accent.

"I am Bill Hernan," the man said, "and this is my wife, Carmina. We are visitors of Mori, just as you seem to be. Where are you from?" The gentleman seemed courtly enough, but something about him made Ana wary.

She didn't want a conversation just now. She wanted to go in and think more about what she would say to Mori tomorrow. Nevertheless, she went through with the superficial pleasantries. "I am Ana Chambeau from Orangeburg, South Carolina. Where are you from?"

Before Bill could stop her, Carmina said, "New Ushuaia, Argentina. My husband is an old friend of Mori's."

Ana grasped for a linkage and searched her memory. *New Ushuaia. That's way down at the tip of South America, isn't it?* Dal had thought his work would involve some place very far south. Ana wondered if this Bill Hernan might know something about Dal, but she wouldn't ask him until she had talked with Mori. That would be best.

"How long are you staying?" Ana asked casually.

"Maybe forever," said Carmina with a sad look.

"Very cute," Bill said. "That's what Carmina would wish for, as would anyone. Right? It's really nice here, so who wouldn't want to stay forever? Very funny, darling. We'd better get inside now, before you catch a chill."

Ana watched the man from New Ushuaia practically drag Carmina down the path toward the house. Carmina looked around gravely, giving Ana a little wave of her hand.

Back in her room, Ana snuggled into the bed, relishing the cool night air coming in through the open window. She looked forward to the natural sunlight in the morning, too. She felt Dal's spirit in the room. She expected to have good dreams for a change, in spite of the constant worry about him that wouldn't leave her alone.

BY 10 A.M. the next morning, Ana had been ready for hours, dressed in her suit and waiting with the bedroom door open. She was just about to go looking for someone—for anyone—when Henri popped his head in. He was wearing what she had only seen in photos before: a "sports" jacket and cravat.

"Miss Chambeau, would you like to come with me?" Henri asked. He looked unhappy.

She jumped up. "Yes, indeed," she said. "Call me Ana, if you like."

They walked through big, airy rooms full of antiques and flowers. Ana had never seen such opulence. She wondered again what Dal had thought about all this. She reasoned that if only one person lived here, Mori ought to sell the place and give the proceeds to orphans, or maybe take in some of the many refugees. When she and Henri passed the library, she took more interest.

"Wait here, please," Henri said, stopping in the anteroom outside a large bedroom with big double doors that were closed. *Henri must be worried about something,* she thought, because he had broken into a sweat and kept rubbing his fingers together as he clenched and un-clenched his hands at his sides. He waved her toward a leather easy chair in the paneled room. On the table was a funny white disc with red and green blinking lights. It certainly drew one's attention.

Henri carefully opened one of the doors just enough to get through and closed it quickly behind him. The sound of muffled voices rising and falling came from behind the heavy, polished doors.

Ana easily made out a number of the words, especially in Henri's voice.

"Boss, I think Bill should go home now. He has his papers and is just a lot of extra work."

The reply was much quieter, unintelligible through the thick doors.

Henri answered: "But, sir, I don't think you will want him to be here when Dal, Naija, and Walt get back. I heard him saying that he wants to get his 'due' share from you, whatever that is. I think the man is trouble." Henri still couldn't bring himself to tell Mori that Bill had broken the Perseus and that it had taken four days to fix it. The news might be a shock capable of killing Mori.

More unintelligible reply followed.

"All right, if you really want, sir. Are you ready for Ms. Chambeau?" Ana could hear these words clearly: "Yes, indeed."

She picked up a book and pretended to be reading when Henri opened the door.

"You can come in now," he said. "Follow me, and please sit in the chair beside the bed. Mr. Taktug will be able to see you better that way. You will have fifteen minutes. Any longer tires him out. It will be time for me to give him his daily injection soon, too. If you are not finished by then, maybe you can come back in the afternoon for another short visit." Henri pushed the door wide open.

Mori sat with a stack of pillows behind him. His hair was white at the roots for two inches, and his face was a mass of wrinkles. His hands lay limply on top of a blue monogrammed duvet. One thin, wrinkled hand peeked out from a cream-colored sleeve with purple piping. His purple bed jacket was open several buttons at the neck. His thin hand held a handkerchief.

A pile of antique books and a carafe of water were on the bedside stand. All the windows in the room were open, and the cool day poured in. A light breeze fluttered thin linen draperies, and Ana could see through them that the sun had come out.

"I wish I could take you to my yurt, young lady," Mori welcomed her. "That is my favorite place to receive honored guests. I took Dal there."

"Then I would like to go there, too," Ana said, trying to sound energetic and share that energy with him. He looked so frail that she couldn't imagine his ever rising from his bed again.

"Where do you live?" Mori asked. "Do you love nature?"

"South Carolina, not too far from Dal and his family. And yes, of course I love nature. Although nature has not been kind down there. The sea is still rising, and both storms and drought come in cycles every year. My apartment is underground. I like it, but here you are still aboveground, and that is very nice. So is your cooler weather."

"Why did you come to see me?"

"My fiancé, Dal Riley, is working for you. I have not seen or heard from him for a long time, and I'm getting worried. It's not good for our unborn child that I worry so much. I can't sleep for worrying. Dal has always done dangerous work, but I never felt like this before. What can you tell me to put my mind at ease? Something tells me that he's in trouble right now as we speak."

"What wonderful news that you are expecting a baby. Does he know?" Mori seemed not to have heard her every word. She would have to try again, another way.

"No, I found out after he left to come here."

"Was it natural, or aggregation and such?"

"It was a complete surprise."

"That is amazing good news, young lady." Mori sat up a little more. "I have been worried for our species, and you give me hope." He stopped for a few breaths.

"I know that Dal contacted you," he continued. "You were good not to try to talk with him before he left on the expedition."

"Expedition to where?" Ana asked.

"That I cannot tell you until it is finished," Mori replied. "In another two weeks or so, I am guessing."

"Guessing? Don't you know?" Ana's voice rose a notch. Henri looked in on them.

"All fine, Henri," said Mori. "I am having a delightful chat. Ana, you must trust that all is going well, and that he will return. Dal is a remarkable person, and he has the best companions possible for what they are doing. I have a foolproof communication system here in case of any problems, and we have heard nothing distressing at all. Go home and rest. Please take good care of yourself. Too much worry is not healthy."

This wouldn't do for Ana. She tried to find another avenue to Mori's inner thoughts. "This is such a beautiful place," she said. "Nature is doing well here, with your help."

"We try," Mori replied. "And Dal is helping, too."

"His mother will be pleased to know that," Ana ventured. "She shows nature films to schoolkids, and they play the films on the walls inside their house all the time. She did that every day when Dal was growing up—all sorts of nature films, some even from way back before the Sixth Extinction."

Then something popped into Ana's mind to try. A real flyer.

"Last night while I was out walking, I met a Mr. Bill Hernan. He made me uncomfortable with the way he treated his wife when she said they were going to stay here forever. She was probably just being polite about the beauty here, but he literally dragged her away. For some reason, I'm afraid of him. He told me he was from New Ushuaia. I think Dal went down there, because he said he was going somewhere far south. I thought this Mr. Bill Hernan might know something to reassure me. As much as he scares me, I would like to look for him and talk with him later today."

She saw Mori's eyes grow wider and sharper and his face tighten.

"Best to stay away from him, young lady. And I will see that he does not come near you anymore."

Mori cleared his throat twice. "This has been delightful, but I am getting tired now, and it is time for my medication." His words were clipped. He leaned over, wincing as he pushed a button set into the bedside table.

"Henri, please show this lovely young woman to her choice of destinations. She can return to see me next week, perhaps. I have other pressing things I must do this afternoon. And Henri, come back in right away. Immediately."

"But—" Ana started to protest the abrupt ending but knew she had no grounds. So she left politely, deciding she would insist on returning tomorrow. For now, she would go walking in the forest. And try to find that yurt, where Mori had taken Dal. Or maybe she would find Bill Hernan, despite the warning.

AFTER HENRI ESCORTED Ana back to her room, he returned to Mori's side. "What would you like me to do now?" he asked. "I just want to keep your stress down and help you live longer, boss." Henri stood wringing his hands.

"Go and comm my solicitor," Mori replied. "I need to think about what to do, and he always has good advice. I have to protect this estate for Naija. And I have a few other ideas as well."

"Yes, sir. Should I comm your shaman—excuse me, I meant to say Angakkug—first?"

"No indeed. I am not at my last breath, Henri. Please give me that injection now, or I soon will be."

"What about the young lady, Ana Chambeau?" Henri asked. "She is going to expect to see you once more. I had told her she might see you again later today or tomorrow."

"Tell her anything you want. No, wait. Tell her that I took a turn for the worse, but that I will be all right. Tell her to go home, and I will be in touch in two weeks. I cannot have her visiting me again right now. If she sees or talks to me, she will figure out that I am upset. She is a very perceptive young woman. And she is gutsy. A perfect fit for Dal. If Naija can only be so fortunate to find a good mate after losing Cornel, I will be a happy man."

Mori fell back on the pillows and gasped through his open mouth. All that emotional talking had exhausted him. Only Bill had been able to agitate him this badly before, and that was nothing compared to the way he felt now. His thoughts were full of Naija. He was terrified for her, and not sure why. Maybe it was Ana's unease that had so filled him with dread.

WHEN HENRI APPEARED in Ana's doorway, stammering that she should go home and that Mori would contact her later, Ana couldn't believe it. "No way," she said. "I'm afraid I am *not* going to go home."

"But Miss, you cannot stay here. It is Mr. Taktug's orders, ma'am."

"Now, you listen to me," she declared. "I am going to have a child. The child's father works for Mori. No one will tell me where Dal is. This is unacceptable, unkind, maybe illegal, and certainly terrible. I will be staying in a hotel in New Churchill until this mystery is solved, and you both *will* see me again. Soon. Please call me a car."

31

Areas with migrants from far-flung locations are more likely to encounter diseases showing confusing symptomatology. An unusual mix of symptoms can be indicative of the victim's harboring more than one disease at a time. The first disease weakens the victim, and even if there is apparent recovery from the first, the second disease may prove fatal.

—*WHO Quarterly: State of World Disease Transmission*, July 2295

DECEMBER 8 AND 9, 2295

ANTARCTICA

Naija did not wake up. She slept and slept, and that sleep deepened to unconsciousness. Dal couldn't wake her, not even with a cold compress on her stomach. He turned her on her side and poured water into the side of her mouth to prevent her from choking on it. At first, she could swallow a little, but later in the afternoon she stopped swallowing altogether. Dal's hands shook when he saw the water slide out of her mouth and run onto the ground.

Naija's skin became hot to the touch, her cheeks flushed bright pink, and sweat no longer poured off of her. Her skin became quite dry. The old mosquito bites that he had assumed were healed merged into a widespread red rash. Naija began to gasp for air.

Dal tried to sit her up so she could breathe more easily. Even then, she didn't open her eyes but groaned and pressed her dry lips together as she leaned heavily against him. All that bright night long, Dal bathed Naija's face, put oil on her lips, and smoothed her matted hair with his hand and a broken comb. Using precious heat cubes to heat the water, he sponge-bathed and covered every part of her body in turn.

The next day, Dal changed Naija's clothes when they became soiled, as she was no longer going to the outdoor bathroom. When she stopped peeing and her face and fingers became puffy, he worried that perhaps her kidneys were failing. Then the rash blistered and covered her back and stomach. None of this looked like any disease Dal had ever heard of.

Everything fulminated quickly, the same way Native Americans had suddenly succumbed to mysterious diseases millennia earlier. He thought of that woman in New Ushuaia talking about new vectors and illnesses. The whole idea made him weak with fear.

Dal couldn't rest. He barely took time to eat. He tied their clothes together to make a wind-and-sun shield for her prostrate body. He could have carried her into the hut, but he was sure Naija would prefer the fresh, open air.

The gravity of her condition was clear, but it wasn't until her breathing took on the erratic Cheyne-Stokes pattern he had learned about in lifesaving class that Dal was sure her end was near. He had used Walt's few clothes in her care. Naija never awoke to notice this or to ask about Walt again.

DAL SAT BY Naija's still, small, lifeless body for half a circle of the sun. He waved the skuas away. Occasionally he rocked back and forth, but otherwise he just sat. His tears were spent. He had no clear idea about what to do next other than to bury her. There was nothing he could think of that would help Naija or Walt any more. His responsibility for their plane wreck overwhelmed any memory of all the good he had done to keep them alive. *What use was any of it if they are gone now? What use am I?*

There was nothing here for him anymore. He hated every bit of the land, the waterfall, the smoking mountains, the sky, and the ocean stretching far beyond the brown bog that he had mistaken for a secure dirt runway. Even more than these, Dal hated the wrecked plane and the trees inside it that had propelled them to this awful place. The bottom line, he felt, was this: what a waste his whole short life had been.

After a period of grief for Naija's family and Walt's, Dal began to grieve for Ana and his parents, who would never know what had become of him. He hoped Mori, if he was still alive, might contact them after a while. Where was Mori now? Dal was angry with both Mori and himself for the pain his family and Ana had in store.

Thank God Ana was at home. He hoped the money was there for her, and that Mori had kept his word. What would his parents do when he didn't come back? This would put his mother over the edge, much more than any dead species had done.

SOME HOURS AFTER making a grave cairn of stones inside the hut for Naija, the pain in his stomach reminded Dal that he needed to eat. There was enough left for a week if he used the extra rations that Walt would have consumed. He felt guilty eating that, though, and really had no appetite. It didn't seem to matter whether he ate or not, as he had nothing to do now except fill the water pail from the waterfall once a day.

The skuas had flown off with the food meant for Naija that he'd left out by mistake when overwhelmed by caring for her. Maybe they had missed something when salvaging from the plane, though. Maybe a crumb of a snack, or anything. Dal thought he'd better make a trip back out there to look before he got too weak to safely navigate the uneven causeway. Even though he saw no hope that he would find anything in the wreck, Dal's ethos demanded that he make every effort.

Once he got back inside the wreck, memories of Naija out there with him—talking about everything, telling stories about her childhood, goading him to lighten up—seemed to echo off of each battered surface. Just for the hell of it, he tried again to call someone with the broken comms system, knowing it was useless.

He sat there for a while, never looking toward the back where the hated trees were.

He blamed them for weakening Naija's health to the point that the disease, whatever it was, took over. He blamed the trees for existing at all so that he, Naija, and Walt would die here. He blamed Mori for setting it all up. And, of course, he blamed himself.

There was no food in the front-seat area. He climbed over to Walt's area; in doing so, he had to get near those sorry trees. There they were, fed and watered by his and Naija's own hands. Ferny green branches peeked out of the sliced-open roof of the plane. Other branches, bent sideways by the crash, appeared less promising, but some trees looked downright healthy.

Anger boiled over, and Dal itched to start a conflagration. Maybe that would bring the Atmospheric Police, at least. Naija hadn't wanted him to do it, but since he didn't believe in an afterlife, he didn't expect her ever to know what he was doing now. Dal walked back to shore, determined to have a tiny meal and get some sleep. And then he would try to start the biggest bonfire possible.

32

Despite our prior optimism and endless effort, it is clear now that not even quantum physics will allow for the safe travel of live humans via teleporting. About 4.4×10^{42} bits of personalized data would need to be transferred perfectly, via disassembling a human being at one end and reassembling, atom by individual atom with absolute accuracy, at the other—an impossibility.

—*Future Science* editorial, November 2263

DECEMBER 10–12, ANTARCTICA

Every night the light was a bit brighter than before. It woke Dal up several times. This time, he had been dreaming about Ana. He stretched happily. They had been making love in his dream.

Then he looked around and experienced again the crushing weight of where he was. The despicable wreck shone in the sun, despite being covered with light dust. The blades twisted rakishly, and a couple of the taller and healthier black-and-white spruces waved insouciantly through the top of the plane, as if waving at him. *If Naija had seen that before she died, she would have been enchanted,* Dal thought. He rolled away from the sight. He didn't even have the energy to act on his anger and try to burn the trees. It would be too hard without a starter, anyway.

LASSITUDE WARPED HIS SPIRIT. Dal realized he had to have something to do or he would get too weak just sitting. Or he might go crazy before he either died or was rescued. He tried going up to see the peat field in the hanging valley, but it really wasn't much more than thin wet moss they had dug up, not compact enough to produce a heating blaze. It had been made-up work anyway. Besides, he wouldn't live long enough to need it.

Dal sat on a rock pondering what to do next. Maybe try to explore the interior? But if rescuers were to arrive, they might not search very far for him. So he stayed where he was.

He laid out an SOS sign with white rocks on the upper shore. Why had none of them thought of this before? That was basic. But would anyone ever see it?

Dal kept thinking back to Naija's and Walt's last days, wishing he could have helped them more. Her devotion to those trees stuck in his mind. He couldn't quite understand it. His mother surely would have, though. Slowly he got up and walked down to the seating ring, where he hadn't wanted to go before. It was too lonely there now. Memories of the three of them sitting companionably around that nonfire ring had to be pushed aside.

Dal found himself absent-mindedly counting the stacked-up tree stakes that remained from the ones they had brought out of the wreck. There were eight. If he used scraps around the campsite, he might put together one or two more. But did he have the energy for his budding idea? Should he waste what little strength he had left on those trees languishing out there in the wreck? Or should he use himself up completely to show his appreciation for Naija and his mother's environmental spirits, and for Ana?

The trees were going to die anyway. And likely so was he. Therefore, why not? Maybe he could plant just the best ones and then burn the unhealthy ones where they stood inside the plane. Maybe that would attract the Atmospheric Police or Black Coats. Burning a couple of small trees would release less carbon than the peat would, but still enough to be detected. He began to think that even the Black Coats might be worth seeing now.

No, he changed his mind again. The Black Coats were too ruthless. They would never help him in any way. But maybe someone else might see the smoke first. Maybe via satellite. Maybe a plane flying at high altitude would get curious. Who knew? Was it worth a gamble?

WHERE TO PLANT those blooming trees? And how to get them out to the shore?

The saplings and root balls were heavy. Dal finally got the small, mangled tree dolly in the plane repaired. He shoved it out and soon had it wobbling across the rocks. This would help a little bit.

Then he climbed back up to the hanging valley and enlarged the holes he had started for Walt. He spent the rest of the day dragging buckets of beach dirt up to mix into the loam of special nitrogen-fixing compost that Walt had prepared.

He wished Walt were there to tell him how much mix and how deep to plant. Dal remembered a phrase from his father: "Plant 'em low, they won't grow. Plant 'em high, they never die."

He had no idea if this axiom was true or not, but he liked the sound of it—and he liked the idea that his father would have a hand in this through him. So that was what he did: planted high.

When hunger gnawed, Dal told himself that even if all of the trees were eventually to die, he still would have completed the mission, and he would have done it against enormous odds. Maybe someone would learn that one day. He wished he and Ana could have had a child who might find out and would care.

He spent the next long days working every waking minute except for the few he spent talking to Naija at her grave cairn and to Walt by the edge of the bog. He told them of his plan. He told them that he was not just a "No Guy" anymore.

Ana inhabited his dreams. Her spiritual companionship made Dal feel a little less alone. He wished teleporting had worked out as a science. He could just imagine her by his side right now, but then again, he was glad she was not around for all this.

He ate very little and stretched his rations out while he struggled to get eight root balls and their spindly trunks and limbs to shore, and then wrestled each one up to the hanging valley. He often fell to the ground panting between exertions. Was his heart giving out like Shackleton's had, or was it just hunger and exhaustion?

As he worked, he thought of what his labors might mean. What if the trees live? If they do, they cannot be removed, by law. They might propagate others. That seemed unlikely. Still, one never knew. Maybe the earth would not have to wait for wind to blow seeds across the sea.

Dal liked to imagine how Ana might benefit from Mori's estate if he could just get this job finished. That gave him another motivation, which in turn gave him more energy. He bent to his labor with increasing pride. He even found a certain joy.

Finally, he was done. His ragged clothes hung on him, and he had only two days' rations left. His eyes were sunken. Maybe he should cut down on food again, now that his big exertion was over. Yes, that was what he would do. But first he would go out to the plane and try to set afire the trees that remained there. Then maybe someone would come. Better than starting a peat fire that might never go out.

Later that last evening of the planting, as the sun stayed up longer and stronger and never went under the horizon at all, Dal hobbled out to the plane. Using Mori's magnifying glass and some dry leaves and needles, he experimented atop the wreck until he managed to concentrate enough sunlight to set the driest needles on fire. Naija had told him that a drop of water on the magnifying glass might enhance the sun's power, so he tried that—and it worked! Dal blew gently and coaxed the frail kindling to a blaze, carried it carefully inside the plane, and lit the remaining trees. The interior quickly grew so hot that he had to scramble out.

Dal hoped the glow from the fire would be seen through the open roof of the wreck by a manned satellite. He knew, though, that at least that burst of unauthorized CO_2, no matter how small, would be caught by the delicate monitors that ringed the earth's atmosphere. Someone would come running for that, he was pretty sure. If they came fast enough, he just might see Ana again.

33

Aviation is the branch of engineering that is the least forgiving of mistakes.
—Freeman Dyson

DECEMBER 16, ANTARCTICA

A distant hum slowly roused Dal from the sleep of the starving. It gradually grew louder until he could no longer credit it to a dream. There was no sound like this in Antarctica. He knew that sound. It was a large rocket, without noise abatement, coming his way. Was it friendly or not?

He jumped to his feet and hobbled toward the mountains, keeping low. Scrambling on painful feet up the stony trail, he reached the path to the hanging valley before he saw the rocket.

Breathless, Dal lay hidden over the valley rim. He raised his head just enough to see what was happening below. He wanted to size up who was coming before he showed himself. Lasers kill instantly, and he certainly did not want to die that way. His plan was to talk them down and get a ride home.

Just as Dal had done many weeks before, the rocket pilot made a hovering pass over the beach and the wide, muddy outflow, which blended into one gently sloping, same-colored expanse. The rocket lingered over the wreck with the charred top. The pilot must have puzzled over the wreck and perhaps the "SOS" written in white rocks as well.

The pilot may have wondered about the bridge to the wreck, although he surely would have determined that the source of the CO_2 he was searching for was in that burned-out plane below. The whole area surrounding the wreck, and far beyond it, looked to be of the same consistency—a solid place to land. Maybe the rocket pilot thought the wreck of the plane had been normal pilot error—just an ordinary, unfortunate crash landing caused by wind or any of a dozen other factors.

At any rate, the rocket pilot throttled up and moved farther out, away from the "SOS" and the wreck. He hovered with his antigravity thrusters down and throttled back to settle about thirty yards beyond the wreck.

Dal could once again see the grim future. He lifted his emaciated, rag-clad body from his hidden crouch and waved his arms high over his head, frantically yelling and standing on the tallest rocks he could find, desperate to be seen. His voice cracked, and he fell off the rock, but he scrambled back up, screaming hoarsely at the rocket again. The rocket was in its last seconds of descent. It settled, and at first it appeared to be stable.

The door of the rocket popped open. Half a dozen laser-armed Black Coats in helmets poured down the steps. Dal peered through his small scope and thought he saw his old friend Andy Thompson on the rocket's steps. The rocket began to list. Dal saw one Black Coat fall into the colloidal moraine quicksand. There were sharp cries of surprise from the men. He watched them tumble, first one by one and then two at a time into the thick, grasping bog, where they thrashed about screaming and quickly disappeared. The sounds were awful. Dal covered his ears.

The rocket listed more to the right. Then Dal saw an escape hatch open on the port side, and twenty or so more Black Coats jumped onto an escape slide to what they hoped would be safety. The second and third ones down realized this was not solid ground. The BCs in the middle or on top of the slide twisted and turned, scrambling to try and get back up to the escape hatch. Those still holding onto the doorframe reached out to try and haul back up anyone they could. Suddenly, the rocket keeled all the way over on its starboard side and slogged noisily below the surface. Cries for help pierced the air. Dal sat with his ears covered until long after it was over.

The breeze continued to lightly ruffle Dal's hair. The few puffy clouds above continued their path to the east. There were no sounds except for Dal's own breathing and the waterfall. He fell down hard where he was, distressed even for those Black Coats. They were human beings, too. One might even have been Andy, although now he hoped not.

Who would come and save him? His only hope was Mori in Canada. Mori. He was probably dead by now, as no one had come in all this time. How would Ana ever find out what had happened to him? Dal hoped she wouldn't think he had deserted her. Or that he had run away. Or found someone else.

He couldn't sleep at all. That night, this irreligious man prayed until morning.

34

A woman is like a tea bag. You never know how strong she is until she gets in hot water.

—Eleanor Roosevelt

DECEMBER 17, 2295, NEW CHURCHILL, CANADA

Ana arranged another taxi ride out to Willow Park with the same driver as before.

"Let me out a little bit before we get there, please," she said. She was wearing all new green-and-brown garb and hiking boots purchased in New Churchill. Ana was taking no chances at being stopped by the sentry.

"What are you gonna do, break in?" asked the driver.

"You might call it that," said Ana.

"You got guts, lady. I'm all over that idea. I remember your telling me before not to even drive around. And here you go, sneaking through the bush to get there. Pretty cool."

"Gotta do it," Ana said. "Please don't tell anyone."

"I wouldn't ever do that," he replied.

"And please drive as fast as you can get away with."

The driver sped up. Soon Ana was throwing bills over the seat to him and slipping out of the car. She jumped over a ditch, climbed a fence, and ran into the woods. Ana had the Willow Park House location on her band finder, so she began threading her way there. Above all, she hoped not to come upon any dogs. She was afraid of big dogs, especially the guard variety.

After pushing her way past some untended ornamental pools overgrown with weeds and then crossing another stream, Ana came to the path grid that meandered through the woods. There shouldn't be anyone else on the paths at this early hour.

Just then she heard a dog begin to bark viciously. It sounded large. She froze. A short woman wrapped in a shawl came strolling toward her. A large German shepherd ran right for Ana, snarling. "Stop him, I'm pregnant!" she screamed.

Carmina called, "Hector, come, *aqui.* Come, Hector." The dog turned and ran back to receive a biscuit and scratching of his ears.

Ana was shaking, but she walked toward Carmina anyway. "Remember me? Is your dog friendly?"

"Yes, he will be friendly now," Carmina assured her. "And I remember you. I do. My husband was angry with me when I met you before."

"Is he like that a lot?" Ana asked.

"Yes, *todo el tiempo* now. All the time. We are in trouble everywhere we go."

"I have a big problem and need your help. Can you help me?"

"Maybe. Let me see. Tell me." The woman patted the dog again.

"My fiancé is in bad trouble. In danger. I can feel it here." Ana put her hand over her heart. "I must get in to see Mori so he can save him."

"I love to help *amantes y bambinos,*" Carmina said quickly, using all the warmth of her rich accent. "Follow me."

As they walked, she talked. "My husband is *muy* unhappy because the time for Señorita Naija and Señor Dal and Señor Walt to return is here. If Señorita Naija comes back, we cannot stay here. I am afraid my husband will try to harm her in some way. And maybe you also, because you are carrying Señor Dal's child. Maybe Mori will like Señor Dal more than he likes my husband. That will make Bill even more angry."

"Why are you telling me this?" Ana asked.

"Because you can stop it all. And keep my husband from going to jail forever. You must tell Señor Mori these things when you see him, *por favor.* Then he will send us back to New Ushuaia today with papers."

"Do you know where Dal and the others went?"

"No, *lo siento*—I am sorry. Señor Mori will not tell my husband where they are. This makes Bill smoke with fury, but he can do *nada* about it except wait for his big chance to have all of this." She swept her hands around.

"What do you want for yourself?" Ana asked.

"I want to go back home, with Bill," said Carmina.

"You get me in to see Mori, and then I will help you, too," said Ana.

Carmina took Ana's hand in both of hers and touched it to her forehead. *"Muchas gracias, mi amiga nueva.* Thank you, my new friend. Let us wait until Mori has received his *medicamentos.* He is clearer and stronger at those times."

ANA HUDDLED IN a linen closet off the hall from Mori's room for ninety uncomfortable minutes. She heard Henri come and go four times. Eventually, Carmina tiptoed up, cracked the door open, and left. This was the signal that it was safe for Ana to slip into Mori's room.

Mori appeared to be the same as before, only perhaps a little thinner, if that was possible. Ana leaned over near his ear and whispered, "Mori, it's Ana."

His eyes sprang open, and he looked all around before seeing her. He brightened. "Ana! I thought I must have dreamt your voice. And here you are. How did you get here, child? How is the real child?" He looked at her stomach.

"We are both fine," Ana replied. "But I had to see you, so Carmina helped me. I've had recurrent dreams that Dal is in huge trouble. The other two, Naija and Walt—that's what she told me their names are— do not appear at all in my dreams. What do you make of that?"

Mori became still and even paler as Ana described her dreams.

"I take these things very seriously, young lady," he said. "Long ago I learned from a wise Inuit woman to listen to one's dreams, and above all to believe the intuition of a pregnant woman, especially when corroborated by facts. We must first learn the facts about this."

"Please send help for them right away," Ana pleaded. "You know where they are."

"I know within tens of miles, but Aron would have to search for them. How did you get in here? And what on earth are you wearing?

It looks like what they used to call 'camouflage' back when we had conventional warfare and trees to hide amongst."

"Just my special walking clothes," Ana said. "Carmina helped me get in to see you. I have an important message from her to you, but you must never let her husband know that she sent it."

"Well, what is it?"

"She wants you to send Bill and her both back to New Ushuaia right away, for sure before Dal and the others return from wherever they are. It must be done quickly, before Bill has a chance to harm Naija or me, although I cannot imagine why she listed me as a target, too. Bill wants your estate for himself. He believes to his core that you owe it to him for 'compounded interest from a land deal' or something like that. She said all this, but I couldn't understand what everything meant."

"Henri!" Mori pushed his call button. "Come quickly!"

Henri barged in expecting the worst and stopped short when he saw Ana standing there in camouflage. He struggled to compose his face. "Yes, Mr. Taktug?"

"Make some notes so that you do not forget anything," Mori ordered. "Use my armband. You are wearing it, after all. Now, first comm one of the grounds guards to be here with me when I talk with Bill Hernan. I am sending him and Carmina home right after we finish speaking. Carmina may have the chance to stay here, but I think she will want to go with Bill. They can fly in my plane with Aron Weeks, who will then go on to find and pick up Naija, Dal, and Walt and bring them back here with all due speed."

Henri began to sweat and shiver. Now was the obvious time to get this burden off his chest. This was the chance he had been looking for. "Boss, since you figured Bill out, I don't guess much else can shock you, so I ought to tell you something. Remember that day when Bill first arrived here? Remember when he ran out in a big huff? Well, when he left, he threw the Perseus relay across the room and broke it."

Mori fell back and clutched his heart. Henri continued. "I didn't realize it at first because of all the commotion. Carmina helped me find it shoved under a chair. I sent the Perseus out immediately to be brought back online. We only missed four days of coverage."

"Four days?!" Mori gasped. "I hope that was not a critical four days for our people, Henri. Why did you not tell me before?"

"You were so upset after talking to Bill that I worried any more trauma might kill you. And then the crew would be as good as lost, being dependent on you if any troubles arose. I reasoned that those four days would probably be the safest of all for them, before they could be detected and all that. Just knowing this has been a big burden. I'm glad to have it off my chest. The Perseus has not gone off at all, not one time, I am sure."

"You have transferred your heavy burden right to my heart, Henri," Mori said. "I wish that I had let them keep their fancy armbands after all, as dangerous as that would have been." He clasped his hands together. "Oh, Naija, my Naija—I hope you are all right. Let's all pray to God for that." His face contorted in anguish. After a few minutes, he regained some composure.

"I must stay cogent here," he said. "Your news adds to the gravity of Ana's premonitions, and together they call for immediate action. First, comm on my band to Aron and have him come here immediately, prepared to fly Bill home and to continue on to look for and bring back Naija, Dal, and Walt. I will give him the probable area.

"Then have my solicitor come back to take Bill out of my will, this time for good, and to make some other adjustments. He will also need to advance funds to Aron for his journey. Last, please notify my Angakkug that I might soon be needing his services.

"And Henri, most important, don't forget to make sure Ana is completely comfortable in Dal's old room. Do not let Bill know or even suspect that she is here. Escort her back there yourself for safety. And—oh, yes—please send out to get her some real clothes."

35

DECEMBER 17, 2295, ANTARCTICA

At noontime, after many days of hard labor, Dal staggered out of his bed to warily observe a skua as it sashayed back and forth, watching him with one beady black eye at a time. It strutted and looked healthy. What on earth did it eat? Maybe Dal should try to follow it and learn something. But instead, he rested. He had only one more day of meager rations left.

Later that afternoon, another apparition appeared. A pair of gentoo penguins waddled into camp from around a bend in the beach where it headed off toward the sea beyond the southeast edge of mountains.

Were there more than just these two penguins? He watched as the gray-coated pair trilled their gentle, raspy calls. They marched up to a rocky perch that Dal hoped might become their nest. Maybe a previous nest had flooded before they'd gotten back to shore. He was happy to see them, having thought they were extinct.

Dal knew his penguins from Risa's films, and he liked these the best of all the subspecies because of their multiple chicks and pleasant calls. He had never expected to see a live penguin, though. In his hungry state, Dal found himself wondering, *What do they eat now that the krill are gone? Maybe jellyfish eggs?* The sight and sound of the two birds provided a rare pleasure for him in this abjectly deserted place. He considered killing and eating them, but because there was no large colony for him to live off of for long, he decided it wouldn't be right to kill these two for only one or two meals that would make little difference in the end. Instead of food, Dal began to think of them as a good omen.

Hope rose in his throat, and he found the energy for one more task—one he wished he'd thought of before the disaster of the BC rocket. He walked slowly over to the wide, solid area of the beach and took up the SOS sign he had printed out with white rocks. Moving slowly, he added more white rocks to the pile; it took him half a day to find enough.

Then he wrote out, large enough to be seen from a long distance: LAND HERE! He hoped that for anyone else flying into the region, this sign would prevent the tragedy of yesterday from happening again. Even if he were dead by that time, they would know he tried to live on.

AFTER THE LAST of the tea was gone, representing his last physical contact with civility, Dal climbed slowly back up to the hanging valley and sat on a rock bench he had made for just this moment. The bench was located on the inland side of the row of eight trees, now all staked and watered. The sun warmed his back up here. He hoped he would be able to continue watering the trees until the very end. But that could not be too far away now. Still, who knew how long a person could survive on just water? He hoped for long enough.

His work was finished. He had done all he could to complete the job that had consumed them. Mori would get what he had wanted: to atone and help nature. Dal's parents would be proud, if they ever found out. He could not think of Ana without breaking down. In a way, by planting the trees maybe he had even made up for the wreck and his failures, perhaps for everything. *Well, no,* he thought, *never for everything—never for Naija and Walt.*

He ate his last one-fourth of an energy bar and drank his cold, clear water while listening to the gentoo penguin pair softly cooing. The sun shone through the gently waving spruce fronds and created beautiful dappled sun designs on the ground in front of where he sat. He remembered a fragment from an ancient, mysterious poem his mother would murmur when putting him to bed.

"Glory be to God for dappled things—
For skies of couple-colour as a brinded cow;
For rose-moles all in stipple upon trout that swim;

Fresh-firecoal chestnut-falls; finches' wings;
Landscape plotted and pierced—fold, fallow, and plough."

Dal had never seen a trout. He had no idea what a brinded cow was. But gazing upon these lovely, sunlight-dappled shadows, he could imagine that they must have been, like so much of nature, beautiful even in their imperfection: the brinded cows and the rose-moles, too.

EPILOGUE

On June 10, 2300, a memorial service was held at Willow Park, New Churchill, Canada.

In early 2296, photographic evidence of eight healthy trees growing in West Antarctica had been presented to the Atmospheric Bureau of the World Environmental Commission. In response to a verification that there were indeed three black spruces, two white spruces, and three *Pilgerodendron* cypress trees thriving on the continent, the entire Antarctic biosphere was hastily declared to be a "Tree Preserve in Perpetuity." No mining or removal of any living thing could henceforth be carried out on the continent.

It happened just in time, for until this discovery the broad consensus had been that nothing of consequence could grow that far south. If trees might make it in Antarctica, well, perhaps there was reason for new hope in a world badly in need of it. Trees on Antarctica would become another carbon drawdown, as well as a source of oxygen for the 10.3 billion humans struggling to live on Earth.

Tree farms sprang up wherever possible, and biologists worked around the clock to propagate species capable of surviving in Antarctica. Tree-planting drones were made capable of the arduous journey and conditions. Scientists cautioned that this was only a preliminary experiment. Nevertheless, headlines everywhere called the discovery of those trees, planted there by some mysterious benefactor, a "Celestial Day."

The migrant camp on the Riley farm in South Carolina, like most other camps, held a yearly springtime celebration. But Risa and Jim

Riley were not in South Carolina for it this year. They came instead to New Churchill for a memorial service, following Dal's path.

Aron Weeks, who had snagged the proving photos of the surviving trees on a dangerous flight to Antarctica, attended the Willow Park ceremony. Henri made sure that everything went smoothly, and he personally drove Risa and Jim Riley in from Akjuit Rocketport. They brought Dal's friend Andy Thompson with them. He managed the Riley Farm Migrant Camp now. Ellie Halamore, Walt's wife, arrived from Saskatoon.

Mori had provided the necessary paperwork of legal cover for the Lapataia tree removal and thus gained Bill Hernan's freedom in southern Argentina. Bill would always be followed closely by the Black Coats but would avoid further beatings or imprisonment. Although the Black Coats questioned Bill about where he had been, he made up a story to protect Mori from ever enduring a Black Coat questioning session himself. They would not have had a chance to do that anyway.

Mori quickly ran out of time. He didn't live to see the outcome of his grand design or to read of the "Mysterious Trees That Saved Antarctica."

On this day, the ceremony was held at Mori's own graveside in his flower-rimmed garden at Willow Park, four and a half years after his death on December 27, 2295. Next to his stone was another, smaller one.

When the Angakkug priest stepped out of Mori's old mansion—now a home for orphaned victims of climate migration—to start the proceedings, a small girl's voice could be heard laughing in the forest.

"You can't catch me," the child cried gleefully. Then more giggles were heard by the assembled. "Naija, slow down, please," a woman's voice called. A little girl with red hair ran out of the woods, where she lived in a yurt with her parents. She laughed and tossed her curly head as she looked back over her shoulder. Ana Riley walked swiftly out of the woods and caught up with Naija to hold her hand. Then Dal strode out of the woods and into the circle. He scooped Naija up on his right arm, put his other arm around Ana, and the ceremony began.

Near the end, Ana whispered something to Naija. The little girl squatted down and carefully laid her handpicked flowers on the other grave. It was the grave with the smaller stone, and the unusual name carved into it—the name just like hers.

They all ate cake, she played with the children who lived in Mori's old home, and everyone smiled at her. She would always remember every detail about this day.

IN FUTURE YEARS, as Naija Riley went on to dedicate her life to helping the earth recover from the ravages of her species, she would often think about that special day. In her old age, whenever she feared for human survival, Naija would sit down and put on the new vid helmet given to her by her son. She would replay her grandmother Risa's nature films, which by then had been reworked to include appropriate sounds and odors, too.

Naija always felt restored by these little experiences of the way the world once was. She felt relief at being just a speck in the grand scheme of so many things that were far out of her control. And she was able to indulge in a tiny hope: hope that, no matter what the ultimate fate of *Homo sapiens* might be, nature on Earth, given many more eons of time, would someday evolve other wondrous creatures again.

THE END

ACKNOWLEDGMENTS

A book this long in the making acquires a lot of helpers over the years. But *A Tree for Antarctica* would not exist at all without the unending encouragement and full support of my husband, Dick, our children, Rick Michaux and Alison Reynolds, all of our grandchildren, and our niece. They are my life. This book is dedicated to them.

Thank you to the librarians at the Library of Congress who found obscure research for me back in the 1990s, after my attention had been snagged by a small *Washington Post* article declaring a scientist had predicted the melting of all Antarctic ice. Thus, an overriding curiosity was born. Thank you to Carol Hoover and her writers group at the Writer's Center for keeping the idea for this novel alive with their support early on.

Thank you to the young lady who lent me her half-ton truck to drive outside of tiny Churchill, Canada, on a dark night in 1997 to luxuriate under the northern lights, and to the helicopter pilot who spent an entire day flying with me on his job measuring water levels out in the frozen wilds, hiking over iced streams, finding caribou and bears, and telling me hair-raising tales of flights he had experienced.

Thank you, Dick Michaux, for that first voyage to Antarctica! Later on, Harlan Crow and Lorie Karnath encouraged me to try and get to the South Pole. In 1999 in Ushuaia, I met and befriended Caroline Hamilton, Zoe Hudson, Pom Oliver, Rosie Stancer, and Ann Daniels—the first all-female expedition to sledge-haul ski all the way to the South Pole. They are excellent role models for exploration by never giving up on anything. Their examples and great friendship continue to spur me on.

In April 2000, renowned explorer and RGS member Pen Hadow provided the experience of a lifetime: accompanying him and Gordon Eadie on a sledge-hauling expedition for the last degree to the North Pole, by transit through Siberia via Khatanga and Severnaya Zemlya (the last archipelago to be discovered on Earth) and finally out onto the ice for our sledge-hauling ski trek, heading due north. This was a reconnoiter trip for Pen, who later completed the first solo ski trek from Canada to the North Pole without a resupply. That April, as we skied along very near the pole, Pen kept remarking on how much open water we were encountering at those latitudes. This was a first, unusual in his experiences to date. That watery spring proved to be prophetic for the entire arctic ocean ecosystem. The story line for the novel in my head was fed once more. Huge thanks go to Pen and Duncan.

Two more trips to the arctic and three to Antarctica added more depth of experience from which to draw.

Enormous thanks for help with this book are especially due to Scott Pelley. He and his wife, Jane, both have big, charitable hearts, which made a 2002 trip to Antarctica and Patagonia with him and his CBS *60 Minutes* crew possible for me and for the wonderful Bob Greene. Also, very big thanks are due to Dr. Paul Mayewski, Dr. Geno Casassa, Dr. Wayne Trivelpiece, and Sue Trivelpiece for sharing their experiences and science. Special gratitude goes to Catherine Levy for her logistical skills. The Polish research base Arktowski provided clean bunks and hearty meals, as well as a farewell party when we left.

Later, Scott allowed me to accompany another *60 Minutes* shoot, this time to Svalbard for the World Seed Bank's installment of its first shipment of seeds from participating nations. Special thanks to Cary Fowler for sharing a small part of his vast knowledge about agronomy in relation to climate change.

A big thank you goes to Al Gore, who taught me how to speak to others about climate in two separate sessions of his Nashville classes. I am thankful also for the many people to whom I later gave presentations about climate change. They sharpened my interest, which kept the novel growing in the back of my mind. It was all the school children and our grandchildren who made me determined to sit down and finish this book.

Once the writing started in earnest, a whole new cast of helpers appeared.

Maura Stevens has been invaluable from the start in so many ways: with logistics, computer help, ideas, and all of the diverse things an assistant does, always keeping good spirit and humor. Ryan Kiplinger at HTA made sure I did not lose the manuscript and saw that the electronics were working. Lise Van Susteran keeps me focused on climate as THE important issue of ours and the next generations. A brilliant advocate for the future, she made astute comments about the first drafts of the book.

Helen Zax read the first early manuscript carefully, and gave detailed recommendations. She in particular taught me how to make a book come together. My terrific editor, Ken DeCell, made the manuscript a smoother read. Big thanks to them all.

To poet and professor of English at Virginia Tech, Bob Hicok, thanks are offered for allowing the use of a stanza from his beautiful and many-layered poem, "The Impulse to Hold."

Thank you to Buzz Johnson, ex-navy fighter pilot and authority on aeronautics, for discussing the flight sequences with me.

Sarah Bereza created the dramatic cover art and the logo for Arctic Tern Publishing, and to her I am immensely grateful.

To Rich Lirtzman and Judy Grace, thank you for encouraging me to continue, after reading the roughest of drafts.

To Chris Crochetière and Julie Allred of BW&A Books, thank you for your beautiful book production and for all your good advice. To Bob and Nick Slater, grateful thanks for sharing your experience on publishing. Thank you to Niki Van Burke of Van Studios for her excellent construction of the website, and to Ariel Mendez for consultation about the publishing maze.

Hearty thanks to all of the special reviewers who wrote in praise of *A Tree for Antarctica*. They are gratefully named along with their credentials in the front of the volume, and on the cover, along with their kind remarks.

V. J. Michaux
MAY 2021

ABOUT THE AUTHOR

V. J. Michaux is a climate speaker, writer, author of climate fiction, conservationist, and explorer. She is a member of The Explorer's Club and has headed their Conservation Committee. Her extensive travels in the arctic and Antarctica helped her prepare to write her new novel, *A Tree for Antarctica*. These travels included skiing the last degree to the North Pole while hauling a sled across the broken ice, and skiing an estimated sixty miles in the interior of Antarctica while there to visit the Amundsen-Scott South Pole Station.

Her passion is working to mitigate the effects of climate change for the sake of future generations. She enjoys hiking, having hiked coast to coast across England and Wales and on all seven continents. She is now at work on her memoirs of those and other adventures, and new fiction.